# Praise for Josephine Myles's
## *Barging In*

"*Barging In* is a book I could read over and over again. Josephine Myles has populated it with loveable heroes, introduced a unique and colorful setting, and infused it with incredible energy and humor. This is a book that just might leave you cheering, and will most certainly reinforce your belief in the power of love."

~ *Top 2 Bottom Reviews*

"I do hope this author gives us more work of this quality, but until then, I'll keep on recommending *Barging In* to my friends."

~ *The Romance Reviews*

"Ms. Myles did a great job of describing life on the water, including all the technicalities of living on a boat... Overall, an amazing book. I loved the characters, the descriptive setting, and the passionate interactions between Dan and Robin. I can't wait to read more from this author!"

~ *MM Good Book Reviews*

"Josephine Myles pulled me into her world immediately with *Barging In*. There's an authenticity to the setting of this story I really liked..."

~ *BlackRaven's Reviews*

"Enjoyable, intimate romantic drama between two memorable protagonists in an unusual and lovingly detailed setting... Readers who enjoy non-US delightful."

~ *Reviews by Jessewave*

Look for these titles by
*Josephine Myles*

*Now Available:*

Barging In
Handle with Care

# Barging In

*Josephine Myles*

SAMHAIN
PUBLISHING

Samhain Publishing, Ltd.
11821 Mason Montgomery Road, 4B
Cincinnati, OH 45249
www.samhainpublishing.com

Barging In
Copyright © 2012 by Josephine Myles
Print ISBN: 978-1-60928-714-6
Digital ISBN: 978-1-60928-592-0

Editing by Linda Ingmanson
Cover by Scott Carpenter

First Samhain Publishing, Ltd. electronic publication: September 2011
First Samhain Publishing, Ltd. print publication: August 2012

# Dedication

To my long-suffering husband and daughter, who were (mostly) patient with my absent-minded behaviour and housework-avoidance when lost in Robin-and-Dan land.

Thanks to Lou Harper for reading my patchy first draft scene by scene, and always being ready to discuss character and plot when I needed someone to bounce ideas off. Thanks to Jamie Merrow for the incredibly thorough and insightful edit that helped me get to a polished final draft. Thanks also to my team of beta readers who read the second draft and gave me their honest reactions: Angharad, Ben, Jill, Julie, Krista and Kristina—I hope to return the favour one day!

Thanks to Josh Lanyon and members of his crit group for helping me get those crucial first few chapters knocked into shape.

Thanks to Charlie Cochrane for encouraging me to "start writing and see where it goes", and to Linda Ingmanson at Samhain for taking a chance on a first-time novelist.

Thanks to all my online and real life friends who encouraged me to keep working on those drafts—your support has been invaluable and much appreciated.

And last but not least, thanks to my capricious and salacious muse—it's been exhilarating getting to know and trust you, and I hope you'll lead me on many more exciting escapades.

# Chapter One

"You still there, Tris?" Dan asked, trying not to stare at the slipstream of muddy water churned up by his hire boat's propeller. The stupid bloody phone kept cutting out—proof, if the general lack of buildings and abundance of trees weren't enough, that he truly was in the arse-end of nowhere. He fiddled with his Bluetooth again. It crackled.

"Can you hear me?" Tris shouted.

"Yes, all right! It's bad enough with you leaving me in the lurch—there's no need to deafen me too."

"Now, now, sweetheart, don't get tetchy. I'm just practising projecting. Anyway, what are you complaining about? With me back here, you won't have any competition when it comes to seducing all those country bumpkins. You on your *Faerie Queen*." Tris sniggered. "They must have seen you coming, giving you a boat called that."

Dan sighed. Tristan Sinclair might well be his oldest friend, but right now he was not in Dan's good books after accepting a part on the chorus line of *La Cage aux Folles*. "It'd be spot-on if you were at the tiller, mate. Fat chance I'll have now, going out on the pull. Can't even manage to take any bloody pictures." Dan eyed his camera with frustration. Even with it hanging around his neck, he was too chicken to let go of his hold on the tiller and take a shot. "I could be up on the roof with some great views, you Judas."

Tris laughed. "Like you'd be standing on the roof! What about the drop into the water, Danny-boy? Or is it not so bad now you're there?"

Why had he ever told Tris about not being able to swim? "You're a total bastard."

"Sorry, darling." Tris did at least sound contrite. "You know me, I just can't resist. But I do mean it—are you okay?"

Dan pulled his life jacket tight and kept his gaze fixed on the canal ahead. There was another narrowboat moored up and a solitary figure standing on the towpath alongside. Looked like a man chopping wood.

"Well, are you?" Tris prompted, and Dan recognised the genuine concern.

"Yeah, it's not so bad if I don't look down into the water. Besides, it's only four feet deep. Even a short-arse like me couldn't drown." Dan shuddered at a vision of himself standing freezing cold in the murky canal, just his head and shoulders clearing the surface.

"You're mad, taking a job on a boat if the stuff scares you that badly."

"It doesn't scare me! And besides, this is the best offer I've had in ages. I've had enough of writing up third-rate Spanish resorts. Besides, they want my pictures too."

"Really? You never said."

"It was all a bit last minute. Didn't get a chance. Couldn't turn down a job like that, though." Despite being surrounded by the wet stuff, Dan added to himself.

"Yeah, well you can't blame me for taking the best offer I've had in ages either, can you?" Tris sniffed. "It's not so easy to find decent parts at our age. On stage, that is," he added, and Dan could hear the smirk. "At least your career is wrinkle-proof. No one cares if the guy who wrote the guide book was a doddery old fool."

"Fuck off, I am not doddery!" Dan flexed his twenty-nine-year-old muscles and checked his course. He glanced at the man up ahead again, then widened his eyes. What he'd taken from a distance for a patterned T-shirt turned out to be tattoos. The guy was half-naked, in October! They must make these boaters out of hardier stuff than him. He'd caught sight of a few of them on the day's journey—weather-beaten, hairy blokes in their baggy, raggedy clothing. Shame that wasn't his type, or he'd be spoilt for eye candy along here.

"Jesus, Tris, you should see this guy up ahead. Wish I could take you a picture."

"Why? Is he hot? Is he—" The line went completely dead this time, not just crackly. Dan cursed, then turned his attention back to the boater.

The inked whorls across his upper back rippled as the man drove the axe down into the log before him. Scratch that about boaters not being Dan's type—this one was just fine from the rear. He wore sturdy black leather boots that reached mid-calf, and his close-fitted combat trousers were tucked inside. His dark hair was cropped short, his tanned back tautly muscled, and his pert buttocks lovingly accentuated by the cut of his trousers. Dan spotted a dark patch on the waistband and imagined licking the sweat from the channel of his spine— picturing himself chasing a bead of perspiration on down, below the waistband and between those enticing cheeks.

Bloody boat engine. The vibrations, combined with the hot man up ahead, had given him the mother of all boners. And stranded on his deck in tight Levis, it was going to be pretty obvious to anyone who cared to look. Wouldn't be a problem somewhere he stood a chance of being able to do something about it, but out here on the bloody Kennet and Avon canal? It was enough to make him wish the bloke away...but it was hard to wish away such a perfect arse. Maybe if he got a look at the front of him. An eyeful of snaggletoothed, bushy-bearded boater would be like a mental cold shower.

Dan strained to catch a glimpse as his narrowboat slowly chugged past. The glint of Tattoo-guy's pierced nipples hijacked his attention, distracting him completely. As he panned up the boater's body, a thud shook through the boat beneath him.

Dan pitched forward, catching a blow to his ribs from the rear door.

"What the fuck do you think you're doing?" The boater dropped his axe and glowered. "Stupid fucking tourist! They shouldn't let you lot out in boats if you don't know how to steer the bloody things."

"God, I'm sorry! Wait a minute, I'll sort it out." Panic coursed through Dan's body. He grappled with the controls, trying to recall how the guy at the hire company had operated the reverse gear. If only he'd been paying more attention! The prow of Dan's boat pushed against the rear fender of the woodchopper's deep red boat. He really did have his nose up the other guy's arse after all. Just not quite how he'd been imagining it. Dan cut the engine—he could remember how to do that much at least.

Tattoo-guy jumped onto the back deck of his own boat and gave Dan's a hard kick, bracing himself against the rear doors. The bulk of the *Faerie Queen* rocked free; then the boater grabbed the rail along her roof to hold her steady. Dan clung to his tiller and gave his rescuer a grateful smile. "Thanks. Sorry, I couldn't find the reverse anywhere."

The boater took hold of Dan's boat and pulled it alongside his, using brute strength to shift the tonne of steel through the water. Dan's smile faltered as he drew nearer to the bloke. Tattoo-guy looked seriously pissed off, his dark blue eyes hostile and his mouth set in a line.

"Watch where you're going in future, all right? You could do serious damage to some of the boats along here. *Serendipity*'s a tough old bird," he said, patting the roof of the red boat, "but some of the others have wood or fibreglass hulls. You could sink them if you're not careful. And slow down a bit, 'cause your wash ends up rocking the boats you pass, understand?" His voice vibrated with controlled anger, but it was surprisingly rich and cultured for one so scruffy.

"Yeah, okay, point taken. I'll be more careful." Dan attempted another smile.

"It's not some fucking joke. These are people's homes. We might not live in brick-and-mortar houses like the rest of you, but that doesn't mean we don't deserve a bit of respect." The bloke folded his arms and glared at Dan.

Whoa! Where had that come from? "Hey, can we start again, please? It was a simple accident. I'm not disrespecting anyone here. I'm just a canal virgin, all right?"

"I suppose you think that makes it all right, then, do you? Steering like a bloody maniac and crashing into my boat?"

"Yeah, wait, no!" Dan could see he wasn't going to win this argument no matter what. "I've said I was sorry. If there's damage, I can pay for it."

Tattoo-guy sneered. "That's exactly the sort of attitude I'd expect from a tourist. You think you can just throw money at a problem and it'll go away, don't you?"

"Look mate, you don't know anything about me." Dan drew himself up to his full five foot six, painfully aware the other guy was still looming over him by about half a foot. "I've just offered to pay for any damage I've caused, so I don't see what your problem is."

"My *problem* is if you've caused any damage with your little stunt, I have to cruise all the way to the nearest dry dock in Bristol and get her lifted out of the water. Then I've got to clean and reblack the hull, which has got to be one of the most backbreaking tasks I've ever had the misfortune to do. It's not like spraying over a nick in your car's paintwork. It's a week out of my life I've got to spend sorting out the results of your sloppy steering."

"Oh. Shit. That is a big deal. Sorry. I didn't know."

"Yeah, well, that's because you're a tosser." Tattoo-guy gave Dan a withering stare, then dropped to his knees and leaned over the water. Dan took an instinctive step back. He relaxed when the man began poking at the side of his hull under the water, presumably feeling around for damage. You couldn't see anything in the murky green canal. Looked more like pea soup than water.

"You're a lucky man," Tattoo-guy said, straightening up again. Funny, Dan didn't feel all that lucky right now, despite being in the vicinity of a gorgeous, half-naked boater. "There's no damage done this time, but like I said, you need to watch out, because some boats are a lot more vulnerable."

Dan nodded. "Right. Gotcha. I'll pay better attention."

"What's your excuse, anyway? Talking on the phone, were you? Or taking a photo? I know you can only go at a snail's pace on one of these boats, but as you're such a beginner, you should have your whole attention on the water ahead, all right?"

13

Dan wrenched the Bluetooth from his ear and shoved it into his pocket. There was no way he was going to tell this miserable git what had distracted him. It was bad enough being shouted at by the best-looking bloke he'd met in ages. He tried for a smile and just about managed it. "Right you are. Any more tips while you're at it?" And he didn't mean for that to come out sounding sarcastic, but it was too late to take it back.

"Yeah. Clear off. There's spots for tourists to moor up in Bathampton."

Tattoo-guy gave Dan's boat a push and turned away, hopping back to the bank and picking up his axe. That would be Dan's cue to leave, then.

He started the engine with a sigh. Bugger, what a way to hit it off with his first real boater. He turned his concentration back to his boat and tried to remember how to get the thing going again. By the time he was confident enough to look back, Tattoo-guy was nowhere to be seen.

As Dan neared civilisation, the canal became much more crowded. Admittedly he wasn't travelling any faster than he could walk, but he'd passed nothing but boats for the last half an hour. It was like a linear city stretched out through the valley, sandwiched between fields of sheep and patches of woodland. There was a conspicuous absence of hire boats, so he couldn't have reached wherever those tourist moorings were supposed to be.

Dan itched to get shooting but didn't dare with Tattoo-guy's words still ringing in his ears. There were so many different styles of boat. He'd assumed they would all be narrowboats, but that was far from the case. There were ones that looked about double the width—too wide for the canal, really, so he had to concentrate on his steering when passing them. There were tall boats with high wheelhouses in the centre that looked like they'd be more at home bobbing up and down on the ocean. There were small white cruisers that seemed to be made of plastic—they must be the fibreglass ones. Dan took extra care when chugging past those, dropping his speed from walking to crawling. But even more surprising than the variety of styles of boat was the range of conditions they were in. Boats that gleamed with fresh paint and polished portholes were moored up next to rust-buckets that looked like they should be sunk to put them out of their misery.

Steering around a curve in the canal's path, Dan caught sight of the white railings of a swing bridge up ahead. He'd passed through only one so far, and someone else had opened it for him so he hadn't had to figure out how to moor up and operate the bloody thing. That was another reason he could have done with having Tristan onboard. Dan scanned the bank. There was a clear section coming up, and the sign said seventy-two-hour moorings. Those must be the tourist spaces, and if he stopped here, he could figure out the bridge on another day—preferably when not half-dead from hunger.

But how the hell was he meant to steer into the bank? The instructor had shown him earlier, but all Dan could remember right now was the guy's meaty paws on the controls. He should have been concentrating, but the sight of the prison tattoos across the guy's knuckles had distracted him, making him wonder what on earth would possess someone to ink "ABBA RULE" as a permanent message to the world.

Did he have to steer the front or the back in first? The burly instructor with the Swedish pop fixation had somehow managed to get the boat to drift in sideways so that the whole fifty-foot length bumped gently against the bank at the same time. Ah well, Dan would just have to see what he could do. What was the worst that could happen?

Getting the front end against the bank was fairly straightforward, even if it did make contact with an ominous grating sound. But then there was the back to steer in, and everything he tried seemed to make it swing out farther. Not willing to concede defeat, Dan crunched away at the gears, swung the tiller arm around and churned up the canal into a muddy soup.

And then he'd gone and done it. Got the boat wedged in diagonally so that he was nearly caught up in the branches of an overhanging tree on the wild side of the bank, while the front end was where he wanted to be—the towpath side.

"Jesus, not again," someone called behind him.

15

Dan whirled around, and his stomach did a nauseating little flip. Sodding perfect! It was Tattoo-guy again, standing astride a beat-up old bicycle with one of his trademark glowers directed Dan's way. Okay, so he was wearing a T-shirt this time, but there was no mistaking that piercing gaze and air of contempt.

"Uh, I don't suppose you could help me out, could you? I seem to be stuck." Dan gave what he hoped was an ingratiating smile.

Tattoo-guy stared at him for a long moment, then shook his head, dismounted and chucked the bike against the fence. He strode over to the front end of the *Faerie Queen* and hopped on deck, making his way down the side of the boat like a monkey. Watching him move along the sticking-out shelf—the gunwales, that's what it was called—Dan couldn't help but admire the economy of his movements. For a big bloke, he was remarkably agile.

Within moments he fetched up on the back deck and loomed over Dan, radiating annoyance. "And what exactly were you trying to do this time? It's not wide enough to turn here. Anyone with half a brain should be able to see that."

Dan bristled. "I'm not an idiot! I was trying to moor up where you told me to, on the tourist moorings." He gestured at the sign, nearly clipping Tattoo-guy's arm. "The stupid bloody thing wouldn't go in the right direction, and then I got stuck on something. Shit, are we going to have to get someone to tow me off it?"

Tattoo-guy raised his eyebrows. "What you've somehow managed to do is get stuck on the shelf. You can't see it, but it runs along under the water to protect the wildlife on the bank." He stared pointedly at the bank behind him, and Dan coloured.

"Oh, bugger. Sorry 'bout that. It was the first time I've had to moor up, and I couldn't work out how to get the back of the boat to go the right way. These crazy things steer all back to front."

Those dark blue eyes gave Dan a look of utter disbelief. "How long did they spend teaching you how to steer? All of five minutes?"

Dan squirmed. "More like fifteen, but I reckon I could have done with longer."

"No shit. Well, I suppose it's not really your fault if they let you go without knowing what you were doing." A weariness crept into the man's voice, and Dan relaxed enough to take him in properly. He was perhaps Dan's age and definitely rough around the edges, what with the frayed T-shirt, the grime in the creases of his knuckles, and the five-o'clock shadow, but there was no denying the bloke had great bone structure, his cheekbones high and his chin strong. Shame he always seemed to be frowning. Dan wondered what it would take to get him to smile.

"So, what do we do now?" Dan asked.

"*You* need to push us off the shelf with the bargepole, and I'll take over the steering, since you obviously can't handle the pressure."

Dan muttered uncomplimentary things that were drowned out by the noise of the engine and took up the cream-and-green-striped bargepole. It was a surprise to discover it still had a use in this day and age. He'd assumed it was there simply to add to the authenticity of the experience, a relic of a bygone age like the traditional roses and castles painted on the door panels. This was good, though. This was one of those moments he could fashion into an interesting little anecdote for the magazine readers. If he left out Mr. Grumpy-pants, that was.

As the bargepole made contact with the concrete lining of the canal, Dan pushed with as much strength as he could muster. The boat shifted a little, but they were still stuck.

"Come on, you'll need to push harder than that. Put a bit of muscle into it."

Dan gritted his teeth and strained until his arms began to shake with the effort but still couldn't rock the boat free. He had a cyclist's body, lean and toned, but built for endurance rather than brute force. He didn't want to come across like some kind of wimp, though, so he gave another thrust, grunting with the effort. And this time he felt it move a little farther. He turned to his rescuer with a smug grin, then realised why. Tattoo-guy's hands were on the end of the pole. Bugger.

The *Faerie Queen* rocked free. Tattoo-guy grabbed hold of Dan's hand and placed it on the tiller. "Right, then, once you've got the front in where you want it, you need to get into first gear and steer into the bank."

Dan watched the towpath bank getting closer, aware of the warmth of that strong hand covering his own. "But all day I've been steering the opposite way to where I wanted to go." Who would have thought a boat with only three gears and two directions to steer in could be so complicated?

"Yeah, but what you need to remember is that you steer in the direction that you want the back of the boat to go in. Going round a bend, that will be the opposite way to the direction you want to follow, but when you're mooring up, you need to steer towards where you want to go."

Feeling his brain start to melt—physics never was his strong point—Dan decided to prove himself by some practical action. Once the boat made contact, he leapt onto the bank, grasped the front mooring rope and secured it through one of the steel rings set into the concrete edge. The effect was somewhat spoilt, however, by the way Tattoo-guy got his tied up first, then came along to tut at and retie Dan's own knot. Dan watched his technique closely, determined to get it right next time.

Tattoo-guy straightened.

"Thanks," Dan breathed, hyperaware that he was standing way too close to one of the most attractive men he'd met in a long time. One who not only hated his guts but was probably straight, he reminded himself, taking a step back. "Dan Taylor," he said, sticking out his hand. "I owe you one."

After a long moment, Tattoo-guy shook his hand. "Robin Hamilton," he said, his voice gruff. "I reckon you owe me two after today, but I don't think you've got anything I'm interested in."

That dark blue gaze roamed over his body, and Dan drew in a sharp breath. Maybe not so straight after all, then. He decided to take a chance—he couldn't likely make things any worse than they already were, could he? "How would you know if you're interested or not if you don't sample the goods?" He gave his cheekiest grin.

Dan could have sworn Robin's mouth twitched at the corner.

A bicycle bell jangled loudly, breaking the moment.

"Robin! I've been looking for you," a deep voice called.

Robin started guiltily, and Dan turned to discover a tiny woman on an old-fashioned bicycle. Dark, skinny limbs, flat chest and short black hair notwithstanding, she was most definitely female. The flowers wound around her wicker handlebar basket and pinned in her hair would give it away, even if her pretty face didn't. She beamed at them, and Dan couldn't help but return the smile.

"Are you going to introduce me to your friend, then?" She had an amazingly throaty, mannish voice.

Robin looked for a moment like he was going to object, and then he gestured to Dan. "Dan, this is Mel. Mel, Dan."

Dan stepped forward when he realised that was going to be it, his hand outstretched. She held him with a firm grip—considerable strength concealed in those delicate-looking fingers. "Dan Taylor, travelling scribe." He looked down at her clunky, water-stained boots. *Please don't let her be Robin's girlfriend.* "And you must be a boater like Robin."

"That's right. Melody Kumar. I'm on *Galadriel*, the little purple tug you must have passed, just before the last stone bridge."

"With the mural on the side?" Dan remembered that one; he'd noticed it not long after his first encounter with Robin. The elf mural had been executed with more enthusiasm than talent, but the boat would make a great subject for a photograph. It had been covered in plant pots, with a line of brightly coloured laundry stretching across between the roof and the bank.

"Hang on, what do you mean, 'travelling scribe?'" Robin demanded. "Are you a bloody journalist or something?"

Dan drew himself up to full height and stared Robin down. "I'm a travel writer, here to write up a boating holiday for the *Observer*. Is that okay, or do I need to get permission from the self-appointed canal police now?"

"So long as you're not sticking your nose into other people's business. We keep to ourselves down here, all right? We don't need outsiders poking around."

Mel rolled her eyes. "Ignore him, Dan. He's not usually quite this grumpy. I'm happy to help you out if you need any information for your article."

"Thanks." Dan smiled at her. "You can start by telling me if there's anywhere around here I can get a decent pub lunch. I'm absolutely starving. It's hungry work, this boating lark."

"Yeah, there's the Queen's Head in Bathampton. It's just half a mile or so that way." She waved in the direction Dan's boat was facing. "It's a bit pricey and stuck up, but I'm sure you'll like it." Dan wondered if that was meant to sound offensive or just came out that way. "Us boaters tend to go to the Hat and Feather, but that's all the way into Bath, a couple of miles further on."

"Maybe I'll give it a go later," Dan said. "Will you be there?" he asked Robin, trying to sound casual.

Robin gave a noncommittal grunt, and Mel shot him an exasperated look. "You're not still moping, are you? I told you, he'll come back to you when he's ready."

Dan wanted to ask who "he" was, but the look on Robin's face warned him to keep his trap shut.

"Okay, well, thanks for the rec. I might see you later."

"Cool. Come find me if you need anything, okay?" She grabbed hold of Robin's arm. "Now I've got to steal this man away from you. Take care, Dan." She beamed at him, flashing teeth that stood out a brilliant white against her dark skin.

Dan watched them walking away, pushing their bikes and deep in intense conversation. So the boaters weren't all surly gits who hated outsiders, then. That was encouraging.

# Chapter Two

"Nice place you have here," Dan told the saggy-faced landlord. Looked like he'd frowned and the wind changed direction, condemning him to a lifelong grimace. Then again, maybe it was because he was such a miserable bastard.

"It would be, if it weren't for all those gyppos out there." The landlord scowled in earnest, creasing a deep furrow between his brows. "Bad for business, they are. Driving the locals away. Never used to be like this. Used to be a respectable village. They're a bloody menace."

"They seem harmless enough. Looked like a bunch of hippies to me. One guy just helped me moor up the boat."

The landlord stared like he thought Dan was a bit simple. "Oh, they've got your number, all right. Putting on that salt-of-the-earth act, was he?" He snorted. "Degenerates, they are. Pagans, criminals and deviants, every last one of them. You want to watch your step along there at nighttime. Little fella like you could easily be taken advantage of by one of those thugs. You'd be shoved on your knees and buggered before you knew what was happening."

Dan blinked, swallowed his beer and tried to keep a straight face. Chance would be a fine thing!

He looked around the Queen's Head instead. Despite the evil menace of the boaters, trade didn't seem to be suffering. The place was packed with diners, and the waiting staff moved between the tables with practised ease. It was one of those traditional pubs that had been recently tarted up. Old wooden beams, brick walls and flagstones co-existed uneasily with the blond-wood tables, faux-continental menu boards and tasteful recessed lighting. Even the customers seemed fake—their sham country tweeds far too clean to convince him they were real farmers. Mind you, the rows of shiny 4x4s and Jaguars in the car park had already dispelled that illusion.

"You seem busy enough."

The landlord sniffed. "It's not too bad today, but trade really suffered over the summer. There were hardly any spots left for the tourists to moor up. Every last one of them hogged by some crusty git in a floating rust bucket. And they empty their waste out into the canal. It's a health hazard. I've been onto British Waterways about it, but they're bloody useless. Say they can only move them on every two weeks. Two weeks! Think of all the trade I can lose in two weeks."

Dan kept his mouth closed, scanning the pub. He was pleasantly sated by the huge roast dinner he'd just finished, but there was another appetite that still needed filling, and the grumpy landlord couldn't help him with this one.

A cute waiter dashed past, his hair a bright enough blond to make Dan's look almost ginger in comparison. The ties of his apron accentuated the curve of his buttocks. Okay, he wasn't as devastatingly gorgeous as Robin, but at least he knew how to smile. Dan tried to catch the waiter's eye and failed. Blondie headed out the back door. Dan mumbled something to the landlord about needing to visit the gents and dashed off after Blondie.

The back of the pub was a labyrinth of crates, barrels and mysterious outbuildings. Dan poked his head around a few corners, hoping he might find the lad having a sneaky cigarette, but there was no sign of him. Sighing, he headed back inside. He'd catch him later. Or maybe just wait until this evening and hit a pub where he could guarantee the guys would be into other guys.

A pillar blocked his view of the bar, but Dan picked up a familiar sound. A rich voice, low but bristling with restrained fury. Fury he'd had directed at him only an hour or two previously.

"What do you mean? You've got other notices up there. What exactly is it that makes mine unsuitable?"

Dan couldn't hear the landlord's reply, but Robin's response certainly carried. "Well fuck you, then, you arrogant cunt!"

Dan stepped around the pillar just in time to see Robin storming out the door, slamming it shut behind him so that the glass rattled in the panes. A piece of paper fluttered to the ground, and Dan picked it up, burning with curiosity. At the top, in careful lettering, handwritten yet set out like type, it said: Missing: have you seen Morris? There was a photograph of a cat underneath. Morris had a huge mane around his serene face, the white nose and bib striking against the dark tabby markings of his body. A beautiful creature—and enormous too—but what really caught Dan's attention was the pair of arms encircling him. The head of the figure might have been cropped out of the photo, but there was no mistaking those tattooed arms. At the bottom of the page there was a plea for anyone with information on the whereabouts of Morris to call Robin on his mobile.

So this was the mysterious missing "he"! Dan folded up the notice and slipped it into his jacket pocket. Turning to the grim-faced landlord, he gave a smile. "I don't know, some people," he offered, shaking his head.

"They should know better than to try and put their notices up in here. I won't have it. I've told them before. They're not getting any favours from me after they drive away my summer trade by mooring their scummy boats outside and letting their dogs run wild. Probably one of them that ate his precious cat."

"No, Nige, it was probably one of the other vagrants. They either ate it or stole it and sold it on. Them pedigree cats are worth a few bob, you know." The old man at the bar leaned towards Dan with a conspiratorial leer. "That lot are bad news, you know. Better steer clear of 'em, if I were you. Nice young lad like you could get led astray."

The mocking laughter followed Dan out of the pub as he made a dash for the fresh air. He ran up the steps to the towpath and looked in both directions, but there was no sign of Robin. Bugger. Still, he had his mobile number, which wasn't bad work considering they hadn't exactly hit it off. He meandered back to the *Faerie Queen*, pondering the tensions he'd just witnessed between the boaters and the local community. There was a story here. He was sure of it.

Now he just needed to get an insider's account of what was going on.

Dan waited until early evening but then couldn't contain his impatience any longer. He cycled out to Mel's boat, relieved to see the lights on inside and her flower-bedecked bicycle resting on the roof. Although the boat was a couple of feet wider than his narrowboat, it was much shorter. He found it hard to imagine how anyone could contain their whole life in such a tiny space.

"You going to stand out there all day or come on in to the warm?"

Dan grinned at Mel, who had stuck her head out of the hatch on the side of her boat. "Wasn't sure if I was meant to knock on the side or if I should climb onto the deck and knock on the door."

"Either way's fine with me, sweetie. We don't stand on ceremony around here. Just hop onboard."

But before Dan had a chance to climb up, Robin pushed his way out of the doors and onto the deck. He gave Dan a curt nod of recognition. "I'll be off, then," he called back to Mel.

"No, sweetie, you should stay. Get to know Dan."

Robin gave Dan a look he couldn't interpret. Dark and complicated and downright intimidating.

"I'm going out, remember? Besides, I've got posters to put up first."

Mel huffed, but she didn't argue. They both watched as Robin cycled off into the gloaming. "Come on in, then. See what a real boat's like on the inside. Bet it's nothing like your hire boat."

It certainly wasn't. *Dark* was the first word that sprang to Dan's mind. Closely followed by *warm*. No, make that *sweltering*. And *cluttered* followed rapidly on as he looked for somewhere to put his jacket.

"Here, let me. The bed's about the only place to throw it." Mel walked the few paces through the crowded living area and pulled back a curtain. A rumpled pile of bedding filled up the tiny bed cabin. It was a totally different layout to his hire boat, where the bed was open to a corridor along the side so it didn't seem too cramped, although maybe he'd feel differently tonight when he actually slept in it. Mel's bed took up the width of the boat and had only a small entryway to climb up onto it—God, it must be like sleeping in a cupboard.

A cupboard that smelled of damp, overlaid with the reek of incense.

"Want something to drink? I've got herbal tea or vodka."

What a choice! Dan eyed the state of Mel's tiny galley. It looked like a crockery and food bomb had exploded all over the narrow strip of worktop and sink. You could catch something nasty just by looking at those mugs.

"I'm fine, thanks. Just popped by to ask you about something." Now that his eyes were adjusting to the dim light, he could make out the knickknacks that encrusted every surface like bohemian barnacles. Was there anything here that wasn't covered in beads and baubles? Mind you, if he could get the lighting right, it would make a great backdrop for a portrait shot.

"Okay. Come on, sit." Mel patted the sofa beside her. There wasn't much room, so Dan would have to squeeze up tight. He hesitated a moment, caught a sharp gaze that made him feel strangely inadequate, and resigned himself to getting up close and personal with Mel.

"So, are you going to tell me what this is about?"

"Right, yes. I was wondering if any of the boaters might be interested in having their photographs taken. On their boats, I mean. Like a portrait of them and their home."

She screwed up her forehead in thought. "Maybe. Depends what it's for and how you approach them."

"I'm trying to break into photojournalism, and it struck me that I could write a social interest piece to go with the portraits. Something about poverty and prejudice on the waterways."

"Interesting." Mel narrowed her eyes, and Dan put on his best earnest face. It usually worked well for him, but Mel seemed impervious to his charms. "I like the idea, but I wouldn't want to sell it to them like that. We're a proud lot. We chose this lifestyle, and you could say we're rich in many ways."

Dan glanced around the claustrophobic space. He wasn't going to argue if Mel thought this heap of junk represented riches, but she was clearly deluded.

"Some of the boats aren't as well kept as yours, though, are they? What about the ones that are like tents on the top?" He'd passed one like that with a crumbling wooden hull and a black tarpaulin stretched out over a central beam. There were a few plastic windows set into the canvas, and the air above the stovepipe rippled with heat, but the sight still made Dan shudder. "Do people actually live on those during the winter? They must freeze."

"Nah, what d'you think stoves are for? If anything, you end up getting too stuffy and have to open the hatches."

"But they've only got a bit of canvas between them and the elements."

"So? Our ancestors used to live in caves. You'd be surprised what your body can take when you put it to the test. But maybe you're too used to your central heating and electrical appliances." Mel gave a mischievous smile. "You've gone soft."

"I bloody well haven't! I cover cycling holidays all the time. They're tough work, especially when you have to camp as well." Dan had once been sent on a gay cycling holiday which was great fun, despite having to get his sore arse back on the saddle each day. He smiled to himself. "That's just once in a while, though, I suppose. What made you choose to live this way?"

"I'm not sure. The way I grew up, I suppose. Mum met my dad while travelling in Gujarat, and I spent my childhood all over the world. Never really learnt how to settle down in one place, but then again, I reckon some people are just like that. You know, they have the wanderlust."

Dan nodded. "Yeah, I spent all my childhood in one house in a South London estate, but I've never been able to settle, either."

"I'm not surprised if you grew up somewhere like that. Rough, was it?"

Dan grimaced. "Could be at times. But like Mum always says, what doesn't kill you only makes you stronger." And in his case, made him want to spend his whole life on the run so he didn't get stuck somewhere like that ever again.

Mel's head snapped up as if she'd had a brainwave. "I'll tell you what angle would work better. You know the main thing that pisses us off? Bloody BW and their poisonous little rules."

"BW?"

"British Waterways. We pay their wages with our licence fees, but they still hassle us to move on every two weeks. One day over and they threaten to take you to court. I knew one poor woman went into labour and had to stay in hospital for a couple of weeks; she got back with her newborn to find her boat covered in court orders. She didn't half kick up a stink."

It sounded unlikely, but then what did he really know about this strange, close-knit community?

"So, can't you just move half a mile or so and moor up again?"

"I wish. Doesn't work like that, sweetie. You have to move to a new neighbourhood, although they can be pretty vague about what that actually means. They're really strict about it around here, though. It's a popular spot with the tourists, and they want to keep the canal clear for them." The way she pronounced "tourists"—just like Robin had—left him in no doubt that there was animosity between them and the boaters. Did that mean the others would be suspicious of him? He wasn't really a proper tourist, but maybe he represented all tourists with his travel writing. The thought wasn't exactly encouraging. He'd have to turn on his high-voltage charm with these people. Should work. They were only used to 12V battery power after all—he'd dazzle them.

"What about marinas? I've seen a few of them on the journey down."

Mel looked at him like he'd said something beneath contempt. "Have you seen how much those places cost? Most of us don't have much. If you wanted to stay in one of those places, you'd have to get regular work, and then you may as

# Chapter Three

Robin stood across the street from the White Hart, trying to get a feel for the place. The Georgian building was typical for Bath. Honey-coloured limestone and tall windows with heritage-green trim gave it an elegant appearance. It rubbed shoulders with the Theatre Royal and looked like somewhere his parents would drink—not his kind of place at all. He was going to look like a proper bit of rough in a fancy pub like that. There wasn't even a whisper of a rainbow flag about the place. Maybe Mel had been wrong. He could always head back to one of the other, more obviously gay bars—but no, he'd been told that this place was definitely queer.

And besides, he didn't want to go into one of those other places. He'd already walked past the Hussars and seen far too many skinny blokes with hungry eyes hanging about smoking by the front doors.

Blokes who reminded him of Jamie.

It was bad enough having Dan-fuckwit-Taylor stir up this old appetite again with his freckles and dimples and cute little arse. He really didn't need to find someone who reminded him of his worst mistake ever.

Robin took a deep breath, glanced around to make sure no one he recognised was there to see him, then pushed open the heavy oak door.

It was quiet inside. And all the drinkers were men.

The well-dressed patrons looked like a theatre-going crowd, but as the play had already started, they couldn't be here for that. Robin glanced over the quietly chattering groups in the booths and the couple of older guys perched on stools at the bar. He didn't have to worry about letting his gaze linger in here, did he? Even if it did make what he'd come here for blindingly obvious. But even after a longer inspection of the room, it was painfully clear that the barman was the most attractive man there, by a long shot.

Smiling—not too ravenously, he hoped—he ordered a pint of bitter and settled down with his elbows on the bar, about halfway between the two other barflies.

"Here you are, sir," the young man purred, handing over Robin's beer with a cute smirk. Shame about the manicured goatee and overly slicked hair, but he had beautiful brown eyes. He might not know where his next lot of cash was coming from, but bugger the cost, Robin had to offer.

"And one for yourself?" he said, handing over all his worldly riches.

"I'd love one, sweetheart, but not while I'm working. The landlord would whip my arse if he found out." There was something knowing in the barman's smile that made Robin feel like he'd been left out of the big joke.

As the barman sashayed over to the cash register, the white-haired man at the end of the bar piped up. "You're wasting your time with him, darling. What the little flirt's not telling you is that he's married to the landlord."

Married? But of course. Just because civil partnerships weren't the kind of thing Jamie and his friends had been into, didn't mean that there weren't plenty of happily married gay couples out there. Looking round the room, he wondered how many of the respectable-looking couples were in civil partnerships themselves. Did this mean he was going to have to start paying attention to ring fingers? With a sudden pang, he remembered Jamie's slender fingers. Would it have made any difference to the way things turned out if they'd been married back then? But there wasn't any point in thinking that way. He couldn't change anything now.

"Don't pout, darling. He's really not worth it, although he likes to think he is," the barfly said. The cute barman stuck out his tongue and flounced off to collect empty glasses from the tables.

"Charles Wentworth is the name, my dear. I don't think we've had the pleasure of your company here before, have we? It's always so pleasant to see a fresh face. And where have you been hiding yourself away?"

Robin took a closer look at Charles as he shook the proffered hand. Silver-haired and ruddy-cheeked, the man reminded him of his dad. It was disconcerting to see the lustful gleam in his eyes. He wore a tweed suit with a bright yellow cravat and probably wouldn't have looked out of place when the building was new.

"Robin Hamilton. I've just come in on my boat. On the canal." It was one of those titbits he'd discovered would either fascinate or kill a conversation dead.

"Oh, you're one of those strapping boaters, are you? How delightful! And what kind of vessel are you the skipper of, my dear?"

Robin smiled despite his misgivings. He could talk about *Serendipity* all day. "She's a beauty. Fifty-five foot, narrow-beam, traditional stern. Lister SR2 engine. Handles like a dream."

"Marvellous, I just adore the traditional narrowboats. Do tell me more. Where was she built?"

Robin allowed himself to be drawn into conversation. Charles was pleasant enough company, even if it wasn't quite what he'd been looking for tonight. He spoke a bit about the work he'd done on *Serendipity* as he drained his pint, Charles hanging on his every word. The man didn't even notice when Robin's breath caught on seeing Dan walk into the pub and take up position at the far end of the bar. Shit, oh shit. What was he doing here?

"I'm buying a house backing onto the canal in Bathampton," Charles continued. "I thought it would be a lovely place to retire and watch the boats go by. You simply must come and visit once I'm settled in."

With this pronouncement, Charles grabbed hold of Robin's hand. His grip was tight, and it was hard to resist the urge to pull away, but Robin's manners won out.

"Thanks, but, umm, I'll have to be moving on soon. Can't stay in one spot for longer than a fortnight. British Waterways's rules."

"Oh, how utterly ghastly!" Charles's face was a pantomime of distress. Robin would have laughed it off if his hand wasn't being squeezed quite so firmly. And, oh God, Charles had started stroking his arm while he spoke.

"But of course!" Charles brightened like a pile of kindling catching light. "You can moor up at the end of my garden. Oh, do say you will. I get awfully lonely, and I'm sure a strong young man like you could make himself useful about the place in return. You look like you'd be good with your hands."

Was Charles proposing what Robin thought he was? He didn't know whether to be grateful or offended. The very idea of being a kept man made his head spin.

"It's a kind offer. I'll have to think about it." His gaze flickered across to Dan, who was watching them with what seemed to be amusement. Robin flushed.

"I'm not letting go of you until we have a definite arrangement, my darling Robin."

Robin stared into Charles's bloodshot eyes. The whiskey fumes on his breath made him want to cough. What was it going to take to get out of this one without causing a scene? The man might be a lech but seemed genuinely kind, and it was nice to meet someone respectable who didn't consider him a threat. Besides, he didn't like the idea of offending someone who reminded him of his dad. He could say yes, then just quietly leave the area without ever seeing the man again. He could even get a shag out of Charles first. He'd been hoping for someone younger, someone more like Dan—although not Dan himself, obviously—but perhaps there was something to be said for the experience of age, and despite having the broken veins of a heavy drinker, Charles wasn't bad looking. Maybe if Robin went along with it, he'd even get his hand back without having to wrench it from the guy's grasp.

"Come along, my dear. Let me show you what a real man can do for you."

Robin felt his resistance cracking under Charles's determined onslaught. Try as he might, he couldn't come up with a totally convincing reason as to why he shouldn't give in.

"Robin, sweetheart, is this man bothering you?"

The voice startled both of them. Robin turned and found himself staring into a pair of twinkling hazel eyes. Oh God, he never would have imagined feeling this happy to see Dan.

"I think you'd better let go of my boyfriend, now," Dan said, placing a hand on Robin's shoulder as Charles reluctantly loosened his grip.

"I'm so sorry, my dears. I didn't realise Robin was already spoken for. Please accept my heartfelt apologies."

Dan smiled breezily, seemingly oblivious to Robin's confusion. "That's all right. I know what a temptation he is, aren't you, gorgeous?"

Robin caught Dan's eye, and it was like he'd been captured by the current, pulled in against his will. It wasn't fair. Someone like Dan shouldn't have eyes that beautiful. He was mesmerised by the flecks of green and amber and that band of ginger freckles sprinkled across the bridge of his nose.

And then, before Robin could say anything else, Dan pulled him into a kiss. His lips pressed hot and soft against Robin's. Perhaps it was the effect of the pint he'd just had on an empty stomach; perhaps it was the sweet, musky scent rising from Dan's body; or perhaps it was simply the relief of being saved from Charles's advances. Whatever it was, against his better judgment Robin sank into the kiss, parting his lips and clutching Dan to him with greedy arms.

# Chapter Four

Dan slid his tongue into Robin's mouth and made a delightful discovery. Not only did Robin have rings through his nipples, but there was a barbell through his tongue as well. Dan moaned as the metal ball made contact with his palate, his tongue. There was a tiny click every time it clashed against his teeth. God, he wanted that hot mouth around his dick so fucking badly. It had been a while since he'd had head from a bloke with a pierced tongue. Wonder if he had piercings anywhere more intimate?

He stretched on his toes to deepen the kiss, wound his arms around Robin's neck and pressed against him, body to body. Robin must be able to feel how much he wanted him, what with the way his prick was starting to harden and rub against Robin's thigh. He rocked his hips to emphasise the point.

Robin froze and started to pull back from the kiss.

Dan thought fast. He couldn't lose his advantage now. Not when he had Robin exactly where he wanted him. He sank back onto his heels, gave his sultriest smile and took one of Robin's unresisting hands, lacing their fingers together.

"Come on, gorgeous, we're running late." He tugged Robin after him and headed for the door, turning to call back to the old geezer with the Robin fixation. "Thanks for looking after him for me. He gets into all sorts of trouble when I'm not there to keep an eye on him."

The pub door swung shut behind them. Dan led Robin around the corner and found a large pillar in the shadows outside a closed shop to push him up against. Robin was still dazed, his eyes hooded and his jaw slack. Yeah, that had been a great kiss. Guys were always telling him he had a talented tongue, and seeing what it had done to Robin made him swell with pride. He dropped his hands to Robin's hips and purred seductively.

"Now, where were we?"

Robin made an alarmed sound in his throat and pulled back slightly, his body trembling. Dan gave a delighted smile. Surely the big guy wasn't out of his depth, was he? But yes, fear lurked in his eyes.

"No need to worry, you're in safe hands. I've done this plenty of times before."

It was as if the words broke the spell his kiss had cast. Robin's eyes widened, and his body stiffened, but not in the place Dan wanted it to.

"How many times?"

"What?"

"How many times have you done *this* before?" Robin snarled, pushing Dan away with a shove to his chest. "You make a habit of picking up strange men, do you?"

Oh God, it was back to Mr. Shouty again, was it? "You're not that strange. I even know your surname, which is more than I do with some guys." He'd been aiming for light banter, but the disgust on Robin's face made him realise he'd misjudged. Dan backpedalled. "I dunno, you just seemed like you needed a hand, and I knew I owed you one, and then I couldn't help myself, you looked so delicious."

"Yeah, well... I was doing fine by myself, thank you very much."

"Didn't look like it from where I was standing. You looked like you were struggling with how to let the guy down without being rude. That's always a recipe for disaster. Best to be honest and get it all out in the open." Dan grinned, but it didn't seem to make an impression on his quarry.

"What makes you think I wasn't interested in him? I suppose someone like you wouldn't shag an old queen like him if he were the last man on earth, although you'd quite happily work your way through every sleazy little whore at a place like the Hussars." Robin's lip curled up in a sneer.

"Look, I'm not a one-man kind of bloke, and I don't see why I should be ashamed of that." Dan stuck out his chin. He was buggered if he was going to let Robin take the moral high ground here. "I'm a player."

"You're a slut, you mean."

"Fuck you."

"Not a chance. I've got a girlfriend anyway. Mel. You remember?" There was no mistaking the challenge in Robin's eyes. It was that defensiveness that fundamentally honest people always betrayed when they were lying through their teeth. "I'd better get going. I'm supposed to be meeting her at the Hat and Feather."

Dan wasn't going to let him get away that easily. "Funny that, I figured you were gay, the way you kissed me back in the pub. The *gay* pub, where you were having a drink with a *gay* man." Bloody hell, if that wasn't a blush spreading across Robin's cheeks and making him look even more edible.

"I'm bi, but that's nobody's fucking business but my own, okay? Not that it matters, anyway, because I'm off to see my girlfriend. Good-bye, Dan." His voice was sharp enough to make Dan wince, and it deterred him from following after Robin as he stalked away.

"See you soon, Robin," he called.

Robin didn't turn back.

Sighing heavily, Dan wrapped his jacket closer around his body and headed off towards the Hussars. Robin was right; that probably was more his kind of place, and there was no point wasting the evening. There'd be plenty of opportunity to get to work on Robin before he had to go back to London. He'd have him by the time his trip was over.

A smirk tugged at his lips.

Robin wouldn't know what had hit him. Dan was going to rock his world.

"Hey, Danny-boy! You just caught me," Tris said. "Lucky for you I'm not on stage for the next couple of numbers. How you doing? Sunk that boat yet?"

"Still afloat, no thanks to you."

"You're such a drama queen! What are you doing calling me at this time of the evening, anyway? Can't you find any better company? Thought you were meant to be checking out the scene in Bath."

"Yeah, I did. It wasn't all that." He'd given up and cycled back to the boat again. Once he'd got the boat warmed up and figured out that there was no television reception in this particular spot, phoning Tris seemed like the best entertainment available.

"So? What gives? Thought you'd be on your knees in a toilet stall by now. Don't tell me you're getting picky in your old age."

"Fuck off. If I'm old, then so are you."

"Yes, but I make more of an effort to look young than you do, sweetness." Dan could practically hear Tris sucking in his cheeks and pouting. "Go on then. Spill it. Or have you already spilt it and come home early?"

"No such luck. Had a great snog earlier—really hot boater guy—but he got the fear, and I couldn't find anyone else who measured up."

"So you are getting picky! I knew it. But Dan, really, a boater? Aren't they all smelly hippies? You hate hippies."

"I don't hate hippies!"

Tris harrumphed. "You once told me you'd never shag a man who wore tie-dye, no matter how well hung he was."

Dan couldn't deny it. "Yeah, well, Robin doesn't wear tie-dye. He looks more like a cross between paramilitary and posh boy. Do you get posh boys becoming boaters?"

"Lord knows, darling. You know me, I try and stay away from all that class nonsense. I love slumming it, so maybe he does too."

Dan pondered Tris's words. So far, Tris was probably the most upper class of all his friends, and the vast difference in their backgrounds had never stopped them getting along. If anything, it gave them more to talk about.

"Anyway," Tris continued, "you'd better not go getting all boring on me and wanting to settle down like everyone else seems to. I was going to take you to this great club I got invited to last night. You'd love it. Full of big men with tattoos. It was a bit...leather, but nothing too outrageous."

"You went to a leather club? Seriously?" Tristan might be a cheap tart, but he was just about the most vanilla man Dan had ever met—didn't even like the idea of threesomes much. Tris made Dan look downright kinky in comparison, even though the closest he'd ever got to bondage was that time he'd let a lover tie his hands to the bed frame. The loss of control had freaked him out so much that he'd never dared try it again.

"Yes, seriously. You know me. Always willing to try new things," Tris said.

"Always willing to try new men, you mean."

Tris laughed. The sound always made Dan chuckle. Tris might put on camp airs and graces like they were going out of fashion, but he had this belly laugh that never sat quite right with the act.

"So go on, then," Tris demanded. "I've got another few minutes. Tell me what I'm missing out on."

Dan looked around the tiny space. Despite using half a box of firelighters, he'd had real problems getting the stove going—good thing the boat had gas-fired central heating or he'd be freezing his nuts off. "You'd hate it. It's cold. The shower's only a trickle, and it's so small in there the curtain keeps getting stuck to your arse. The bed's about the size of a single even though it's meant to be a double. God knows how we'd have both fit in it."

"We'd have had to snuggle, babe. I'm sure that's what the boaters do. Must help them to keep warm as well."

"Yeah. Tell you what, I wouldn't mind snuggling up with this Robin fella. Bet he'd keep me warmer than your skinny arse would."

"Darling, I'm wounded. Mortally. Can't you hear the death rattle?" Dan held the phone away from his ear as Tris made a vile noise.

"You finished yet?"

Dan heard a voice in the background, and Tris stopped pretending to die.

"Oh shit, that's my call. Gotta go. You just go after this sexy boater man. I want to hear all about how you seduced him next time you phone, okay?"

"Will do. Break a leg, Tris."

"Love you too. Ciao!"

Dan stared at the phone display for a moment, but there was no one else he wanted to call. Tris was his oldest, closest friend and the only one he felt he could really open up to. Plus, he was brilliant at phone sex. He worked on one of those chat lines when he was between jobs—said it was just another form of acting. Dan had been hoping he might have the time to work his magic over the phone tonight. It had been ages since they'd done that.

For some reason it was much easier to get off with Tris over the phone than it was in person. Maybe they just didn't fancy each other enough to make the sex spectacular, or maybe it was something else. Maybe they couldn't be what the other one needed. Dan always had to top and got the feeling that Tris wanted him to be even more dominant. It just wasn't his style, though, so they very rarely bothered these days. Much better to flirt outrageously and go out on the pull together.

He shivered and pulled the blanket tighter around his shoulders. Why hadn't he gone home with one of the guys who'd offered? He'd have a warm bed and even warmer company. Fact was, though, none of them had measured up to Robin.

He couldn't shake the memory of that kiss.

Bugger. Perhaps he really was getting old.

He went with the flow and got an early night, stumbling into bed fully clothed. Maybe it was all the fresh air and exercise that was to blame, but sleep claimed him almost as soon as his head hit the pillow.

Morning found Dan warm and cosy in his nest of blankets. He surfaced from a dream of tussling with three sweaty, naked men and went to touch himself while still half-asleep.

Why was he wearing his jeans?

Dan sat up and looked around. Oh God, still on the bloody boat. What's more, it was fucking freezing. He burrowed back under the blankets and tried to recapture his dream.

But the dream guys were gone and he could only conjure up Robin. He went with it, remembering the image of Robin chopping wood. Those muscles had been beautiful—lean yet defined—and obviously the result of real work rather than steroids and protein supplements.

Dan unzipped his fly and stroked his cock. Memories of Robin's scent and taste assaulted him. Smoky, spicy, musky... Whatever it had been, it drove Dan wild. Would the rest of him taste as good as those luscious lips had? He imagined them wrapped around his dick. Imagined that tongue stud teasing his slit just before every plunge down. He used his thumbnail as a substitute, and the delicious pain made him hiss with pleasure. As his hand started to slip on precome, he sped up, his breathing shallow and rapid. The blankets were stifling, and he threw them back, no longer bothered by the frigid air.

He pictured Robin crouched down, pinning him to the mattress. The tattoo on his back undulating as he bobbed up and down, his cheeks hollowed. His dark eyes meeting Dan's.

Dan arched his back and came with a cry, spunk spurting between his fingers and pooling on his stomach.

He gave a wry smile. He could have woken up next to one of those blokes from the pub last night but turned them down for a date with his hand and an imaginary Robin. It felt like the start of one of his infatuations. Dan had grown to recognise them by now—this overwhelming interest in one particular man, which would last only for as long as it took him to shag it out of his system—no more than a couple of weeks. At that point, some of the gloss wore off the previously perfect man, and Dan would start to get bored and restless, looking around for someone new to divert him. The first few times he'd assumed that he'd fallen in love, but now he was older and wiser, he'd come to the conclusion that he just wasn't capable of that. It was probably for the best, as he'd hate to get tied down like his mum had been with his dad. He wasn't about to let an infatuation with one man—no matter how soulful his eyes were—wreck his perfectly happy lifestyle.

The come on his belly cooled and rapidly became uncomfortable. Dan sighed. No point trying to figure out the Robin thing on an empty stomach. Much easier to work on it in the presence of the guy. He'd get over him quickly enough.

After a hasty encounter with the clammy shower curtain, Dan pondered the options for breakfast. He ended up eating cold couscous salad out of the plastic tub from the deli, along with a torn-off piece of the now rather stale ciabatta loaf. He needed to get to a supermarket for some proper food—none of this fancy middle-class grub he'd been hoodwinked into eating over the last few years. He felt like a return to the food of his youth: chips and baked beans, pie and mash, sausages and gravy... Good honest food to fill you up and give you energy. Grimacing, he abandoned the rest of the ciabatta.

By now the sun was filtering through the rather thin curtains, so Dan decided to welcome it in. Unfortunately, he'd forgotten which side of the boat was which and ended up opening them on the towpath side. The elderly woman out walking her dog gave him a rather sweet, if decidedly startled, smile. Mind you, his towel had slipped pretty low on his hips... Shame it hadn't been one of the male boaters, really. One in particular.

By the time Dan was dressed and had checked over his camera, the sun was high enough to have boiled away most of the mist that hung above the water. It was going to be another fine autumn day. Humming to himself, he cycled off in the direction of Mel's boat. After checking in with her, he wanted to wander down to the river and get shots of the Dundas Aqueduct from that angle. And who knew, maybe a certain sexy boater would be up and about and ready to carry on their conversation from last night.

That way he could have his fun and get Robin Hamilton out of his system for good.

Dan framed the composition of the stone aqueduct towering over the river below and fired off a few shots. They'd be good but not striking. What he needed was to find an angle where the vivid reds of the trees were partially obscuring the ochre limestone and adding interest to that side of the scene. He scrambled up the valley side, slipping on the leaves covering the slope. Bugger. Now he had a muddy knee to match his soiled trainers. The countryside was bloody murder on his clothes—it was no wonder these boaters all looked like they'd been dragged through a hedge backwards, then rolled in a ditch for good measure.

Eventually Dan found a tree he could lean into and use to brace himself while he composed his photographs. It wasn't comfortable, leaning sideways onto the rough bark, but at least it was secure enough so that the slight give of the springy trunk didn't alarm him.

The leaves above his head rustled. Great. There was a creature up here with him. Dan tried to remember if any dangerous animals climbed British trees. As far as he could recall, he should be safe. Probably just a squirrel or something that sounded a lot larger than it really was. He peered nervously up into the crisscrossing branches and saw a furry face staring back. A familiar furry face.

"Morris?"

The cat just eyed him a few moments longer; then its lids blinked shut. Dan rooted around in his jacket pockets and found the folded-up poster liberated from the floor of the pub. Yep, that was Morris all right. The markings all matched. What the bloody hell was he doing lurking halfway up a tree, halfway up the side of the valley, when he could be curled up by a stove on a nice warm boat? Dan knew where he'd rather be.

"Here, Morris! Come on down. Your daddy's worried about you, you know."

Morris blinked slowly, giving Dan a look that suggested he found him beneath contempt but resolutely refused to budge. He'd been missing for a couple of days now, Dan remembered, so he might well be injured.

43

Dan pondered his options. There was really only one way of checking on the cat, and that involved climbing the sodding tree. It might be one of those skills every man was supposed to absorb during childhood, but his hadn't featured many trees. Still, there was a branch just above his head, and he was light and limber. It would have to be enough. After packing his camera away, Dan grabbed hold of the branch, relieved to discover the bark was crenellated deeply enough to provide decent traction for his feet. He found other hand and footholds, eventually seating himself on the same branch as Morris, some eight feet off the ground.

Dan eyed the cat. "You're coming with me, you know," he said with rather more certainty than he felt, looking down and wondering how on earth he was going to get them both safe on solid ground without causing further injury. He reached out and gave a tentative stroke to Morris's back. The cat hissed and bared his teeth. Bloody marvellous. Then Dan noticed what looked like blood matted into the fur there.

"There's no point getting pissy with me, catkins. I'm taking you down, and there's nothing you can do about it."

Turned out there was plenty Morris could do about it, including yowling, swiping out with bared claws, then sinking them into Dan's chest when he finally grasped the ungrateful monster by the scruff and held him close. "Ow! You bitch! I'm only trying to help."

Morris turned his head to bite Dan's hand, and any consideration of how best to get down from their perch became purely academic as Dan lost his balance and toppled off. He squawked, arms flailing, then hit the ground with a jolt that knocked all the breath out of his lungs. Fortunately he landed on his back, forming a human cushion for Morris. A human pincushion, more like, he thought to himself, wincing as claws dug in dangerously close to a nipple.

Still, it was better than landing facedown and having to explain to Robin why he had a squashed dead cat attached to his chest by its claws. But it wouldn't do to lie around in the woods all day. Not now that he'd effected his heroic rescue and could take Morris home and claim his reward, whatever that might be. Dan smiled to himself. He'd go for another kiss, followed by something more intimate once he'd got Robin warmed up. Yeah, that was worth dragging his arse up off the ground and wrestling with the world's most ungrateful rescuee.

Morris had gone limp, so Dan took the opportunity to haul himself up and then button his jacket around the furry lump. God, he looked like he was pregnant, and he was fairly sure the denim of his jacket, designed more for posing in clubs than rugged outdoor use, was going to stretch all out of shape trying to support Morris's weight. He slung his camera bag over one shoulder and experimented with adjusting the straps, eventually fashioning a platform for the unwieldy creature's bum.

As he stumbled up the valley side, Dan lost himself in daydreams of an insanely grateful Robin. Better that than panicking about the fact that Morris hadn't moved since their fall from the tree.

# Chapter Five

"Fucking bastard piece of shit!" Robin glowered at the half-assembled plate rack. It didn't defend itself; it just sat there on his workbench maintaining a stubborn silence. Really, it wasn't the plate rack's fault that Robin was having so many problems working today, but since it couldn't stand up for itself and accuse him of being a moody bugger, it was having to bear the brunt of his bad temper.

"You just watch it, plate rack. Right now you're nothing but fancy kindling." Robin picked the wooden construction up, half inclined to just chuck it on the fire and start again, but Smiler was expecting it to be ready by tomorrow—he had his daughters coming to stay and wanted to be able to impress them with his new-found domesticity. Perhaps it wouldn't seem so utterly hopeless if he took a break and came back to it. Okay, so he'd cut one of the pieces to the wrong size, but it had been bloody difficult to read his scrawled notes, especially after he'd spilt beer on them.

Robin downed tools and kicked the leg of his workbench. He needed fresh air and grabbed his jacket and bag on the way out. It was still bright and mild for October, but there was a chill breeze, and he knew that it would be that much cooler in the shade of the woods.

From his boat he headed towards the swing bridge at Smiler's, tramping over the springy boards and into the rundown car park. He could see Smiler knocking in fence posts over by the caravan but didn't want to get into a conversation about the buggered-up plate rack, so he picked up his pace, hoping to escape unseen. No such luck.

"Oi, Robin! Over 'ere, mate, I need a hand with this." Smiler's tone was commanding, and Robin bristled at it but didn't think it a good idea to fall out with the man. Not when he sold the cheapest fuel in the Bath area.

Smiler lived in a caravan on the land he owned—a narrow strip between the road and the canal—and had set himself up as some kind of landlord-cum-chandlers. From the inside of an old shipping container you could buy sacks of smokeless fuel, gas bottles and all manner of boat supplies. You could even fill up with marine diesel if you moored your boat up next to the bridge. There were car parking spaces and private moorings to rent in a small marina he'd had built. It would have been a good place to overwinter if Robin could have afforded the rates...and put up with having a miserable git as his landlord.

"Come on, Robin, get a fucking move on. I need you to hold this bastard post still for me. It's being a right bloody nuisance, the little fucker."

Smiler's hard eyes glared at the post from under bushy brown eyebrows. Robin remembered his own altercation with the plate rack and smiled. God, he hoped he hadn't looked that much of a twat when he was yelling at a defenceless piece of wood. He knelt down and took hold of the post, careful to keep upwind of Smiler, because the man reeked after his morning's work. Fresh sweat Robin didn't have a problem with. In fact, on the right person, fresh sweat could be downright sexy, but stale sweat clinging to clothing that looked like it hadn't been washed for the whole summer was another matter.

"This okay?" Robin asked. The sooner Smiler finished the job, the sooner he could get away and sort his head out.

He was answered with a swing from Smiler's sledgehammer, which gave a satisfying thunk when it hit the wood. He strained to hold the post straight as Smiler continued his swings. Adrenaline flooded his system and his heart raced. All it would take would be for Smiler to succumb to his scrumpy hangover, miss, hit Robin's head, and he'd probably be dead. And for all the crappy things he'd had to put up with over the last few years, Robin wasn't ready to throw in the towel just yet.

"Right, that's done. Nice one, mate. Got the fucker beaten into submission at last." Smiler grimaced as he turned to his roll of fencing wire.

Robin let go of the post and stretched his fingers out, letting his breathing return to normal before he rose. He wondered if he could just leave now, but the well-brought-up son in him knew that some small talk was expected.

"What's the fence for? You getting livestock?" God help the poor animals if he was. He wouldn't trust the man to look after a hamster, let alone a chicken. The thought of animals brought Morris to mind, and he scowled at the idea that he might never see him again.

"Nah, can't be bothered with all that animal-welfare crap. This is to keep the nippers safe when they visit. Their mum's bloody paranoid about them getting hurt or drowning in the canal, the stupid cow. Don't know why I even bothered fighting for access."

The expression on his face was contemptuous, but even though they'd only got to know each other a few weeks ago, Robin knew that Smiler was thrilled about seeing his girls again. He'd mentioned them practically every conversation they'd had. He felt sorry for the girls, really, for having a dad like Smiler. Mind you, when he looked around the giant play area the man had constructed, he had to concede that a lot of thought had gone into it. There was a tyre swing dangling from a branch of the overhanging oak tree, a sandpit made out of an old tractor tyre, and some kind of assault course cobbled together out of logs and bits of old farm machinery. He stifled the traitorous thought that his own father had never built anything like that for him. He was always far too busy, and anyway, his surgeon's fingers were far too valuable to risk doing manual labour. There'd always been plenty of expensive toys for Robin to play with after all.

"It's looking good. See you later." Robin started for the gate out to the main road, but Smiler wasn't yet finished with him.

"Oi, what about that plate rack? I needed that by about fucking yesterday, mate."

Really, the man was a complete arsehole. "Yeah, don't worry. I'll bring it over later. Just got to put the finishing touches on it, so that it meets my high standards."

"Right, well, you make sure you do that, Robin Redbreast."

Robin ground his teeth as he headed up the incline to the wrought-iron gates that led out onto the main road. His life would be a hell of a lot easier if he didn't have to deal with people all the time. Somehow he'd had the idea that the boating life would be a way of getting away from people, but even though you kept moving all the time, you still found yourself getting involved in close-knit communities whether you liked it or not. And then there were those people who weren't part of the boating community at all, but who somehow managed to get past Robin's defences. Well, okay, that one person...

As he headed into the woods on the other side of the road, Robin let himself mull over the problem of Dan properly for the first time that day. Impertinent, maddening Dan with his dirty little smirk and mischievous eyes... Not forgetting his wicked tongue and sinfully squeezable arse. Robin groaned, feeling his cock stir in interest when he remembered the press of Dan's hard body against his own.

Fuck! He really didn't want to fancy someone like Dan. Someone who was obviously such an unrepentant slut. He couldn't go there, wouldn't go there. No way. Not after what happened with Jamie. Blokes like that were way too risky.

As he headed deeper into the woods, Robin scuffed up the leaf litter with his boots and cast his eyes around for edible mushrooms. He'd brought a bag with him out of habit, and now he was here, he might as well do some foraging. It was free food, and who knew when his next pay cheque would come in? After Smiler's plate rack was finished, it could be weeks before anyone else wanted his skills, and he was buggered if he was going to ask his mum. At twenty-five it was mortifying to still be reliant on your parents, but it was almost impossible to sign on when you had to keep moving all the time. Besides which, the last time he'd managed to force his way past the gaggle of junkies and drunks who blocked the door of the DSS, the woman at the desk had thrust a massive stack of paperwork at him. He'd been too embarrassed to admit his difficulties and ask for help filling it in, choosing instead to dump it in the nearest bin when he got outside. It wasn't worth the humiliation. He'd rather be penniless.

His mobile rang, the sound jarring in the quiet woodland but making a welcome distraction from his circling thoughts. Robin pulled it from his pocket. It was bound to be yet another progress update from his mum on his sister's pregnancy. Now the birth was only weeks away, she had been phoning him almost every day, gabbling on about Braxton Hicks contractions, doulas and the appalling state of the NHS hospital in Cheltenham. That was just about durable if he tuned it out, but the minute she started on about his life and plans for the future, he had to resist the urge to throw his phone into the canal.

*Unknown Number*, the display read. Frowning, Robin dropped his bag and lifted the phone to his ear.

"Hello?"

"Hey, Robin? It's Dan. Listen to me, I've—"

"I'm not interested in anything you have to say, and how the hell did you get this number?" It had better not have been Mel. He'd have to have words with her about Dan.

"No, you've gotta listen to me." Dan sounded urgent, almost panicked. "It's Morris. Your cat. I've found him."

Robin clutched the phone to his ear and leant back against an oak's sturdy trunk. "Is he okay?" He held his breath, trying not to jinx things by second-guessing Dan's answer.

"He's been hurt, but I can't tell how badly as he won't let me look. He's resting now—looks exhausted."

He was alive. Thank God he was alive! Robin swallowed against the lump in his throat. "Where are you? I'm going to come and find you."

"We're near your boat, down in the field at the bottom of the valley. Are you home?"

"Not yet. I'll be there in ten minutes."

"Okay, I'm probably closer than you. D'you want me to take him back to the boat, then?"

"If you think you can manage it without hurting him. Just leave him where he is if you think moving him will make things worse."

"That's not really an issue. He seems to have welded himself to my T-shirt. He's coming with me whether I like it or not." Dan sounded serious, and Robin hoped he was capable in a crisis. The evidence of the previous day hadn't been encouraging.

"If you get to the boat first, then just let yourself in the doors on the front deck. It's all unlocked."

"Okay, then. See you soon."

Robin took a few moments to try to calm his racing heart, but realising it was probably futile, he set off down the hill at a gallop.

# Chapter Six

Dan pushed his bike with one hand, the other supporting the weight of the injured cat. He could see Robin's boat up ahead, gleaming red like a beacon. Morris was now a dead weight inside his jacket.

"Come on, cat. Don't you go dying on me now." He'd rather have claws and teeth sinking into him than this freaky torpor.

He threw his bike against the hedgerow, leapt onto the boat and tried the doors. They opened, just as Robin had promised, letting out a gust of warm air.

"Robin? Are you back?" There was no reply. He took a deep breath and stepped into the sanctuary of another man's home.

After the bright autumn sunlight, the interior was dim, but his vision soon adjusted enough to take in his surroundings. He was in the galley, a counter with the hob set in to his right and the sink over on the left. All manner of cooking utensils and crockery hung from hooks set into the wooden ceiling and walls. Dan stepped forward a couple of paces to where an open set of shelves made a barrier across half of the boat's width, and he was in the saloon, the stove kicking out heat. He sank down onto the welcoming sofa with a sigh and opened his jacket.

Morris had curled into a ball against him, looking like a picture of innocence, although Dan's hands and chest told a different tale: the scratches bloody well smarted.

"I was only trying to help you, you know. There was no need to get rough with me."

Morris opened his eyes, blinked and closed them again. A rumbling sensation started up on Dan's stomach. After all that, the creature had the cheek to start purring! Dan chuckled. Robin was going to be thrilled. He wondered how Robin behaved when he was happy. Was he gregarious, or would he keep it low-key, showing his gratitude with a smile? Dan knew so little about the man. Not that he was normally all that bothered about the life history of a potential shag, but Robin had him intrigued. He cast his eyes around the boat, trying to get more of a sense of the man from his dwelling.

It was almost like being inside a tree, the walls and ceiling lined with wavy-edged boards—the bark still attached—and the floor constructed from smooth, honey-coloured planks. There was a warm sheen to it all from the light that filtered through the porthole windows and the large, raised skylight. The saloon was mostly filled with the built-in sofa that ran along one side, with the wood-burning stove angled back against the kitchen to cast its light and heat into the saloon. Opposite the sofa was a long, upholstered bench, also built-in, which looked like it would make a good footrest. Pulling a cushion behind his back, Dan stretched out his legs and lounged backwards.

The clean simplicity of Robin's home was a pleasant surprise. Like himself, Robin had a refreshingly minimalist approach to possessions, but whereas Dan's London flat felt empty and barely lived in, Robin's boat was cosy and welcoming. Weird. He felt more at home here already than he did after nine years in his own flat.

Beyond the sofa, bathed in the light from the skylight above, was a space roughly as long as it was wide. It had been set up as a carpenter's work area. A workbench extended from the wall that divided the back of the boat from the saloon, and above it hung an array of hand tools that Dan vaguely recognised from his grampa's shed. There were planes, fretsaws, coping saws, chisels, files and other things he didn't know the names for, all gleaming in the sunshine. Indeed, the only thing that didn't look so well cared for was the floor, which was littered in curly ribbons of wood shavings and sawdust.

"Hey, Morris, is your daddy a carpenter, then? That's pretty smart. I like a man who knows how to use his hands." He stroked the fur on the top of Morris's head, and the cat arched up against the pressure, purring even louder. He was just contemplating whether he had time to sneak a look down at the end of the boat to check out Robin's sleeping quarters, when he felt the boat rock towards the bank and then back again.

The doors swung open.

"How's he doing? Is he okay?" Robin's voice was urgent, breathless, and he closed the space between them before he had finished speaking. He fell to his knees beside the sofa and leaned over to caress Morris with trembling hands. His voice dropped to a low murmur, but Dan could still hear it shaking. "Hey, how's my naughty boy, then? You gave me quite a scare, you did. Oh, but you seem all right now, don't you?"

Dan studied the top of Robin's head. Although it was cropped to less than half an inch, the hair was naturally thick and lustrous. The urge to reach out and stroke Robin's head was something Dan had to struggle against. Maybe he'd get a chance later. While checking Morris over, Robin's hands brushed against Dan's arms and chest, every accidental touch stirring a response in Dan's body. He looked down at those strong hands with the network of raised veins on the back and the dark hairs encroaching from the wrists. They'd look great against Dan's own smooth flesh. He breathed deeply, inhaling Robin's smoky, earthy scent.

But it wouldn't do to get overexcited right now. Dan tried to focus on Morris instead. "I found him halfway up a tree down in the valley. I think he must have climbed up there to keep safe from whatever attacked him."

"He was attacked?" Robin gazed up at him with wide, watery eyes. Christ, he was really cut up about this cat, wasn't he? "I can't find any injuries."

"I think he might be lying on it. There was something matted in his fur that looked like blood. I couldn't see any more than that because he went mental when I tried to pick him up." He held out his right hand, which had received the worst mauling. Robin's eyes flicked to it for a brief moment before returning to the cat.

"We'd better turn him over so I can get a look."

Right. Not a lot of point in angling for sympathy at the moment, then. Not unless you had four legs and a tail. Dan swallowed his pique and helped to lift the cat, who seemed even heavier now fully relaxed. He shifted over on the sofa so that Robin could sit next to him, and held Morris gently as Robin searched through the long fur. "I think it was down by his hind leg. Yep, that's the place." Dan felt the cat tense in his arms, but a few gentle words and strokes from Robin soon calmed him down again. The next time Robin tried to inspect the wound, Dan distracted Morris by tickling him under the chin, which seemed to go down well if the volume of purring was anything to go by.

"I'm going to have to clean this up to get a proper look, but I don't think it's too serious." Robin's eyes were clearer and brighter this time when they met Dan's. "Just hold him for me a little bit longer, please?"

"Always happy to help you out," Dan said, and he didn't even have to make a conscious effort to give his most charming grin—it just happened. This man with his peculiar mixture of arrogance, good manners and vulnerability seemed to call it forth from him.

His gaze roamed over Robin's body as he turned away and stretched in a peculiar, folded-limbs fashion no doubt adopted by all boat dwellers. Dan had already whacked his knuckles on the boat ceiling more times than he cared to recall. Must be a nightmare for a big guy. And wasn't Robin just deliciously large?

It probably wasn't a good idea to mentally undress a drop-dead-gorgeous man when you had your arms full of injured cat. Made it bloody tricky to hide a hard-on, for a start. Dan could have shifted Morris over to cover it, but that just seemed wrong, not to mention dangerous, considering those sharp claws. Robin made no comment though, and perhaps he didn't even notice with his attention focused on cleaning the wound. As Robin wrung out the cloth, rusty particles of dried blood swirled out into the bowl. Dan could feel some of the excess water soaking into his Ralph Lauren T-shirt. That was going to stain, although it was probably already a lost cause what with the claw damage from earlier.

But Dan's concerns about his clothing were forgotten the moment Morris sank his claws into his stomach. That fucking well hurt! He grunted, biting his cheeks to keep from giving a girly whimper. Not that Robin noticed. On the plus side, at least his cock was behaving again.

The more blood Robin cleaned away, the more Dan could smell its metallic tang. Eventually the fur was clean and they could see what lay beneath.

"Is that it?" Dan asked. How could such a tiny wound have bled so profusely?

"Looks like it. Hey, Morris, it's all clean and I think you're going to be fine." Robin tickled the cat, who pulled his claws out of Dan, turned over and wriggled, demanding more attention.

Dan had never felt jealous of an animal before, but God, he wanted some of that affection lavished on him. However, when Robin looked up to him with sparkling eyes and a warm smile, he forgot all his uncharitable thoughts. The love Robin had for that cat shone out of his face, blessing Dan with some of the second-hand radiance. Surely this was time for his reward kiss? To say thank you properly. To say—

"Thanks, Dan, I really appreciate all your help." And then Robin picked Morris out of Dan's arms and cuddled the cat close, flopping back against the sofa and closing his eyes as the last of the stress drained out of his face.

Nope, that definitely wasn't a man in the mood for seduction. He should get a grip—just make the most of being here and getting to know Robin better.

"Would you like a drink?" Dan asked, pleased to see the lazy smile curve Robin's lips as he opened his eyes. "How about a cuppa? I'm sure I can find my way around your kitchen."

"I'd love one, but I should be doing all that, really." Robin looked like a man who had no intention of getting up any time soon.

Dan grinned. "No worries, you just look after Morris and I'll sort us both out with a nice cup of tea." Oh God, he was turning into his mum. A woman convinced that the world's problems could all be solved if only people would take the time to sit down together and drink a cup of PG Tips. Possibly with a digestive biscuit on the side. At the thought of food, his stomach rumbled. It felt like a long time since he'd breakfasted, having spent his morning photographing Mel in her boat and then being shown into several other boater's homes. They were a friendly bunch, once Mel introduced them, although he had the suspicion she'd started him off with the easy ones.

"Tea bags are in the tin on the top shelf, and the fridge is next to the sink."

"Thanks. Umm, any biscuits by any chance? I'm famished."

"I see, you're expecting feeding now, are you?"

Dan's eyes flicked up to Robin's, and he was relieved to see humour in their depths. "I think I've earned at least a biscuit, don't you think? Possibly more." Although he wasn't going to detail what just yet.

Robin chuckled. "I think you'll have to settle for the biscuit, as anything else is going to need cooking. Look on the shelves under the glasses. There should be a new pack of Hob Nobs."

With everything prepared, there was nothing to do but wait for the kettle to boil. Dan peered out of the porthole above the hob, wondering what it must be like to live life with such tiny windows. It was almost like seeing the world through a fish-eye lens.

Shit—his camera! There was two grands' worth of equipment in his camera bag, and he'd just left it out there on the back of his bike. His unlocked, cost-a-small-fortune, custom-built bike. A terrible certainty sank through him like a stone. It wasn't going to be there, was it? One of these gypsies would have made off with it, and he'd have lost his whole morning's work as well.

"Fuck!" He crashed his way through the doors and off the boat.

# Chapter Seven

What on earth was all that about? Robin stared at the half-open doors. The boat rocked gently in Dan's wake, and his eyelids soon started to feel heavy. The comforting warmth of Morris on his lap lulled him into a dreamy state—it was only when the kettle started whistling that he pulled his strands of attention together enough to realise it was up to him to sort it out.

"Sorry, Morris, you old lump. You'll just have to do without me for a moment." By now Morris was so fast asleep that he didn't even stir as Robin hefted him onto the sofa. Robin stood and stretched, then turned off the gas and opened the doors to look out.

"Shit! Watch it! You nearly knocked me over," Dan said, grinning as he hopped onto the deck. "Sorry about that. Just realised I'd left my kit out there where anyone could have helped themselves, but look!" He held up a rectangular pannier bag. "All here! I'm a very lucky man today." Dan winked.

Robin turned away to the kettle, flustered. His body tingled all over in response to Dan's proximity. He tried to focus on Dan's words to take his mind off it. What had he said? Something about the canal being risky. A typical outsider's presumption.

"Things are usually pretty safe down here. We're not all thugs and criminals, you know." Memories of some of the suspicious glares he'd received from the villagers nearby rose unbidden, and he slammed down two mugs onto the worktop before realising that Dan had already got some ready.

"Hey, I know that. But this is an expensive bit of kit I've got here, and it's my livelihood, so I can't go losing it partway through an assignment." Dan's voice came from right behind him. It would take only one step back to bump into him, and a quick turn to have him pinned against the counter.

But he wasn't going to go there, was he? Not with a bloke like this. Not with someone who flirted with the confidence of a man used to getting whoever it was he'd set his sights on. Robin gripped the edge of the worktop and forced his mind back to the tea and whatever it was that Dan just told him. "Assignment?" He kept his eyes firmly on the water as he poured it out of the kettle, willing his hand to stay steady and his misbehaving body not to betray his excitement.

"Yeah, it's a good one. Mostly I'm just given the contract for the writing, but this time they want my pictures too."

Robin grunted in response, but after he'd slopped some milk into the mugs and given them both a quick stir, there was no excuse left to keep turned away. He found Dan leaning back against the sink counter, his legs planted wide and hips canted forward in a suggestive manner. God, did Dan always wear such tight clothing? He could see practically every muscle, every rib through his T-shirt. Dan might have been slight, but his physique gave the impression of great strength and agility. It was the kind of lean, lithe body Robin had always lusted after. The kind of body that made his hands itch to reach out and grab.

Holding the mugs out in front of him like a shield, Robin suddenly remembered his manners. "Oh, ah, I forgot to ask if you take sugar."

"Nah, I'm told I taste sweet enough already, but I guess you'd know." Dan's cheeks dimpled as a particularly mischievous smile played across his lips.

Robin really didn't want to be reminded of the delicious warmth of Dan's mouth and the way that tongue had tasted as it slid against his own. He took a big gulp of tea to distract himself, scalding his palate in the process. He winced. At least it should help to take his mind off that exquisite kiss. Rather than look directly at Dan's face, he focused on a bit of leaf matter that had somehow found its way into Dan's carefully styled hair, but rather than making Dan look less appealing, it somehow had the opposite effect.

"So you're taking photos of the canal?" Robin asked.

Dan's smile faded a little, then recovered. "A few, but I'm more interested in the people. You're a fascinating lot, you know that?" And then the glint in his eye was back. "I spent an hour with your 'girlfriend' this morning, you know? Very interesting shoot, that one. Very informative."

The way Dan was smirking at Robin left him in no doubt that he'd been rumbled. Shit, he should have seen that one coming. Mel wasn't really a gossip—she had too much goodwill towards others to spread malicious rumours—but she certainly loved talking. He could just imagine the two of them discussing him and all his hang-ups. He scowled down at his tea.

"Mel has a big mouth. I wouldn't believe everything she says about me."

"Now who says we were talking about you, Robin Hamilton?" Dan's tone was teasing. "Although I must say, Mel was rather surprised to find out that she's your girlfriend."

Robin continued to stare at the surface of his tea, blaming the rising steam for the heat he could feel spreading across his cheeks. "It's none of your business."

"No, you're quite right, but I'd say it was hers, wouldn't you? Anyway, you'll be pleased to know that she didn't tell me anything much about you. She was too busy trying to convince me about all the other boaters I 'need' to go and photograph."

Despite himself, Robin smiled. When she had her mind set on something, Mel wouldn't let anyone else get a word in edgewise.

"She didn't even tell me you were a carpenter," Dan continued. "Did you fit out the inside of this boat?"

There was so much admiration in Dan's tone Robin dared to risk looking up into those inviting eyes. "Yeah, she was just an empty shell when I bought her. I spent five months working on the inside. She's designed just how I wanted her." Warming to his favourite subject, he started on the usual tour he gave to visitors the first time they stepped onboard. Dan made all the right comments when Robin pointed out the space-saving design features he'd built into the galley, the nifty mechanism to pull out the sofa into a spare bed that spread across the saloon, and his workbench that could be folded up to hide all the tools and turn a working area back into a living area.

"And the wet-room and bed cabin are at the end of the boat," Robin finished, reluctant to show Dan down there. "Why don't you have a look by yourself? There's not really room for two." Not unless you were already intimate.

Dan pouted a little, but his eyes still twinkled. "But how will I know what to appreciate if you aren't there to guide me?"

Robin kept his face as stony as possible, but could feel his lips trying to twitch into a smile. "I'm sure you'll figure it out by yourself. You don't need me to hold your hand."

"You could hold something else, if you'd rather." Dan reached out to run his fingers lightly over Robin's hand where it gripped the edge of his workbench. When Robin made no response to the flirting, Dan sighed theatrically. "Okay, I'll show myself around, then, shall I?"

Once Dan was out of sight, Robin exhaled and leant back against the wall. He'd have to ask Dan to leave after he'd seen the rest. Having the guy here was stirring up too many conflicting emotions.

Dan's voice rang out from the back of the boat—a welcome distraction. "So what made you decide to take up the boating life? It wasn't just to show off your woodworking skills, was it?"

He should have a pat answer to that question by now, but lies never tripped easily off Robin's tongue. They tended to stick in his throat, and he was always convinced that people could see his falsehoods written on his face. At least with Dan out of sight it was easier to respond with a half-truth.

"My grandmother gave me some of my inheritance early, to avoid the taxes." That bit was true, at least. "It wasn't enough to buy a house, but I'd always liked the idea of living on the water and travelling around." That might have been a childhood dream, fostered by obsessively watching pirate films, but it had hardly been the motivating force for buying *Serendipity*.

"You're like me," Dan said, appearing in front of Robin. "I never want to get stuck in one place for too long. Variety is the spice of life, wouldn't you say?" His smile pinched up at the edges, turning from friendly to lascivious in an instant. "I guess you would, seeing as how you like it on both sides of the fence. Tell me, Robin, are you versatile? 'Cause I am."

"I fail to see how that's any of your business."

Dan threw up his hands, feigning innocence. "Okay, okay! I can see it's a touchy subject for you. It's fine. Like I said, whatever way works for me, but I don't expect the rest of the world to be as easygoing." Maybe Dan was picking up on Robin's vibes now, because a sheepish expression passed over his face, and he gave a strange laugh that jangled on Robin's nerves. "Look, it's cool. I'd better get going now, I reckon. Will I see you at Mel's party tomorrow? Sounds like it'll be a blast."

Oh for fuck's sake! Was he ever going to get rid of this man? Robin muttered a noncommittal reply which Dan accepted with a knowing smile before clasping Robin's hand briefly and racing off the boat with a cheery, "See you tomorrow, then!"

Robin glared at his fingers. They burned from Dan's touch, craving more contact. They wanted to explore every inch of Dan's body. They wanted to tangle in his hair.

It just wasn't fair.

Sluts shouldn't be so fucking enticing.


"Bleedin' hell, she's here." Smiler turned to Robin with a grimace, the net curtain falling back into place. "Sorry, mate, you'd better get going. Trust me, you don't want to meet the cow."

"Nearly done and I'll be out of the way." He'd have been done about half an hour ago if Smiler hadn't been so keyed up about his daughters. The man couldn't stop pacing about the caravan and regaling Robin with anecdotes. Katie and Sarah sounded like two little wildcats—always racing around and driving their mother crazy.

Robin concentrated on driving the last two screws home. Yesterday's huge problem with the plate rack had turned out to be easily solved by gluing in an extra strip of wood and turning it into a design feature. Funny how things could be so simple when you'd woken up happy. His day had got off to an almost perfect start with Morris draped over his legs, and he spent at least half an hour petting the cat silly before the desperate urge to piss finally forced him out of bed.

Maybe something was in the air today. Smiler was as close to cheerful as Robin had ever seen him, and even the prospect of having to greet the ex didn't seem to have made too much of a dent in his mood. The man was actually living up to his name, beaming as he left the caravan. Robin shoved his screwdriver, tape and pencil back in his tool belt and followed him out into the car park.

There was a sour-faced woman in a designer suit standing next to a shiny Mercedes. Two pale blonde girls hid behind her, prim and proper in their matching pink coats, shiny shoes and white tights. Robin gawped. He hadn't realised they were identical twins. It was hard to see anything of Smiler in them— they definitely favoured their mother. Either Smiler had really let himself go since his divorce, or the ex-wife had moved up in the world. Must be similar to what people thought when they saw Robin with his own family.

He would have just slunk away over the swing bridge if it weren't for the fact that Smiler hadn't paid him yet and he needed the cash. He walked over, trying to ignore the way the woman glared at him.

"All done now," he said.

"Cheers, mate. Great job." Smiler reached into his pocket and pulled out a roll of notes. Robin watched the woman's eyebrows rise. Smiler peeled off four twenties and handed them to him. "And here's another for your trouble." There was a sly smile on his face as he handed Robin another twenty.

One hundred pounds! That was almost double what they'd originally agreed. Robin grinned and clapped Smiler on the back.

"Thanks. Anything else you want doing, just ask."

He grabbed his bike and made a quick exit. God knew what those two girls would make of the assault course. He hoped Smiler wouldn't be too disappointed.

A pleasant afternoon cycling out to the village of Avoncliffe and spending some of his windfall on a few pints in the King's

Arms next to a roaring fire had followed. Under those circumstances, with the pleasant buzz of the alcohol in his veins and the warmth of the fire against his skin, the Dan situation didn't seem like such a big deal after all. It wasn't like Dan would be around for long, and he wasn't a part of this lifestyle. Their paths would never cross again, so would it really be so dangerous? It wasn't like they'd be emotionally involved. Dan wouldn't do a Jamie on him. Wouldn't be able to tear his heart out and trample on it. Robin would never let him get that close.

Robin took another deep gulp of beer and tried to banish Jamie from his mind. Dan wasn't all that much like him anyway. The surface charm was similar, but on Jamie it had barely been able to gloss over his neuroses and self-loathing. Dan was different; he seemed optimistic to the point of lunacy, with a sense of self-worth bordering on the smug—both qualities Robin was drawn to against his will. Dan wouldn't be the type to risk destroying his health and that of those around him. Still, Robin would have to be careful.

He bought two packets of condoms from the machine in the gents: one extra-strength and one strawberry flavoured. It never hurt to be prepared.

He was whistling when he sauntered back into the bar, and when he returned to *Serendipity* he made a snap decision to cruise half a mile or so until he reached a deserted stretch in the reed beds. It wasn't as far as he was supposed to have moved, but he wanted somewhere with no neighbours peering through their portholes. Morris curled up on the roof above the engine, and Robin petted him as they chugged along, possibilities for later drifting through his mind like smoke in the still air.

# Chapter Eight

Dan could see the flickering glow of the fire below through the branches. He took a moment to lean on the fence he had chained his bike to. The night revealed a different terrain, the many shades of green, red and gold reduced to a stark contrast of light and dark, the river a silvery ribbon reflecting the full moon back at him. Shame he hadn't brought the Nikon, but he didn't want to be weighed down with the responsibility of taking photos. He had other ideas about how to spend his evening.

The light of the bonfire was the only warm thing in the whole vista. It drew Dan's gaze. There would be warm bodies down there. People laughing, drinking, flirting and making merry. Maybe some of the boaters he'd photographed earlier in the day—Chris and Zoe with their brood of mischievous children, all happily crammed into one of the large Dutch barges; Tigger with his soot-blackened, dilapidated old barge, the dim light inside picking out the map of wrinkles on his bearded face; pink-haired Flora with her crystals and half-baked theories about the spirits of trees. Yes, there were the artisans and the terminally unemployable that he'd expected to find living in this way, but some of the boaters were a real surprise. Chris was a physics lecturer up at the University, and Zoe was an educational psychologist—although they both worked part-time in order to share child-care duties. Clearly the boating community was more varied than he'd first expected.

As he vaulted over the stile and made his way down the barely visible track, Dan's stomach started to flutter in that pleasant way it always did when he was on the brink of making a conquest. The possibility that he wouldn't be going back with

Robin later was unthinkable. It was obvious that Robin fancied him, even if he was doing his best to deny it. And now that he'd been the means of returning the beloved Morris to him... Well, he figured that Robin would be feeling much better disposed towards him. A bit of alcohol, some suggestive banter, and the man would be putty in his hands. Maybe not putty, exactly—he was after something harder than that—but certainly malleable, pliant and accommodating. Right now, he wanted nothing more than to bury himself in that sweet arse and fuck Robin so hard he forgot his own name...but he could be patient. He could wait and bide his time if he had to.

Several voices called out to him from the circle of firelight.

"Dan, sweetie, it's lovely to see you! Come and meet Aranya—you just have to get some shots of his boat—it's unbelievable!" As Mel tugged on Dan's hand and pulled him towards the lanky, dreadlocked guy with the guarded expression, Dan searched the groups of chattering boaters for the one face he really wanted to see. He came up with a disappointing blank.

"What is it you're taking your pictures for?" Aranya asked, his narrow eyes fixing Dan with a glare that made him want to squirm. Fortunately Mel pressed a bottle of beer into his hand at that moment, so he had a little longer to frame his reply.

"It's a piece for the *Observer* magazine," he said, hoping the left-wing liberal credentials would help him win the guy over. "I'm meant to be covering a narrowboat holiday for the travel section, but my agent asked me to get character shots as well. The idea is to have an article about British Waterways versus the boaters. Show the human side of the situation. People in their own homes. That sort of thing." He gave Aranya his least flirtatious grin, but the man's face showed little responding emotion. Shame, really—with those long blond dreadlocks and Nordic features, he could be quite a looker if he lightened up.

"It might be alternative now, but when the oil runs dry, we'll all be living like this. Current Western lifestyles are totally unsustainable—we are living in Babylon, man, and the end times are coming. Did you know it would take three earths to supply everyone with the resources to maintain the status quo?"

Oh Christ, just what he needed. A white Rastafarian tree-hugger with an evangelical bent. Dan let the eco-brainwashing attempts wash over him as he tried to make the right noises in response. Asking Aranya about energy-saving measures on his own boat proved to be a good move, earning Dan more opportunities to scan the group for Robin. He idly watched one of Chris and Zoe's brood running around with a stick, poking it into the fire and chasing his younger sister while brandishing the smouldering wood. A couple of identical blonde girls with wild hair joined in the game. No one seemed to care that they were quite literally playing with fire, but no one seemed to get hurt, either. The adults were all relaxed and happy. A few of them had brought djembes down and were sitting in a circle, beating out a rolling, primitive rhythm on the large drums. No one was out on the pull as far as he could tell; well, no one other than himself. This was just friends, chilling together. No agendas. No ulterior motives. He could get used to this.

"And another thing you can put in your article is the criminal lack of recycling facilities along the canal." God, Aranya was still going on. "I have to cycle for miles to get to a bottle bank sometimes. And we need composting toilets. Those pump-out stations feed the shit straight into the main sewers. We can do better than that. Some of us already do."

Dan wrinkled his nose. He'd smelt some pretty honking toilets that day. Mel had lectured him that it wasn't considered polite to use another boater's toilet unless you really had to. Pissing in the woods didn't bother him too much, but how could you deal with the shit?

Aranya must have read his mind. "I go out every morning with a shovel. It's the only way, man. Put back into the ecosystem everything you take out of it. I don't even use paper. I wipe with my hand and then wash it."

Okay, that was way too much information. He really didn't want to be picturing Aranya squatting in the woods like some kind of animal.

When Aranya offered him a joint, he gave it a suspicious once-over. The guy's hands looked clean, but he wasn't sure he wanted to put anything into his mouth that had been handled by a man who wiped his arse with his bare hand. Then again, he wouldn't think twice about rimming a hot bloke, and surely that was no better. Mind you, most of the guys he picked up were pretty scrupulous about hygiene. But what the hell, he wasn't going to catch anything nasty, was he? Not from the world's most responsible hippie.

He took the joint, pulled in a hot lungful and choked. As he doubled over, desperately trying to calm his overactive diaphragm, Dan remembered exactly why it was he'd given up smoking.

But when he straightened up, eyes streaming and face burning, there Robin was on the other side of the fire, gazing at him with an inscrutable expression. His face may have been set like a mask, but there was no mistaking the blaze in those dark eyes.

Robin turned away and Dan fought to regain control of his breathing. He needed to keep steady, keep focused, keep his wits about him. This was going to be his lucky night.

Robin's hopeful mood had evaporated by the time he arrived at the party. He couldn't see Dan anywhere, his eyes scanning the fire-lit figures for a shock of spiky, fair hair. And then he heard coughing, saw the doubled-over figure, and ached to rush over there and pat Dan's back for him.

Their eyes met, and there was no denying the need that boiled inside him—he hadn't felt this alive in so long. He was desperate to stride over there and grab hold of Dan, then drag him back to *Serendipity*. And then... And that was the point where his mind stubbornly refused to let him go any further, so he stayed where he was. He dropped his gaze, scuffing the toe of his boot against the ground, his every nerve painfully aware of just where Dan was in the group and how much distance there was between them.

Smiler had approached Dan, and he wasn't looking happy.

"What's all this I hear about you snooping around asking questions about BW? You a fucking spy or something?"

Shit, that wasn't fair. Before he realised he was moving, Robin had closed the distance, ready to step in between the two men.

Dan looked bewildered in the face of Smiler's ferocity. "I'm a travel writer. Freelance. I'm just looking for an angle for a piece I'm writing."

"Yeah, right. Heard it all before, mate. You're one of them."

"He's not." Robin's face grew hot as they both turned towards him. "He's telling the truth. Honest to God, Smiler. No BW grunt would be so useless steering a boat."

Smiler grumbled under his breath and turned back to Dan. "Good thing for you you're friends with Robin, here. I'll take his word, but you put one foot out of line and you'll be sorry." His eyes scanned the gathering. "Where've them two wildcats got to now? God, their mum's gonna kill me if they fall in the river."

As Smiler moved away, Dan turned to Robin with a smirk. "Not sure I like my defence being based on how incompetent I am. I think I deserve a chance to show you where my real talents lie."

Robin gulped hard. He didn't want to flirt in front of all these people. But oh God, he wanted...

"Dan, over 'ere mate." Chris grabbed hold of Dan's arm and dragged him off. "Rusty's up for you taking some pictures of his boat. You don't want to pass up on this one. It's a beaut."

Dan threw an apologetic glance over his shoulder, mouthing *later*.

Robin stood by the fire, watching the group around Rusty to see when Dan would be free. Every now and then Dan would cast a heated gaze in his direction that kept him rooted to the spot.

"Hey, sweetie, I hear that cat of yours is back at last. Told you he would be."

Robin looked down at Mel's smiling face, and allowed himself to be momentarily distracted. "Yeah, he's fine. He had a little cut, but it doesn't seem to have caused any permanent damage. Dan found him up a tree." Robin's cheeks grew hot as he mentioned Dan's name to Mel, his gaze skittering around between her, Dan and the ground. When he looked at Mel again, she was studying Dan, who Robin realised was looking at him. He met Mel's eyes and flushed at the understanding he saw there.

Mel raised her eyebrows. "Well, Dan is quite the man of the moment, isn't he? Seems like everyone's a bit taken with him." Robin said nothing, developing a sudden fascination with the toes of his boots. "Oh, looks like he needs to answer a call of nature. Maybe you'd better give him a hand, make sure he doesn't get lost."

Robin followed Mel's gaze to see Dan heading off towards the trees bordering the field. He was walking in the direction of the stile Robin had entered the field by.

"I, uh..." He looked down at Mel, not knowing how to phrase his excuses.

"Just go, Robin. I don't expect to see you back here tonight, okay?"

Robin nodded. He didn't know how she'd managed to work everything out so quickly but was grateful that she understood. He bent down to kiss her cheek, then turned and took off after Dan as fast as he could manage without actually running.


It was dark under the trees. As Robin waited for his vision to adjust, he concentrated on listening. There was a faint splashing sound off to his right, and he waited until Dan was finished before clearing his throat.

"Dan?"

A dark shape detached itself from the shadows and moved towards him. The next thing he knew, arms were snaking around his waist and he felt warm breath on his cheek.

"Robin? I hope that's you." Dan's voice was low and seductive, but he held himself back as if expecting Robin to make the first move.

"It's me," Robin whispered, not trusting his voice to stay steady. All he could concentrate on was the press of Dan's warm body against his, the scent rising from him, sweet and heady. His hands rose of their own accord, pulling Dan's head closer as he closed in for a kiss.

Dan tasted of lager and marijuana, with that underlying sweetness Robin remembered from before. He moaned into Dan's mouth, growing hard so fast it was painful. He grabbed hold of Dan's arse and pulled him in tight, willing him to feel how much he wanted him. Dan responded by grinding his hips, and their erections rubbed together with an intense friction. Made Robin want to rip Dan's clothes off and have him on the damp leaf litter.

But Dan had his own ideas, and Robin found himself stumbling backwards as Dan broke off the kiss and pushed him, his fall broken by a tree trunk. He panted, slightly winded by the unexpected blow. That was uncalled for! But then Dan slid a cool hand down the front of his trousers, and all other thoughts fled.

"Oh! This is a pleasant surprise," Dan said, fingering Robin's Prince Albert piercing in a way that made him whimper and push into Dan's hand. "I think I'd better get a closer look."

And when Dan sank down, unzipped Robin's fly and exposed his aching prick to the cold night air, Robin needed the support of the tree behind him. Dan's hot breath against the head of his cock made his knees buckle as he trembled with anticipation.

But Dan seemed determined to tease him, nuzzling, licking and touching him so gently it was an exquisite torture. Dan paid special attention to the piercing, and the way the ring moved under his tongue sent jolts of pleasure racing through Robin's body. He gasped, his hands clawing at the bark. He had to stop himself from grabbing Dan's hair and thrusting into his mouth. He wasn't going to be that needy. He wasn't that desperate. He wasn't.

When Dan finally enveloped him in the moist heat of his mouth, Robin had to bite down on his hand to prevent a howl escaping. The relief that the torture was over barely registered— now he had to concentrate on not coming too fast. To hold back, to make it last. No matter how good. And oh, it was good. Dan knew what he was doing, taking him deep and making happy noises like Robin's dick was the most delicious thing he'd ever tasted.

Fighting to keep a grip, Robin stared wildly around. His eyes fixed on the distant fire. There were figures silhouetted against it. Figures getting closer.

"Fuck! Dan, stop, please!" Robin grabbed hold of Dan's hair on the upstroke, preventing him from sucking his cock down again.

"What? Don't tell me you're not enjoying it, because I won't believe you." Dan sounded smug and gave a lick to the head of Robin's cock that made him gasp.

"Stop it, someone's coming." By now he could hear voices. "Shit, it's Smiler and his girls." That got Dan's attention, and he rose to his feet, muttering curses.

"Bet my jeans are ruined. Bloody countryside."

Robin ignored him, zipping his fly over his rapidly wilting erection and starting off towards the stile. He wanted to get over it before they were seen. But more than that, he wanted Dan with him. Realising he was alone, Robin halted, looking around the dark woods. Shit. He'd lost him.

"Dan?" Robin called softly.

But this time no dark figure approached through the trees. This time he was on his own.

# Chapter Nine

Of all the bloody times to be interrupted! He'd nearly had him. Dan could still taste Robin's arousal, salty on his tongue. He'd been eagerly anticipating that moment of release, of feeling Robin's cock pulsing in his mouth; of hearing the sounds Robin made while coming; of holding Robin's jerking hips steady as he drank down his prize.

And now Robin was running scared again.

"Robin?"

Oh, that was just perfect! Left here on his own with a raging hard-on and not a sexy boater in sight. Dan reached down to adjust his jeans. They chafed against his erection—he'd have to finish off by himself if he didn't find Robin soon. Didn't think he could bear the idea of having to resort to that, though. Robin would have to be around here somewhere. Dan thought quickly, looking down the valley to the group making their way up towards him. Robin wouldn't have gone that way. No, he'd probably be heading back up to the canal.

Dan set off at a swift pace, tripping over only one tree root before breaking out into the moonlit clearing by the stile.

The stile with a dark figure sitting astride it.

A dark figure with cropped hair who was panting as hard as Dan was. Dan strode over, placed a foot on the stile and hoisted himself up to where Robin was perched. When Dan saw the dark wells of Robin's eyes, he knew that words wouldn't be necessary. He dived in with a hard, biting kiss, grinding his chin against Robin's stubble with all the force of his thwarted lust.

When they heard the whooping of the approaching children, Robin pulled back.

"My boat's closer," Robin said.

Dan grinned.

Dan pushed his bike to *Serendipity*. Robin had left his own bike with his boat, so Dan was the only one with his hands occupied. His fingers felt mutinous, desperate to start exploring Robin. He studied Robin's profile instead, marvelling at the fine bone structure that made such an intriguing contrast to the scruffy clothing and military haircut. What had made a man so obviously well-bred end up living on a boat like a feckless hippie? Of course, there was always the possibility that Robin really was a feckless hippie at heart, but the evidence of his dedicated craftsmanship and the distinct lack of crystals and joss sticks on his boat suggested otherwise. And he'd never once mentioned apologising to the spirits of the trees whose wood he used.

"Here she is," Robin said, pointing at *Serendipity*. She was moored up in the middle of what looked like a dying reed bed, with a narrow plank between the bank and the deck.

Dan swallowed hard, concentrating on locking his bike so as not to think about having to walk the plank. He was light and lithe. He didn't need to worry about falling in. Besides which, the canal was shallow and Robin was here to look out for him.

Yet when he made his way to the end of the plank he paused, his heart pounding like the drums still sounding in the valley below. Robin was watching him from the deck. Bugger. He refused to play the effeminate queen like Tris did, but there were times when his manliness deserted him.

"Uh, any chance of a hand?" Dan asked, his eyes closed so as not to see the mockery that would be filling Robin's by now. "Not that I'm scared or anything…"

Robin answered with a low chuckle, and Dan felt the board shift under his feet and warm hands wrap around his.

"Just step. There's no need to watch your feet," Robin said.

And so Dan walked, two regular steps bringing him to the deck where he collapsed gratefully into Robin's arms. "Thanks," he breathed into Robin's neck.

"That's all right. I expect you just couldn't wait to get your hands on me again, could you?"

"Yeah, something like that." Dan pulled back to give Robin a lopsided smile. He didn't really want to explain about the swimming thing right now.

"Shall we?" Dan asked, nodding his head towards the doors. Robin answered by opening them, disappearing into the dark boat as warm, woodsmoke-scented air escaped from within. When the dim light flicked on, Dan followed.

Robin crouched down in front of the stove, opened the door and stabbed inside with the poker. Dan stepped behind him, watching the flames licking up around the coals inside. Robin added more fuel using a small shovel. Eventually the fire seemed to be stoked to his satisfaction, and he shut the glass door, leaning back on his haunches and staring up at Dan with an impenetrable expression.

Dan gave in to temptation and stroked Robin's hair, the short crop surprisingly soft and thick. Robin's lips parted as he shifted position, leaning back against Dan's thigh. The sight of Robin kneeling before him sent blood rushing to Dan's cock. It was just a shame he was facing the wrong way, but it didn't stop him from pulling Robin's head closer and canting his hips forward, brushing his denim-clad erection against an ear. Robin gave a shuddering exhalation, craning around farther and mouthing against Dan's cock, making him groan and roll his hips.

"Think now you've heated things up, maybe I need to take some clothes off," Dan said, not sure whether he wanted to get his own or Robin's clothes off first. Robin gave him a look that he couldn't decipher and made a cut-off noise in his throat. If that wasn't just the sexiest sound...

Robin stood and stepped over to the kitchen counter, leaning his head down on the surface and breathing heavily. Was he all right? Dan was torn between an urge to frot wildly against that temptingly thrust out arse, and the possibly more sensible course of checking that things were okay with him. Wouldn't do to push his luck.

Sense won out. "Are you all right? We can slow things down if you're nervous." He reached out a tentative hand to stroke Robin's back.

The effect was electric. Robin straightened and spun round. "Fuck off!"

Dan reeled, stepping backwards and stumbling as his legs hit the sofa. He ended up lying back along the length of it, propped up on his elbows as Robin loomed over him. Dan's thoughts spun out of control. What the hell? Wasn't he interested anymore?

Robin leant over him, his breath hot against Dan's face, his voice a low snarl. "I'm not fucking nervous, and I will let you know the minute you're doing anything I don't want, all right?"

Dan nodded, his heart hammering, the adrenaline burst ramping up his lust until he didn't know if he were more scared or horny. Not wanting to say the wrong thing, he kept his lips firmly sealed until Robin's tongue thrust between them insistently. Demanding hands tore at his clothing. Eager to avoid another ruined T-shirt, Dan scrabbled to help, only to have his hands swatted away. Once Dan's fly was yanked open, Robin broke the brutal kiss and stood, pulling all those layers of T-shirts off as one. Dan took the opportunity to kick off his trainers and finish removing the top that had been shoved up to his armpits.

He looked up. Robin was staring down at him with dark eyes, breathing hard. Dan shivered despite the blazing fire. Looking into Robin's eyes was like gazing into an abyss, and he didn't want to know what dark secrets lurked at the bottom.

He lowered his gaze to Robin's heaving chest, admiring the way those pecs bulged enticingly. Then there were those two nipple rings, glinting in the low light. Taking a deep breath, Dan rose to his feet and clamped his mouth around a nipple, sucking hard.

Robin hissed, his hands clawing at Dan's back even as his hips thrust forward. Dan pushed, shoving Robin back against the wall and making the whole boat rock in the water.

If Robin wanted it rough, Dan would give as good as he got.

Dan's well-practised fingers made quick work of Robin's fly. As his tongue flicked against the nipple ring, he pulled out Robin's cock. He took a firm grip of the shaft with one hand, the other squeezing Robin's balls—gently at first but steadily increasing the pressure.

"Ahh! Fuck!" Robin gasped, grabbing hold of Dan's head and forcing it back. Dan eased the pressure on his balls and slid a finger back towards Robin's hole, watching his face all the while. Robin had his eyes screwed closed and was chewing on his lower lip. When Dan circled his entrance, Robin made a choked-off sound, and his body jerked. Grinning, Dan licked the other nipple—the one that wasn't yet red and shining with saliva. He closed his teeth around the piercing.

Dan's arms bloomed with pain. Robin had him in a viselike grip around his biceps, using it to manhandle him onto the sofa and hold him there. Robin stared down, his expression all lust and anger jumbled up together, then yanked Dan's jeans and thong off in one swift movement.

Jesus, this guy was savage. Dan's heart hammered, the frisson of fear only turning him on even further. Dan hoped Robin would put as much passion into giving head. He hoped he hadn't made a big mistake coming here, all alone and out in the middle of nowhere with a man who could so easily overpower him. But no, Robin wasn't like that, was he?

As if he'd sensed Dan's unease, Robin paused, panting hard as he stared down at him. Dan smirked, taking advantage of the momentary break to spread his legs wide, stroking himself and giving an obscene moan. Was Robin a man who liked to watch? Dan was always happy to put on a show.

Dan couldn't help wincing as he saw Robin's hand reaching out for him but was surprised by a very gentle stroke down the crease of his groin.

"You shave your pubes?" Robin asked, his voice hoarse.

Oh, so that's what it was. It was such a commonplace occurrence among the guys he usually slept with that he'd forgotten about the novelty value.

"Not shaved, waxed. And I don't do it myself." Dan glanced at Robin's shock of dark hair, admiring the way it contrasted with his ruddy dick. The sensation of a lover's hair rasping against his denuded skin was always a turn-on.

As Dan continued to slowly pump his own cock, he moved a hand down to lift his balls, watching the way Robin's eyes darkened even further. "Why not have a feel? You know you want to."

Robin knelt between Dan's legs, and when his hand came back, he was cautious, exploratory, running his fingertips down Dan's prick to circle the base, then ghosting over the sac, one hand moving down to tease Dan's hole while the other slid back up to take a tentative hold of the shaft. Dan kept watching Robin's face, puzzled to see raw pain warp his features. The man obviously had some issues, and Dan felt a surge of anger at whatever guy had fucked him over so badly in the past that he couldn't even enjoy giving a simple hand-job. Shit, Robin's hand was trembling, and he looked like he was about to cry.

He reached out his spare hand, stroking Robin's cheek. "Hey, it's okay. This is meant to be fun, you know."

"Fun?" Robin stared at him, the anger Dan had seen earlier rising to blot out the sorrow in his eyes. "You think this is fun?" The hand that had been stroking Dan's cock didn't feel so gentle anymore. "You think it would be fun to have me fuck you?"

"Uh, yes?" Although maybe fun wasn't quite the right word, judging by the violence with which Robin grabbed hold of Dan's hips, dragging him to the edge of the sofa and humping against the crease of his arse. Looked like this was going to be hard and fast. Dan whimpered as Robin's cockhead bumped against his arsehole.

Robin paused a moment. "You want this?" he asked, his voice rasping. "You'd better tell me now, 'cause I don't think I'll be able to stop otherwise."

"Condoms and lube are in my jeans pocket." Dan pointed to where they lay on the floor. Robin better not push on ahead without them. Dan wasn't into taking risks like that, no matter how desperately he wanted that thick cock inside him.

Robin dug his fingers into Dan's flesh and gave another sharp thrust before letting go and searching through the clothes on the floor. Dan took a moment to compose himself, breathing deeply and consciously relaxing his muscles. He loved a good hard shag but he didn't want it to hurt too badly, and right now Robin didn't look like a man who would pause to prep him. He looked like a man hungry to fuck the living daylights out of him.

"Turn over," Robin said, the commanding tone making Dan shiver.

"I'm fine like this," he said, spreading his legs wide and watching Robin step out of his trousers and roll on the condom. Robin grabbed hold of Dan's legs and pulled him off the sofa so that he thunked down onto his arse.

"Ow! All right, all right. Jesus, you only had to ask."

"I did," Robin said, lifting Dan up and turning him round before pushing him back down onto his knees.

Dan leant forward onto the sofa, spreading his legs wide as Robin settled down behind him. Bugger, he'd wanted to be able to watch Robin's face while they fucked. There were so many conflicting emotions passing over it, it was fascinating viewing. That, and the guy was so hot he'd get off on just being able to see him.

But Dan's mind stopped bothering about that when he heard Robin spit, then felt that meaty cock breaching him, sure and steady, and all that mattered was relaxing his muscles enough not to tear. It smarted, being taken like this, but it was good too. Good to feel the solid presence inside him, the inexorable pressure surging deep into his guts. When he felt Robin's hips pressing against his arse, he pushed back, and there was a brief moment when all he could hear was the gasping of their breath. It was getting hot in the boat—hard to breathe. His body dripped with sweat. Then hands squeezed his hips hard, and Robin pulled back before slamming into him again and again.

Dan grunted with each punishing thrust, pushing back to meet Robin and feeling the delicious sting as their balls slapped together. He had to brace himself with his hands, so he couldn't pump his cock like he wanted to, but there was enough friction against the side of the sofa to get him to the brink. All he needed was a little more, a little more...

Robin changed the angle of his entry, hitting Dan's prostate over and over, making him whimper and writhe and forget all about keeping up with the rhythm. Then strong hands closed around his cock, and with two short jerks, he was spilling his load, bucking wildly and cursing with the force of the orgasm crashing through him. Robin's rhythm faltered, and with a final, painful slam into Dan's arse, he came too, falling forward onto Dan's back and biting down on his shoulder with a muffled shout.

Dan felt the pain through the haze of endorphins but couldn't care less. His body was bruised and tender, but he had a hot, sexy man draped over him, shuddering with the aftershocks of his orgasm. It didn't get much better than this.

And then, when he felt Robin kissing his neck, it did get better.

# Chapter Ten

As his racing heart slowed, Robin realised what he'd just done.

Shit.

There was a livid red mark where Dan's neck met his shoulder, the imprints of Robin's teeth clearly visible. The anger was gone now, swept away by his climax, leaving an empty space for the guilt to resurface. He shouldn't have been so rough. Shouldn't have taken out his rage at Jamie on Dan. What would Dan be thinking of him right now? That he was an animal? A brute with no finesse? It was impossible to tell with Dan's face buried in the sofa.

Before he could think about what he was doing, Robin craned forward and kissed the mark his teeth had left. Dan's skin tasted good, a sweetness underlying the tang of sweat, and Robin gave in to the urge to taste again. He licked a stripe up Dan's neck towards his ear. Dan sighed deeply, heaving beneath Robin while he made amends by kissing and nibbling, words way too awkward to consider. It was only when he sucked on an earlobe that Dan dissolved into giggles. What the fuck?

"Stop! Ticklish." Dan turned his head at last so Robin could see the side of his face. He seemed happy—if his smile was anything to go by. "Now, if you could just move, maybe we can cuddle up properly."

As Robin withdrew, Dan hissed in a sharp breath, his body tensing. Robin winced. Had he hurt him? He was feeling pretty tender himself—Dan had been tight, much tighter than he'd expected. He wanted to apologise, but the words knotted up inside him. Instead, he gave the curve of Dan's arse a gentle caress and pressed a kiss to his tailbone.

"Hmmm, thanks for that," Dan murmured, sounding close to sleep. He rolled over and gave a lazy grin.

Robin bit his lip and hurried off to his wet-room without a word.

What was he meant to do now? He had a naked and thoroughly fucked man on his boat. He couldn't just throw him out, and what's more, he didn't want to. But neither was he sure about sharing his bed for the night. About waking up next to another man again. Robin leant his head against the wall and groaned.

"Hey, Robin, any chance of me getting something to clean up with?"

Robin spun around, startled. Dan was standing at the open door, less than a foot away, but Robin's thoughts had been so noisy he hadn't even heard him approach. He showed Dan how to operate the foot pump for the sink water and handed him a flannel. There wasn't enough water in the tank to risk taking a shower now—not if they wanted one in the morning.

Robin realised that he was picturing himself soaping down Dan's back. His stomach lurched. Suddenly, being in the tiny room together was almost too much to handle. But Dan was blocking his way out, wiping himself clean with a total lack of shame. Of course, Dan probably did this sort of thing all the time, but Robin felt terribly exposed. He closed his eyes and leant back against the shower wall. Everything was fine. Dan obviously didn't have a problem with it, so why should he?

"You okay if I stay tonight?" Dan sounded casual, but there was something about the way he looked at Robin that seemed wary.

"Yeah, sure." It would be fine. It would be reassuring to feel another body next to his. To hear steady breathing in the depths of the night.

He realised that Dan was still giving him that wary look. "I'd like that," he added softly, and Dan gave a slow smile.

But Robin wasn't quite ready to go to bed. He pulled on a T-shirt and jogging bottoms and headed back into the saloon. The scattered clothing on the floor was a stark reminder of how ruthless he'd been, and he gathered it up quickly, folding Dan's clothes neatly and leaving them in a pile on the sofa.

"Would you like a drink?" he called out. "Tea? Or something stronger?"

"Tea sounds great."

Robin wasn't going to drink alone, so he put the bottle of rum back in the cupboard and took out his stash tin instead. He needed something to soothe the jitters inside him. When Dan came back through, there were two cups of tea sitting on the bench opposite the sofa, and Robin was busy rolling a joint. It gave him an excuse not to look up and see Dan naked again, and he kept his eyes averted until Dan was dressed. Even then, he caught glimpses of smooth, tanned legs out of the corner of his eye.

"I don't really smoke much these days," Dan said when Robin offered him the joint, but he accepted it anyway, his fingers brushing over Robin's. He took a short drag before handing it back but remained standing, gazing down at Robin.

"Sit down. You're making me nervous," Robin said, then instantly regretted it when he saw how gingerly Dan lowered himself onto the sofa. He flushed, looking down at his hands. "Fuck. Sorry. I didn't mean to hurt you."

"I'll be fine, but next time you nail me that hard, you should use some lube. Spit doesn't really cut it."

Next time? Robin looked up in surprise. Dan smiled—there wasn't a trace of accusation in his eyes.

"Sorry. I didn't find any." He hadn't been thinking straight, overwhelmed by the driving need to fuck Dan until everything else disappeared for those few glorious moments.

Robin took a deep drag while Dan dug his hand in his pocket. It was a tricky manoeuvre, what with his jeans being so tightly fitted.

"Here, look. Sachets of the stuff. I'm always prepared, just like a Boy Scout."

The image of Dan as a scout swam before Robin's eyes, and he started to chuckle. Dan would look pretty cute in the uniform, what with his freckles and boyish physique.

Dan gave him a quizzical look, so he calmed himself down. "Sorry. I've just... I've never seen lube in sachets before."

Dan raised his eyebrows even farther. "And that's funny? That must be some strong shit you're smoking." Dan shook his head, smiling, but then his expression turned more serious. "Robin, how long has it been since you were with a man?"

Too long. Robin stared at the flickering flames in his wood burner. Years and years. He shivered despite the heat on his skin, transported back to those black months after things ended with Jamie.

"Sorry. It's none of my business. Wish I could learn to shut up sometimes."

Robin heard Dan slurping his tea. What would it cost him to confide? He hadn't wanted to with Mel. Hadn't wanted to risk seeing the tenderness in her eyes cloud over—her affection replaced with contempt. But Dan? Dan was still a stranger, really.

They were silent while Robin finished his joint. He reached for his tea but found it was now only lukewarm. He put it down with a sigh.

"Four years. It's been four years. His name was Jamie, and I don't really want to talk about it right now." He glanced up at Dan, who was gazing at him with something that looked like sympathy. It made him want to curl up and hide away.

"How old are you, Robin?"

"Twenty-five. You?"

"Twenty-nine. I'll be thirty next March. Hard to believe, eh? I should probably be settling down and finding the man I want to marry, or something." Dan gave a short chuckle. "Reckon it'll be a cold day in hell before that happens, though." He sighed before reaching out and squeezing Robin's hand. "Come on, you, let's go to bed."

The bed was chilly, but Dan turned down the loan of a T-shirt and jogging bottoms, so Robin went without them too, reasoning that the extra body under the covers would help to keep him warm. And when Robin curled up, facing away from Dan, he was absurdly grateful to feel Dan spooning behind him. He drifted away into a dreamless sleep, soothed by the warm breath against his neck.

Robin woke on his back, the sensation of a smooth leg thrown over his, a warm arm over his chest. Mel...no, Dan!

He studied his bedmate. Dan appeared even younger when sleeping, his face soft and his hair a fluffy mess. There was a faint haze of stubble on his cheeks, the hairs glinting with reddish tints in the soft light that filtered through the blinds in the portholes.

Light. If it was light already, then Robin had slept in much later than usual. He must have been worn out after last night... The memories flooded back, shot through with a heady mix of guilt and lust. Of Dan, sucking him off under the trees. Of Dan, spreading his legs with a come-hither smile. Of Dan, trembling on his knees as Robin pushed deep inside him.

Bollocks. He was getting hard just thinking about doing that again. He rolled over to face Dan, who stirred and mumbled something. Robin pressed himself closer, running his hand up a hairless leg and over a temptingly pert buttock. He squeezed on the smooth flesh, not caring if he woke Dan. Not caring about anything except the desire that was building inside. It welled up, threatening to spill over all his carefully constructed barriers. They'd held fast for all those years since Jamie, but against this need, they didn't stand a chance.

Dan mumbled again. Robin watched his face as he stroked Dan's cock. It was already half-hard, lying heavy and thick in his hand.

Dan's eyes sprang open. "Morning, gorgeous." He yawned, giving a contented sigh as he undulated his body, pushing into Robin's grip. "Mmm, that's my favourite way to wake up. How did you know?"

"Lucky guess," Robin said, shifting closer so he could rub his own shaft against Dan's. The contact set his nerves on fire. He wrapped his hand around both of them, swallowing back a moan, and searched hungrily for Dan's lips.

"No, wait, morning breath," Dan said, turning his head with a grimace.

"Don't care." And he didn't. Didn't care about yesterday's sweat still clinging to their bodies, about the sleep crusting Dan's eyes or the sour taste in both their mouths. All Robin cared about was the roaring blood in his veins and the need to kiss, caress and generally make up for his behaviour last night. He concentrated on Dan's neck, licking and sucking the skin there while his hand set a slow and steady rhythm, the other hand snaking underneath Dan's head to tangle in his hair. He felt Dan's body quiver, heard him gasp, and then Dan's hands joined in, kneading Robin's buttocks and playing with his nipples. And this time, when he went for Dan's mouth it was open and willing, their tongues sliding together as they kissed deep and hard.

Holding Dan's head steady, Robin pulled back and dragged his teeth along Dan's lower lip. He forgot everything but this driving need, this desperate urge to press himself against Dan's slim body, to make him pant and groan and give those husky whimpers that drove Robin wild. And when he felt Dan's fingers sliding between his buttocks, he couldn't stop himself, his hand working them fast and hard until the world whited out and his grip turned slippery.

In the afterglow, Robin was barely aware of Dan's hand joining his and holding it tight as he thrust into their combined grip. There was a wordless cry as Dan convulsed and shuddered to a halt, panting hard.

Lying there, hot and sticky, with Dan's face resting on his chest, Robin found an unfamiliar peace. A knowledge that there was nowhere else he would rather be right now. And then he heard a purring chirrup, and felt Morris's heavy weight land on his legs. The cat pushed up between them, licked Dan's arm and settled down on Robin's chest, purring like an outboard motor.

"Oi, cat," Dan said, wriggling around and propping his head up on one hand. "You're gonna have to share your man with me, you know."

Something inside Robin leapt at Dan's words, but he pushed it down, squashing it out of the way unexamined. Dan wouldn't be around for long.

Dan was pulling faces at Morris—holding up a hand, slick with their come.

"Don't you go expecting any petting, now. Oh God!" Morris had butted his head against Dan's sticky hand. Dan's face twisted with barely contained laughter. "Sorry 'bout that."

Morris's fur stood up in wet spikes, rather like Dan's had the previous day, but the cat was still purring despite the mess on his head. Robin turned to Dan, whose cheeks were dimpled and whose body had started shaking. An answering laughter bubbled up inside him, quaking through his chest. When Morris stalked off in disgust, he pulled Dan close, hugging him tight as he shook and shook until it felt like he was going to fall apart.

And if he did, if he truly let go, would he ever be able to put himself back together again?

# Chapter Eleven

"That is some sandwich," Dan said, amazed at the height of the thing. "You really think you can fit it in your mouth?"

Robin gave a wicked grin and opened wide. Dan caught a brief flash of his tongue stud before he chomped down on the triple-decker, ketchup and egg yolk running out of the opposite side. Mmm... Dan shifted on the sofa, imagining those lips wrapping themselves around his cock. He'd have to drop some serious hints about that later, once he'd been back to the *Faerie Queen* and showered, of course.

"You gonna eat yours, then?" Robin's voice was muffled around the mouthful of greasy food, but it still sounded sexy. There was something about a man trying to talk with his mouth full that always flipped a switch deep inside Dan. Maybe he had a food kink he'd never really explored in any depth. Maybe he could explore it with Robin. That'd be fun.

Turned out Robin cooked a mean breakfast, and Dan liked that in a man. None of that muesli and grapefruit rubbish—this was a proper feast to make up for all that strenuous exercise they'd been having. Robin's "Cholesterol Sandwich" consisted of three slices of fried bread, layered up with bacon, two fried eggs and slices of cheddar cheese, not to mention the lashings of ketchup and mustard.

"Just looking at it makes my arteries shudder," Dan said, picking up his own Cholesterol Sandwich. His taste buds tingled in anticipation, and he took a bite. It was amazing, the crisp bacon perfectly complemented by the soft egg yolk and crumbly cheese. He gave a deep groan of contentment, looked up and found Robin gazing at him with twinkling eyes.

"This is bloody gorgeous," Dan said, although he could just as easily have said Robin was bloody gorgeous and it would have been equally true. Now that they'd finally done the dirty, Robin had relaxed and started enjoying himself. Dan had even heard him whistling as he cooked, and the man could certainly hold a tune. Made him wonder about that guitar propped up against the worktable.

But best of all, there was a warmth in Robin's eyes when he looked at him—one which Dan felt sure he could kindle into blazing passion whenever he felt like it. Not right now, though. His arse was still tender after the pounding Robin had given him last night.

Dan washed down the last of his greasy feast with a slurp of strong black coffee and grinned. This was going to be a great week—beautiful scenery, willing models and a fling with a handsome man who had a kink for rough sex. Hard to imagine now why he'd been so reluctant to take the job.

Robin had also finished his sandwich and was licking his fingers clean. Dan watched for a moment, not sure if this was a show designed to tantalise or if it was typical atavistic boater behaviour. But then he decided he didn't care and reached out to grab Robin's hand, pulling it to his mouth and sucking in the first two fingers. Robin stared at him, eyes wide, but when Dan swirled his tongue around the bacon-flavoured digits, those eyes fluttered shut and Robin moaned in a way that made Dan's cock begin to swell.

Dan hummed happily before pulling Robin's fingers out of his mouth. "Much as I'd love to carry on with this, I should be getting back to my boat. I reek of sex."

Robin's pupils had flared wide and hungry. "You could shower here. With me." The way his voice caught on the last two words made Dan want to pull him into a greedy kiss and start stripping all their clothes off. But he had work set up— people he'd arranged to shoot—and he needed to get the camera out of the boat's safe as well as change into some fresh clothing. Robin would keep. Maybe he'd be even more delicious if Dan gave him a few hours to stew.

"Sorry, work to do." Dan stood and walked towards the doors. Robin moved fast, blocking his way off the boat. Interesting. Was he going to get all dominant again?

Dan smiled, slipping his hands around Robin's hips and cupping his arse. Robin's breath came fast against his forehead, and Dan craned his neck to give him a quick kiss, pulling back as Robin's tongue flicked out. "Uh-uh, I'm sure you can wait a few hours. It'll be that much more exciting, what with the anticipation and all. Maybe, just maybe," he craned his neck again to whisper in Robin's ear as his hands kneaded his buttocks, "you'll let me get a piece of your sweet arse later."

Uh-oh, wrong words. Robin tensed in his arms, and Dan brought his hands up slowly, carefully. Must be one of those rare beasts, a total top. Still, that was fine. He could cope with being bottom for a week as long as Robin remembered the lube.

"It's okay, no pressure. I'd like to fuck you, but I'm just as happy with you topping."

Robin had his eyes closed, and that furrow was back between his brows. "I can't... I don't... Fuck! I just can't, all right?"

"It's fine, like I said. Not a problem." Part of him was curious as to why Robin couldn't, but another part refused to get drawn into emotional complexities. That was always the point where the fun dried up and his relationships fizzled out. Easier to stick to the sex and the banter—he was good at that. And cuddling too... He pulled Robin close and hugged him, offering the warmth of his body instead.

"No hard feelings, eh? Well, hopefully later there will be, when I've had a chance to recover." That was better, Robin was smiling now—only a glimmer, but it was a start.

Before Robin had a chance to rethink things, Dan steered him to one side and walked to the doors.

"I'll be back later, okay? Say, five-ish? I can bring us some fish and chips if you like, to say thanks for breakfast. Get a bit more cholesterol down us."

"Yeah, great." Robin stayed where he was, leaning back against the side of the boat. His face was impassive. Why'd Dan always go for the moody and monosyllabic ones? But then

Robin turned towards him, and a warm smile transformed his face for a brief moment.

"Later," Robin said. "I'll make it good for you this time."

Dan shivered at the intensity in his eyes.

"Believe me, it was good last night."

Robin raised his eyebrows, and Dan made a swift exit before either of them said anything they would later regret.

"And what sort of time do you call this, Mr. Taylor?" Mel made a tsking sound as she leaned back against the *Faerie Queen*. "My, don't you look like you've been dragged through a hedge backwards. Good night, was it?"

Dan flashed her a grin before kneeling to lock up his bike. "Marvellous, cheers. That was quite a party." He was tempted to brag, but it wouldn't be fair to out Robin before he was ready.

"It's no good pretending it was that. I saw you leave early."

"Oh?" Yep, he could be subtle and keep secrets if he wanted to. No matter how much he wanted to grin.

"Robin was pretty hot on your tail, as I recall." Mel's smile was more of a smirk, and he couldn't help but answer it with one of his own.

"Was he?" He tried to sound innocent, but her eyes were knowing. She wasn't about to give up easily—Dan recognised the type. "Yeah, he was, wasn't he?" His smile grew even more salacious as he remembered just how "hot on his tail" Robin had been.

"Seriously?" Mel looked like she was going to explode with excitement. "I've been thinking for a while that what Robin needed was a good shag, but I didn't know it was gonna take a man to do it. That's fantastic! You've got to tell me all about it."

Christ, she was one of those straight girls who got off on blokes shagging each other. Dan had met a few of them over the years. Most were fine, if a little odd, but he'd been really freaked out by one who cornered him in a gay bar wanting explicit details of his sex life. Mind you, Mel seemed genuinely happy for her friend, although he wasn't about to furnish her with any more intimate details.

"Mel, can I take a rain check on that photo shoot you've set up? I need to get a shower and a change of clothes. How about…" He glanced at his watch. How'd it get to be ten thirty already? He'd better get a move on if he wanted to do any work today. "I can be ready in half an hour. Want to come in and make yourself a cuppa while you wait?"

"I thought you'd never offer. You'd better be quick, though. Don't want to keep Aranya waiting. You'll love his boat, but that guy's the most uptight hippie I've ever met. Think his dad's an investment banker, and it shows."

"Are you saying he's a proper trustafarian?"

"I don't know if he has a trust fund, sweetie, but he's certainly come from money. No need to look so surprised. There's all sorts along here. Robin's much posher than he looks. Not that I've ever met his family." She gave a rueful smile. "I get the impression they're not all that keen on us boating folk."

Dan held out a hand to help Mel up onto the deck, which she looked at with amusement but took anyway. "I can be a gentleman," he said.

"I don't doubt it, darling. Now let's get into the warm, and while you get ready, you can give me all the juicy details about last night."

Dan gave a theatrical sigh. "You don't give up easily, do you?"

Mel grinned. "They call me the Terrier."

Someone who was used to getting what she was after? Yeah, Dan could recognise that. After all, didn't he usually end up getting exactly what he was after? He smiled to himself as he pushed back the hatch and unlatched the doors. Yep, he knew what he wanted out of Robin this week, and he was determined to use all his charm to get it.

# Chapter Twelve

The water tank ran dry while Robin was in the shower. It always seemed to do that. Good thing Dan hadn't taken him up on his offer after all. He stepped out of the stall and rubbed the remaining soap off him with the towel. Christ, it was all crusty from when they'd cleaned up last night. He'd need to pay a visit to the launderette. Those sheets on his bed wouldn't be much better, and he didn't have any storage space for spare linen.

He stuck his head out of the boat, whistled, and after a few minutes, Morris appeared from out of the hedgerow. His head still looked a little tufty, but when Robin reached out to stroke him, he realised the cat was just wet. The clever creature must have gone and given himself a dew bath. Morris circled around Robin's legs, purring loudly, before trotting inside the boat and looking around.

"Oh, you're missing Dan too? He's not here, but he'll be back later. He promised. Said he'd bring you some fish, mister." Robin left Morris curled up by the fire and shut the hatches to keep him inside while they cruised. It probably wasn't necessary, but after losing him the last time, he really didn't want to take any chances.

Robin started the engine with the hand crank he'd installed, grinning in satisfaction at the loud chugging and belch of black smoke from the exhaust. There was nothing more irritating than a flat battery, and he'd modified his engine accordingly. He pulled in the plank and made a flying leap over to the bank to untie the lines, using them to hold *Serendipity* steady before jumping back.

Remembering Dan's face as he walked over the plank brought a smile to his face. It'd been good to see the oh-so-worldly Dan drop the act for a moment and ask for help. Good to feel the rapid beating of Dan's heart as he pulled him close afterwards.

Robin tried to clear his mind of Dan and observe his surroundings as the boat puttered along. This was a great spot, being deserted most of the time. Although they were only five miles from the city, it felt like deep countryside. The local villages were small and quiet, the majority of the canal passing through sleepy farmland and woods. Most of the other boaters preferred to moor up near the villages where there were concrete banks allowing them to pull their boats in tight. This might stop the boats rocking so much when others passed, but Robin avoided those kinds of moorings as it brought him too close to the towpath and the nosy passersby—not to mention the other boaters, who all seemed to know one another's business. Would they have seen his boat rocking last night? Or heard Dan's uninhibited noises? Robin felt the flush spread over his face and frowned. It was ridiculous; he'd lived with Jamie for years and been out and proud, so why had he spent the last few years hiding away?

A kingfisher darted across in front of the boat, a flash of iridescent blue cutting through his unsettling thoughts. Robin steered his mind from dangerous memories and focused on *Serendipity*, noting the way the shimmering blue of the solar panels echoed the kingfisher's feathers. The sun might be shining, but at this time of year the photovoltaic panels were next to useless. Still, the cruise would help to recharge his battery bank, meaning there would be no need to run the generator this evening. There was something about its incessant drone that annoyed Robin at the best of times, and he certainly didn't want a passion killer like that spoiling his plans for the night...

And he did have plans. So many things he wanted to do to and with Dan. It was an unfamiliar feeling, this rush of lust, and he found himself wondering just what Dan's eyes would look like when Robin went down on him for the first time. He frowned again. Bugger those pretty eyes. He wasn't going to fall for them, no matter how brightly they sparkled. He spent the rest of the journey lost in memories of Dan's body instead— much safer that way, even if it did give him a stiffie. It took a good few minutes of mental cold showering to sort himself out when he neared the water point.

But first things first, there was a swing bridge in the way. They were a pain in the arse without a hapless passerby to charm into helping, but his last couple of years cruising alone had given him plenty of practice at operating them by himself. Robin steered into the mini-marina and left the engine chugging away as he stepped onto the next boat—a wooden-hulled, steam-powered monster that was a hobby craft for one of the well-to-do weekend boaters living in the village. He hitched *Serendipity*'s line around a cleat on the *Mayflower*, then hopped from boat to boat until he reached the bank. This particular bridge took a good bit of elbow grease to get moving—Robin stripped off his shirt before starting to push, knowing he'd be uncomfortably hot otherwise. His head dropped as he put the weight of his body into pushing the beam, and it wasn't until the bridge started swinging round that he realised he had observers on the towpath side.

Dan and Mel were standing there, Dan's bike laden with his camera bags, both grinning like morons. Dan gave a wolf whistle, and Robin flushed, getting even more flustered as he saw Dan get his camera out. Once the bridge was fully open, he went to put his T-shirt back on.

"Don't you dare cover up that gorgeous body," Dan shouted across the canal. "I need a photo of you driving your boat like that." Mel said something Robin couldn't hear. "Sorry, *steering* your boat. And don't worry, you can sign the release form later."

Release form? What the fuck? But the heat in Dan's gaze stirred something inside him, and Robin had the sudden urge to flaunt himself.

"Watch this," he said, grinning at Dan before running and leaping onto the first of the boats. He landed on the deck with a *thunk*, sprang up onto the gunwales and launched himself onto the small cruiser that was next in line. A couple more jumps, a momentary pause to whip undone his hitch, and he was back on *Serendipity*. He ran down the roof, vaulted over the woodpile and landed with a twist on the tiny back deck. He could hear the clapping from the other side of the canal and looked up to meet Dan's admiring gaze...and a decidedly knowing smile from Mel.

"Better get your camera ready," he called to Dan over the noise of the engine before putting *Serendipity* in gear. He steadfastly refused to look Dan's way as he steered through the narrow passage, keeping his face set in a serious expression, but it was hard to resist the smile that twitched at his lips as Dan called out instructions like an uber-camp fashion photographer. At one point he had to turn away and hide his face.

"That's beautiful, darling. We'll have a pout next time, okay? That's it, oooh, sexy. Now, imagine you're a tiger."

"Piss off!" Robin's laughter broke the surface, and he turned to see Dan still watching him through the camera's lens with a mischievous grin. He turned away again, concentrating on steering *Serendipity* into the short stretch of bank on this side of the bridge. This time there were no boats to leap over, but Dan continued snapping away as Robin swung the bridge back across the canal. It was hard to know where to look. He'd never been particularly at ease with having his picture taken— every year growing up, his mother had complained about yet another scowl in their annual family portrait shot.

The bridge was still moving as Dan stepped onto it and strode over with an expression that did funny things to Robin's insides. He leant on the other side of the beam as Robin wiped the sweat from his brow with his T-shirt before pulling it on over his head.

"That was quite a performance. I had no idea you were so athletic." Robin could hear the lust roughening Dan's voice, and he swallowed hard. He looked down at Dan's chest, displayed provocatively in a tight red T-shirt with "flirt" written across the front in bold script.

"There's a lot of things you don't know about me."

"I look forward to finding them all out. Later..." Dan ran a finger along Robin's forearm, and Robin wanted to pull him closer. But he couldn't. Not here. Not in public. He looked across to where Mel was tapping her foot, hands on her hips.

"So where are you off to?" Dan asked. "Not trying to escape me, I hope. I'm pretty persistent, you know."

"We're already late," Mel called, "so if you could stop chatting up the locals for five minutes, we need to get to Smiler's before he changes his mind about this."

"Smiler? I thought you were only interested in boaters?" Robin said.

"Oh, I am, don't you worry," Dan purred, his finger tracing a line over Robin's jaw. "But as he's a splash of local colour, I figured I should go and investigate. I do love those crazy, rustic types, even when they threaten me."

"Not sure what he'll say." Robin apprised Dan's figure-hugging outfit, which screamed GAY at the same time as making his mouth water. "Probably tell you to 'get orf' his land."

"Well, I'm hoping he'll let me take a little break. I'm not finding my bike seat too comfortable today." Robin flushed, and Dan took advantage of his mortification by planting a quick kiss on his lips. "See you later, sexy."

Robin closed his eyes and deliberately calmed his breathing. When he finally opened them, Dan and Mel were both mounted on their bikes, watching him. He raised his hand in a feeble wave, and they blew him kisses before setting off, the mock grimace on Dan's face as he lowered himself onto his seat no doubt all for Robin's benefit. Bastard.

But Robin couldn't tear his eyes away. He kept watching until the red of Dan's T-shirt disappeared into the distance.

"Robin, darling, have you been avoiding my calls? You know how I worry about you all alone on that awful boat."

Robin held the phone away from his ear and could still hear his mother's strident tones blaring out at him. He walked back to the boat to check the level of water in the tank before interrupting her torrent of words.

"Don't worry, I've just been moored up where there's no reception. I called you as soon as I got your messages. There was no need to leave so many." He hadn't bothered listening to the last six, deleting them straight away.

"Well, don't you think you should be moored up somewhere with the basics of civilisation? What if there was an emergency? You know I'm only saying it because I care, darling. Why not get yourself a place in a marina? I've been looking into it, and there's one down by the Aqueduct that looks lovely. Your father and I would pay for you."

For crying out loud! "It's not about the money. I don't like living so close to everyone else. What's the point in living on a boat if you don't keep moving around, seeing new places?"

He heard a loud sniff. "Well, I've never been able to understand the appeal of living on one of those death traps anyway. Honestly, Robin, wouldn't you prefer a proper house somewhere? I don't like the idea of you living like some kind of gypsy. It was bad enough when you got all those tattoos and decided you were part-time gay. Do you plan on spending your whole life doing things that make me worry about you?"

Robin ground his teeth and bit back all the things he really wanted to say. "This isn't about you, Mum. It's about what I want. Now, do you have something to tell me about Miri or not?"

Fortunately, the chance to speak about the impending grandchild was irresistible to his mum, and Robin's mind drifted as she chattered on about the designer nursery décor and developmental toys that Miranda's lawyer husband had been able to provide for the baby. Poor little Patrick Oswald, not even born yet and already his whole life was mapped out for him. They'd probably hothouse the kid so he could turn into one of those freaky child prodigies and make up for Robin's fucked-up life. He shoved the phone between his ear and shoulder as he turned off the water tap and reeled in his hosepipe, barely paying attention to the aural onslaught.

"I said, will you be around on Saturday? Your father has a ticket for the rugby, and Miranda and I are going to hit the shops in Bath for baby things. They have some of the cutest little outfits. Then I thought we could all go for lunch together."

Saturday? Robin realised he had no idea if Dan would still be around on Saturday. "Umm, I'm not sure, I might have plans."

"You might have plans? You either do or you don't. Why not check your diary?"

"You know I don't keep a diary."

"Yes, well, I give you one for Christmas every year, so I don't know why you don't use the bloody things. Honestly, Robin, your handwriting isn't that bad. I remember your tutors saying that you just needed to put in more regular practise rather than spending all your time fooling around with that hooligan boyfriend of yours."

He really didn't want to have this conversation right now. "Fine! Look, I'll be there. Just leave a message to remind me. I might be out of reception for a while, but I'll cycle somewhere with a signal every day."

"What a time to decide you want to be out of range! Honestly, I don't know where you get it from. I'm sure your father and I were never this awkward when we were young. As a matter of fact, I distinctly remember—"

"Bye, Mum." He took a perverse pleasure in hanging up on her in mid-flow and immediately switched his phone off. But all the simmering anticipation he'd been feeling about his evening with Dan had evaporated at the mention of Jamie, and his thoughts swirled dark and gloomy as he cruised to the winding hole, turned and set off back to the mooring spot.

But this was no good. Wallowing in it never got him anywhere. Fortunately he knew just how to cheer himself up. Robin moored up, then went to get out his tools.

# Chapter Thirteen

The setting sun cast warm rays into the clouds, leaving the valley in shadow as it dipped down behind the hill. As he cycled out to Robin's boat, Dan inhaled lungfuls of fragrant woodsmoke, occasionally varied by the sharper scent of smokeless fuel. The boats were already lit up inside, casting warm lozenges of light onto the grass bank. The stretch out towards Robin's boat was lonely and dark in comparison. It was a world away from cycling through the choking fumes, dazzling lights and hectic noise of London. Absolute quiet reigned. It was almost...spooky.

Dan shivered, glad that he'd thought to pack his panniers with spare clothing this time. He had the bag of fish and chips tucked into his jacket keeping him warm—no doubt it was also making him smell like a chippy, but he had a feeling Robin wouldn't hold it against him. The guy always seemed to smell of fresh sweat himself. Dan thought back to their encounter on the bridge that afternoon and the hot, smoky tang rising from Robin's body that had made his mouth water.

*Serendipity* was pointing the wrong way, confusing Dan for a moment. But of course, part of the general weirdness that was boat living, no doubt—constantly changing which side of your home looked onto land, and which onto water.

He faced the plank. It shone pale against the dark reeds and even darker water beneath. His pulse raced at the idea of crossing it alone. But he couldn't call Robin out to hold his hand. He'd managed to cross it earlier on when leaving, so he could do it again now. It wasn't any more dangerous in the dark. And there was absolutely no need for him to jump out of his skin just because some fucking owl had hooted. He stepped onto the springy board and stumbled onto the front deck with a surge of pride, despite his jelly knees.

Should he knock? Robin must know he was here. The whole boat rocked like a fairground ride after his clumsy arrival. Might as well make a grand entrance. Dan flung the doors open and entered with as much of a flourish as was possible while laden with panniers, camera bag, and the chips down his jacket.

"Come and get 'em while they're still warm! There's a man-size portion of delicious hot, salty treats hidden away under my clothing for some lucky fella to ferret out."

Robin was closing the lid of the farther-away, built-in footstool, and he straightened with an indecipherable expression on his face. "Hi," he said, closing the space between them.

Dan couldn't breathe for a moment after seeing the blaze in Robin's eyes. Robin's hands closed over his, and Dan inclined his head for a kiss. But instead of the pressure of lips against his, he felt his hands relieved of their load. Robin turned away to place the bags on the floor beyond the sofa. Stupid to be disappointed about that—it wasn't like they were a couple or anything.

"Quite a load. Planning on moving in, are you?"

It was hard to know whether Robin was teasing or not when Dan couldn't see his face, but he went for his usual banter. "Well, if you insist, I suppose I could for the rest of the week. Your bed's so much more comfortable than mine." His stomach clenched in anticipation. Oh God, he hadn't realised how much he wanted to stay until he was slap-bang up against the possibility of Robin saying no.

Robin turned to face him, and Dan relaxed when he saw the smile tugging at his lips. "Is that all you're after? A decent night's kip?"

"I was rather hoping you'd keep me up half the night instead." Robin flushed slightly, but Dan saw his eyes grow darker. "First things first, I reek of battered fish, so how about helping me find some plates and things?"

A huge plate of fish and chips later, Dan licked the grease off his fingers and cast a sly glance at Robin, who was mopping up the last of the ketchup with a chip. Robin's lips were coated with an oily sheen. Dan salivated as he imagined running his tongue over them, then down over the bristles to the smoother skin of Robin's neck and chest. Would he have the opportunity to explore Robin's body tonight? It was always so delightful to get to know a new lover's body in intimate detail. To find out what touch where would send him into ecstasies; to discover just what sort of noises escaped him when Dan's tongue went wandering; to revel in all the different flavours of a new man.

Robin looked up at Dan; then his eyes dropped and he bit his bottom lip. Curious, to be so hesitant after his behaviour the previous night. Rather charming, though, the way Robin kept surprising him.

"So, are you too stuffed to move, or do you fancy working off some of those calories?" Dan asked.

"I think I need to let my food go down first." Robin stuck out his belly and rubbed it slowly. "Mum always said you shouldn't exercise on a full stomach. How about a film instead?"

Dan looked around the boat, puzzled. There was no evidence of any entertainment system. "You'd better not be suggesting we cycle out to the cinema. I'm far too cosy for that right now." He emphasised his words by shifting closer and dropping his head onto Robin's shoulder. The effect he was after was somewhat spoiled by the plate falling from his lap and onto the floor, but Robin just chuckled and wrapped an arm around him.

"I'm not a complete Luddite, you know. I have technology. I have DVDs."

"Where are they, then?" From the looks of his home, you wouldn't think Robin had any interests beyond woodworking and playing the guitar. There weren't even any books.

"My feet are on them."

"Ah, so that's what you were doing when I arrived. Hiding your technology."

Dan felt Robin's body tense slightly and had to move as Robin stood and lifted the lid of the bench nearest the fire.

"I prefer to keep it hidden, as I don't like to have to lock the boat. I'm less likely to get burgled if no one can see anything worth taking." Dan watched as Robin carefully lifted out a smallish flat-screen television and placed it on the other footstool. "What do you want to watch?"

"Got any porn?"

Robin turned towards Dan, amusement twitching his lips. "I've got a couple of discs, but I don't think you'd like them. They've got women in them too."

Dan screwed his face up. "Eww, what do you want to watch straight porn for?"

"It's not straight, it's bi. I told you I was bi, didn't I?" Robin's cheeks flushed as he pulled out a DVD with a lurid screenshot of a woman and two men entangled on the front.

"I thought that was just a cover story. You set my gaydar off big-time."

"I've slept with girls plenty of times."

"Yeah, right." Dan gave Robin what he hoped was a penetrating stare. The guy was protesting too much.

"I have. You think I've been celibate the last few years? Think again. I can prove it. Ask Mel. She'll tell you."

Was Robin saying what he thought he was? "You've slept with Mel?"

"Yeah. A few times. We had fun." Robin was holding something back, though, he could tell.

"As much fun as you had with me?" Dan kept his tone light, but he really wanted to know. For some reason it was terribly important that Robin was as into this as he was. "You sure you're not really gay after all? Sure you haven't been secretly lusting after cock all this time?"

"I expect you reckon you can convert me with the power of your dick or something." Robin grinned. "Okay, no porn with girls in. How about a kung fu movie instead? That's got lots of half-naked men getting all physical with each other. Will that do?"

"I'll give it a go, but I've never been that keen. The stuff my brother liked was just mindless violence—all muscley guys with dead eyes beating the shit out of each other." Dan had hated the way Pete and his mates would get wild-eyed and aggressive after watching them. Even as a child, he'd been afraid of being on the receiving end of a beating if Pete found out what Dan really thought about some of his friends.

"Right, then, something with a storyline and a sense of humour. I know, you'll like this one. It's got Jet Li in it, back from before he went all Hollywood." Robin held up a disc with a picture of the actor in traditional Cantonese garb and one of those bizarre half-shaved hairdos. Dan nodded, wondering what he was letting himself in for.

Dan watched Robin plugging everything in—it turned out he'd built in a decent speaker system and hidden it behind latticework—and pondered what it must be like to live full-time in a space like this. You could stand with your arms stretched out and touch both walls—everything was easily accessible if you had the right storage. In some ways it wasn't too different to his tiny flat in Balham, but so much cosier. No draughty sash windows and crippling gas bills for Robin. Here, you just had to chuck a fresh log on the fire every half an hour or so and had all the fun of watching the flames rather than your gas meter spinning around.

The tinny Chinese music started up, and Robin slumped beside him, remote control in hand. Dan looked at the menu screen and caught Robin selecting the dubbed version.

"You don't have to do that—I'm fine with subtitles."

Robin kept staring at the screen. His jaw worked, but no sound came out.

"Just 'cause I'm not posh like you, doesn't mean I can't cope with subtitled foreign films. I've seen a few. Got a bit of a thing for some of those French actors. It's much better when you can hear their proper voices instead of some bloody ridiculous American translation that doesn't match their lip movements." Dan kept babbling, but something wasn't quite right, and he didn't know how to approach it.

In the end, he shut up and waited, watching the way Robin's fingers clenched around the remote. His knuckles were white, and Dan reached out to lay a hand over them. Robin gave a long, shuddering sigh and began talking in a low voice, his eyes on their hands.

"We could put the subtitles on, but I won't be able to read them fast enough. I'm dyslexic. Pretty fucking severely dyslexic." Robin's laugh was a short bark, devoid of mirth.

"I didn't know."

Robin stared at him. "Why would you? It's not like I go around broadcasting it."

"Sorry, I—"

"I was twelve before my Mum managed to bully the school into getting me properly tested. Up until then, everyone told me I was thick. I used to get lippy with the teachers to hide the fact I couldn't read properly. First time I got expelled, I was eight years old."

"Eight?" Jesus Christ, Dan had been a model pupil at eight. Not that it stopped the teasing from the other kids, but he didn't think it politic to mention that right now. Robin's brow was furrowed deeply, and he looked like he was trying to bore a hole in the floor of the boat with some kind of death-ray glower.

"Do you know what that's like, Dan? To have everyone ripping the piss out of you about something you can't help?"

"I've got an idea." Yeah, those childhood bullies had sniffed out his homosexuality before he'd even realised it himself. "Is that why you don't have any books? I did wonder."

Robin shot him a glare. "I can read. I'm not an idiot."

"I didn't say you couldn't." Why did this man have to be so bloody complicated? "I just figured you probably wouldn't enjoy it much."

"Yeah, well..." Robin seemed mollified, and his scowl softened. "It's hard work, and it takes me a long time to get through a page. I can't really read for pleasure." His fingers still gripped the remote, and Dan began to unlace them slowly, slipping his own between them.

"That's a shame. I can't imagine how I'd have survived my teens otherwise. I used to get picked on by Dad for always having my nose in a book. Reading wasn't the most popular pastime in our house."

"You'd have fit in better with my family." Robin gave a wry smile. "Mum sent me off to a fucking boarding school the first chance she got. Special place for those who were 'differently abled'. What a right bloody waste of time that was."

"They couldn't help you, then?"

Robin sighed again, and Dan wondered if he was going to answer at all. When he spoke, the words came slowly, as if forcing them out was causing him pain.

"I learnt a lot there, but not what they were teaching. It's where I met Jamie." The expression that darkened Robin's face at the mention of that name was a curious one, mingling guilt, nostalgia and a deep sorrow. Dan wanted to wrap his arms around him and tell him it would all be okay, but as he didn't even know what "it" was, the best he could do was to squeeze Robin's hand and lean against him.

"Do you want to talk about him?" What was he going and offering now? He didn't do all this emotional-baggage shit. But as Robin shook his head, disappointment tightened Dan's chest. Bugger; he actually wanted to know about Robin's big dark secret. Stupid, really. He should steer well clear of those kinds of confidences. It would make it so much harder to leave if he knew this man deep down and inside out.

Robin heaved a huge breath and visibly composed himself. "How about this movie, then? *The Legend of Fong Sai Yuk*, complete with cheesy American voice acting and half-naked Chinese men?"

Dan snuggled closer, curling his legs up beneath him, wrapping an arm around Robin and resting his head on his shoulder. "Sounds good to me. I like a big dollop of cheese with my half-naked men."

Robin snorted. "You'll get that all right."

"Ooh, is that a promise?" Dan nipped playfully at Robin's shoulder. "I might have to take you up on that later."

"Piss off, you randy bugger." Dan grinned as he felt Robin's shoulders drop farther, the tension leaching out of his body.

But though he laughed at the film and enjoyed the balletic fighting despite himself, there was a little part of his mind that couldn't help dwelling on Robin's confession and what the fuck this Jamie fellow had done to mess him up so badly.

If Dan ever met the guy, he wouldn't be held responsible for his actions.

# Chapter Fourteen

As the end credits rolled, Robin pondered his next move. He'd somehow ended up with his head resting on Dan's lap. What's more, Dan had started stroking his hair, making it a real challenge to concentrate on the last few scenes. The heat of Dan's thigh made Robin's head sweat where they touched, and he was hyperaware of just how close he was to Dan's groin. His breath came harder, and he stroked his hand up the denim-clad thigh, his callouses dragging at the fabric.

Dan cleared his throat, and Robin looked up at him. There was a playful glint in his eyes, and he raised his eyebrows as if challenging Robin to do something.

Robin gulped. He'd had some nerves the previous night, but nothing like this. It felt like his insides were fluttering so hard they'd break out and fly away. He wanted. God, how he wanted. He slipped down to the floor and settled on his knees between Dan's legs. Dan's lips parted with a sharp-drawn breath, and Robin found it hard to tear his gaze away from them. He wanted to bite and suck and taste but held himself back. Who knew what a kiss would mean on top of all the cosy intimacy and the confession he'd made earlier? Better to stick to purely sexual contact.

And so he lowered his head, nuzzling into Dan's groin and feeling the swell of that cock grow stiffer against his cheek and lips. The musky scent was overwhelming, and his fingers seemed to be working on autopilot, scrabbling at the button and zip while he rubbed his face against Dan's erection. A moan welled up inside him, all needy and turned on and bloody embarrassing.

"Fuck, yeah." Dan's voice was husky, and he placed a hand on the back of Robin's head, the touch gentle but firm enough to let him know that this was exactly what he wanted.

Dan's jeans were off in moments, and then there was just that skimpy little thong preventing access. Under any other circumstances, Robin would have found the scrap of red cotton amusing—it was too small to contain Dan's erection, and his cockhead poked out the top. But right now it was in his way and had to go.

Dan's dick sprang free, and Robin froze. There was no way he was going to fit all of that into his mouth. Dan was longer than Jamie had been, and other than him, Robin had never sucked another guy's dick before. But he wanted this so badly. His chest grew tight with anticipation, and the whole world narrowed to the idea of his lips around Dan's shaft. Of taking him deep and forcing some of those absurdly sexy noises out of him.

"Robin? You there?"

God, how long had Dan been trying to get his attention?

"There you are! Thought you'd gone into a trance for a minute. Here, let's get your shirt off." Dan's hands began tugging at the fabric. "I want to see your gorgeous body while you're sucking me off. I've been thinking about it all day. I've been draining my camera battery looking at those pictures of you at the bridge."

When Dan's voice went low and sultry, Robin's body responded with a delicious tingling. He let Dan pull off his T-shirt, then returned the favour. He pulled the fabric over Dan's head and watched the way those pupils flared as Dan caught sight of his inked skin.

*Beautiful,* Dan mouthed. Was he really? Robin looked down at the patterned skin with its trail of dark hair, then over at Dan's smooth body, honey-coloured and suspiciously free from tan lines. Indeed, the only lines there were some livid scratches on Dan's chest.

"That wasn't me, was it?" Robin asked, running a fingertip over the marks, his stomach clenching. God, he hadn't really been that rough, had he?

"Nah, it was that cat of yours. This one was you." Dan pointed to a bruise on his neck. "And these. Pretty sexy, huh?"

Robin was about to apologise for the bruises on Dan's hips when he felt himself being pulled up and in, closer and closer towards the haven of Dan's mouth.

Robin gasped as Dan's lips brushed hot against his own. He had to kiss him, had to—his tongue pushing in to taste that sweetness before his teeth closed to tug on Dan's lower lip. The moan Dan gave started a chain reaction in Robin's body, his pulse racing as the blood rushed to his groin and made him harder than ever. He dragged his lips down Dan's neck and chest, pausing to nip in places, the pressure of his teeth causing Dan to groan and buck his hips. But that reaction was nothing compared to when Robin sucked at Dan's perked nipple, baring his teeth just enough to graze over the skin. Jesus! Robin thought his were pretty sensitive what with the piercings, but that was nothing compared to Dan's reaction: writhing and whimpering and begging Robin, "Please, God, please, fuck, please!"

Robin couldn't help himself. He sucked hard at the skin just below Dan's nipple. He needed to mark him again but couldn't think why. He just needed. Robin sat back on his heels to admire his work. The dark red bruise stirred something deep inside. Something wild and dangerous. Something primal.

Dan took a while to calm down, his body stilling and breathing returning to normal. A flush had spread over his chest and up to his cheeks, his eyes shining bright and liquid.

Robin couldn't remember anyone ever having this sort of response to his touch; no recollection of ever having this level of power over a lover. It made his heart pound, and he had no idea if that was from fear or arousal or a heady mixture of both.

Dan rubbed the back of his hand over his eyes. "If you're gonna suck me off, you'd better do it quick or I'm going to embarrass myself."

"Right." Robin eyed Dan's cock, watching as a bead of pre-come formed and then broke, trickling down. He salivated, desperate to taste but not daring to. Not when he knew the sort of man Dan was. He'd put the condoms in his pocket earlier and pulled one out. Strawberry flavour—well, it seemed unlikely. As far as he could remember they all tasted of rubber, despite the packet's claims.

"What are you doing?" Dan asked, a trace of annoyance in his tone.

"What does it look like?" Robin found the tip and pinched it closed, taking hold of Dan's cock with his other hand and trying not to notice how silky smooth it was, because otherwise he wouldn't be able to bear covering it up. He tore open the packet and began rolling.

"You don't need one. I'm negative, and even if I wasn't, the risk from oral is tiny."

Dan definitely sounded pissed off now. Robin looked up to see him frowning.

"How many men have you fucked?"

"What, since my last test? I dunno, a few. Not that many. It was only a couple of months ago. I'm careful, though. I'm always safe. Come on, Robin, I want to feel you properly."

Dan's pout was adorable, but Robin wasn't about to be swayed that easily. "You shouldn't ask me to do something I'm not comfortable with."

Dan glared at him. "What about you last night? Fucking me so hard I've been sore all day. That wasn't very comfortable for me, was it?"

Robin's face grew hot. "I'd have stopped if you'd asked me to." The words came out louder than he'd intended. Regret twisted sharp in his guts as he watched Dan wince.

But then the fight drained out of Dan, his shoulders slumping, even his cock starting to droop. "No, you're right. Sorry. You have every right to want to be safe." Dan closed his eyes and fell back against the sofa cushions. "Way to kill the mood, eh?"

The sight of Dan, defeated, pierced Robin through. He knew he was being pigheaded, but he wasn't about to apologise, so he leant in and licked along the seam of Dan's lips instead. It took a moment for Dan to react, but then those arms snaked around Robin and pulled him closer as the kiss deepened. When they eventually broke apart, Dan was panting again, his erection pushing hard into Robin's belly.

Dan gave a half smile. "I'm sure I'll be able to feel things just fine with that tongue stud of yours."

Robin ran the stud along his teeth so that Dan could see it, gratified by the lust that darkened Dan's eyes. His own was still high, stoked rather than quenched by the heat of his anger. He lowered his head straight to Dan's crotch this time, wanting nothing more than to slide that length into his mouth and wipe out the memory of their argument. But first he took a moment to explore Dan's balls, filling his mouth with the flavour of him in the hope of combating the artificial strawberry scent that was already invading his nostrils.

He couldn't put it off forever, though. If he wanted to do this, he'd have to brave the condom. He took a firm grip of Dan's shaft with his hand while sucking gently at the tip, and when Dan's moans grew fevered, he plunged his mouth down as far as it would go.

Robin almost gagged on cloying strawberry when Dan hit the back of his throat, but he pulled back, working his tongue stud against the head and relaxing his jaw. The next time was easier, and by the third plunge he was confident enough to increase the suction and even try swallowing, wriggling his tongue with every pull to give Dan the full benefit of his piercing. He had to brace his hands on Dan's hips to stop him thrusting, digging in his fingers and setting his own pace. Dan complained, pushing down on the back of Robin's head but too far gone for the words to make any sense.

The sounds Dan was making and the sensation of him filling Robin's mouth were so intense that even without the taste and texture of him on his tongue, Robin's balls started to draw up. He held Dan down with one hand as the other tore at his fly, releasing his aching cock.

"Shit, Robin, coming, please!"

Robin relaxed his hold on Dan's hip, allowing him to fuck his mouth while coming. It was so good, being used like that. So good to hear Dan's uninhibited howls of pleasure ringing in his ears. To feel Dan pulsing in his mouth, twitching and stuttering. Once Dan had finished, Robin crawled up and straddled him, pumping his cock hard until the fire flashed through his veins and he drenched Dan's body with his seed.

The sight of creamy jizz dripping down that smooth skin and over the bite mark he'd left earlier sent another surge of heat sweeping through Robin, and he convulsed with a sound he wasn't proud of. Seemed his body wanted to keep on going. He rode out the racking spasms, burying his face in Dan's neck and letting the world around dissolve into a haze of overwhelming sensation.

When things started to make sense again, Robin collapsed in a loose-limbed sprawl, hooking a leg over Dan's. He closed his eyes, content to drift in a post-orgasmic haze, until he felt Dan's weight shift and a gentle touch on his shoulder.

"What do they mean?" Dan asked.

"Huh? Who?"

"Your tattoos. They look tribal. Do they have a particular meaning?"

"Umm, not sure. I was only eighteen when I got them done. Spent all my birthday money on them. Mum went ballistic when she found out." Robin chuckled at the memory. Baiting his mother had been a full-time hobby when he was a teenager. "She wanted to pay for laser removal."

"You mean you had your body covered in patterns and they don't mean anything to you?" Dan sounded appalled, and Robin opened his eyes to check on him. Dan was staring at him, wide eyes glittering gold in the dim light.

"Does it matter? Why d'you get yourself waxed? And I don't reckon that tan's from the sun, either."

"Just a little aid to my natural beauty." Dan's lips curled in a smile as he ran a hand over his own chest, smearing Robin's come around before reaching down to pick up a T-shirt and wipe himself clean. "We're not all gorgeous hunks of masculinity like you. Some of us have to work at it."

Robin's face grew hot at the compliment. "I reckon you'd look pretty good without the sunbed tan." His voice came out gruff, surprising them both.

"Pretty good?" Dan pouted, his eyes creasing at the corners. "Baby, you're going to spoil me. My head will swell so large I won't be able to ever leave your boat."

Despite the weirdness of being called "baby" by another man, Robin found himself chuckling as Dan mimed getting his head stuck in the door. Funny, he didn't mind the odd camp affectation on Dan. It was kind of cute.

Dan grinned at him and began stroking over Robin's tattoos again, tracing around an armband and up over his shoulder, following the sweep of an inked line over Robin's back. "So why d'you have them done, then?"

"Not sure. Lots of reasons, probably." Robin waited for Dan to lose interest in his line of questioning, but he continued to trace over the inked patterns and made no comment. Eventually, Robin sighed. "Jamie dared me to get the first one done. This armband." He held up his right arm so Dan could get a good look at the armband, now partly subsumed by the surrounding whorls. "He thought I'd look hot with tattoos and piercings."

Robin watched Dan's brow crease as he examined the armband. "And what did you think about it all?"

The memories threatened to flood back, and Robin did his best to resist them. "It was fine. I wanted to be a rebel, so it all fit."

Dan's hand stroked up to Robin's cheek, cupping his jaw and moving it so that he found himself staring into those hazel eyes. He couldn't hold the gaze, preferring to focus on Dan's lips, which were slightly parted and still swollen from their kisses.

"You kept them all, though. You could have had them removed. They must mean something to you," Dan said.

"Reminders." Of all the things he didn't want to think about. Reminders not to trust. Not to lose himself in someone else like that ever again. Not to be a fool.

But as he felt Dan's tongue moving on his skin, following the curve of an inked line , Robin remembered that there were other reasons for keeping them. Maybe he could overlay old betrayals with new associations. He gasped as Dan sucked on his skin, the sweet pain stirring something deep within him. Maybe things could get better. If he let them.

Maybe it was time to try something new.

# Chapter Fifteen

Dan finished up his second shoot of the day—an old geezer called Rusty who owned a traditionally painted narrowboat that fit his name perfectly, listing to one side with moss growing on the windows. The inside had been as dark as a crypt, but with clever use of reflectors and his able assistant, Mel, Dan had taken some atmospheric shots of Rusty's grizzled face looming out of the darkness. He'd been alarmed by Rusty's cough, though, and they'd had to stop several times while they waited for him to hack his lungs up.

"Is he okay?" he'd whispered to Mel during a particularly loud coughing fit.

"He's better off here than in a hospital," was all she would say.

Dan begged to differ. The man was living in filth, and his stove belched black smoke whenever he opened it to chuck another log on. But then again, it was his home. There was a fierce independence in Rusty's demeanour, and Dan did his best to capture it in the photographs.

As Dan folded up his tripod, his phone started blaring Ricky Martin: Tristan's ringtone. He gave Mel an apologetic smile as he answered. He wouldn't want her to think that his taste in music was quite that camp; he'd chosen it only to annoy Tris, and it worked a treat.

"Danny-boy! How are things out in the wilds of Somerset? Caught yourself that hunky boater yet?"

Dan glanced over at Mel and Rusty. Tris was so loud he wouldn't be surprised if they could hear him. "I'm just taking this outside," he told them before making a hasty exit.

"Go on then, darling. Spill the beans. How did you manage to charm you way into your hot boater's pants in the end?"

"And what makes you think I did?"

"Oh come on, I know you. The guy didn't stand a chance."

"True. Okay, so I wore him down in the end."

"I knew it!" Tris shrieked. Dan held the phone away from his ear and watched as Mel stepped off the boat and put the bags down in front of him. "Come on, I want details! Who did who? How well hung? What rating on the Sexometer?"

Dan groaned. He'd forgotten all about the Sexometer. They'd invented it when they first met as a scale to rate their hookups by. Points were scored for size, inventiveness, willingness, noisiness, enthusiasm, cleanliness, designer underwear, depth of throat and all manner of criteria they'd considered important at the time. Points could also be taken away for a range of heinous offences such as bad breath, love handles and garlic-flavoured spunk. Strangely enough, conversation, kissing and cuddling hadn't figured at all.

"I've no idea. You're not still using that thing, are you? I thought we were too old and sophisticated these days."

"Quit stalling, angelface. I want to know all the juicy details."

But he didn't want to share Robin with Tristan yet, and not just because Mel was doing a particularly unconvincing job of pretending not to listen. Actually, she wasn't pretending at all and raised her eyebrows at him as he looked at her.

"We'll talk about it when I get back, okay?"

"That's not fair! Right, well you are so not going to be hearing about this Alex I met at the leather club, then. We had a little date last night. You should have seen some of the things he got me doing! I had no idea I was such a pain slut, I can tell you."

Dan smiled. Although Tristan had always been very vocal about his opinion of the whole "ghastly" S&M scene, he was beginning to suspect the superior attitude masked a deep fascination. Maybe it would do Tristan some good to finally get it all out of his system. Maybe it was what he needed. If it took his mind off the Sexometer, it had to be a good thing.

"Another time, Tris. Listen, the reception's not good out here, but I'll call you when I get back. We'll go for a drink. Catch up properly."

"Dan Taylor, you're lucky I'm such a good friend that I'm not going to take offence at being brushed off."

"Bye, Tris."

Dan distinctly heard a rather huffy "Judas" as he hung up.

Mel was still watching him. "Anyone special?"

Dan caught an edge of something in her voice. "Just a friend. An old friend." He didn't want to share Tristan with Mel any more than he'd wanted to share Robin with Tristan. He was on a holiday from his normal life at the moment, and the phone call had been an unwelcome intrusion. As he swung his leg over his bike, he realised that it was Tuesday already. He had five days left to spend with Robin. Five days longer than he'd usually spend with one guy.

Trouble was, it didn't feel like it was going to be long enough.

"So, are you planning on visiting us again at some point, once you've swanned back to London?"

Dan knelt in the grass and fumbled with his lens, irritated with Mel's tone as well as her interruption of his task. She'd been distant ever since overhearing his phone call with Tristan, and he had the feeling that she was looking down her nose at him. Tricky, what with her being even shorter than he was, but she seemed to be able to manage it.

"I don't know. Maybe. If I have time." He inserted the wide-angle lens back into the correct compartment and carefully lowered the body of the camera into the bag. They'd finished the final shoot Mel had arranged for him, and he thought he had enough shots to illustrate the article, or perhaps even for an exhibition. The rest of the week was his to spend as he pleased, and there was only one way he wanted to do that: with Robin.

He looked up to meet Mel's gaze and quailed at her stony expression.

"Robin's a good mate. I don't want him getting fucked around," she said.

"He's a big boy, Mel. He can look after himself." Dan stood, stretched and went to attach the bag to his bicycle. He hoped the sight of his back would signal the end of the conversation.

"Maybe so, but he's still hurting from something that happened years ago. I don't want you making it worse."

Could Mel help him make sense of it all? Dan turned to look at her. "What happened between him and this Jamie fellow, then? If I knew what it bloody well was, I might be better at avoiding putting my foot in it."

Mel's face went pale at the name. "Jamie?" Her voice was quiet, hesitant. "I couldn't tell you anything about him."

"Fine. I know how you boaters like to look out for each other and repel the evil outsiders. It's not a problem if Robin fucks around with one of you, is it?"

"Just what are you getting at?" Mel put her hands on her hips and glared. That woman could win any staring contest, hands down. He decided he didn't want to bring up the fact that she'd been sleeping with Robin after all.

Dan fumbled in his wallet and pulled out a wedge of notes, counting out a hundred and fifty pounds—not bad for a couple of days' work. Okay, it was a lot less than he'd have to pay a proper assistant, but he wasn't exactly rolling in money himself and hadn't planned on paying Tristan anything other than treating him to a few nights out and possibly some sexual favours. "Here, I owe you for all the help."

Mel sneered at the notes in his hand. "I don't want your money, Dan."

He shoved them back in his pocket, exasperated. "Well, what do you want, then? You'd better tell me, because I can't figure it out."

She gave him a level stare, and Dan felt like he was being weighed up and found wanting. "I just want you to be good enough for him, that's all."

"I can only be myself."

"Yeah, well, just don't go raising his hopes for something more than you're prepared to give, all right?"

"Okay. Okay," he repeated in response to her continued glower. "Look, I really like him, but he knows the kind of guy I am. It's all out in the open, okay?"

Mel nodded, and Dan was relieved to see her face soften. She was pretty when she smiled, all white teeth and crinkled nose.

"Sorry, Dan. I just... I care about him, you know? He might be a bit of a grumpy git at times, but he's got a good heart."

"Yeah, I know." It was blindingly obvious as soon as you scraped back the surface—the moment you got past Robin's shallow defences. Dan wanted to see more of that Robin—the one who smiled and laughed and threw bread to the ducks. The one who told him things about his past, even if they were cryptic references to a relationship he was still mostly in the dark about.

Maybe Dan looked pensive, thinking about Jamie, because Mel gave him a hug which nearly knocked him off-balance.

"I'll see you around over the next few days, I hope. Don't you go hogging Robin all to yourself, you hear?"

Dan mumbled his good-byes, then headed off towards town. Now that Mel had refused his money, he had an idea of what he could do with it. He smiled as he pedalled, humming tunelessly under his breath. A little shopping trip was in order. He had someone he wanted to treat.


Robin startled at the rocking of the boat. He hadn't been expecting Dan back so soon and lunged to hide away his wood and carving chisels in the footstool. He lounged back on the sofa, trying to look wanton. His body tingled at the idea of Dan's proximity, and he began idly rubbing his dick through his trousers, feeling it swell.

The doors swung open.

"Hey, sweetie! Oh!" Mel's mouth stayed open as her eyes raked over Robin's pose.

"Shit! I...uh... Hi, Mel. Wasn't expecting you." Robin grabbed a cushion and held it over his now rapidly deflating erection.

"No. I can see that. He's a lucky man, that Dan is." Her eyes sparkled with amusement, but Robin heard something darker in her voice.

"Cup of tea?" he offered, rising, and was glad to be able to busy himself while she sat in front of the fire, warming her hands.

"Things are going well, then?" Mel asked. "Everything happy in Robin-and-Dan land?"

Robin frowned at the kettle. "Everything's fine. I'm fine."

"You like him." It wasn't a question.

"Yeah, he's a nice guy." He had to stop himself from slamming down the mugs onto the work surface. It really wasn't any of her fucking business.

"But he's going back on Sunday." Mel said it quietly, allowing the full meaning to sink in slowly.

Because he didn't want to think about it, Robin blustered, "Yeah? You think I don't know that? It's fine, Mel. We're just friends with benefits. You don't need to worry about me. I'm a grownup."

"That's what he said." Mel gave a wry smile, and Robin glared.

"You've been talking about me behind my back?"

"Don't be silly, it's not like that." Mel spread her hands in a pantomime of innocence. "I just want you to make sure you don't expect too much from Dan. He's going back to his life in London. He's told me a bit about it, and it's a pretty wild scene. I've heard his shrieking friend on the phone going on about all the men he's slept with."

"If you're trying to warn me that he's a slut, then I'm one step ahead of you." But even as he said the words, a knife twisted inside him. He didn't want to consider the idea of another man with his hands on Dan. Another man screwing Dan. Of Dan risking himself with a parade of random strangers, any one of whom could easily be a violent, diseased nutjob.

He didn't realise how tightly he was gripping the handles of the mugs until the whistle of the kettle roused him from his dark fantasy. He let go, feeling the ache in his fingers on the release.

"Robin? How about you two come around to my boat for dinner tomorrow." She sounded concerned, but Robin had had enough.

"What? One minute you're warning me off him, and the next you want us to come around and play happy families? What the fuck?"

"For God's sake, Robin, it's not like that! I'm just looking out for you. I don't want you getting hurt."

Robin felt Mel's hand on his arm, gently massaging the tensed muscles. He was gripping the edge of the work surface this time. He wanted to tell her to mind her own business, but she was a friend, and as far as he could remember, this was what friends did. He was out of practise when it came to friendship, having kept pretty much to himself for the last few years. When her head leant against his shoulder, he inclined his to rest on top, taking deep, calming breaths.

"Sorry. I'm sorry. I shouldn't have shouted," he said.

She put an arm around his waist. "Who's Jamie? You never told me about him."

Robin froze, the shock of the question rendering him speechless. What on earth was Dan doing, talking to Mel about Jamie? He knew how Robin felt about that. He knew it was private.

"Was he your boyfriend?"

"I don't want to talk about him." It was amazing he'd ever said as much as he had to Dan. No one else had been able to prise anything out of him over the past three years. Not even the shrink his mum had insisted on sending him to in a last-ditch attempt to lift him out of his depression. It had worked, in a roundabout way. He'd fled the appointment early and, after half an hour's meandering walk, had found himself staring out over the river. Thoughts of plunging into the icy water had been sidetracked by the appearance of a narrowboat chugging past. The man at the tiller had given him a nod, and Robin had watched as the little boat disappeared into the distance. The self-sufficiency and privacy of the lifestyle had appealed to his jaded mind, and so he'd spent the money he'd had left from his inheritance. The money that Jamie hadn't already squandered, that was.

"Robin?" He realised with a start that Mel was still leaning against him and expected some sort of response. He didn't have the words, so he pulled her closer, squeezing her skinny body and breathing in the scent of patchouli and incense that lingered in her hair. Eventually she sighed, tilting her head back to look up at him.

"Look, just make sure you don't go falling for him. Spend a bit of time with your other friends over the next few days. Don't let it get too intense with Dan, all right?"

Robin didn't respond. It wasn't advice he wanted to hear.

"I'm just looking out for you. Believe it or not, I care about you."

"I know."

Robin couldn't meet Mel's eyes when she repeated her invitation to dinner but made a noncommittal noise that seemed to satisfy her. At any rate, she gave up the subject and chattered on about other news as they drank their tea. Apparently BW had made a whole new section of canal into winter moorings, so there'd be even fewer spots where they could moor up without the proper license. Robin listened with half an ear, turning over ideas as to how to get Dan all to himself for the rest of the week. They needed a holiday from reality, from interfering busybodies and other distractions. They needed time to get to know each other, inside and out.

# Chapter Sixteen

Once Mel had gone, Robin cycled out to the grocers at Bathampton and stocked up on supplies. His panniers and rucksack full of food and beer—and his wallet disturbingly empty—he set off back to *Serendipity*. His heart leapt when he saw Dan's bright yellow bike leaning against the hedgerow. He leant his own beat-up old bicycle against it, and the two looked just right together. He beamed as he threw open the doors to find Dan in the galley, frying something that smelled mouthwateringly good.

"The wanderer returns! I was hoping you'd be back soon. This is nearly read—"

Robin covered Dan's mouth with his own, kissing greedily. Dan kissed back, then pulled away, brandishing the greasy spatula like a weapon.

"Oh no you don't. This is my mum's specialty, and I'm not willing to burn it just because you're feeling horny." Robin looked down into the frying pan to see a sizzling mix of bacon pieces, potato cubes and slices of onion. Dan stirred it up again, and Robin contented himself with just resting a hand on the swell of that tempting rear as Dan threw in crushed garlic and a generous handful of fresh parsley.

"Your mum's a good cook, then?" Dan hadn't spoken much of his family other than to say he was the youngest of five children.

"The best. She was a dinner lady at my primary school and even managed to make school lunches edible." Dan smiled affectionately, and Robin tried to imagine what it would be like to have a dinner lady for a mum, rather than a "lady who lunched".

"You get on well together?" he asked.

Dan's gaze flickered to him, then back to the pan. "Yeah, I mean, we don't live in each other's pockets. I pop round for tea every Sunday when I'm not working, but she doesn't call me all the time like your mum does. She's great, though. Not got a bad word to say about anyone."

"Definitely not like my mum, then." Robin brooded as Dan stirred the hash. "Does she know about you?"

"What about me? My secret life as a superhero, rescuing stray cats?" Dan quirked an eyebrow at him, one cheek dimpling.

"You know what I mean. Have you come out to her?"

Dan laughed. "Do I strike you as someone who's hiding in the closet, babe? Of course she knows. She knew before I did. Said she used to catch me making my Action Men snog each other."

"And she doesn't mind?" Robin rested his chin on Dan's shoulder, watching the deft movements as he stirred and flipped over the potato pieces, exposing the crisp golden undersides.

"No. She's cool. Dad was a different matter, though."

"Was?"

Dan was quiet for a long moment.

"He died when I was nineteen. Never had time to get over his disgust at having a 'shit-stabber' for a son."

"I'm sorry."

Dan gave a tight smile. "Not your fault, was it? Anyway, Mum's fine with it all, even if she does keep hassling me about when I'm going to bring a boyfriend home to tea. Can't seem to wrap her head around the idea that it's not gonna be like that for me. I'm never going to do that whole monogamy thing. Don't reckon men are any good at it."

Robin tried to ignore the way his guts twisted at this pronouncement. "They can be. If they're in love." But he didn't really want to dwell on that. He remembered his own coming-out speech instead—not really necessary after his mum had blundered in on him and Jamie in his bedroom with their hands down each other's pants. "My mum kept going on about grandchildren, how I'd regret it if I never had kids of my own."

"Yeah, well, my mum already had eight grandkids by the time I came out, so she didn't need any more. Christmas was expensive enough already."

"You've got eight nieces and nephews?"

"I've got eleven now, and I don't reckon Sarah's had her last yet. I should probably start thinking about Christmas shopping myself. Ooh, speaking of shopping, I got you a present today. Hope you don't mind, but the bed sheets were getting a bit crusty." Dan's nose crinkled in mock disgust. "Go take a look in your bed cabin while I finish cooking. You're a distraction in here." Dan wiggled his arse, and Robin grudgingly removed his hand.

His curiosity piqued, Robin made his way to the bed cabin. Everything looked the same, but when he pulled back the quilt, he saw that the bed had been made up with new sheets, the creases from the packet still visible. He ran his hands over the deep blue brushed cotton, admiring the quality. He'd grown up with expensive bed linen and knew this was a world away from his old set of cheap, supermarket bedding, which had worn into scratchy bobbles around his feet. He'd been meaning to head down to the launderette earlier but had allowed himself to get absorbed by his woodcarving, and the day had run away from him before he'd realised.

What did all this domesticity mean? Robin didn't want to read too much into it, but it didn't seem like the actions of a heartless slut only after a quick shag. Then again, maybe the meal and the fresh sheets were as much about Dan looking after his own creature comforts as they were about Robin's. He shook his head. It wasn't like it mattered. They had a few days together and then it would end. Best just to enjoy it while he could.

And a good meal, a couple of beers and some hot, sweaty sex to christen the new sheets sounded like the perfect way to spend his evening... So God knew why he still felt twisted up inside.

Dan woke from a dream about trying to outrun an earthquake to discover his bed really was shaking. The groan of the earth ripping apart was the deafening roar of the engine which sounded like it was slap-bang under his pillow. He could smell diesel and there was a definite draught coming in from the ventilation shaft in the wall above his head.

Dan rubbed his bleary eyes, sat up and tried to make sense of the boat's rocking. A loud thudding sounded right above his head. He cringed, but it was only Robin's footsteps on the roof. As the engine's noise changed pitch, the boat rocked some more, and the queasy sensation in his stomach told him they were on the move. He pulled out the blind in the porthole next to him and watched the reeds drifting past.

Jesus Christ, it was too early for this. A dim memory surfaced of agreeing to cruise somewhere even more deserted— Robin had never mentioned anything about it being at the crack of dawn, though. Shivering in the cold, Dan staggered across the tiny hallway to the wet-room, located his watch and saw that it was quarter past six in the morning. Bloody early risers and their antisocial ways. He much preferred the way Robin had woken him the last couple of mornings, fondling and kissing him into awareness before ravishing him. Robin fucked like he'd been starved of sex for an eternity and wanted to gorge himself on Dan, over and over. It was thrilling—Dan could get used to that ravenous gaze boring into him, promising he was about to be eaten alive.

He looked down at his chest and saw evidence of Robin's hunger written on his flesh in red marks. Just looking at them heated his blood. Funny, he'd never found that sort of thing appealing before—had always thought it rather spoilt the unblemished look he was going for. Now, though, seeing the effect they had on Robin—the way the guy just about exploded with lust when tearing off Dan's clothing to expose the bites before adding some more—well, maybe he was kinkier than he'd realised.

Or maybe it was just something about Robin.

The thought was unsettling, and between that and the wandering around naked in the cold, he managed to stave off his morning wood. Dan went in search of his clothing, discarded in the saloon the previous night. He really needed to bring over a few more changes of clothes from his boat, since it didn't look like he'd be sleeping there for the rest of the week. He found his jeans and T-shirt neatly folded next to a set of red, ribbed thermal undies. There was a small piece of paper on top, with "Come outside—U can were these—its cold" printed on it in an uneven hand. Grinning to himself, Dan stood in front of the crackling fire—Robin really had thought of everything—and suited up.

The long johns were a little too lengthy in the leg and the thermal vest was baggier than Dan's usual, skintight attire, but when he lifted his arm and inhaled, the fabric exuded a delicious, Robiny smell—all smoke and maleness. It felt as if he were wrapped in a warm hug, the sensation remaining even with the rest of his clothing over the top. Once he'd shrugged on his leather jacket and donned his trainers, he felt brave enough to open the front doors.

Frigid air washed in over him, stinging his eyes and making him gasp. But the canal! There had been a frost overnight, and all the grass and dead stems along the banks sparkled like they'd been dusted with glitter. The water steamed slowly, mist rising in lazy curls that hung diaphanous in the damp air. Dan looked out over the valley, a sea of mist with the tops of trees rising out here and there like islands. He popped his head up to wave at Robin—who appeared to be wearing some kind of knitted monstrosity on his head—and ducked back inside for his camera.

Half an hour later, Robin had turned the boat in the nearest winding hole so that they were heading towards Bath, and most of the mist had evaporated in the morning sun. Dan's fingertips and ears smarted with cold. He realised the dull throbbing at his temples was a caffeine-withdrawal headache coming on. Who would have believed he'd be up this early, working, without the aid of his morning cuppa? Maybe if you spent long enough on a boat, these early nights and mornings just became natural. He waved to catch Robin's attention and made a T shape with his hands—receiving a thumbs-up—and headed in to make them both a drink.

It was only once he had the two steaming mugs of tea in his hands that he realised he had absolutely no idea how he was going to get one of them to Robin. Maybe he could persuade him to pull over so that he could run along the bank and drop one off with him. Stepping up onto the front deck and placing the mugs on the roof, Dan pondered his options. He couldn't yell—Robin was fifty feet away, and the engine was deafening down at that end of the boat. Dan looked at the gunwales—the narrow shelves that ran along each side of the boat where the hull met the top. They were about four inches wide and looked alarmingly slippery in their glossy black paint.

He'd seen Robin walk along them without any qualms, but could he do it? Could he make his way to the back of the boat, clinging one-handed onto the narrow wooden rail at the edge of the roof? Above all that water? No, that wouldn't work. The roof was another possible route, but it was piled high with logs, sacks of coal, coils of rope and, bizarrely enough, a wheelbarrow. The idea of scrambling over a frosty obstacle course on the top of a moving boat did not appeal. Not with a plunge into icy-cold water as the penalty for any misstep. He still found it hard to believe it was shallow enough for him to stand up in.

Robin beckoned, then pointed insistently towards something on the roof. Dan held his hands out in a "What?" gesture, then looked down the side of the boat to where Robin was now pointing. Of course, there were the two side hatches down at the far end of the boat; the ones in the passageway that divided the wet-room and bed cabin. Okay, he'd be almost there if he could open one of them. Maybe he wouldn't have to risk life and limb scrambling around outside at all.

The passageway flooded with light as he opened the hatch, and the view was spectacular. Dan climbed the steep stepladder and carefully lifted the full mugs up onto the roof of the boat. When he finally stuck his head out and caught Robin's warm grin directed his way, he realised how close he was to his goal.

Close, but not close enough.

"Come on, then. You'll have to bring it to me," Robin shouted over the drone of the engine.

That was easy for him to say, but how the hell was Dan going to do it? There was about ten feet of gunwale left to inch along. He looked up again, about to protest, but when he saw the teasing glint in Robin's eyes, he rebelled against his fear. There was no way he was going to let a man in a bobble hat with ear flaps laugh at him. Especially not when it was a bright orange one with pom-poms on the end of the ties.

The first step was the hardest as he had to simultaneously twist his body so he faced the boat, leaning against the side and gripping on to the pallet stacked with logs. Rough splinters scratched at his palms. As his racing heart began to slow, he eased his grip, gaining confidence in his secure footing. He'd be fine so long as he didn't look down at the water. He looked at Robin instead, surprised to see the mischief had been replaced by concern.

"You okay?" Robin asked.

Dan gave him a nod. Yeah, he could move his head, no problem. It was the rest of his body that was going to prove difficult, especially as his stomach was doing its best to convince him that he was plummeting from a great height. He took a deep breath and let go of the pallet completely, transferring his right hand to the rail while his left scooted the mugs along the roof. As soon as both hands were on the rail again, he attempted a shuffling step sideways, moving like a decrepit crab. Why the fuck wasn't he wearing a life jacket? Hadn't the hire company told him he should? Mind you, a life jacket wouldn't be much help if the shock of being swallowed up by freezing water stopped his heart beating. He wondered if Robin knew any first aid.

"Dan? Just keep moving. You're nearly here."

Dan lifted his gaze, grateful for the distraction of Robin's face. He didn't think he'd ever get tired of watching those handsome features. He pushed the mugs along and took another step sideways. There were lines of concern on Robin's brow, but his gaze locked onto Dan, pulling him inexorably closer.

Just two more steps.

Just one.

And then it was done. Dan's foot found the relatively wide expanse of the back deck, and Robin's arm wrapped around his waist, pulling him in close for a hug. He let himself fall against Robin, his bones liquefied by the ordeal. Even with the tiller arm intruding between them, he felt more comfortable than he would ever have imagined possible. Dan nuzzled into Robin's neck, breathing in deeply to try to find his scent. It was there, hiding beneath the diesel fumes, and as he breathed in Robin's unique smell, he felt safe, even though he was still standing on a tiny platform over the water.

Robin's bristles grazed against the side of his head.

"Your ears are freezing. You okay?" Robin's voice rumbled through him, the vibrations rivalling those of the engine below them.

Dan nodded again, raising his head to prove it with a weak smile. "They don't feel cold. They feel like they're on fire."

Robin chuckled softly, his breath burning Dan's cheek. "You went white for a minute there. Thought I was gonna have to rescue you."

"Are you saying my tan needs a top-up?" It was a pathetic effort at humour, but Robin grinned, squeezing him closer. His gaze flicked between Dan and the route ahead, and the arm that wasn't around Dan's waist rested on the tiller, making small adjustments to their course.

"You're shivering. Here, have this." Before he could protest, Dan felt the warmth of the knitted hat descending on his head.

"God, no! The thermal undies are bad enough. You're trying to turn me into one of you lot, aren't you?"

Robin chuckled, loosening his grip around Dan's waist. Any sense of disappointment was swept away when Dan felt a hand insinuating itself down the back of his jeans. A hand with icy fingertips. He squirmed and squeaked in protest but felt strangely bereft when it withdrew.

"Glad to see you put them on. Can't have you messing about on the river in your flimsy city clothes. I'll help you peel them off later, shall I?" Robin's smile went a lot further towards heating Dan up than the hat had managed. "Now, since you went to all that trouble, how about tea?"

By now it wasn't nearly as hot as Dan would have liked, but Robin gulped his down with enthusiasm.

Dan watched the canal coming to life around them. Once they'd negotiated the swing bridge—Dan instructed by Robin to hop off the boat and open it—they entered the busy stretch down at Bathampton. Already stovepipes were smoking and hatches flung open. He saw a lanky, dreadlocked man in a ratty dressing gown step off the deck of a small tug painted in red, gold and green. He knew that boat—had spent an hour or so trying to coax a smile out of its owner for the photographs. Aranya gave them a quizzical stare and a half wave before dumping his tray of smouldering embers into the hedgerow and turning his back to them. Dan felt snubbed but then noticed the cloud of steam rising and realised why. Jesus, some of these people were so primitive.

"Robin? My boat's coming up. Would you mind stopping so I can grab some more clothes?"

Robin smiled warmly again, and even though his hand was now back on the tiller rather than around Dan, it still felt like they were connected. Dan's stomach did a little flip. Funny, he'd never felt anything quite like that before. Must be hunger. Maybe he should grab something to eat off his boat as well.

In the end there weren't any spaces left to moor up. Robin brought *Serendipity* to a gentle stop alongside *Faerie Queen* and held the boats together with a foot on each deck.

"You'd better be quick. We're blocking the canal."

Dan threw the rest of his clothing into his shoulder bag, along with a couple of packets of crisps and a chocolate bar—not a balanced meal, but it was all he had onboard. He caught sight of himself in the bathroom mirror as he left. "What the fuck are you doing, Dan?" he asked his reflection, pulling the ridiculous hat off his head and putting it into the bag. He wasn't sure if he meant the hat or the whole situation with Robin. He wasn't even sure if he cared, and stuck his tongue out at his reflection as recklessness rushed through him in a giddy stampede.

When he returned to the deck, Robin held out a hand to pull him back onboard. Dan hesitated for a moment. Did he really want to spend the rest of the journey on that tiny deck?

There wasn't even a safety railing. Then again, the only other option was to spend it on his own down on the front deck.

He looked doubtfully at Robin.

"Come on. I want to teach you how to steer. You need to learn how to cruise properly."

Dan pouted and stuck out his hip. "Baby, there ain't nothing you can teach me about cruising."

Robin stared blankly for a moment, and Dan worried that he'd overdone the camp. He felt a surge of relief as Robin broke into surprised laughter, saying, "Get your arse over here, now!"

"Aye, aye, Skipper."

Dan saluted as he hopped onto the back deck, then stepped up onto the small shelf that hung over the noisy engine room. As he did so, he felt Robin's hand squeeze his arse.

"Cheeky tart," Robin murmured into his ear.

Dan grinned and did his best to concentrate on Robin's patient instructions as they negotiated the twists and turns the canal made through the Bathampton flood plain. He clearly wasn't the most attentive pupil, however, as Robin had to keep his hand on the tiller as well. What he was most aware of was the warmth of Robin's body so close to his, and the way Robin's breath tickled his ears as he spoke.

With the sun on his face and the world waking up around them, it was just about the closest Dan had ever felt to perfect happiness.

He wasn't going to ask himself what that meant.

They closed the lock gate behind the boat, taking opposite sides of the canal. Robin pushed slowly, not wanting to show up Dan, who was obviously putting all his strength into his side, judging by the colour in his cheeks and his laboured breathing. It was the sixth lock they'd tackled in an hour and a half, and Dan looked exhausted. He'd been quiet for the last three locks— a sharp contrast to his initial enthusiasm at watching the water rush out through the sluice gates and snapping pictures of *Serendipity* slowly moving down as the water level dropped inside the narrow channel.

As soon as the gates were fully closed, Robin walked over the top of the lock. Dan was standing, slumped back against the heavy oak balance beam, and Robin hopped up on it to sit next to him. The height of the beam put his knees at Dan's shoulder level, and Robin put out a hand to stroke the exposed flesh of Dan's neck. The muscles were knotted up with tension, and Robin began to massage without really considering what he was doing.

"Mmm...don't stop. Feels good."

A dog barked. Robin snapped his head around. Just a woman walking her terrier along the opposite bank, but he realised how exposed they were. This last lock was right in the city centre and although the screens of trees and walls gave an illusion of privacy, it was still a public area.

But then again, what did he care what people thought of him? They already had him down as an illiterate, scumbag gypsy with designs on their property, so why not prove just how depraved he really was?

Robin lifted his leg and scooted over so he was seated with Dan between his thighs. There, much easier to give him a proper massage now. He dug his fingertips into the knots and worked them loose, glad to be able to do something to help Dan that didn't involve having to talk.

Dan gave a happy moan, his head lolling as Robin worked wider circles with his hands, sweeping his thumbs up either side of Dan's spine and stroking firmly across his shoulders and down again. It would be easier without the T-shirt in the way. Maybe later he could treat Dan to a proper back massage.

"That's good. Where'd you learn to do that so well?" Dan asked, his head still lolling and his eyes closed against the sun as Robin's strokes eased into feathery touches.

"Mel taught me. She's a qualified masseuse. It works better with oil, though." Robin gazed down at the top of Dan's head and stilled his hands. There was a whorl of hair on Dan's crown that drew his attention. The hairs shone gold and copper in the weak sun, and he had this powerful urge to lean down and kiss him there. Before he could, Dan's head dropped back and rested against his thigh. Robin's gaze wandered over the freckles dusting Dan's cheeks and nose, the crescents of those eyelashes and the curve of those lips. Why on earth had he ever considered Dan plain? The man was beautiful.

Just looking at Dan made him ache with a terrifying joy.

A low growl interrupted his reverie, and Robin looked up to see a man restraining his German shepherd. Shit, he knew that dog. The owner raised his head, and Robin stifled a groan as he recognised the unwelcome features of Nigel Truman, landlord of the George. Nigel's lips curled in a sneer as he walked past them, and Robin heard him mutter something about "fucking arse-bandits".

Dan didn't seem to notice, still basking in the sun and smiling, but Robin's mood was shattered. He couldn't enjoy sitting like this any longer. He shifted, gently pushing at Dan's shoulders.

"Come on, we should get going and moor up somewhere before lunch."

Dan's eyes sprang open. "I think I should stay inside for the next bit. Keep Morris company."

"Might be better on the river anyway. You need to keep your wits about you in fast-flowing water." Robin felt Dan shudder against him. "You all right with this?"

"It's a proper boating holiday this way, isn't it?" Dan gave a strained smile before heading over to the iron-rung ladder that led down to *Serendipity*, now nine feet below them.

It was only after Robin had watched him inch his way back along the gunwales to the hatch that he realised Dan hadn't actually answered the question.

Robin frowned as he steered out into the Avon. Just what was eating Dan?

# Chapter Seventeen

The river worked its charm, as always, and Robin revelled in the sensation of freedom. The water was wide, and the current pulled them along much faster than *Serendipity's* engine could manage alone. You saw a different side of Bath from the river. None of your tourist spots here. Most of the old buildings in this part of the city had been razed in World War Two, meaning the waterside was a mixture of tangled undergrowth and the squat boxes of industrial buildings and retail parks. He didn't mind it, though. He found a desolate kind of beauty there—not the manicured charm of some of the rest of the city.

As they passed a patch of scrubby trees glowing in the autumn sunlight, Robin spotted Dan's camera lens poking out of the side hatch.

He grinned to himself. Dan certainly took his photography seriously but seemed to have a lot of fun with it as well. Last night Dan had loaded the day's shots onto his laptop and shown them to Robin, who was totally unprepared for the artistry of them. He'd kind of assumed that the pictures would be like Dan himself—fun and colourful without much substance. Although that probably wasn't fair; Robin had caught some hints of deeper feelings lurking under the surface gloss, but whenever he thought he'd connected, Dan shimmered back into brightness again.

Dan's photographs, though—they had depth. Robin saw the boaters in a new light—something about the way Dan shot them highlighted both their vulnerability and their pride. Their tiny, cluttered homes had a dignity in Dan's compositions, and there was great strength in the way the boaters stared down the lens—sometimes laughing, sometimes haughty, sometimes serene.

Robin cruised out of the city into open countryside until he reached the bend he remembered was just wide enough to turn *Serendipity*. The lack of rain over the last month of fine weather meant the river was flowing slowly enough for him to make a controlled turn, and he cruised back against the current until he reached a picturesque spot where the banks were steep enough to get the boat moored up tight. A row of ash trees lined the bank, a small patch of woodland beyond them. It was a private spot, the nearest footpath on the other side of the wood. After securing *Serendipity* with the anchor, he jumped over to the trees and tied the mooring lines to the slender trunks.

His last line made fast, Robin turned to find Dan watching him from an open hatch.

"What do you think? Nice spot, isn't it?"

"Yeah, it's beautiful." Dan smiled, but something about it didn't ring true. What the hell was wrong with him?

Robin frowned. "You want to go for a walk? Reckon there'll be a great view from the top of the hill there." The Avon valley spread wide here, the floodplain a patchwork of fields divided by hedgerows in gold and yellow.

"I'm fine for the moment. How about you join me inside?" There was a lascivious tilt to Dan's smile this time, but it still wasn't totally convincing.

Robin leapt back onto the boat and found Dan in the back, stripping off his T-shirt in the dark passageway before the bed.

"Hang on, you want to see this first," Robin said, throwing open the hatch looking out onto the river. "Take a look at that view."

As Dan remained motionless, Robin pulled him to the open hatch. Dan didn't resist when Robin pushed him against the ladder but was curiously listless. Robin wrapped his arms around him and rested his head on Dan's shoulder. That tension was back again. He pressed a kiss into the knotted muscles.

"You want to tell me what's the matter? You've been acting weird ever since the locks."

"Bugger, and there was me thinking you hadn't noticed." Dan gave an abrupt laugh, but some of the tension left his body as he leant back against Robin. "It's going to sound really stupid, and I should have told you earlier, but..."

"But?" Robin prompted, trying to ignore the sinking sensation in his guts.

Dan sighed. "But I can't swim, and all that water, well, it's a bit, uh, intimidating."

Robin wanted to laugh with relief but stifled the urge, smiling into Dan's shoulder instead. "You should have said something. We didn't have to come onto the river."

"I know, I know. I think I just wanted to believe I was over it now. I was fucking terrified of water when I was growing up. Mum said I used to scream bloody murder if she tried to get me down the pool." Dan shivered. "I was dead skinny as a kid. Mum always said it was 'cause I was born six weeks early, didn't get my first bath until I was out of the incubator and that's why I was so scared."

"What do you reckon it was?" Robin prepared himself for a tale of water-based trauma. A near drowning, perhaps?

Dan just chuckled. "Like I said, I was skin and bone. Not an ounce of fat on me. Used to sink like a stone in the water. Still do, even though I've put on a bit of weight."

Robin ran his hands down Dan's sides. There was no denying Dan had great muscle tone, but as for body fat—there wasn't any evidence of that. He'd be worried about breaking him if it wasn't for the way Dan responded with wild enthusiasm when Robin got rough in bed. Dan was definitely tougher than he looked.

"Can't you swim at all?"

"Well, kind of. I can tread water. I had lessons in my early twenties. Special adult learners classes. Most embarrassing thing I've ever done." Dan paused a moment, then angled his head so that Robin could see into his eyes. They had a mischievous spark in them. "You should have seen the lifeguard, though. Talk about sex on legs! Mind you, it's bloody hard work trying to seduce someone who's just been watching you doing doggy paddle while clinging on to a float for dear life."

Robin couldn't help the laughter this time. It bubbled up inside him, escaping in a peal that surprised them both.

"Oi! That's my humiliation you're laughing at, bastard."

Dan didn't sound upset, and after a moment Robin felt him begin to shake with laughter as well.

"Sorry, sorry," Robin said, recovering his equilibrium. "I was just trying to picture it."

"Well, if it's any help, I was wearing the skimpiest, tightest pair of Speedos I could find. They were bright red. Looked pretty sexy, I thought, but I don't reckon the lifeguard agreed." Dan sniffed dismissively. "Reckon he must have been straight after all."

"Mmm..." Robin nuzzled into Dan's neck, the thought of him in tight swimming trunks having an effect that made his own clothing suddenly feel about three sizes too small. "You do have a thing for skimpy undies, don't you?"

"You got a problem with that, Mr. Thermal Long-Johns?" Dan wiggled his arse as he spoke, grinding back against Robin's erection.

Robin groaned, acutely aware of Dan's naked chest against his arms. The clean scent of cedarwood shower gel mingled with Dan's underlying sweetness and wrapped itself around him. Funny thing was, he really didn't find Dan's taste in underwear as ridiculous as he had a couple of days ago. Somehow, those thongs were just right for Dan, and that made them all right for Robin too—so long as he didn't have to wear them himself.

"Nope, no problem. Think you look better out of them, though." As he spoke, his hands began wandering, one rising to pinch Dan's nipple while the other reached down to find a tempting bulge. Dan moaned, arching back and pushing against his hand. He palmed Dan's half-hard cock through the denim, then slipped his hand beneath the waistband. Dan was naked underneath.

"What happened to the thermals?"

"Took 'em off, didn't I? I was bloody roasting in here with Morris on my lap. Besides, they're not exactly sexy, are they?"

"Hey! I'm still wearing mine." It was no wonder he was so hot and sweaty. He didn't stand a chance of keeping cool between those and the gorgeous, half-naked man in his arms.

"Yeah, well, you could make an old sack look hot. Some of us aren't so blessed."

Robin blushed. "You're the sexiest man I've ever met," he mumbled into Dan's neck.

"Mmm, you're just saying that 'cause you want to get into my pants."

"I already am."

Robin grasped Dan's cock and used his other hand to pull Dan's head around, devouring him with a messy, openmouthed kiss. Their breath was coming hard and fast when Dan broke away and tried to turn around properly.

"Bedroom, now," Dan said.

"Uh-uh. I want you here." Robin stripped off his own layers of T-shirts as one, keeping Dan pinned against the ladder.

Dan protested when Robin began to pull down those indecently tight jeans. "It's cold. Someone might see us." It didn't sound like a serious objection, and Robin finished stripping Dan before dropping to his knees behind him.

"I'll keep you warm," Robin said, lifting one of Dan's feet up onto the ladder so that his legs were spread. "And who cares if someone sees?" Dan's buttocks were right in front of his face, and he was seized with the urge to mark them. He sucked hard on one smooth cheek, revelling in the way Dan gasped and quivered whenever Robin did this to him. He didn't understand this craving to mark Dan as his, but the need was powerful. It wasn't like he'd have him for long. The bites would fade. Like Robin, they'd soon be nothing more than a memory for Dan. The thought hurt, so he thrust it away.

Robin pulled back to examine his work. The mark burned livid against Dan's skin. He licked over it, soothing the reddened flesh, then worked his tongue into the cleft between Dan's cheeks.

"Oh fuck! Robin!" Dan's voice trembled as Robin spread those cheeks wider and found what he was after, running his tongue over and around that sensitive flesh until Dan was panting and writhing, thrusting back against him eagerly. The effect he was having on Dan was such an aphrodisiac that Robin forgot all of his paranoia about infection, all of that safety advice he'd been given that was apparently out of date, and he decided to do something he hadn't done in years. He delved his tongue into Dan's twitching hole, relishing the earthy, musky flavour and the sensation of Dan fluttering around him, the whimpers and moans. Yeah, Robin could remember how good that felt, having Jamie rim him until he felt so fucking horny he thought he'd be able to come from that alone.

"Don't stop," Dan pleaded.

But he didn't want Dan to come yet. He wanted to feel Dan's body rippling around him as he pounded his arse. He licked up his spine and found Dan resting his head on his arms, hands clutching at the edges of the hatch. Dan half turned towards him, his face flushed and sweaty, eyes unfocused.

"Stay there," Robin told him, licking Dan's ear. "Be right back."

Robin emerged from the bed cabin—sheathed and lubed—and took a moment to drink in the sight of Dan braced against the open hatch, legs spread wide and arse thrust out. And beyond him, the sunlit river glinting and casting shimmering reflections onto the inside of the boat. He didn't think he'd ever seen anything more erotic. A lump formed in his throat and tears threatened, so he fucked Dan instead—pushing into that hot, tight channel with a steady slide he now knew Dan loved.

Robin gripped those hips firmly, right where he'd left bruise marks before. Dan gasped and thrust back. He watched his cock disappearing into Dan's hole and admired the perfect mark he'd made on that smooth, smooth skin. He ached to ride Dan hard but held back for as long as possible, sliding in and out excruciatingly slowly. But it was impossible to resist picking up the pace and slamming into him, the slap of flesh on flesh and Dan's incoherent cries all he could hear beyond the rushing blood in his ears. The tide rose high inside, his balls drawing up tight.

Not yet. He wanted to feel Dan's orgasm first. He grabbed hold of Dan's cock and pumped him again and again, heard his name chanted over and over in a broken voice. Dan pulsed in his hand, shuddering and bucking against Robin as his grip grew slippery. Robin came hard, swept away by the current, biting down on Dan's shoulder to stifle the howl that wanted to escape as he spilt himself over and over again.

And then everything was quiet and still—everything except for their rasping breath and heaving chests and all those crazy things in Robin's head that he wanted to say but never would. Never could. So he kissed Dan instead, drawing him close as the sweat on their bodies cooled in the river breeze.

# Chapter Eighteen

"Arrgh!" Dan hopped off his bike and let it fall against the hedgerow as he doubled over. He sucked in air and tried to concentrate on getting enough to breathe rather than on the excruciating pain in his balls.

"Dan? What's up?" Robin asked.

Dan felt Robin's hand land on his shoulder. It was another few moments before he was able to reply.

"Landed on my nuts. Chain must have broke. Fucking kills."

"Ouch." Robin's hand squeezed him before letting go.

When the pain had reduced from oh-my-God-kill-me-now to merely don't-want-to-have-sex-ever-again, Dan straightened up to see Robin examining the broken chain.

"You've lost a link. Got a spare?"

Dan groaned. "I used it a couple of weeks ago. Bloody thing!" He kicked the back tyre. "After the amount of money I spent on you, you'd think you could hold it together for one sodding holiday!"

Robin looked like he was trying to hide a smile.

"It's okay. You can afford to shorten the chain by one link. I'll do it for you, if you like."

"No, no. I can do it. Just because you're Mr. Fix-It and I'm a city boy, doesn't mean I can't mend my own bike chain."

"I never said you couldn't."

"I'll prove it."

"Go on, then." Robin was definitely smirking now.

"Right." Dan rummaged through his panniers. He had one of those handy little multi-tool thingies in there somewhere. "Ah, there you are!"

Robin watched him as he pushed out the broken link and joined up the two on either side.

"Good thing my dad taught me some useful stuff before he gave up on me, eh? I may not be able to strip a boat engine or build a kitchen, but I can mend a bike chain all by myself."

"Must have been nice, having your dad teach you things." Robin sounded wistful. He was staring off over the river, but Dan didn't think his eyes were focused on the scenery. Especially as the scenery was the backs of some warehouses at the arse end of Bath.

"Yeah, well, depends how you look at it. He never missed a chance to let me know he was disappointed in how girly I'd turned out, but I think he thought he could put it right by teaching me bloke's stuff. He always hated the fact I wasn't into football and had my head stuck in a book all the time."

Robin didn't respond. Dan nudged him. "What about your dad? He must have taught you loads."

Robin snorted. "Yeah, right. Do you know how much an eye-surgeon's hands are worth?"

Dan stared. "Your dad's a surgeon?" That explained a hell of a lot. The posh accent, the chip on his shoulder about the dyslexia, the rebellion.

"Yep. His hands are far too valuable to risk doing DIY. His time was too valuable to spend much of it on a loser like me, either."

"That's rough."

Robin shrugged and kept his eyes fixed on that distant point. "I managed. Learnt a few things at school and found other boaters to teach me what I've wanted to know since then. I picked up enough."

Robin hugged his arms around himself and chewed on his lower lip. He looked so young, so vulnerable like that. Why did some parents have to fuck up their children's lives so comprehensively?

Dan wanted to hug Robin tight, but his hands were covered in grease from the chain. He wiped them off as best he could on his jeans. They were already ruined from the mud, soot and general canal dirt. He didn't even want to think about the state of his trainers. If he were going to spend much more time here, he'd need to get a pair of boots like Robin's: big, sexy, lace-up leather boots Robin tucked his trousers into. But he wasn't going to be here for longer than a few days, was he?

"Finished?" Robin said. He turned to look at Dan for the first time since their conversation had started. The inscrutable expression was back. The one that Dan now realised meant he had his barriers up again. "I'm dying for that pint. Can you manage to get back on the saddle?"

Dan winced at the idea. Between yesterday's shafting at the open hatch and the abuse his balls had just suffered, it wasn't the most appealing prospect.

"Can we walk for a bit? That way I might just be up for a ride again later." Dan let his voice drop low and waggled his eyebrows.

That earned him a smile.

"Come on, then," Robin said. "Better get a move on if we want to get there while they're still serving lunch."

They walked side by side, pushing their bikes along. Robin was quiet for a long while, and Dan was content to watch the scenery change as they journeyed through the industrial hinterland at the edge of the city. There was a narrow strip of steep bank between them and the fast-flowing water, with scrubby bushes and trees clinging there insistently. Dan was grateful for the steel railings along the side of the path that lent the illusion of safety. Buildings separated them from the main road, but traffic murmured in the background. On the other side of the river, some thirty yards away, the backs of the warehouses butted straight up to the water as if daring it to do its worst. Beyond them the twin gas towers added their defiant protest against the picturesque Bath skyline.

"Look, witches' knickers," Robin said, pointing to the bushes festooned with ragged carrier bags.

Dan couldn't help a chuckle, despite his irritation at the way the litter spoilt the view.

"Fucking arseholes, chucking their rubbish into the river and blaming us boaters." Robin pointed at a large, floating object making its way downstream towards them. It was caught in the slower water at the edge, snagging on low-hanging branches as it spun its lazy way towards the ocean. "It's not like they don't have enough bins around to use."

Dan squinted at the humped object Robin had indicated. It looked like a floating bin bag from a distance, but as they drew nearer, he realised that the black plastic was in fact black fabric, shining because it was one of those puffy, nylon bomber jackets. Humped because it had something underneath it. Floating because that something was buoyant with air…

Dan's guts plummeted as cold fear slid down his spine. He froze.

"Robin! Wait!"

All his attention was focused on the floating object. His arm shook as he pointed to it. Now it was closer, he could see a second hump, barely visible, covered in dark, sopping wet hair.

"It's a body," Dan said, his voice coming out in a croak.

"What the—"

The next thing Dan saw was Robin running to the water's edge, vaulting over the railings and throwing off his jacket. Then time slowed, Robin's body arcing gracefully through the air. Powerful, muscular, yet so fragile compared to the river's relentless surge. Dan's stomach tied itself in agonising knots as he watched Robin disappear into the dark water.

The water still flowed, the birds still sang and the breeze still blew soft on his skin, but Dan was frozen to the spot. He couldn't breathe, staring at the river's darkly glittering surface, willing it to give up its hold on Robin. Promising anything just to have him back on dry land and safe in his arms.

Robin's head broke the surface near the body. Dan exhaled, taking ragged breaths as he stumbled to the river's edge and clung on to the railings with white knuckles. Robin's jacket lay on the ground before him. He picked it up, barely aware of what he was doing. He wanted to call out, bring Robin back to him by the power of his voice, but nothing would come out. Robin struggled with the misshapen lump, hauling it around so that the head broke the surface. It looked like a young man, waxy white, with a vicious gash on his temple.

Now that the body was a person rather than a thing, adrenaline coursed through Dan's system. Galvanised into action, he drew out his phone and thumbed in 999. Holding it to his ear, he ducked under the railings, his legs spread wide and knees bent low as he edged towards the riverbank. In the water below, all that was visible were the two heads moving slowly closer to the bank even as the current swept them downstream. Dan cursed. He'd have to move farther along if he was to be of any help hauling them onto the bank.

"Hello, Emergency Services Operator. Which service do you require?"

"Ambulance! I need an ambulance. And, oh God, I don't know…some kind of river rescue?"

"What's the nature of your emergency?"

"He's in the river, trying to save some guy. I… I think he's drowned."

"I'll connect you to the Ambulance Service, and if you still need rescue help, then they'll put you through after they've taken the details, okay?"

"Okay."

Dan jogged up to the towpath and followed Robin as he was swept downstream. Just then the operator cut in.

"Ambulance Service, what's the address of the emergency?"

Bugger. He remembered passing an industrial estate just before they stopped, a furniture factory belching its cloying fumes out onto the towpath.

"We're on the river. J-just past a factory on the river bank in Bath. Going towards the city. Shit! I, um, I can see a bridge ahead, right next to the gas towers."

"Thank you. I think we can pinpoint your location from that." The woman's voice was calm and steady. Could she not tell this was urgent? "And what is the telephone number you're calling from?"

All Dan could focus on was the sight of Robin struggling in the water.

"Hold on there, Robin. I'm calling for help." His voice was louder than he'd expected, and the sound gave him confidence. He gave the operator his mobile number.

"What's the problem? Tell me exactly what's happened."

"There's a body, in the river. Young guy. Drowned, I think. Robin dived in to rescue him. He's struggling. Getting swept along."

"Is the young man conscious?"

"No. I...oh God, I think he's dead. Looks like he hit his head."

"And do you think your friend will be able to get him out of the water?"

"He'd better! He's pretty strong." Robin had better be strong enough. "I'm going to have to hang up and help them out in a moment."

"Please don't put yourself at risk. I've already arranged for the ambulance and the police. I need you to be able to liaise with them when they reach you. Would you be able to go and stand by the main road so they can find you?"

Dan glanced over at the rows of buildings standing between him and the main road. "No fucking way! I'm staying where I can help Robin."

He thought he heard a sigh, but when the woman spoke again, her tone was firm and professional. "Do you have any first-aid training?"

"It's been a long time." Memories of fooling around when he had to blow into the plastic dummy's mouth resurfaced. "I'm not sure how much I'll remember."

"The first few minutes can be critical. Stay on the line and I can talk you through resuscitation."

"That's not going to be any fucking use if he's still in the river, is it?"

Dan hung up on her, determined to ignore the advice about risk. Robin was closer to the bank now, only about four feet from the edge, but didn't seem to be making any further progress.

"I'm coming," Dan shouted. "Just stay where you are."

"'Kay." Robin's shout was breathless.

"Don't waste your breath. Just stay alive, all right!"

The handrail came to an end where the bank was lined with scrubby trees. Dan scrambled down between them, grabbing hold of thicker branches to slow his headlong rush. A boulder jutted out into the water. He knelt on the rock. Reached out. His hand grazed the water, and an icy chill shuddered up his arm. So cold!

"Robin, you're nearly there, just a little bit closer." Robin was facing away from him, his head bobbing lower and lower in the water. Dan looked around him for something that might help. It was all just nature. Trees and bushes...and branches.

Dan picked up the largest he could see. It crumbled, rotten in the core. His gaze skittered over the other branches littering the ground. One stood out as shinier than the others, and even though it was slender, he grabbed it and tried to snap it in half. The branch bent but held. It felt right in his hand. He turned back to the river, his heart skipping a beat as he saw Robin's head duck almost completely below the water. Why the fuck was he still clinging on to that deadweight? Even Dan could see the lad was quite clearly not breathing.

"Robin! He's dead. Let go of him. Please! Grab this stick and I'll pull you in."

He thrust the stick towards Robin, poking at his shoulder in his haste. Robin's head disappeared beneath the water again.

Fuck, was he going to have to jump in there to save him? He stripped off his jacket and took a deep breath. He'd do it. For Robin.

Robin resurfaced with a gasp. Dan gave a silent prayer of thanks to whatever or whoever might be watching over them.

"Please don't make me get in there! Grab hold of the stick." Thank God. Robin clutched the stick with one pallid hand.

Dan hauled. The weight of their two bodies against the drag of the current was enormous, and he just wasn't strong enough.

"Fucking hell, Robin. Let him go!"

But Robin wouldn't listen. Slowly but surely, Robin's fingers began to slip from the far end of the branch. Dan watched it happen, and bile rose in his throat. His body broke out in a cold sweat.

"Don't you dare drown on me, or I'll fucking well kill you!"

Robin's hand tightened, and with a final burst of strength, Dan managed to pull him close enough to reach. He lay down on the rock and grabbed Robin's cold hand. He squeezed it hard and felt a faint answering twitch. Robin's mouth was just above the surface, his arm still wrapped tight around the corpse. Dan summoned up every last ounce of strength and pulled. Robin either wouldn't or couldn't loosen his grip on the body. But then, with a last, muscle-screaming heave, they were out, lying on the rock, water streaming off their clothing.

Dan lay back, Robin cradled in his arms. Dan's heart was trying to hammer its way out of his chest. He lifted Robin's arm. It was stiff with cold. He gave a shove, and the drowned lad rolled off Robin to sprawl on the ground.

Dan stared at the corpse. There was a clean graze on the bloke's temple, but no new blood welled up. Perhaps that was what did him in. An accident? Suicide? Murder? Dan shivered and tried not to think about swallowing water—tried not to imagine watching the sky grow dim as the river claimed you. He attempted to focus on concrete facts—the bloke's eyes were open but unseeing. He was heavyset—no wonder Robin had struggled—and he couldn't be any more than twenty. So young. And so dead.

But Robin—Robin was shaking in Dan's arms, trembling and gasping and reaching for him.

And alive. So very alive.

"Why didn't you let go? I nearly lost you."

Dan grasped Robin tight. He'd willingly give Robin every last bit of body heat he could. He kissed his forehead, telling himself that those weren't tears in Robin's eyes. Robin was too strong for that. It was just water. Same as in Dan's eyes. Just salty river water, running down their cheeks as their bodies shook with sobs.

# Chapter Nineteen

A round-faced woman and a skinny blond lad in green appeared at the top of the bank. It wasn't until they called to him that Dan recognised them as paramedics. The woman tried to persuade Dan to let go of Robin. He fought her off, snarling, but she plied him with offers of blankets for Robin. He followed as she led Robin up to the pathway. He didn't see what happened to the body. He didn't care.

"D-Dan? Where are you?" Robin's voice was weak, almost hoarse.

In a couple of strides, Dan was at Robin's side, wrestling him out of the paramedic's grasp.

"Please, Dan, we need to get your friend some medical attention." The woman attempted to loosen Dan's hold on Robin. "We need him to get into the ambulance. You can come too."

Dan clung on tighter, pressing his body against Robin in an attempt to transmit his warmth through the sopping-wet clothing. He buried his face in Robin's neck, his head shaking as Robin's teeth chattered by his ear. Robin's arms came around to circle him, the grip almost as tight as his own. Eventually the paramedic gave up trying to separate them, and sometime later Dan felt a warm blanket being draped around them both.

"Dan, my love, could you tell us your friend's name?" It was the woman. The one whose face reminded him of his mum. He told her, hoping she'd leave them alone.

"Robin? Can you hear me? My name's Julie, and I'm here to help you. We need to get those wet clothes off you and check you over. Can you please ask Dan to let go?"

Reluctantly Dan complied, but he refused to let go of Robin's hand, forcing Julie to work around him in the confined space of the ambulance. He wouldn't let her strip Robin's clothing—that was his job. Robin's skin was damp and clammy—the touch of it almost too much to bear.

Warm, dry clothes miraculously appeared, and Robin obediently lifted his arms for the Pfizer T-shirt, then stepped into the faded jogging bottoms when Dan asked him to. There weren't any spare socks, but there was a fluffy towel for Robin's feet. Julie draped another dry blanket around Robin, this one powder pink and full of holes like something his baby nieces would have come wrapped in. They sat on the two flip-down seats by the back door as the other paramedic wheeled out the gurney; then Julie shut the door behind him, keeping the warmth inside.

Robin's reactions were slow to begin with. Julie took his pulse and temperature, all the while asking gentle but insistent questions. Dan needed to keep reassuring himself that Robin was there—it had been such a close call. He twisted up inside every time he thought about it. He squeezed Robin's hand, watching the animation and colour slowly return to his face. Julie brought them both lukewarm tea in plastic cups. It tasted like the inside of a Thermos flask, but Dan didn't care. All he was concerned about was the way Robin's hand shook as he lifted the cup to his mouth. But then Robin looked up and gave him a hesitant smile.

"Thank you," Robin whispered.

Dan's heart swelled. The world's soppiest grin took over his face and wouldn't let go.

"You are the bravest, stupidest man I've ever met. You ever do something crazy like that again and I'll kill you myself." He kissed Robin firmly on the lips.

"All right, then, lovebirds. Break it up. You'll make me all weepy if I have to watch much more of that." Julie was smiling fondly, and Dan pulled her close for a peck on the cheek. She chortled. "Stop it, you! I'll forget what I'm meant to be doing.

Now, Robin my love, I want to take you back to the hospital to keep an eye on you. We don't want you going into shock."

"No." They both spun around to stare at Robin. His face was calm, but his eyes were flinty. "I'm not going into hospital. No fucking way."

"But poppet, it's just for a little while. You'll be in safe hands." She reached out to pat Robin's shoulder.

"Dan can look after me."

Dan caught Robin's gaze, the intensity of it cutting right into him. It was hard to bear, so he made light of it. "You just want to get me on my own again, don't you? Play a bit of doctors and nurses."

Robin's gaze faltered for a moment; then he laughed, the unexpected sound ringing harshly in the small space. "Okay. You can be the nurse."

"But I'm always the nurse!" Dan pouted and did his best impression of an aggrieved queen, complete with hands on hips and gratuitous hair flicking.

Julie eventually managed to make herself heard through their giggling. "All right, all right. You've convinced me! Just make sure you give a statement to the police before you leave. I don't want them on my case about it."

The hysterical laughter died on their lips as they stumbled out of the ambulance door.

Robin stared. A shiver ran down his spine.

There was a body on the gurney. A dead body. In a bag.

He'd failed.

His stomach churned. He leant on Dan's shoulder. He'd probably feel better if he could throw up, but there were people everywhere. Most of them in uniform.

An officer with dark rings under his eyes and slumped shoulders approached.

"He's dead?" Robin's voice came out as a whisper. It was obvious now. It was what Dan had been trying to tell him when he'd been struggling in the water. But maybe, just maybe, someone would tell him it was all a mistake. Maybe that was something else in the bag. Maybe his mind was playing tricks on him.

Dan clutched his hand as the officer filled them in.

"There was nothing you could have done, sir. He was probably dead as soon as he hit the water. Took a plunge off North Parade Bridge and knocked his head on the way down. We've had fatalities there in the past."

"What was his name?" Robin tried to suppress the trembling in his voice. He needed to know.

The officer looked at his pad, frowning. "Ben Parker. We've been looking for him after a report of him falling. Apparently he'd been drinking with friends in the Huntsman and someone dared him to walk along the parapet." It wasn't hard to guess what had happened next. Robin tuned out the officer's voice and tried to concentrate on the way Dan's fingers laced through his. Dan was warm and alive. Dan was here right now.

Old ghosts had no business trying to resurface now.

"So it wasn't a suicide?" Robin asked. Dan squeezed his hand, his face a picture of puzzled concern. Robin tried his best to ignore it. He owed Dan an explanation, but he couldn't give it here in front of all these people.

"Doesn't look like it, sir. Just a case of youthful high jinks gone wrong. You'd think they'd know better, these university students, but get a few drinks inside them and they all think they're bloody Superman."

It didn't take long for them both to give their statements, and the officer seemed satisfied, if his grim smile was anything to go by. Taking their details was a different matter. Dan received a raised eyebrow for his South London address, but Robin was given a look of barely concealed contempt. The officer muttered "no fixed abode" while writing in his pad.

Someone had retrieved their bicycles and propped them up against the back of the ambulance. Robin's wet clothes were in a carrier bag hanging on the handles of Dan's bike.

They pushed their bikes back to Serendipity, neither of them saying much.

"Would you really have jumped in there to save me?" Robin asked.

Dan was quiet for a long while. Robin had just about given up on an answer when it finally came.

"I don't know. I think so. I was fucking petrified, but I couldn't face losing you." Dan's voice cracked as he spoke. "Why'd you do it? Why didn't you let go of him?"

Dan had been willing to face his fears. All for him. It was about time Robin returned the favour.

"I thought if I could save him, it would make up for Jamie. I'm ready to talk about him. If you still want to know."

Dan just nodded, his lips set in a thin line.

"When we get back, I'll tell you everything. I promise."

Robin's stomach knotted up. This was going to be much harder than plunging into a cold river.

This was terrifying.

# Chapter Twenty

"We met at boarding school. My first day there. We were roommates, and he took it upon himself to show me all the shortcuts and the best places to sneak out for a smoke. He smoked like a fucking chimney if he got the chance."

Dan watched Robin take another drag on his joint. They were in a clearing in the woods next to the boat, sitting side by side on a tarpaulin next to the fire they'd built. Close, but not touching. Robin didn't seem to be able to meet Dan's eyes and stared at the flames while speaking. They were out here because Robin had complained of feeling too claustrophobic inside. Probably best to be outside, anyway. Dan had a yearning for dry land after the day they'd had.

The river was still visible through the tree trunks, glittering amber with the setting sun. The evening's chill would soon start creeping in around them. Dan threw a pine cone into the flames and watched it flare brightly as it shrivelled. Robin held the flask of rum out towards him, but he turned it down. He didn't mind how much Robin needed to drink to get this out of him, but he wanted to remain clearheaded and give his best as a listener.

"I didn't know what it was I felt for him at first. I mean, I'd always fancied girls, but I kept watching his mouth when he smoked. Kept wondering whether he'd taste like an ashtray if I kissed him. It was freaking me out, but I told myself I was definitely straight. Just a bit...homesick."

Dan nodded. It was hard to imagine what being sent off to boarding school must be like. Tristan had told him it was a blast, but then Tris claimed he'd always known he was gay. Maybe this Jamie had been more like Tris.

"What was he like?" Dan asked.

"He was larger than life, you know? If he was in the room, everyone knew about it. He used to go on about how ADHD was just another term for party animal, but he'd get antsy if he'd been doing the same thing for more than a few minutes. Letting him fuck me was one way of keeping his attention on me for a little bit longer. He could concentrate on that all right."

Had Robin just implied what he thought he did? Dan didn't like to ask such a blunt question, so he just watched Robin's face. A flush spread over those cheeks as Robin met his gaze.

"Yeah, he always topped. His stepfather had raped him. He said it would bring it all back again if he bottomed."

"Were you happy with that? Must have been weird, if you still thought you were straight."

Robin gave a wry smile. "I figured out I wasn't straight the first time I tasted his cock. Nah, it was fine. It was good. It felt good."

Robin's eyes were watering. Dan's heart clenched painfully. He hated seeing Robin undone like this. Hated the thought that this Jamie could have hurt him so badly.

"You loved him." It wasn't a question. It was obvious from every word Robin spoke.

"Yeah. Just goes to show what an idiot I am. Picked the one guy who was even more of a fuckup than me. He was so charming, though. Seemed so together. I thought he had it all figured out, the way he could talk about all those bad things that had happened to him. I didn't know how much he was still hurting.

"I took him home that first Christmas. Mum couldn't stand him. You should have seen the look on her face when she walked in on us together. That was my coming out. She sent him packing, and I followed him back to school. Didn't go home for any holidays after that.

"I got my inheritance from my gran on my eighteenth birthday. We both left school that day and got on the train to London. Spent a few weeks in a bed-and-breakfast in Soho before we found this little flat to rent. I would have preferred somewhere quieter and cheaper, but Jamie loved it there. So many distractions. So many people. Just his sort of place."

Robin ground to a halt. Dan's mind buzzed with questions. Why the hell hadn't Robin told him about living in London? And what on earth happened there? He desperately wanted to understand, but it was so hard seeing Robin suffering like this, his voice brittle, naked, raw.

"Things were great for a while. Jamie wasn't capable of holding down a job, and my money was getting eaten up, so I had to find work, but that was okay. Had to work in a factory putting together executive desk toys, but I didn't mind. So long as I had Jamie to come home to, it didn't matter what I had to do. We'd go out clubbing every weekend. He'd flirt with other guys, but we always went home together. I thought we were solid...happy. Shows what I know."

Robin's mouth twisted in an ugly smile. Dan wanted to kiss it away. Wanted to tell him he didn't have to carry on if he didn't want to. Then again, maybe he needed to. Maybe Dan would just have to keep quiet and listen.

"I'd been working these awful shift patterns, doing lots of nights. I figured Jamie was just out down the pub with our mates—that's where he said he'd been. Then one day it hurt to piss, and I had this discharge..." Robin took another drag of his joint before jumping up to pace around the fire.

Dan stayed seated but watched Robin closely. He was ready to leap up the moment Robin needed him. He just hoped he'd be able to tell when that moment arrived.

"The doctor told me I had the clap. He wanted to know if I'd been sleeping around, then said I should get Jamie in to see him so he could be treated too. He made it pretty fucking clear that Jamie must have been screwing around." Robin turned to the trees and continued in a low voice. "You know what the worst thing was? If he'd asked me first, I probably would have said it was okay. I'm not saying I would have been happy about it, but if I'd known how hard it was for him to stick to one bloke, I'd have made allowances. It was...it was the betrayal. That was what really cut me up. He said he'd never promised to be exclusive." Robin snorted derisively and shook his head.

"Said he still loved me, but he couldn't help himself. I asked for an HIV test and started getting really strict about condoms, even for oral. He hated that."

It was all starting to make sense now. Robin's paranoia about infection. His insistence on using those awful strawberry condoms. But there was more to come, Dan could see that. Robin's shoulders were hunched up like he was being crushed under a heavy weight.

"He fell in with a bad crowd. At first it was just the booze, but he didn't have any willpower, and they were all on smack. It slowed him right down—he didn't even seem like my Jamie anymore. I used to get home from my shifts and find him crashed out with all his kit spread out around him. I was always worrying about stepping on infected needles. Things kept going missing, so I changed the PIN number to my account and kept my wallet on me all the time. He refused to see a drug counsellor. Said he was self-medicating because of his fucked-up childhood." Robin's voice wavered dangerously, and he wrapped his arms tightly around himself.

That was Dan's cue. He got up and walked around to stand in front of Robin. It hurt to see those eyes brimming with tears.

"Come here," he said, holding his arms out. Robin fell into them, and for a long moment, all he could hear was their uneven breathing. Dan buried his face in the crook of Robin's neck. Dan had seen childhood friends fall to addiction before. It was hideous, what it did to them, how it ate them up from the inside out. He couldn't imagine what it must be like to watch someone you loved destroyed in that way.

When Robin started talking again, his voice was a rough whisper, barely audible above the hissing and crackling of the fire. Dan pressed his ear to Robin's chest and felt the words fighting their way out.

"It was like living in a crack den. The squalor. I tried to keep things clean and look after him, but I had to go to work. Then one day...one day I was so tired I gouged my finger and got sent home early. The TV was finally gone. I'd been wondering how long it would take him to sell that, and I went into the bedroom to lay into him, only...only, he wasn't alone. He was off his nut, being fucked by some mean-looking arsehole. At first I thought it was rape. Wanted to help him. But he was enjoying it. He was—" Robin broke off with a choked-back sob.

"You don't need to tell me anything you don't want to." Dan kept his voice calm, his eyes fixed on Robin's, trying to pull him back to the here and now. To the sky, fading to purple, and the dark trees and their warm circle of firelight.

Robin nodded, sniffed and blinked the tears out of his eyes. "I think I need another drink."

Dan led Robin back to the tarp and sat, Robin settling between his legs and leaning back against him. Dan found the flask and handed it over, but not before taking a quick swig himself. He hadn't realised how hard this would be. How ripped apart he'd be feeling after hearing Robin lay his life bare. He hoped he was giving at least the illusion of strength and capability, because right now he felt tattered and bruised by the raw emotions pouring out of Robin.

"How long ago was this?" he asked.

"Four years. Pathetic, right? I should be over it by now."

"No, no. I was just thinking how young you must have been. That's rough."

"Yeah, you should hear the rest, then." Bitterness warped Robin's voice.

Dan pressed a kiss against the side of his head. "I'm listening."

The words tumbled out. "I ran. I left him all alone and holed up at my parents' place. I even changed my mobile number. Didn't want anything to do with him. Told myself someone else would help him. If I wasn't there, he'd go and get the professional help he needed." Robin sniffed loudly and rubbed his eyes. "Yeah, right. Who was I trying to kid?

"It was six months later when he finally called their landline and I picked up. He told me he had HIV. He said it was my fault. Said he'd had to sell himself. Wanted to know why I'd left him to rot.

"His breathing sounded funny. Like he was falling asleep or ill or something." Robin shivered, and Dan hugged him tight. "Said he'd taken an overdose. Said it felt like he was wrapped up in cotton wool. He laughed. That laugh...it sounded all wrong.

"I should have called an ambulance, but I just thought if I could keep him talking, it would all work out. That he'd pull through. I started talking about our school days. All those sneaky cigarette breaks and snogging on the fire escape. He remembered some of it. Said he fell in love with me back then. It was bullshit. He never said anything at the time.

"But then he slowed right down, and I was shouting at him, but he couldn't hear me. They told me he was dead by the time the ambulance crew arrived. I've always wondered if...if the last thing he heard was me yelling at him. Calling him a selfish cunt." Robin's body quivered as he spoke. Dan could hear the tears welling up behind his words.

He sighed and rested his head on Robin's shoulder.

"Have you been blaming yourself all this time?"

Robin gave a single nod. He didn't seem able to speak. His body thrummed with tension.

"It wasn't down to you. You didn't force him into doing anything. He chose that course."

"I let him down. I—"

"No you didn't. You stuck by him all those years." Dan's voice was fierce. He needed Robin to understand this. "Fucking hell, Robin. You can't carry on beating yourself up for this. There's nothing you could have done to stop him. I've seen it happen to families round where I grew up. You might have been able to keep him going for a bit longer, but that's it. People that fucked up always find a way of destroying themselves and bringing down everyone around them. At least this way you managed to keep yourself safe."

Robin laughed, a harsh, croaking sound that turned into a sob.

Dan held him fast as the pain flowed out in jagged wails, welling up and spilling over and over and over until he was spent.

His head rested on Dan's chest. Despite the rawness of his throat and eyes, Robin felt more peaceful than he had in a long time. Somewhere inside a door had been opened, a chink of light slicing through the darkness. Dan's arms were still solid around him. Robin raised his head and felt Dan's breath hot against his nape.

"For a minute there I didn't think you were going to stop," Dan whispered, nuzzling at his ear. "Thought I'd have to resort to distracting you with sex."

Robin laughed, more from relief than at what Dan said. He snorted and wiped his nose on his sleeve. "I'm a right fucking mess. Should probably just go stick my head in the river and have done with it."

He felt Dan's hands pull away from his body and turn his head.

"Nah, I like a bit of snot. Tastes good and looks even better."

Robin managed a crooked smile. "Charmer."

He risked meeting Dan's gaze and saw that familiar lust glinting. But there was something more there this time. Something unlooked for that made his skin prickle and his thoughts reel. He shouldn't read too much into this. He knew what kind of man Dan was. Here today, shagging someone else tomorrow. It was what made this safe—this intimacy. He couldn't get hurt, because he certainly wasn't going to fall for the bloke.

He knew, though. He knew as he twisted around to meet Dan's lips with his hunger. This was more than just sex. This man in his arms had listened to it, all of it, and still thought he was a decent guy. Dan was still able to look at him with respect and understanding, and something more burning deep in those hazel eyes.

They crushed together, wild and needy. Robin pushed Dan back on the ground, straddling him and grinding against him. He craved Dan's touch all over his skin to wipe away the chill of the river and the grime of his memories. He stripped off his shirt, heedless of the cold night air.

"You're going to freeze," Dan warned, his hands rising to stroke over the planes of Robin's chest. "Not that I don't appreciate the view. Jesus! Do you not feel the cold?"

Robin freed his cock with a sigh of relief, then stood to get rid of boots and trousers. He had to smile at the dazed yet alarmed expression on Dan's face.

"Wouldn't you rather go inside?" Dan stood, looking between Robin and the boat. "Robin?"

Robin threw a couple more logs on the fire. He turned to Dan. He knew exactly what he wanted.

Everything was different now.

Dan's eyes shone with curiosity, drawing him close. The air was chill, raising goose bumps on his skin, but it made Robin feel alive and tingly all over, increasing his sensitivity. He ran his hands down Dan's back and pulled him closer. Dan felt so good—warm and hard and pliant all at once.

"What is it you want?" Dan murmured into his ear. "It better not involve me getting naked out here."

"I want you to fuck me."

Dan's breath halted for a moment; then Robin felt a long exhale against his ear.

"You sure?"

"Yeah. I'll tell you if I need you to stop."

Dan didn't say or do anything. Time stretched out and Robin's heart hammered wildly. He felt like he'd just thrown himself off the top of a cliff—he needed Dan to be his safety net, or he was going to hit the water hard. He didn't want to have to beg for it, but if that was what it was going to take…

"Please," he said, grabbing hold of Dan's hand and drawing it to his mouth. He sucked on the first two fingers, coating them with saliva. "Will you just fucking well get on with it?"

Robin felt the desire shudder through Dan's body. He pressed himself closer, squashing them together and grinding against Dan.

"Can't help yourself, can you?" Dan said. "Still ordering me around. Right, Mister, you asked for it." Dan's hands came out to push Robin to the ground.

A thrill shivered down Robin's spine as he gazed up at Dan towering above him, eyes glinting in the firelight. He propped himself up on his elbows as Dan sank down between his thighs.

Dan gave Robin a wicked smile before swallowing him whole. The surprise made him gasp, distracting him from the fingers pushing their way back from his balls. When Dan made contact with his hole, the shock was like a lightning bolt. Robin stiffened, torn between the urge to bear down and to pull away.

"This still what you want?" Dan asked, his fingers circling gently.

Robin closed his eyes against the concern on Dan's face. He'd had it with being fragile today. He'd had it with being rescued and coddled and understood, and now he needed to be taken, hard and fast and without pity. He grabbed hold of Dan's hand and pushed down against his fingers, desperately trying to impale himself, gasping for air.

"Okay, okay. I get the message."

It was as if a switch had been flipped inside Dan. His motions became purposeful, commanding, as he lifted Robin's hips and deliberately sank his fingers in deep. Robin hissed with the burn but gave himself up to it, to the glorious pleasure that was sure to follow. And it did, Dan's fingers unerringly finding the most sensitive spot inside him and giving him a massage that made his toes curl. Robin moaned, arching his back and fucking himself on Dan's fingers until the whole world shrank down to the sensation of them moving inside him and the warm, liquid pleasure spreading from that spot.

A kiss broke the spell, along with a rude withdrawal that made Robin groan in frustration.

"Simmer down, sweetheart. You'll get a good fucking in just a moment, I promise."

Dan lay next to him, kissing him deeply, masterfully. Robin felt Dan's sheathed and lubed erection pressing against his belly and trembled in anticipation. He'd never thought he'd want this again. Never thought he'd get that urge to be taken, that need to be fucked senseless, so strong it turned his insides to a writhing mass of desire and his voice to a cracked whimper.

"Please," he asked, closing his eyes.

"Look at me," Dan said.

Robin shook his head. He couldn't, because Dan would see the violent need written in his eyes and it would scare him off for good.

"Look at me."

The power in Dan's voice startled Robin, and his eyes sprang open.

But Dan was smiling, looking at Robin with unconcealed desire. Then Dan rolled onto his back. "Climb on. I want to watch you while I'm fucking you."

Robin scrambled on, straddling Dan's hips and trying to push his jeans farther down.

"Uh-uh, too cold."

"Wimp."

"Hard case."

But Dan wouldn't let Robin push his jeans back any farther. Fine, well, if he had to have an arse full of rivets and buttons, he'd just have to try and enjoy it. Robin lined himself up, the press of Dan's cock against his arsehole making him quiver. He was going to be sore, but fucking hell, he needed this. As he sank down, filling himself with Dan, all the other cares of the day were pushed aside. There was only room for the simple fact of Dan inside him, stretching him wide and filling the void. Taking the space inside him for his own.

Robin paused, but it was too late for pulling back. It was already done, and with a groan he took in that last inch, grinding himself ferociously against Dan. Dan gasped, bucked his hips, and it was just what Robin needed to goad him on. He took control of the pace, lifting slowly but dropping hard and fast. He looked down in amazement at Dan's body still clothed, and his own naked, his cock aching to be touched by more than the night air.

"Looks so good," Dan said, his voice hoarse.

Robin felt Dan buck again and picked up his pace, leaning forward to hold himself over Dan. Dan's hands slid up his sides, reaching behind to pull him down.

Robin felt himself falling. Falling into Dan's eyes, so dark and round and perfect. He fell into the kiss, letting Dan fuck him with his tongue just as he was claiming him with his dick.

Heedless, reckless, grunting; Robin moved faster and harder. And just when he thought he couldn't bear it for a moment longer, Dan's hand found him and squeezed.

Robin's orgasm exploded, the spasms racking him as he spurted into Dan's grasp and sobbed into his mouth. The aftershocks were still resounding as Dan gave a cry, and Robin felt the pulse of his cock deep inside as Dan heaved and thrust.

The balance had shifted. Robin felt it, inside him. More than simply the physical invasion—he'd opened up to Dan fully, body and soul.

It was fucking terrifying.

He shook, and then Dan was lavishing him with kisses, his arms wrapping around him and pulling him tight.

"Come on, let's get you inside."

Robin nodded, gathered his clothes and followed Dan back to the dark boat.

# Chapter Twenty-One

Dan was uploading his recent photographs onto his laptop when Robin's phone rang. He stared at it for a moment, then picked it up to check the caller.

*Mum.*

Dan listened to the chug of the engine as Robin steered them back towards the canal. He wondered whether Robin would go apeshit if he answered. He could make up all sorts of plausible excuses for doing so, but truth be told he was fascinated by the formidable woman Robin had described. Would the reality live up to Robin's account?

Bugger it. He'd have to risk Robin's anger.

"Hello, Mrs. Hamilton. This is Dan Taylor, friend of Robin's. He can't get to the phone right now, I'm afraid." That was good. He'd managed to erase most of his South London accent. All those years of hanging out with Tris had given him an insider's knowledge of posh folk's talk.

"Oh! Good afternoon. Oh goodness! Dan Taylor, did you say? I don't believe we've met, have we?"

Dan smiled to himself. "I haven't had the pleasure yet. How can I help you, Mrs. Hamilton?" At least Robin wouldn't be able to fault him on his phone manners.

"I was hoping to speak to that absentee son of mine. I've been trying to contact him for the last couple of days. Doesn't he realise how much I worry when I can't get hold of him?"

"I do apologise. We've been moored up out in the middle of nowhere and there was no mobile reception. I'll make sure he stops somewhere where he can talk to you."

"I see. And you've been staying with Robin, you say?"

"That's right." Dan grinned. The next question would be the one about how long they'd known each other. He hadn't decided whether to evade that or not. He looked down at the candid photos of Robin currently being uploaded. They might not have known each other long, but they certainly knew each other well. Since that fireside confession, it felt like they were real friends, comfy as old socks but much more sexy.

"And what is it you do?" There was just that faintest hint of snobbery in her voice—a wariness rather than outright unfriendliness.

"I'm a freelance travel writer and photographer."

"Oh! I see. And you live on the boats, do you?"

"No, I'm just visiting from London, working on a piece for the *Observer* magazine."

"How fascinating." There was definitely warmth creeping into her tones now. "It's good to know that Robin's making some better-connected friends. Maybe he'll be persuaded to leave that death-trap boat one day." She sighed. "And how is my darling son? He never really tells me anything these days."

"He's well. Very well. He's been whistling all morning." Well, most of it. There were the parts when his mouth had been otherwise occupied. After his outpouring of grief, Robin had decided he didn't need to bother with the strawberry-flavour condoms anymore, much to Dan's delight. And Robin's too, judging by his contented moans as he lapped up every last drop of Dan's come. "He seems really happy."

"That's marvellous! Oh, you don't know how thrilled I am to hear you say that. I've been so worried about him. Now, I need you to pass a message on to him about tomorrow. We're going to meet at Popjoy's at one, and he'll need to dress smarter than last time. Shirt and tie, no jeans. And if he could refrain from sticking his tongue out and scaring the waiting staff with that awful jewelry I'd certainly appreciate it."

Dan chuckled. "He never told me about that."

"Yes, well he was going through a particularly difficult stage at the time. It nearly gave his father a heart attack when he saw it. Especially when Robin explained what it was for. Really, I had no idea." She sniffed.

Dan fought down the laughter. "Mrs. Hamilton, I'll make sure I remind him to be on his best behaviour."

"Oh please, call me Rosemary, darling. Actually, I've just had a marvellous idea. Are you free tomorrow afternoon? Why don't you join us? It would be lovely to meet one of Robin's friends."

Dan shut his eyes. He knew exactly what he was going to say, and Robin was going to kill him. "Thank you, Rosemary. I'd love to. And I promise I won't scare the waiting staff. I haven't packed a suit with me, but I should have time to go and get one tomorrow morning. I'll make sure Robin has something decent to wear too."

Rosemary rang off after giving Dan a genuinely warm good-bye. He sat there, looking at the phone in his hand and wondering what he'd just agreed to. The idea of meeting Robin's family was so appealing, but he'd never, ever wanted to meet the family of any of the guys he'd been with before. Still, it was just curiosity. Nothing wrong with that.

Just idle curiosity.

Yeah, right.

Morris interrupted his chain of thought by purring and leaping up onto his lap, obscuring the view of the laptop screen.

"Hey there, Morris. What am I getting myself into here, eh? I'm buggered if I know."

It was easier not to think about it, so he petted Morris for a while, then went to look through Robin's clothing and see if there was anything respectable enough for lunch with his parents.

Not a chance. They were going to have to hit the shops.


"You did what?" Robin glared at Dan from across the lock. Dan had waited until they were on opposite sides of the canal before broaching the subject. Good thing too, considering how Robin was reacting.

"I accepted your mum's invitation to lunch. It seemed like the polite thing to do."

"You answered my fucking phone! I didn't give you permission to do that."

Dan's body wanted to flinch, but he stood his ground through sheer force of will. "I didn't realise it would be such a big deal. I was just taking a message."

"I've got voicemail for that. And anyway, you didn't just take a message, did you? You invited yourself along to a family lunch."

"No, I was invited, and your mum makes it very hard to say no. It took me by surprise. It was the first I'd heard about your plans." And Dan didn't mean that to come out sounding resentful, but somehow it did.

"I didn't tell you because I wasn't going to go." Robin folded his arms over his chest. Dan could feel the anger boring into him even at this distance.

"Why not? They're coming especially to see you."

"They're coming so my dad can go to a rugby match and my mum and sister can go shopping. It's got nothing to do with me. I'm just expected to go along and be the dutiful son. And anyway, I'd rather..."

"You'd rather what?"

Robin was silent for a long moment; then he looked around. There was an old couple sitting on the nearby bench and taking an obvious interest in their argument. A woman walking her dog passed behind Dan. Dan watched Robin's shoulders straighten as he lifted his head high and fixed Dan with his gaze.

"I'd rather spend the time with you," Robin said, his voice low and intense.

Dan shivered. He'd been hoping for Robin to say that, but he didn't know if it was for his sake or for Robin's. It was great that he was coming out of the closet more, and if Dan could help him with that, then it would be a week well spent. But it didn't explain the way his chest felt fit to burst when Robin admitted how much he wanted to be with him.

Dan stared down into the lock. The narrow channel was slowly filling up with water, raising Serendipity to the level of the canal above. It was the famous Bath Deep Lock and the nineteen foot drop was giving him vertigo. Before he could ask himself what he was doing he started off across the lock gate, his hand tightly clasped to the rail. He didn't look down, just kept his eyes fixed on Robin. When he stepped onto solid ground, he realised he was shaking and his heart was ready to pound its way out of his chest.

Robin's arms folded around him, keeping him steady. The weird thing was, Robin seemed to be trembling too. Not shaking like Dan was, but thrumming like a wire under tension.

"You shouldn't have done it," Robin said, his voice softer now as he gently released Dan.

"Hey, I'm okay. I didn't fall in."

"That's not what I meant." Robin's brow was still furrowed, but bemused affection danced in his eyes.

Dan plastered on a smile and aimed for a light tone. "Look at it this way, your folks get to see you, and you can still spend time with me." He thought he did a pretty good job of hiding his agitation.

Robin sighed. "Come on, then. You'd better fill me in on what you said to her."

"Me? Nothing incriminating came out of these innocent lips. Picture of discretion, I was."

Robin gave him an incredulous look.

Dan smirked. "It's not me you should be worried about. What's all this I hear about you scaring the waiters with your tongue stud?" The flush that spread over Robin's cheeks made Dan chuckle. "I hear you gave them an explanation of what it's for as well."

"Um, I may have done. It was a while ago."

"Care to give me a demo?" Dan cocked his hip and tilted his head. It was so much easier to steer clear of this bewildering intensity and stick to the flirting. Fortunately, Robin always responded well.

This time Robin reached out and pulled Dan close, arms tight around his waist. "I thought I'd already shown you this morning."

"I think I'm in need of a refresher."

For the first time, Robin initiated a kiss in public. A slow, deliberate and deep kiss. A kiss that made Dan's knees weak. When Robin finally let him go, Dan had to turn away to hide his confusion. He didn't want to feel like this. It wasn't wise—not when he had to leave the day after tomorrow. He shouldn't have let himself get so involved.

Yet when he looked at Robin—striding over the lock gate with supple grace before turning to grin back at him—he couldn't bring himself to regret one moment of their time together.

Not one single sodding moment of it.

"We're not mooring up here, are we?" Dan shouted, making his way down towards Robin. The engine cut out while he was speaking, his voice ringing out embarrassingly loud across Smiler's car park.

"No, I just needed to stop for a pump out. The tank's getting critical."

Dan frowned, trying to figure out what tank would get filled rather than depleted. Oh yeah, the sewage tank. That would explain the ripe smell last time he flushed the toilet. Gross.

He definitely wasn't going to offer to help with that one. But then again, he really didn't want Robin thinking he was such a dyed-in-the-wool city boy he couldn't cope with getting his hands dirty. God, he really hoped this wouldn't involve getting his hands dirty.

"Want a hand?" Oh bugger, he'd gone and offered and couldn't take it back now.

Robin's mouth twitched. "You think you can handle it? You've gone green."

"I have not."

Robin just raised an eyebrow. "Okay then, I'll sort out the hose and you can press the button. How does that sound?"

"Sounds fine." Buttons he could cope with, no problem.

"We'll have to go find Smiler first."

They strode across the car park. It was populated with an odd assortment of cars, mainly old, a few downright vintage—although that term was a rather generous way to describe the mismatched bangers.

"Do many boaters have cars?"

"A few, why?"

"Just wondered. Seems odd to have a car when you've got to move around. Bit of a liability."

Robin nodded.

"How come you don't have one?"

Robin looked away. "Like you said. A liability. What about you?"

"Huh?"

Robin turned back to him. Dan couldn't read his expression, yet again. "Do you have a car?"

"No. Not a lot of point in Balham. The parking's a nightmare, and it's much quicker to get around on the bike. Besides"—now it was his turn to look away—"I never took my test."

"You can't drive?"

"There's no need to sound horrified. And anyway, I can drive. Dad taught me, but we fell out before I was ready for my test, and then I moved out soon after. Never really needed a car since then. Tris drives me places if I really need a lift."

"Tris. That's your best mate, isn't it?" Robin sniffed and looked away again.

What was this? Surely Robin couldn't be jealous of Tris! But then Dan remembered showing him the portfolio shots he'd taken for Tris. Robin had merely grunted, but then immediately afterwards, he'd set about giving Dan a brand-new set of love bites. He hadn't connected the two things at the time.

"That's right. I know him like the back of my hand."

"Not your boyfriend, though?"

Oho, this really was jealousy. Dan grinned. It was too cute. He had an evil urge to bait Robin and see if it made him all growly and possessive again.

"I wouldn't call him a boyfriend, exactly. I mean, we shag occasionally, a bit like you and Mel, but we don't let it get in the way of being friends."

But Robin didn't take the bait. He just brooded silently and picked up his pace.

Bugger.

Robin stayed surly all through the transaction with Smiler, turning down the offer of a few hours' work in the chandlery point-blank. They walked back to *Serendipity* in an uncomfortable silence. Dan started to wonder how they were going to break it.

It was the pipe that did it, in the end. Of all the unlikely things, a clear plastic sewage pipe. Dan was aghast.

"You mean we've actually got to watch it all being pumped up the tube?"

Finally, Robin smiled. "I thought you said you could handle it. Go on, then, press the button."

"Yeah, I...uh... That's disgusting! Oh my God, it stinks!" He screwed his eyes shut and clapped his hand over his nose and mouth. He could still hear the squelchy sound of the pump, though. That and Robin pissing himself laughing.

"All right, all right, I admit it. I'm not man enough to deal with this. Just shoot me now!"

Robin strode over with that look in his eyes. The one that made Dan's knees go weak. He reached out.

Dan jumped back. "Not until you wash your hands, Mister."

Robin planted a wet kiss on his lips instead. Dan found himself shoved back against the pump-out wall. It was a good thing the air stank of sewage and the pipe was still making that nauseating sound. Even with those passion killers, he was half-hard and dazed by the time Robin pulled back.

"You're man enough for me," Robin said.

Dan's head swam.

Best blame the smell. Any other explanation was plain disturbing.

# Chapter Twenty-Two

"Jesus, do we have to?" Robin asked, glaring at the front doors of the restaurant.

"They're your family." Dan gave his hand a quick squeeze before dropping it. "I think we probably do."

Robin rolled his eyes. "Fine. Don't say I didn't warn you." He pushed open the heavy doors before Dan could make any smart comments.

Popjoy's was situated on the ground floor of an enormous Georgian building. It was the kind of place Robin's mum loved: high ceilings with elaborate wedding-cake mouldings picked out in historic colours, enormous potted palms and a hushed calm that lay over the diners while the waiters dashed around seeing to their every last demand. His family were already seated, and the maitre d' led them over.

"Robin! Darling! You look wonderful." His mum was practically gushing in her effort to lavish praise on him. Most unexpected. "Doesn't he look smart, Edward? So much better than last time we visited."

"Leave him be," Robin's dad said. "You won't be able to nag him into a better wardrobe. You should have realised that by now." Robin flashed him a grateful smile, but he'd already turned his sharp gaze on Dan, holding back and assessing while his wife unleashed her maternal affection on the unsuspecting newcomer.

"And you must be Dan," she simpered. "It's a pleasure to meet you. I can see you've been a good influence on my boy already."

Robin watched him fielding the cheek kisses and fawning attentions and hoped Dan would end up with a great big lipstick mark on his face. It would serve him right, forcing Robin into going shopping and insisting on buying a brand-new outfit. He'd felt humiliated accepting the gift, but even Robin had had to agree that he really didn't own any clothes suitable for Popjoy's, and he'd conveniently forgotten to take out his wallet. Not that there was anything much left in it, but Dan didn't need to know that.

It wasn't a bad outfit. He'd insisted on his usual style of combat trousers, but these were from Gap rather than the army surplus store. They probably wouldn't last as long, but at least he'd get some use out of them over the winter. Dan had picked out a black collarless shirt for him, which he had to admit looked good, but he felt odd. It was like wearing some kind of disguise or costume—the sort of thing he'd wear to a wedding or funeral. Or perhaps a christening, which was the most likely celebration to be coming up soon. Could you wear black to a christening? No doubt his mum would have something to say on the matter. He glanced at her tastefully coordinated ensemble of neutral-coloured clothing that looked deceptively simple but, knowing her, cost a small fortune. She'd always tried to bully him into polo shirts and chinos like his father wore, which was why he took such pleasure in thwarting her by wearing scruffy combat gear.

Robin bent down to kiss his sister, who was too big now to get up easily, or so she said. It was a shock to see her like that—so large and round, her cheeks glowing and her eyes bright.

"How's my nephew getting along in there?" he asked.

"Oh just fine. We think Patrick junior's going to be a rugby player when he's older. He already seems determined to throw his weight around as much as possible." Miranda smiled up at Robin, and for the first time he could remember since they were kids, it seemed genuine. "You're looking well, little brother. Your friend Dan here must be a good influence after all. So, are you and he...?"

Thankfully she didn't seem able to finish the sentence, because Robin didn't have a clue how to answer. To be honest, he wasn't sure he could say whether he and Dan were anything more than fuck-buddies, and he didn't think that term would go down too well.

"He's very dashing," Miranda continued. "Quite a catch, I should say." She winked at Robin, who hid his confusion by fixing his eyes on the dashing Mr. Taylor. Even though Robin didn't have the fashion consciousness to fully appreciate the cut of Dan's new suit, he could certainly enjoy the way the cream wool hung on his slim body. The salesman had called the colour ecru, and it looked drab on the hanger, but when Dan tried it on, it had made his skin and hair radiant. Yeah, he could probably get into the idea of having a boyfriend who looked that good in smart gear. But of course, Dan wasn't his boyfriend, so thinking like that was a pointless waste of time.

They all sat down at the round table, Robin between Dan and Miranda, with his mum on the other side of Dan. He eyed the white linen tablecloth and array of eating implements with trepidation. God, he hoped Dan knew which forks to use for which course. Trust Mum to book them into somewhere this stuffy and staid. The bloody waiters were in smarter clothing than he was, for Christ's sake.

The tiny, cursive script on the leather-bound menu danced in front of Robin's eyes. He scowled. How the hell was he meant to read that? He'd have to order steak and chips. Every restaurant seemed to be able to cope with that one, although it did get dull, always having the same thing.

But then Dan squeezed his thigh, gently kneading the flesh as he carried on his conversation with Robin's mum, and the pressure was reassuring. It wasn't until he felt his shoulders ease that he realised just how tense he'd been.

"What are you going for, Robin?" Dan asked. "I can't decide between the salmon fettuccine, the lamb burger with roast potatoes, or the mixed grill."

Dan must have ended up mulling over almost every item on the menu before Robin finally realised what was going on. He selected a lemon sole with thick-cut chips and roasted baby vegetables, giving Dan a grateful smile. It meant a lot to be helped out in an unobtrusive way. No one else had ever managed to do that without him ending up feeling patronised.

The first couple of courses went well. Surprisingly well, with Dan keeping his mum distracted with a constant stream of chatter. Dan seemed far more interested in the Hamilton family history than Robin himself was, and it pleased her no end. Even his dad smiled a little, and when Dan asked him about the rugby match, they had a whole conversation over Rosemary's head.

"I didn't know you liked rugby," Robin said when there was a lull.

"Yep, certainly do. I could pretend it was purely for the love of the game, but really, have you seen some of those players?"

"Not my type," Robin mumbled, staring down at his half-eaten fish. Did Dan really have to flame quite so brightly in front of his dad? If there had been any doubt about Dan's sexuality in their minds, there certainly wouldn't be any longer. Now they'd all be wondering what was going on between the two of them.

Not that his dad seemed bothered. "I suppose you like that Gareth Thomas, then, do you? Must say I was a bit surprised when he came out, but just goes to show you never can tell."

His mum butted in. "That's right, darling. Like with our Robin here—you never would have thought it to see him as a teenager. He was always such a lad. Running around, getting into trouble, swearing and drinking. You should have seen him then, Dan. A right little tearaway, he was. Not even a trace of a limp wrist."

Robin glared at her. Was his mum determined to wreck whatever this thing was he had going with Dan?

This thing that would be over tomorrow when Dan went back to London. Back to his other fuckbuddy, Tris. Bile rose in his throat at the thought.

"Excuse me," he said, almost knocking over his chair in his haste to get away.

He made for the gents.

The stomach acid burnt his throat, but the food stubbornly refused to make a reappearance. He stared into the empty toilet bowl. Just dessert to get through now.

Dessert was always a disaster with the Hamilton family. Too much wine consumed for his mum to keep it civil. Too much for Robin to resist taking the bait. Dan would want to run away as fast as he could, and Robin wouldn't blame him.

His heart dragged as he made his slow way back to the table.

Dan watched Robin stalk back through the tables with a face like he'd been sucking on one of those scented urinal cubes. When Robin sat down again, Dan tried to take his hand under the table, but he pulled away and refused to make eye contact. Dan wasn't able to draw anything more than a monosyllabic response from him, eventually giving up and concentrating on talking to Rosemary instead. It was fascinating to observe just how much Robin had taken after his parents, no matter how far he'd tried to remove himself. While Robin had Rosemary's dark colouring and eyes, it was obvious he favoured his father in conversational skills and facial expressions. By contrast, Rosemary was all smiles and flirtatious, breathless confidences.

She became even more voluble over the dessert course, her cheeks glowing as she leant towards him.

"So, Dan, darling, tell me, do you have a boyfriend back in London?"

"No, nobody special. I've searched London far and wide but not had any joy."

"You don't want to go looking there. Much better men to be found in the countryside. I met Edward on a walk in the Cotswolds, didn't I, darling?" Edward gave a noncommittal grunt, but Rosemary didn't seem in the least bit bothered. Maybe he could learn something from her about how to deal with Robin's moods. "So, how long have you known my Robin?"

"Only for the past week, but I feel like it's been much longer."

"Oh, I see. Just a week." Did she really sound disappointed, or was that just his imagination? "But I expect you'll be seeing more of each other in the future."

Dan gazed at Robin, getting a blank stare in response. How was he meant to know how to respond if the guy didn't give him any clues?

"If that's what Robin wants."

"Well, Robin? Are you going to carry on seeing Dan? I think you should. He's a very nice young man, and he's worked wonders on you in a short time already. He might be able to help you get your life back on track."

Robin's face twisted as Rosemary spoke. Funny how hurt that made Dan feel. Not that they'd been planning to see any more of each other after this week, but the thought that Robin was disgusted by the idea was more painful than Dan would ever have expected.

But when Robin started speaking in a low, dangerous voice, it wasn't about Dan at all.

"How can you say that when you treated Jamie like he was shit? I loved him, I really loved him, and you wouldn't even have him in your house. You kicked him out, remember?" Robin was getting louder and people at the nearby tables turned to look. "Now you want me to shack up with a guy I've only just met? A guy who's the biggest slut in the whole of London? Well, excuse me if I don't go taking your advice on men."

Robin knocked his chair back as he stood, then whirled around and stomped out of the restaurant.

Fuck. What was he supposed to do now?

Dan looked around at the faces of Robin's family. Rosemary's mouth hung open, Edward studied his tiramisu with a frown, and Miranda stroked her bump and made soothing baby talk. Useless, all of them.

Dan leapt up and made after Robin.

He caught up with him down a crowded pedestrianised shopping street.

"Robin, wait!"

Robin halted and stood with his head hanging. Dan fought his way past a group of tourists laden with cameras and shopping bags and eventually fetched up next to him. Robin met his eyes for only a brief moment, but long enough for Dan to see the hurt lurking there.

"I'm sorry. Shouldn't have said that. About you, I mean."

Dan shrugged. "Nothing I haven't heard before, babe, and it's not that much of an exaggeration, although I reckon Tris could give me a run for my money."

Robin turned his face away again, and Dan stepped closer, taking hold of both his arms.

"How about we go back in there, you smooth things over with your folks, and then we can both head back to the boat and make up properly?"

Robin gave a small smile. "How about we skip straight to the last bit?"

"She's your mum. She obviously loves you like crazy or she wouldn't want to get so involved. How about you give her a break just this once?"

"You're only saying that because she likes you."

"Yeah, okay, I'm a sucker for flattery. Now come on. A little apology won't hurt you. I'll make it worth your while later, all right?"

Robin closed his eyes for a moment, then nodded and opened them. He turned back towards the restaurant. "Come on, then, the sooner we get this over with, the sooner you can make good on that promise."

Dan followed in his wake.

Family.

He was getting way out of his depth here.

# Chapter Twenty-Three

Dan woke to the sound of raindrops pattering against the steel roof above. He was awake earlier than Robin for a change. There was none of his usual grogginess while the world swam back into focus. No, today the situation was crystal clear from the moment he opened his eyes.

It was time to leave. The hire boat was due back later today. He needed to get back to London, write up the assignment and edit his shots. He wanted to do this—he wanted to seize the opportunity and further his career. The only problem was, he didn't want to go.

It would be stupid to pretend he didn't know why. There was the weight of Robin's arm thrown across his chest that felt so right. There was the warmth of Robin's body, fitting against his own so perfectly. And most of all, there was that urge he had to kiss him awake so that they could fuck again and again. Yeah, he had it bad, all right. But he'd been infatuated with guys before and it had never lasted long, so why should this be any different?

Was it because he knew he'd be just as happy to wake Robin up, skip the sex and go straight to the cuddling and confidences? Okay, maybe not just as happy, but this wasn't all about sex. Not anymore. The previous night had made him realise that. After fucking him long, slow and thoroughly, Robin had lapsed into a brooding silence, and Dan had lain awake for an age after Robin's breathing had settled into the rhythm of sleep. He'd berated himself for not coaxing words out of Robin; he hadn't wanted to promise what he couldn't give, but he felt like he owed Robin something.

No, scratch that. He didn't owe Robin anything, but he wanted to prove to both of them that he was more than just an easy lay. A cheap slut. Thing was, he wasn't sure he knew how to be anything else. He wasn't good enough for Robin, and he knew it, even if he'd never treat him as shittily as Jamie had.

But maybe they could try and salvage something out of this week—something more than just a memory and a crazy longing for what could have been if he'd let himself go.

Trouble was, Dan was bloody well terrified.

He was still paralysed by indecision when Robin's breathing changed.

"Hey, morning, sleepyhead. I was hoping you'd wake up soon." Dan batted his eyelashes and wriggled, rubbing his hip against Robin's ever-present morning wood.

He quailed under the intensity of Robin's gaze: those eyes were like two dark pits, swallowing up the early morning glow filtering through the skylight.

"You're leaving today." Robin's voice sounded rough. He must have had too much to smoke last night.

"I have to."

Robin closed his eyes and nodded. Dan watched the way his brow furrowed and reached out to smooth it. Robin caught his wrist, rubbing lips and cheeks against his palm, and for some stupid reason the rasp of stubble against his skin made him want to cry. He fought back savagely, assaulting Robin with his lips and tongue so that he wouldn't break down. His lust rose thick and fast, blotting out everything else, and he bit down on Robin's neck before scrambling down to latch onto his cock.

Dan scraped his teeth along the heavy length. Robin hissed, grabbing handfuls of his hair. Dan's scalp burned as Robin yanked his head back and glared at him.

"Don't you ever hurt me again, slut!"

Dan blinked, wanting to make a sharp retort about how he'd put up with Robin biting and scratching him all week, but he knew even as he started to speak that he'd loved every minute of it. "Well then you shoul—"

Robin's fingers pushed into his mouth, effectively silencing him. "Listen to me carefully. I'm going to fuck your mouth, and if you dare use your teeth on me again, there'll be trouble, all right?"

The steel in Robin's voice made Dan shiver, but not in an altogether bad way. Yes, there was fear, but not the big, life-changing fear he'd been contemplating before Robin woke. No, this was a small fear, a delicious frisson. Robin was just playing with him, wasn't he? But the darkness in Robin's eyes made him doubt.

Robin must have sensed his confusion, and he loosened his hold on Dan's hair. "Is this okay?" he asked in a hoarse whisper.

"Yeah." Dan nodded and was about to say more when Robin pushed into his mouth.

He relaxed his jaw, opened his throat and let Robin fuck him. This wasn't something he normally enjoyed all that much. He'd always thought guys who took over a blowjob like this to be boorish. But when it was Robin, it was somehow different. The sensation of his hair being pulled and Robin's cockhead bumping against the back of his throat set his whole body on fire, his own dick throbbing with anticipation. He snatched his breaths quickly between strokes, the lack of oxygen making him dizzy.

"Look at me," Robin commanded.

Dan's eyes sprang open. Robin was staring at him in a way that made him even more confused. His eyes shone with a wild mixture of jumbled-up desire and sorrow and rage and...tenderness.

"Touch yourself, please."

There was nothing Dan wanted to do more, and he wondered why he hadn't already. But when his damp palm made contact with his burning cock, all thoughts evaporated. There was only this here, this now, with Robin pounding into him and his own hand pumping himself up and down. This cocoon of hot, sweaty bodies and the constant drumming of rain and rasping of breath.

Robin's rhythm stuttered, and Dan stared into his eyes, losing himself in their depths. Their gazes remained locked, even as Robin convulsed, cursed and rammed into Dan's sore throat. Dan felt Robin's cock pulsing in his mouth and swallowed hard, grateful for the way the jerks dragged the flavour across his tongue. And still Robin's gaze bored into his own, and he could feel the heat of it deep inside him.

The sensation reverberated through him, thrilling down every nerve ending and shaking his fragile control apart. Dan thrust hard into his hand, barely aware of the tightening of his balls as the world contracted to that glimmer in Robin's eyes, that spark that he held on to even as the orgasm swept through his body. A fuzzy whiteness invaded the edges of his vision, but Robin's eyes were the centre of the storm, holding him there while the world burst into fragments.

He didn't remember clambering up the bed and curling back into Robin's body, but he must have done. Breath puffed hot against his face, arms gripping him tight as their heaving slowly subsided. Dan opened his eyes to find Robin gazing at him. It was too much to bear, so he closed them again.

"I should take a shower, then head back to my boat. Got to get it back to the hire centre by midday."

"Stay. Please. I don't want you to go." Robin's voice rasped, as if the words hurt on their way out.

"I don't know. It's getting on a bit. I should check..." But when he looked up and saw the naked fear and longing in Robin's face, he knew that wasn't what was meant. "Shit. I...I can't. I'm sorry. My whole life is in London." He watched Robin roll onto his back, close his eyes and bite his lip. Why did Robin have to ask so much of him? "I'll come back soon. I'll visit. Next weekend. No! Bugger, not next weekend, I'm busy. The one after. But I will, I promise. I want to see you again. I can get the train up every couple of weeks and spend some time with you."

Dan watched Robin's face closely for clues. He had no experience with this, of being the one trying to reassure the other that they cared. He felt clumsy and inadequate. The silence stretched out between them, so taut it felt as if the air could snap at the pressure of a single word.

"Is that how you think this is going to work?" Robin said, his voice heavy. "I hang around here waiting for you to show up every now and again?"

Dan blinked. "That's not what I meant. You can come and visit me, too. You could bring your boat closer. There's places you can moor up in London. There are marinas."

"I'm not coming to live in London, all right? I'm not staying cooped up in some bloody marina surrounded by buildings and noise. I couldn't stand it."

"Okay, okay. Sorry I spoke. Well, you'll just have to wait for me to visit you, then."

Robin stared up at the skylight, grimacing. "I've got to keep moving every two weeks. I'm not always going to be moored up near a train station."

"Then I'll buy a fucking car!" Dan paused, as surprised at his outburst as Robin seemed to be.

"You can't drive." Robin was looking at him again now, which was an improvement, although Dan still couldn't read his expression.

"I'll learn to drive. I'll pass my test. I can do it, all right?" Dan sighed deeply, wondering if that was scepticism or hostility in Robin's eyes. "Look, if you don't want to see me again, then just tell me now."

"It's not that. It's... Fuck!" Robin slammed his fist into the wall.

Dan flinched.

He'd had enough of this. He shuffled to the end of the bed and looked about for his clothes. He was pulling on his thong when he heard Robin's voice, low and defeated.

"I just can't bear the idea of you fucking around with other guys while I'm left behind. I can't do that again."

Jesus, it would have to be that, wouldn't it? Dan slumped on the end of the bed, his head in his hands. "You want me to be monogamous, is that it? Christ, you don't ask much, do you?" Dan tried to laugh, but it came out jagged and bitter, so he stopped and concentrated on breathing deeply.

"I'm not asking that. I'm just saying, the idea of you and this Tristan bloke... I don't think I can handle it." Robin's voice was flat, as if all the fight had leached out of him. The sound of it wound Dan up further.

"Well, it bloody well sounds like an ultimatum to me. Sounds like you're saying if I can't stay faithful, then you don't want anything to do with me. Do you even realise what you're asking, Robin? I've never done a relationship before. I don't know if I've got it in me." Robin's silence was unnerving. Dan turned to look at him. The sight of him lying with his eyes screwed shut and his lips clamped tight hurt him more than he could have imagined. "Shit. Look, does it have to be this complicated? Can't we just be friends? Can't we chat on the phone and meet up occasionally for mind-blowing sex? Or just to watch a DVD and chat some more, if that's what you prefer?"

"You'd come all this way just to watch a DVD?" Robin sounded incredulous. Did he really think Dan was only after one thing?

"I'd come all this way to see you."

"You would?"

There was a softening of Robin's expression, and Dan's heart did a stupid bloody somersault. "Yeah, believe it or not, I do like you, even if you are a moody git. I wouldn't have spent the whole week with you if it was just about the sex, not that it hasn't been the best I've ever had."

"Now I know you're lying."

But there was something in Robin's expression that led Dan to believe he just wanted convincing. "No lie." He looked down at the marks Robin had left all over his chest and thighs. He gestured at a particularly livid love bite. "I'm not usually into this kind of thing. Never been turned on by it, but it's different with you. You're different. I dunno." He sighed, flopping down on the bed again and shivering now that the heat of his anger had subsided. "I just want to spend some more time with you, figuring it all out. If it's gotta be over the phone, I'll cope, but I'd rather see you in person. What do you say?" He reached out for Robin, absurdly grateful to feel Robin's arms snaking around him in return.

When Robin's voice came, it was a whisper. "What about Tristan?"

"What about him? He's just a friend."

"Yeah, but you fuck each other."

"Not very often. Not for ages. We don't really do it for each other, you know? Better as friends than lovers. I'll stop it altogether if it bothers you." And that really wouldn't be a hardship. He and Tris were only ever a last resort for each other, anyway. "Now, are you going to let me come and see you again? If I'm not going to be doing anyone else and you won't let me visit, I'm gonna end up with a nasty case of blue balls."

Robin smiled at last. Only a small one, barely curving his lips, but it was there. "Okay, you can call me. Just...give me some time to think about you visiting."

It wasn't the answer Dan wanted, but with the heat of Robin's body against his own and the scent of him filling his nostrils, it was hard to concentrate. He made a last-ditch effort, as Robin's cock was growing hard again and he desperately wanted to feel it inside him one last time before leaving.

"I'll give you time, so long as the answer's yes." And then he kissed Robin before he had a chance to respond, trying his hardest to give him something to remember him by.

Something that was more than just bodies moving together. Something to tide them over until they could do this again.


"I'll call you when I get back home. Let you know I didn't sink the boat," Dan said.

Robin tried to smile, but his mouth refused to cooperate. He'd walked Dan back to his boat, then helped out by checking over the weed trap and the engine while Dan tidied inside. It didn't take Dan long—probably because he'd spent nearly all of his time on *Serendipity.*

And now they were here, standing on the deck while the engine idled. Robin wanted to grab Dan and drag him back to his boat. He wanted to throw his arms around him and sob. He wanted to rage at the world for tearing them apart so soon. And so he stood there, paralysed, gazing at the still water. It had stopped raining sometime during their hurried breakfast, leaving the deck slippery.

"You should wear your life jacket." It wasn't what he'd meant to say, but he didn't want Dan taking any unnecessary risks.

"I don't think it does me any favours with this outfit, but if it makes you happy." Dan fastened it up and pulled a face. "God, you'd think they could redesign these things to be a bit more flattering. I look ridiculous."

"You look safe." *And you look beautiful, and that look you get in your eyes when you smile makes me want to hold you tight and never let go.* But he couldn't say any of that, so he attempted a smile and then tried to ignore the prickling in his eyes when Dan hugged him tight.

"Look after yourself, babe. I'll miss you."

"Yeah." It was the only word he could trust himself to say, and it came out harsh and abrupt.

Dan let him go at last, and then Robin turned, stepping onto the bank and untying the mooring lines. He coiled up the last rope down at the stern and looked up to find a reflection of his own feelings written on Dan's face.

*This isn't fair,* he wanted to say. *Don't go. Not yet. I don't want to lose you to the city.*

And then a dog barked, and the moment was broken. Dan gave a crooked smile. "I'd better be off, then. Thanks for everything. I mean that."

Robin nodded. There was a lump in his throat he didn't think he could speak past. And then Dan walked to the edge of the deck, pressed a last, fleeting kiss to his lips and loosened Robin's hold on the rail with an apologetic smile.

"See you soon," Dan said, sounding confident at the prospect.

Robin nodded.

The *Faerie Queen* and the lone figure at the stern blurred hopelessly by the time they reached the stone bridge. Robin waved anyway, just in case Dan looked back one last time before turning the corner. If he did, Robin couldn't tell.

# Chapter Twenty-Four

Robin stared at the ringing phone. If he didn't pick it up soon, it would go through to voicemail and he could listen later. Or not, if that was what he decided.

But then he really wanted to hear Dan's voice again, and so he grabbed it and answered without even checking the display.

"I'm here," Robin said, his heart racing.

"Oh, darling, that's such a relief!"

When he heard his mother's tones, Robin's cheeks flushed. "Listen, Mum, I'm really sorry about yester—"

"Don't worry about that now. It's Miranda. She's gone into labour early. They're not saying anything to us, but I think she might lose the baby. Little Patrick might be...might be... Oh Christ!"

Surely that wasn't a sob? But the choked-back sounds continued, and they couldn't be anything else.

"Hey, Mum, don't cry. They'll be doing everything they can for him. Lots of babies get born this early. Dan was six weeks premature, and it hasn't done him any harm." Okay, Robin was no expert, but his words seemed to do the trick as she sniffed and the sobs subsided. "Who's there with you?"

"Your father's here, but he'll have to go soon as he's in theatre first thing tomorrow and needs his sleep. Patrick's on his way back from Aberdeen, but it's going to take a few hours."

Shit, she was going to be left alone there, in this kind of a state. A memory rose, unbidden, of her holding him tight in the days after Jamie's death. He'd barely been aware of it at the time, and once he'd recovered from the worst, she'd pulled back from being too demonstrative, resuming her usual habits of lecturing him about his life. But she'd been there for him when he'd needed her most.

"Mum, you wait there. I'm on my way."

"You're coming here? How are you getting here? The trains are terrible on a Sunday."

That was the challenge. He thought for a moment, remembering the emptiness of his wallet and the distance to Cheltenham. "I'll have to get a taxi." He squashed down his pride. "Mum? I'm completely skint. Would you be able to meet me outside the hospital and pay the driver?"

"Yes, yes, of course. I'm waiting in the maternity-unit foyer. There's a drop-off point right outside the doors."

After reassuring her a few more times, Robin hung up and threw some clothes and a wash bag in a rucksack. He tucked his mobile into his pocket and took one last look around the boat, feeling sure that there was something he'd forgotten.

His gaze fell on the bundle of fur curled up on the sofa.

"Sorry, Morris. Looks like you'll be staying with Auntie Mel for a few days."

Robin called Mel to make the arrangements while he took one last look over *Serendipity*. He hated to leave her at this time of year when burst pipes were a very real threat, but there was nothing else to be done. He just had to hope that the temperature wouldn't drop too low and that BW would cut him some slack if he went over his time in this spot. Family came first, after all.

The sense of having forgotten something important continued to niggle as he dropped Morris off with Mel.

Robin was halfway to Cheltenham before he heard his phone give the low-battery warning pips, and remembered what it was he'd left behind. His charger.

And then his phone rang again, and he used up his last bit of power reassuring his mum that he was on his way. He stared at the blank screen, knowing what Dan would think when he didn't answer.

"Sorry, Dan," he whispered.

"Fuck you, Robin Hamilton!"

Dan flung his phone across the room. Last night he'd put Robin's unavailability down to him having drunk himself into oblivion, but there was no excuse for him not to have responded to Dan's messages by now. Well, he was buggered if he was going to leave another one. He wasn't going to beg for Robin to call, no matter how much he wanted him to.

He took some deep breaths to calm down. It didn't get rid of the turmoil in his guts, but at least his hands had stopped shaking.

The doorbell sounded. It was Tris. Dan buzzed him in, glad for the distraction.

"Well, hello, sailor. How the devil are you?" Tris spun Dan around and lavished kisses on his cheeks. The man was a whirlwind of floppy-haired, razor-cheekboned flamboyance. Only today, dressed entirely in black rather than his usual tastefully coordinated colours.

"What happened to your clothes? You look like someone died."

"Only the old me, darling. Meet Tristan, mark two. Now available in any flavour you want, except vanilla." Tris raised an eyebrow, cocked his hip and pouted.

Jesus. Dan couldn't help smiling.

"That's better. Now what's the long face all about? Don't tell me you're missing your studly boater already? Well I've got something to take your mind off him. Remember Brett? The guy with the teeth and the huge tits you were dancing with last time we hit Heaven?"

Dan shook his head, already dazed and confused. Tristan barely paused.

"Oh, you'll remember when you see him. You really got his hopes up, then ditched him for that hairy Greek god. What was his name? Micky?"

"Mikolas." Dan remembered him, all right. Hung like a donkey, had a marathon runner's stamina and barely spoke a word of English. It had been a great night. He still couldn't quite picture Brett but had a vague impression of oiled muscles, gleaming teeth and bleached hair. Or was that gleaming muscles, bleached teeth and oiled hair?

"Well, Brett's been asking after you. Seems he's rather besotted, God knows why—I did try to warn him about what a sleazy old tart you are. Anyway, it's his birthday, and he specifically asked—no, make that begged—to make sure I bring you. So go get your glad rags on and we're off."

"I don't really feel like a party tonight."

Tris stared like Dan had just announced he was going to get married and have kids.

"Of course you do. It's just the ticket if you're feeling glum. Now come on. I want to see you in your sexiest jeans and a shirt Brett's going to want to rip off with his teeth. You'll get to meet Alex too, and if you're extra-specially nice to me, I might share him with you. Come on, chop, chop!"

Tris bounced into Dan's bedroom, and he followed with a sigh. There wouldn't be any peace unless he went along with this. And if the only way to get Robin Hamilton out of his mind was to let some other guy fuck him senseless, then so be it.

By the time they reached the Tube station, he'd almost convinced himself he was all right. Buoyed up by Tris's constant stream of chatter, he felt almost normal. It was only when he saw his reflection in the train window that he realised there was a vertical crease between his eyebrows and his right hand was still plucking at the pocket containing his phone.

"It's okay, you can put your hand in there to touch him. It's good for prem babies to get as much skin-to-skin contact as possible." The ICU nurse smiled at Robin as she checked the monitoring equipment. It was just him keeping vigil in here at the moment, what with Miranda in the ward, his mum visiting her, his dad working and his brother-in-law catching some much-needed sleep. When all the others had been around, Robin hadn't dared touch the tiny baby in the incubator. It was enough just to watch him, marvelling at the skinny limbs and tiny fingers. There wasn't much of him visible, as he was bundled up in so many layers of clothing, but the squashed-up face and fragile hands were astonishing by themselves.

"Go on with you. He'll like it. Might help settle him down a bit."

Robin looked doubtfully at the ground-in grime in the creases of his knuckles.

"Are you sure my hands are clean enough?"

The nurse gave him a sharp look. "Did you wash your hands and use the sanitiser when you came in? Well then, they're clean enough. Go on now, you don't need to fret."

Patrick Junior was wriggling around all over the place. Robin supposed the weight of his hand might be enough to keep him still for a moment. With trepidation, he pushed his hand through the hole at the side of the incubator.

His nephew was so delicate. So small. Robin could feel the heartbeat fluttering under his hand. The enormity of the task facing Miranda and Pat hit him for the first time. They had to keep this tiny, helpless creature safe and alive and bring him up to be a functioning member of society. He didn't envy them. No, not one bit. He had enough in his life trying to keep himself sane and healthy, let alone trying to look after someone else.

But then Patrick opened his mouth, made a plaintive mewling sound, and Robin was captivated.

When his mum came back in, Robin was grinning like a madman, Patrick's tiny fingers grasping one of his. He looked up to find an expression on her face that he didn't remember ever seeing directed at him before.

"You're going to be a wonderful uncle," she said.

Robin stared at her, trying to work out how even though she wasn't groomed and made-up like usual, his mum radiated beauty. He realised it was love, love shining out for baby Patrick but also for himself. He smiled back, a deep smile that welled up within him, warming him through.

"You'll make a fantastic grandma."

"Thank you, darling. I'll try my best. He's not going to want for anything, this little one. I'll spoil him rotten."

They both watched Patrick squirm some more, batting ineffectually at the feeding tube coming out of his nose. Robin stroked Patrick's tummy, and that seemed to help him settle down again.

"Do you think you'll ever want one yourself? You'd make such a lovely father, you know."

Robin shook his head. "I don't think I could cope with what Pat's going through right now." His brother-in-law had been utterly haggard when he left the ward earlier on. He'd seemed lost without Miranda by his side, and for the first time, Robin had realised how much the career-driven lawyer relied on his wife.

He'd expected protests from his mother, but when he looked up, she was eyeing him in a strange way, like she was really seeing him for the first time. It made him uncomfortable, so he looked down at the sleeping baby again.

"You're stronger than you think, darling, but maybe you're right. It's not for everyone. But there's nothing to stop gay couples from adopting these days."

"Mum! I'm not..." But he wasn't sure how he wanted to finish that sentence. "I'm bi, not gay."

Rosemary huffed, and Robin saw a little of her usual combativeness return. "Look, darling, you say that, but I've never met any of your girlfriends, and the only times I've ever seen you in love, it's been with men. I'm not bothered by that anymore, so I don't see why you need to deny it."

"I'm not denying it. I just..."

She'd said "times" he'd been in love. The plural. His stomach went into free fall.

"I'm not in love with Dan. I barely know him."

"It didn't look that way to me, darling. Now why don't you go and phone him and let him know everything's okay? He must be worried sick about you."

"My phone's dead."

"Robin, you should have said! We'd have sorted you out a charger if we'd known."

Robin didn't want to point out that everyone had been so wrapped up in Miranda and the baby's plight there would have been no chance of anyone popping out to buy him a charger.

"Honestly, darling, you need someone to look after you, you really do. Get yourself back home and give Dan a call so he'll know you haven't dropped off the face of the planet. You don't want to let that one go, sweetheart. He's a great catch." She ransacked her handbag, and Robin sighed. Looked like she was back to her usual ways, then.

"How come you don't mind Dan? I thought you hated the idea of me having a boyfriend."

"I can tell Dan's a decently raised young man. He'll treat you well."

"But..." She knew so little about Dan. "He's working class, you know. No money in the family. No connections."

She gave him a look tinged with regret. "You don't really believe that's going to make a difference to me, do you? There are more important things in life than money and connections, darling, as you so vividly illustrate." She offered him a wedge of banknotes. "Here you go. Plenty to get you back home and tide you over for a while. Maybe you can get on the train to London and pay Dan a visit. And let him know the invitation for Christmas still stands, despite your little outburst."

Robin flushed at the memory but wasn't in the mood for arguing about it. Not with his nephew in the room. He gave Patrick's slender body one last, gentle stroke before taking the notes. He peeled off enough to cover the train journey back, an extra forty for food and phone credit, then handed the rest back. She raised her eyebrows but made no comment.

"I'll pay you back, Mum. I promise."

"Oh, sweetheart, you know you don't need to." She now had her hand in the incubator and was making soppy faces at baby Patrick even as she spoke.

"I do need to." More to the point, he needed to make his own way so that Dan didn't end up having to buy things for him either. Shame rose hot in his guts when he thought of how he'd had to accept charity from Dan. He'd pay him back for the bed sheets and smart clothes. There was no way they could have any sort of relationship if Dan ended up treating him all the time. Robin wasn't after a sugar daddy. The thought made his skin crawl.

On his train journey back to Bath, Robin pondered the work available to him. Manual labour hadn't been hard to find in London, but there wasn't the same industry in Bath. Shops and restaurants usually wanted GCSEs, not to mention employees who could read and write confidently. But perhaps... Smiler was always talking about needing more help with his chandlery. Robin didn't relish the idea of working for such a moody, unpredictable git, but he could handle him, couldn't he? *Takes one to know one*, he thought, giving a wry smile.

Of course, it was going to be bloody difficult to work if he kept having to move on every fortnight, but maybe he could manage it for a few months if he stopped for a fortnight at every neighbourhood into Bath and then back out again. So long as he didn't mind a long ride into work at some points. And what's more, it would keep him near enough to Bath railway station for Dan's visits.

He grinned, imagining the expression on Dan's face when he told him the news. He couldn't wait to get back and get his phone charged again. The train just couldn't get there fast enough.

# Chapter Twenty-Five

Dan stared up at the cold, white ceiling. Just looking at it made him shiver. It was miles away. He wanted something close and wood-panelled, with the warmth of Robin's body next to his own.

He should get out of bed and write. He knew he should. So why did his limbs feel like lead? It wasn't like he'd had much to drink the previous night. Okay, it was a pint or two more than he'd usually have, but he'd needed it to unwind enough to chat and flirt. Brett had been an incredibly attentive host, and he wasn't a bad-looking guy either—even if his porcelain veneers shone so brightly Dan had found himself wishing he'd brought his shades.

As he'd turned up empty-handed, it seemed only polite to offer the birthday boy a blowjob, but Dan's heart hadn't been in it. Even his dick had been only mildly interested, and he couldn't help but compare it to the last time he'd had Robin in his mouth. With Robin he'd been on fire, aching and throbbing, relishing the sensation of Robin's pierced cock fucking his mouth. With Brett, it was perfunctory at best; a predictable sequence of sucking and licking that he hoped would bring the bloke off as quickly as possible. The man's moans seemed as phony as his teeth, and Dan had gently declined his offer to return the favour. Fortunately, the rapping on the bathroom door had provided the perfect excuse, and Dan had left the party early, pleading a headache. Tris had given Dan a funny look on his way out but was too entwined with his leather daddy to chase after him. Just looking at the two of them, so bloody happy together, had made him want to vomit.

Eventually he hauled himself out of bed and headed for the shower. He was covered in suds when he heard the foghorn blast coming from his phone. He pictured it, perched on the living room table.

"Bollocks!"

Dan scrambled out of the shower, slipping on the tiles but grabbing hold of the sink in time to stop himself going arse over tit. He had three more blasts before it would go through to voicemail. He got there before the second.

"Robin!" He wanted to say more, but his heart was pounding from the adrenaline rush, and he needed to sit down. Sod it, he'd clean the soap suds off the sofa later.

"Dan, sorry, I...I got your messages."

"Really." He'd only left three of them. Dan tried to remember what he'd said in the last one, but all he could recall was hanging up feeling so pissed off he wanted to wipe Robin's number from the phone's memory. He hadn't, though. Couldn't bring himself to do it.

"Yeah, I just got them. I've been away for the last couple of days and forgot to take my phone charger. Sorry."

"Oh, right. I see." Yep, that was just like what he knew of Robin. Despite his tidy and organised home, Robin was hopeless at remembering stuff like that. Kept forgetting his wallet, leaving Dan to pick up the tab. He wanted to be annoyed, but the sound of Robin's voice was too reassuring. The warmth of it melted away the lump of anger that'd been weighing him down for the last couple of days. "Where have you been?"

"Cheltenham. Miranda had the baby six weeks early. He's fine, they're both fine now, but Mum was really worried for a while."

Dan breathed a deep sigh of relief. So that's why Robin had been unavailable! It wasn't until he felt himself buoyed up on a wave of joy that he realised just how upset he'd been. Anxious, even.

"Hey, that's fantastic! So you're an uncle now. And your mum's a grandma. I bet she's loving that." Dan tried to picture the formidable Rosemary cooing over a baby. It was a challenge, but he bet she would, if his own mum's daft behaviour over her grandkids was anything to go by.

"Yeah, she is." Dan could hear the smile in Robin's voice and had a sharp longing to see it too. Robin looked his age when he smiled, all the severity wiped away in a breathtaking transformation.

Robin was still talking, unusually garrulous. "She's decided she's going to let me off having any myself now."

"Well, that's a mercy. It's much better to be the gay uncle. Trust me."

"She says we can always adopt when we're ready."

"What? But...what?" Dan had the sense that the conversation was rapidly spinning out of his control. Maybe it was being wet, soapy and naked that had him at a disadvantage, even if Robin couldn't see him.

Robin burst out laughing. "That's pretty much what I said too. She likes you, you know. Still wants you to come over for Christmas. If you're interested."

Dan heard the hesitation in the last three words. Did Robin want him to?

"What, and give up a houseful of nieces and nephews all trying to leap on me at once? Not to mention all the comments from Mum about how I should find someone nice to settle down with. Or my brothers-in-law thinking if they pour enough beer down my throat I'm going to somehow catch heterosexuality just by watching *Top Gear* with them."

Robin chuckled. "It's not that much better with my parents, trust me. Mum loves that settling-down speech, but she might let me off it if you're there."

"Would you like that?" Dan wished he could see Robin's eyes. He'd be able to read the answer there without even having to ask.

Robin paused, and when he spoke, his voice was quiet. "Yeah, I'd like that."

"Okay, then. Just let me know what to expect. I'm used to Christmases where everyone gets wasted, bickers and slumps in front of the telly. I've never done a middle-class one before."

"It's not that much different, believe me. You'll be able to handle it. Probably better than I can."

Dan smiled, remembering Robin's flare of temper at the restaurant. "Yeah, I reckon I could."

They were both silent for a moment. It could have been awkward, but Dan was still too happy to have Robin on the other end of the line to feel uncomfortable. It would be better to have him on the other end of the sofa, though, and the idea of "having Robin" anywhere sent blood coursing south. He wondered if Robin would be up for some phone sex. Wondered if he'd ever done that sort of thing before. It had been a long time since Dan had, but he reckoned he could remember a few of Tris's tricks.

"Sooo..." Dan began, making his voice low and sultry.

"What have you been up to?" Robin asked.

Bollocks. He could lie. Tell Robin what he wanted to hear. If he were here, Dan would distract him by licking Robin's neck and playing with his nipples, something he'd found always worked a treat. But he had the impression that relationships went better when you were honest with each other, and Robin deserved honesty.

"I went to a party," he said before he could chicken out.

"Oh yeah? A gay party?"

"A birthday party. But yeah, it was fairly gay. At least ninety percent by volume, I'd say." Probably more. He couldn't remember having seen any girls at all, which was odd.

"Have a good time?"

Dan wished he could see Robin's face and know if that was jealousy turning those innocent words into an accusation. Or maybe it was just him feeling guilty.

"Not really. I left early."

"On your own?"

Yep, he deserved that. It didn't make him feel much better to be able to tell Robin that yes, he had left on his own, because there was the reason why that needed explaining. If he could bring himself to open his mouth.

"What is it, Dan?"

"Look, I was missing you, all right? I was angry that you hadn't answered my calls." Robin kept silent, but Dan could hear him breathing heavily. "Fuck. Look, I didn't enjoy it, and I kept thinking about how much better it would have been with you. I wanted him to be you."

"Am I supposed to feel flattered?"

Dan had expected anger, bracing himself to defend his actions, and the weary monotone of Robin's response made him pause.

"Yes. No. Shit, I don't know. But it's not every day I turn down a blowjob from a hot guy."

"You turned him down? I thought you said—"

"I just sucked his cock. That's all."

"I don't like the idea of some other guy's dick in your mouth." Robin's voice was practically a growl. "It should have been mine."

"Yeah, and I would have preferred that too, but you weren't there! Look, it was his birthday, all right? I'd turned up empty-handed, and I thought he deserved a little something."

"Is that your usual birthday gift? Most people go for a bottle of wine."

Was that amusement he could hear in Robin's voice, lurking there under the annoyance? "Yeah, I know, and I'm sorry, but never let it be said I'm not generous. So...when's your birthday, gorgeous?"

Robin was quiet for a while, and Dan began to worry that he'd pushed it too far.

"It's pretty soon. November third."

The weekend Dan had earmarked for returning to Bath.

"Interesting you should say that. I think you're going to have to let me come and give you your gift in person as it's a bit tricky down the phone. But we could always have a trial run and see how it goes." The sound of Robin's laughter was better than anything he could have imagined, short of being with him in person. Dan grinned, leaning back against the sofa cushions and relaxing fully.

"By the way, did I mention that I'm all naked, wet and soapy?"

# Chapter Twenty-Six

Winter was coming. You could smell it in the air; a scent of rotting vegetation underlying the tang of the woodsmoke that pervaded the canal. Most of the trees had been stripped bare by the high winds, and dark clouds blanketed the sky. Robin stood with an axe in his hand. Smiler had given him instructions to split and bag up as many logs as he could, but Robin faced the enormous woodpile with a smile on his face. He loved this hard, physical labour. After only six weeks at the new job, his shirts were starting to feel tighter, and it was costing him a fortune to feed his newly bulked-up muscles, but it was worth it to see the appreciative glint in Dan's eyes. He'd work until five and then head into Bath to meet Dan off the train. That's when the fun would really begin...

"Oi, Robin! Get your lazy arse back to work. I'm not paying you to bleedin' well daydream about your boyfriend."

Robin rolled his eyes. The twins were hiding inside—who could blame them?—so he gave Smiler the one-fingered salute and got on with bagging up the wood.

The canal grapevine being what it was, news about Robin and Dan had spread fast. Robin had noticed the other boaters giving him weird looks, but it wasn't until he'd gone to Smiler's to say he'd take on the work that his suspicions had been confirmed. Never one to mince his words, Smiler had come straight out with it.

"So, I hear you're taking it up the arse these days. Funny. Never had you down as the type."

Robin bristled. "I didn't know there was a type."

To his surprise, Smiler paused and his gaze seemed to lose focus. A smile twitched at the corner of his mouth. "Nah, maybe there isn't. I mean, I used to think there was, but you see all kinds of things when you spend a bit of time inside. Big tough guys like you going all queer when there's no birds around."

They negotiated a ten-'til-five shift, weekends only, so that Robin could cover the chandlery when Smiler had his girls over. It was fine for him as Dan could usually visit just as easily during the week, although Robin did wish they could be together at the weekends too. He didn't care what Dan said about things being purely platonic between him and Tris; he still didn't like the idea of them spending time together. Okay, so Dan said Tristan had a boyfriend now, but what's to say Dan wouldn't get drawn into some sordid threesome with the two of them? That's the kind of thing gay blokes did, wasn't it? Especially kinky ones like this Alex bloke supposedly was.

No, it was a discordant note in his otherwise-harmonious life, but Robin shook his head and did his best to try and ignore it. Right now Dan would be on the train, so theoretically wouldn't be with another man, but Robin couldn't stop his mind generating crazy scenarios of some nameless stranger seducing Dan and dragging him off to the train toilet to shag his brains out. Or worse yet, Dan doing the seducing... Robin put the brakes on that train of thought. It did no good to torture himself like this. He turned his attention back to splitting logs instead.

Smiler had been surprisingly generous with the hourly rate of pay but told Robin that he was going to work "like a fucking ox" for it. It was a shame it wasn't enough for Robin to afford a winter mooring, but at least he could keep himself in food, beer and pot, as well as having a bit to put aside to pay back his mum and Dan, and for emergencies like when his boots finally gave out. Shaking on the deal, Robin had felt his shoulders straighten. The pride of having steady work again had probably added another inch to his height. If he kept at it, he'd have to duck to get into his boat.

Robin was filling his twelfth bag when he heard a familiar voice.

"Hey, sweetie! Can I buy a couple of bags when you've got a moment?"

Mel was grinning up at him, and Robin returned her smile. She'd proved to be a brilliant friend. He'd finally summoned up the courage to tell her about the dyslexia, and she'd taken it upon herself to start giving him reading support in return for guitar lessons. With her patient presence and encouragement, he'd discovered that he wasn't quite as illiterate as he'd thought, and reading was getting easier day by day as his confidence grew.

"You're getting to be a right old socialite these days, aren't you? Just found a fella looking for you on the towpath. I expect he'll be along in a minute."

"Oh yeah?" Robin wasn't particularly curious. "Need help getting this to your boat?" he offered, once Mel had handed over the cash for the sacks of firewood and bundle of kindling.

"Robin, you're such a sweetheart! I could do with a hand. I need to get back quickly and check on the veg. I'm making us nut roast tonight."

"Us?" Robin furrowed his brow. Nut roast with Mel was the last thing on his mind for tonight.

"Yep. You and Dan are coming over to dinner. I've asked Sparky as well. Have you met him yet? Just came in last week on the little tug, *Albion*. He's a quiet one. Kind of cute. I thought if anyone could bring him out of his shell, it was Dan."

"Umm... Sparky? Isn't that a dog's name?" God knew why he was focusing on that. He should be protesting about having his evening hijacked, but sometimes it was just easier to go along with whatever Mel had planned.

"He's a welder, silly. I think he might be batting for Dan's team, but if not, I want to get in there quick before someone else does. I figured this way I should find out before wasting too much time trying to get into his pants." She gave a cheeky smile and winked at him. "Not that it was all a waste of time, sweetie."

Someone save him from women and their manipulative ways!

"Dan and I have plans for tonight." Plans that involved not wearing any clothes and doing some of the things they'd been describing to each other on the phone.

Mel slapped his arse playfully. "I'm sure you have, but you can wait to shag each other senseless until after you've had dinner, can't you? Besides, it's all organised. You're coming over at seven. Dan's already agreed."

"He has?"

"Yep. Called him earlier. So you can't wriggle out of it."

Robin sighed as Mel blew him a kiss and bounded off in the direction of her boat. Irritating though it was, he couldn't help feeling flattered that Mel had phoned Dan to ask them out as a proper couple. Chucking the sacks of wood into a wheelbarrow, he realised he was actually looking forward to the evening, even if meals with strangers were not his usual sort of thing.

He was whistling by the time he'd crossed the swing bridge.

"I say, what a sight for sore eyes! Robin, isn't it?"

Robin whirled round in surprise. A silver-haired man in tweeds and a rather jaunty red cravat stood before him. It was the old geezer from the White Hart. The one who hadn't wanted to let go of his arm until Dan came in with his tall story about them being a couple. Not such a tall story anymore, mind you. Robin's cheeks grew hot. He couldn't for the life of him remember the man's name.

"Charles Wentworth," the man said, extending a hand. "That lovely young Melody told me I could find you here."

"Of course, Charles. Good to see you." Robin was officially out of polite conversation. God knew why his school tutors had tried to convince him that having dyslexia led to you developing better verbal skills. It didn't seem to have worked for Robin. Fortunately, Charles seemed perfectly content to ogle him. Eventually he remembered a snippet of their conversation. "Did you buy your house in the end?"

"Yes, darling, I did. So kind of you to remember. Actually, to tell you the truth, that's one of the main reasons I was trying to track you down." Charles leant forward, putting a hand on Robin's arm. "There's so much that needs doing to the old heap, and I can't find a reliable carpenter for love nor money. Oh please, do say you can help! I'll pay cash in hand, if you like."

Robin did like, but he wasn't so sure about working for an old lech who didn't seem to be able to stop his gaze from roaming all over his potential carpenter's body. If Charles was this bad during the negotiations, Robin dreaded to think what would happen if he was alone with him in his house. He didn't want to have to resort to using his chisels to defend his honour.

"I'm sorry. I have to keep moving on all the time. BW regulations. I'm not going to be about here for much longer."

"Gosh, what a terrible bore for you. Oh, but of course, you said before." A sly glint transformed Charles's eyes. "You know, there's always that mooring spot at the end of my garden. Very secluded. Just perfect for when your boyfriend comes to visit."

Robin tried to keep his face blank—what Dan called his "inscrutable" look. A secluded garden mooring and cash in hand work sounded perfect, but at what cost?

"I'm not sure. I'd need to see the place and what needs doing first."

"Of course, darling. I wouldn't expect anything less. I'm sure you need to measure up and do all your estimates and so on. Here, just take my card and give me a call when you have the time."

The card he handed over was simple and elegant, and Robin could tell from the quality of the stock must have cost a fair whack. The typeface was easy to read, the address for one of the huge houses that backed onto the canal in Bathampton.

"Thanks. I'll think about it."

"You make sure you do that. Au revoir, my dear." Charles took his hand and planted a slobbering kiss on it. Robin had to fight not to wipe it off again. Not until Charles was facing the opposite direction, anyway.

He contemplated throwing the card into the canal. Becoming Charles's handyman wasn't an altogether tempting prospect—not if he had to put up with more sloppy kisses and being mentally undressed—but then again, if it made things easier to be around for Dan... Maybe he could give up Smiler's job and earn enough to travel up to London at the weekends, all the better to keep an eye on things there.

He slipped the card into his pocket. He'd have to give it some thought.

# Chapter Twenty-Seven

Dan could never stay in his seat when the train neared Bath. It was like his stomach had a bunch of small creatures turning somersaults inside it, preventing him from settling. He moved down through the carriage and waited with his bike in the vestibule at the end. Instead of watching the city pass by in a graceful sweep of honey-coloured limestone, he was glued to the other window. The one that looked up at the canal. From this angle in the falling dusk there was little to see, but every now and then he spotted a boat roof from between the trees, and he grinned.

And then they were drawing into the station, and Dan hung his arm out of the window so that he was ready to open the door the moment the locks were released. He scanned the platform, experiencing a giddy rush when he saw that familiar, much-dreamed-about figure slouching against the station wall.

"Robin!" he shouted, and when their eyes made contact, he felt it all the way down to his toes.

They were separated by the crowds pouring off the train towards the exit, and Dan had to push his way through the mass of bodies. It wasn't easy with a bicycle—he ended up wheeling it over a few toes and earned some dirty looks. But then there was Robin, still leaning back, the casual illusion of his pose betrayed only by the heat of his gaze. Yeah, that was the kind of dirty look he'd been craving.

Dan tried to keep his walk casual, but it was bloody impossible when his body screamed out to run. And in the end, he ran the last couple of paces. The ones that took him right into Robin's personal space and fetched him up against that long, hard body. He let his bike fall against the wall. Robin's arms came round to meet him, and he pitched forward into a crushing embrace.

Robin spun them round and Dan found himself up against the wall, his breath stolen in a blistering kiss. He could feel himself trembling with need, his body pressed against Robin's, and in the end he had to tear his lips away.

Robin growled and ground his hips against Dan's, letting him feel the strength of his arousal.

"Hey. It's good to see you too, but don't you think we should take this somewhere more private?" Dan asked, looking up and down the platform. The guard was very conspicuously watching them. Dan gave him a big grin, but the bloke refused to look embarrassed, scowling at them instead.

"Think I might have problems walking," Robin said, panting hard. "Where do you want to go?"

"Back to yours?"

"Uh-uh. You've promised Mel we'll be round for dinner in about twenty minutes, and it'll take us about that long to get there. We'd have to cycle past her boat to get to mine, and she'd spot us, believe me."

"Bugger! I forgot about that. I didn't think I'd be this fucking desperate for a shag the moment I saw you."

Robin raised an eyebrow. "I suppose that's meant to be a compliment?"

"Oh yeah. Big compliment. Can't you tell how big it is?" Dan gave a lewd smile and pulled Robin's hand around to his crotch. Screw the platform guard.

Hearing Robin's chuckle, Dan realised just how much he'd missed it over the last couple of weeks. Sure, he'd heard it over the phone, but it wasn't the same thing as being able to feel Robin's body shaking and watch the laughter transform his face. It was why he'd waited to tell Robin about their upcoming holiday in person, but he'd do all that later. There was no telling how Robin would react to the news initially, and he didn't want to risk spoiling the reunion.

Dan saw the platform guard approaching and tried to school himself into a respectable pose. It wasn't easy, what with Robin's hands clutching his rear.

"All right, lads, that's enough. Move it along, please."

"Sorry," Robin said. He didn't look very sorry, and he gave Dan's arse a good squeeze before finally letting go. "We'll 'move it along' somewhere else, shall we?" He winked, looking more roguish than Dan had ever seen him before. "I know where we can go."

They cycled along the towpath until they reached a white metal gate. Dan remembered seeing a park beyond it but had never ventured inside. Now Robin led the way through the gate and into the gloaming. He followed, his headlight picking out the reflective panels on Robin's bike. They hadn't gone far before Robin told him to stop and propped his bike up against the back of a bench.

Dan let himself be pulled by the hand into the dark under a low-spreading tree. Branches snagged on his hair as Robin spun him around and slammed him into the trunk. The air rushed out of him, and he gasped as he felt a sharp nip on his neck.

"Now, where were we?" Robin asked.

It didn't seem like Robin needed an answer, though, as he picked up where they'd left off. His tongue invaded Dan's mouth as if claiming it. The heat of his desire was plain in every movement, every groan, every thrust. Dan felt it deep in his marrow, the yearning that had been building for the past fortnight cresting high inside him.

Robin's erection ground against his own, the layers of fabric accentuating the friction. It was delicious. Just this. Nothing more than the overwhelming presence of Robin pressed up against his body, the scent of him sharp in Dan's nostrils, the taste of him hot on his tongue. Dan's skin was hypersensitive, registering every scrape of stubble on his chin, every breath ghosting over his cheeks.

"Fuck!" Dan gasped as Robin broke the kiss. "You're gonna make me come in my pants if you're not careful."

"That's the idea." Robin's voice rasped, thrilling through Dan's body.

It was like Robin gave him permission to take what he needed. After all these years of trying to be a fantastic lover, of holding back and making it last. Of trying to impress yet another random stranger with his technique. With Robin he didn't need to do anything other than feel and enjoy it. Dan's lust spiked high, and his balls began to ache. He rutted hard against Robin, trying to relieve his need even as the teeth on his neck made it surge higher.

Dan felt Robin's hands clutching at his buttocks and lifting him up, increasing the exquisite friction. Between those bruising, grasping fingers and that sucking, biting mouth, he was undone. His breath came in ragged gasps as his desire peaked in a flood of sensation. He bucked his hips, almost knocking Robin over with the force of his orgasm, then was slammed back against the tree as he rode out the waves.

"Robin!" he called, his voice hoarse.

Robin grunted in response, and then he too was jerking his hips hard, thrusting against Dan's body and biting down on his neck. As their shudders subsided, Dan started to laugh, the sound breathless and startling.

"Been a good few years since I've done that," Dan said.

"Yeah, me too. How long?"

"Dunno. Since I was a teenager, I reckon. Tell you what, two weeks is probably the longest I've gone without a shag since then as well." But Dan knew that wasn't the only reason he'd come so fast from just a kiss and a frot. It was being with Robin again. The sheer intensity of the way Robin made him feel. He wanted to put a word to it, but the only one that came to mind was too frightening. "That was...intense."

"Worth waiting for?"

"Oh yeah." Dan felt his chin being lifted and a lazy kiss pressed to his lips. He shifted his hips, uncomfortably aware that the mess in his pants was going to get chilly before long. "We're going to have to go back to yours to get changed now."

"No need. I've got a couple of hankies."

"That's not going to deal with two weeks' worth of spunk. And my undies will still be wet. And we'll stink of sex."

"Like anyone's going to notice over the incense and burnt nut roast," Robin said, sliding a hand down the back of Dan's jeans and plucking at the undies in question. "If you're that bothered, stop being such a wuss and take them off."

"Oi, watch it! You're giving me a wedgie."

With hindsight, it probably did sound like a challenge, but by then it was too late and they'd collapsed on the ground in a sniggering tussle.

"You're late. I hope you have a good excuse." Mel leaned out of the door to brandish a kitchen knife at Robin as he climbed onto *Galadriel*'s deck.

"The best," he said, giving her a kiss on the cheek. "That's not burning I can smell, is it?"

"Bollocks!" She turned back to the stove and gave something ominous-looking a stir.

Robin started to wish they'd eaten something before coming. Mel's cooking was a pot-luck affair at best, and this didn't look like one of her more palatable efforts. Maybe she'd been distracted by the bloke sitting in the saloon.

Robin sidestepped around Mel and figured he would have to introduce himself. Sparky looked like he'd walked straight out of some 1980s punk band, right down to the safety pins through his ear, studded leather wristbands and the bright pink Mohican. He was smiling—perhaps just a little too brightly—and seemed to find it hard to make eye contact. God, he'd better not be freaked out by Dan. There wasn't any subtle way of asking Dan to tone it down now they were inside the tiny boat.

"Hi, I'm Robin." He held out his hand.

"Sparky," the punk replied, taking Robin's hand and shaking it briefly. But his voice sounded warm enough, so maybe it was just nerves.

"This is Dan. My...uh...boyfriend." When was he going to get used to saying that? Hopefully never. He loved the butterflies it gave him every time he used the word. He wasn't quite so keen on the flush of heat, though, and began stripping off layers and trying to work out where they were all going to sit. He had to move a bag of knitting and a heap of water-damaged anatomy textbooks to make space for him and Dan on the beanbag. It would be intimate, but as the only other space was the sofa, he figured he'd rather squish up with his boyfriend than with Sparky. Dan was considerably less likely to accidentally spike him with dangerous bits of jewelry, for a start.

Sparky didn't speak much during the meal, but with Dan and Mel rabbiting on, it wasn't like anyone else had a chance to get a word in. Robin concentrated on balancing his plate on his lap when Dan seemed to be doing his best to climb on there as well, and trying not to accidentally knock knees with Sparky.

"So, are you a writer or something?" Sparky asked Dan when there was a gap in the conversation.

"Yep. Travel writer, and it's really not as glamorous as it sounds. Robin will vouch for that, won't you?"

Would he? Dan had mentioned roach-infested hotels and bouts of food poisoning, but it wasn't like Robin had been along to see it firsthand. All he really knew was that it was one of those jobs that threatened to take Dan away from him at unpredictable intervals. He gave a noncommittal grunt in reply.

"Actually, I need to fess up, hon." Dan turned to him, dislodging the plate at long last. Robin made only a halfhearted attempt to catch it. No one was going to expect him to eat the last bits now they'd been on Mel's floor. "Ooops! Sorry 'bout that. Anyway, I've been asked to go and cover a gay resort holiday in January. It's a bit last minute, I know, but I've written for *Attitude* before, and the guy who was meant to be going has gone and broken his leg skiing. D'you want to come to Gran Canaria with me? They usually provide an extra-cheap ticket for partners."

Dan gave him such an appealing smile, and the feel of his body pressed up close was so distracting that it took Robin a moment to process what he was saying.

"You're going away in January? How long for?"

Dan looked shifty. "Don't be mad, okay, but Tony reckons he can get me a Rough Guide gig as well, photographs and checking out places for their updated guide book. I'll be out there for a month. But like I said," he added hastily, "you can come too."

"A whole month?" It felt like the bottom had just dropped out of Robin's world. "I can't leave *Serendipity* for a whole month. Not in the middle of winter."

"Why not?"

Robin looked over to Mel and Sparky for support. Neither of them seemed to want to meet his eyes. He sighed. There was just so much Dan didn't understand about boats and boaters. He tried to explain about ice damaging pipes and the potential for the bilges to overflow if they weren't regularly pumped out. Dan's eyes glazed over, brightening only when he mentioned leaky prop shafts. Robin refused to be distracted by smutty innuendo.

"Then there's the need to keep moving. And there's Morris. I can't do it."

"Surely someone else could keep an eye on Morris and the boat for you?"

Now Mel and Sparky were studiously avoiding Dan's imploring gaze.

Something else occurred to Robin. "Did you say it was a gay resort?"

Dan gave an impish grin. "Yep. Great fun. Well, they are if you're single, anyway. Or there as a couple, I expect."

"I'm not going to a gay resort. No way." He shuddered. It would be full of guys like Jamie. Guys like Dan used to be before they got together. Or maybe like Dan still was when he wasn't with him. The thought stabbed him in the gut, and bile rose hot and bitter in his throat.

"We'll talk about it later, okay?" Dan said, squeezing his shoulder.

Robin just nodded, and everyone seemed relieved when Mel brought out a pack of cards and set up a tiny, rickety table between them. No one seemed to notice that he didn't say anything more than the bare minimum after that. No one except Dan, who kept trying to make eye contact.

Robin glared at his cards.

# Chapter Twenty-Eight

"'Ello, love. What's all this about? Not like you to phone on a Friday evening."

It wasn't, and Dan felt distinctly guilty about interrupting her favourite telly night, but he couldn't lie to his mum. "I know. It's just, I'm not going to be able to make it on Sunday, so I wanted to give you notice. I know Chantal's expecting me." He'd promised to take his favourite niece to the zoo next time he had a free Sunday.

"You're gonna break that little girl's heart, you know. It's all she's been on about for the last fortnight."

Could she make him feel any worse than he already was? "I know, I know, and I'm sorry. But I've been given a really good commission. I can't turn it down. You understand, don't you?"

She sniffed, and the noise of the television suddenly ceased. "All I know is, we've hardly seen 'ide nor 'air of you for the last month. Family's more important than your career, love. You should know that."

Dan deserved the guilt pooling heavy inside him.

"I'm sorry. I've just been busy, but it's not all been work, I promise." He took a deep breath. He'd been avoiding telling her about Robin because he wasn't sure how to describe this thing they had going on. Truth was, he'd wanted to wait until he was sure he wouldn't just mess it all up by going back to his old ways, because disappointing his mum always made Dan want to crawl away and die of shame. "I've met this bloke. A boater. Robin, his name is. I think you'd really like him."

There, it was out in the open now.

"Are you sayin' what I think you're sayin'?"

"If you think I'm saying that I'm seeing someone, then yes."

"Like, a proper boyfriend? Oh love, that's smashing." That was better. Her usual warmth was back in spades. "Tell me all about 'im. Did you meet on that boat holiday? I thought you seemed a bit bloody mysterious when I asked you about it."

"That's right. I've been going back there whenever I can. It's... It's early days yet, but I think this might be something."

"You don't know how 'appy I am to hear you say that. My little boy, fallen in love at last!"

"Mum! We're not 'in love'. It's just... I dunno. We're just seeing what happens, okay?"

"Whatever you say, poppet. So go on, what's this Robin fella like? Good lookin', I s'pose, knowing you."

"I hope you're not saying I'm shallow."

His mum giggled. "I just know you've got a keen eye, even as a littl'un you did. Always noticed the way you perked up when an attractive fella came on the screen."

Yep, that sounded about right. His mum may have dropped out of school pregnant at age fifteen, but she'd always been an acute observer of people.

"He's tanned and fit. Amazing body. All natural, not like he's all pumped up on steroids either. Umm, what else? Tattoos and piercings, could do with a complete wardrobe overhaul. I'm gonna have to say tall, dark and handsome, even if he's only tall compared to me. Gorgeous dark blue eyes. Sound good to you?"

"Sounds lovely. But what's he really like? D'you get on well?"

"Oh yeah. Really well. We have great fun, and he's kind and thoughtful, even if he doesn't like people to notice. I mean, he can get moody, and I don't always know what he's thinking. Last time I saw him, he tried to pay me back for some stuff I'd bought him and got really grumpy when I wouldn't take the money. Couldn't figure out why, because he wouldn't talk about it. And there's other stuff he won't explain..." He trailed off, thinking of Robin's point-blank refusal to come with him to Gran Canaria.

"Is something the matter, love? You know these relationship thingies take some work, but it's well worth puttin' in the effort."

"Yeah. I dunno. I can't really figure him out, to be honest. He's had a really messed-up past, a junkie boyfriend who cheated on him and then killed himself, but I don't know... It's like he's scared of being gay. I asked him to come out to a gay resort with me. Thought it could be a holiday for us both while I get paid to write it up, but he won't even consider it."

She made sympathetic noises. "I always thought they sounded like abominable places, and I *know* you only gave me the edited 'ighlights. God knows what you really got up to. Different man every night, knowing you."

That was certainly true. At least one a night. And he'd given only the carefully edited version to Robin as well.

"I'm not like that anymore, Mum. I've changed. I don't even go clubbing anymore. I've grown up." If he kept saying it, then maybe it would be true. Stop him from making a really stupid mistake and ruining things between him and Robin.

"I'm glad to 'ear it. So let's figure out what you're going to say to Chantal now, shall we?"

Dan sighed. She was right, of course. Family should come before his career, as should Robin.

It was just so unfair that he couldn't have it all at once.


In mid-December, the weather closed in.

*Serendipity* rocked in the gale. Robin peered out the galley porthole, hoping he'd driven the mooring pins in deep enough. When the ground was soft and wet it could be a real challenge to get the bloody things to stay put. He probably should have stayed on the official moorings where he could have pulled the boat in tight against the bank and stopped it rocking quite so sickeningly. At least he'd remembered to pull in the plank. It could be a real bugger fishing one of those out of the canal the next day.

"I hope Mel and Sparky found somewhere decent to moor up." Robin couldn't help worrying about Mel. She'd gone off with Sparky, who was cruising back towards Oxford to spend time with family at Christmas. What if she never came back again? He must be getting used to company, as the thought of being alone had never bothered him this much before.

"They'll be fine, and stop pacing around, will you? Come on, I need some comforting over here."

Robin was about to berate Dan for being a great big wuss, but when he saw the look on his face, he kept that to himself. Dan's eyes were haunted, his arms hugged tight around himself.

"Hey, it's okay. Just a storm. We're safe in here, I promise." He sat next to Dan and pulled him close. Dan shivered, climbed onto his lap and seemed to melt, head nestled in the crook of Robin's neck. He could feel Dan's hot breath gusting against his skin, heating his blood.

"Pathetic, aren't I?" Dan whispered. "It's just, there's all that water out there, and I can hear it sloshing around. I keep thinking we're gonna sink in the night."

"Rubbish. Not a chance. It would take more power than the wind to push a narrowboat over. Just doesn't happen."

"You sure?" The hope in Dan's voice made Robin feel all warm inside. It was such a high to be able to comfort him.

"I'm certain."

But Dan wasn't completely reassured. "What about the...prop shaft? Didn't you tell me water could get in through there?"

"It's fine. I packed it good and proper the other day."

"You packed your prop shaft?"

There was a definite cheekiness to Dan's tone. Robin figured he should make the most of it. He dropped his voice and slid his hands to Dan's waist, caressing lightly.

"Yeah, I got the ring all greased up and packed it in there hard. That prop shaft didn't know what had hit it."

Dan undulated against him and lifted his face. Robin looked straight into his mischievous eyes.

"Sounds like I should be jealous of this thing you've got going on with your boat, Skipper."

Robin nodded gravely. "A man's relationship with his boat is sacred. But I'll tell you what." He dropped his hands farther, grabbing himself a double handful of Dan's arse. "Packing her isn't anywhere near as much fun as packing you."

"Mmm, glad to hear it."

There wasn't a trace of fear in Dan's voice anymore. Robin revelled in the husky warmth of his moans as he pulled him into a kiss. Dan tasted sweet as ever, with just a trace of lager cutting through his familiar flavour. Robin tried to keep things slow and steady, comforting rather than stimulating, even though his cock was starting to take an interest.

Dan obviously had other ideas, though, and wriggled around until he sat astride him. Then Dan broke the kiss and pulled off his T-shirt.

What a sight. Dan looked so fucking sexy like that, so debauched, all kiss-reddened lips and wild eyes. Robin's dick stiffened as he traced a finger over the trail of love bites he'd left on Dan's chest. His heart beat faster. That Dan let him do this, let him make his mark and claim him, let him take just what he needed and seemed to find it every bit as exciting and overwhelming as he did...

It blew his mind.

If only Robin could explain it all, but when he looked up into Dan's eyes, he realised that maybe he didn't need to. Dan felt it too. Robin could see it in his face, hear it in his moans, feel it in his every movement.

Dan's hands were deftly unbuttoning his fly.

"Stay right here," Dan said, then got up and stumbled his way through to the bed cabin.

Robin humoured him and stayed put—he had a pretty good idea what Dan was fetching—but as Dan hadn't mentioned anything about clothing, he took the liberty of stripping off, then sat back again with legs planted wide and his hands behind his head.

The delighted surprise on Dan's face made Robin's heart swell.

"Great minds think alike," Robin said, because Dan was every bit as naked as he was.

"Oh yeah. Hold that thought. In fact, hold it just like that."

Robin's hand had moved to his cock, and he kept it there, watching Dan sway closer. A fierce gust of wind shook the boat, and Dan fell onto him, narrowly missing planting an elbow in his groin.

"Whoa! Careful there. You nearly ruined your chances of getting lucky."

Dan giggled breathlessly but soon righted himself and straddled Robin.

"Like this, okay?" Dan asked as he rolled the condom onto him.

Robin had no complaints. It was always a buzz to let Dan take a bit of control back from him, and if that's what he needed to ride out the storm, he could have it.

He held himself firm as Dan lowered his body, pulling him in with rippling muscles. Exquisite heat enveloped him as he drank in the incredible sight of Dan wincing and gasping and shuddering with pleasure as he sank down.

Dan came to rest, his forehead pressed against Robin's and his breath shallow.

Robin waited for him. He could give him all the time he wanted. It felt right, just having Dan around him and pulled in against him. He could feel the damp heat of Dan's cock and balls pressed up against his belly.

The wind gusted hard again, and something rattled against the outside of the boat. Dan's head whipped around.

"Shhh, just a twig or something. Sounds worse than it is." Robin could tell what all the sounds were: the tarpaulin snapping in the wind, the stovepipe rattling, the logs shifting, the intermittent raindrops. All perfectly normal sounds but no doubt alarming to Dan's city-boy ears. "Just try to ignore it and listen to me."

Dan shifted, and Robin looked up into his eyes. They were so trusting it made him long to live up to whatever it was Dan was expecting.

"Well, go on, then," Dan prompted.

Shit. He was going to have to talk. He didn't do talking during sex. But he'd have to try, what with Dan looking at him with those big puppy-dog eyes.

"See these?" he said, running his hand over Dan's chest. "These marks? Just looking at them turns me on. Sometimes I want to rip all your clothes off just to check they're st-still there. Oh God, that's good!"

Dan had started moving, lifting right up, gyrating his hips and driving down on him with force.

"Keep going, and I'll keep moving," Dan said, pausing.

It was going to be bloody hard work concentrating, but he'd give it his best shot if it meant more of that.

"They look so fucking sexy on you. The bites. Sometimes I want to make other marks. I want to..." Oh God, could he actually admit to this? But Dan stopped moving, and he wanted more. Needed more. His voice came out gruff and demanding. "I want to bend you over and smack your bum until it's red, and then—and then fuck you so hard it stings and you c-can't sit down for days."

Dan was panting almost as fast as him, and Robin's hand found its way to Dan's cock. It was slippery already, and he knew it wouldn't take much to tip them both over the brink.

"Any more?" Dan asked, not really pausing this time but slowing down a little.

"You need more? Shit, I...I've never wanted anyone like this. Scares me. All the things I want to do to you. With you. Yeah, like that. Dan, I, I think I—"

*I love you.*

The words were lost in a rush of sensation. Robin felt Dan go first, spattering the space between them with hot seed. He braced himself against the floor and thrust up into Dan's pulsing, twitching body, determined to milk Dan's orgasm for as long as he could. To help him push back the fear and the wind and the rain.

He didn't let himself follow until he felt Dan collapse against him.

He hadn't said it. He couldn't, not even then.

But he knew the words inside him were true.

Just three little words that scared him stupid.

# Chapter Twenty-Nine

Robin was going to blow a gasket.

Probably.

Dan pulled himself together and dialled his number. He knew exactly what he was going to say—that he was helping out a friend in distress and Robin hadn't wanted the spare ticket anyway. He'd put it better than that, of course.

But he knew Robin still wasn't going to like it.

He was right.

"You've invited Tris? Are you serious?"

"He's really upset, babe. His stint in *La Cage* ended, Alex dumped him just before Christmas, and he needs something to cheer him up."

"Needs a shoulder to cry on, more like."

"Yeah, well that's what friends are for, isn't it?"

The silence stretched out.

"You tell me what friends are for," Robin said, his voice hard and bitter. "According to you, friends are for fucking as well. According to you, we're just friends. What's to say Tristan doesn't want a bit of that kind of cheering up too?"

"I expect he does, but he's not going to be getting it from me!"

Dan heard Robin mutter something that sounded suspiciously like "Yeah, right".

Charming. Well, he could do angry every bit as well as Robin could. In fact, he could do righteous anger.

"Oh, for fuck's sake. We're more than friends, and you know it. When was the last time I slept with anyone other than you?"

"I don't know. You tell me. You're the one who has trouble keeping it in his pants."

Shit, that hurt. That really hurt. It felt like Robin had just stabbed him in the chest, twisted the knife and spat in his face.

"Is that really what you think of me? You really think I'm screwing around behind your back? I'm not like your precious Jamie, you know. And anyway, you stuck with him for ages even though you knew he was a no-good junkie slut."

As soon as the words were out, Dan wanted to claw them back again. It was obvious Robin had worshipped the ground Jamie walked on, and those feelings still lingered. Dan should have known better than to insult the guy, even if every word was true.

Robin was silent for a long time. Dan could hear harsh breathing, but it gradually slowed. He hated to be the cause of such distress. He should have waited, told Robin in person when he could have reassured him physically. Shown him the honesty in his eyes.

"Sorry," he said. "Didn't mean to bring him into it. What you had going with him is none of my business."

"No." Robin's voice was softer now, the anger replaced by pain. "You're right though. I did. I trusted too much. I can't go through that again."

"You don't have to. Look, we'll see each other in a couple of days. It will all look better by then, and I can show you how there's nothing to worry about."

"Yeah, maybe."

They talked of other things for a while, but Robin sounded tired, and they said their good nights earlier than usual. When Dan put down the phone, he realised his shoulders were still tensed up. He'd been way too stressed just lately, what with the mountain of work to get finished before going away, the prospect of no Robin for a whole month, and now this stupid argument...

What he needed was a night out. A chance to blow off some steam before seeing Robin again.

He dialled Tris's number.


"It's like he doesn't fucking well trust me. He thinks you're gonna seduce me while we're away and I'm...I'm just a cheap slut who can't keep it in his pants." Dan hiccupped and sloshed back another mouthful of Sex on the Beach. He wasn't used to drinking this much, but the boozy fruit juice was sliding down easily.

Tris stared at him over the cocktail umbrellas. "Sounds like he's got a pretty accurate picture of you, darling, if your track record's anything to go by. How many different guys was it last time you went to one of these resorts?"

Dan scowled. He didn't need to do the mental arithmetic as he could remember bragging about it on his return. "'S'not the point. I'm a reformed character. When's the last time you remember me fucking anyone other than Robin?"

"Hmmm..." Tris was doing that really annoying thing where he pursed his lips and looked like he was seeing right into Dan's fucking soul. "Okay, granted. But what is it about this Robin that's keeping you faithful? I mean, I want to believe in true love and all that bollocks, but I've never seen you as the type."

"You wouldn't understand."

"Try me."

Dan glared at Tristan, wanting to resent his oldest friend but not able to summon up enough anger at him to make it work. In the end, he just sighed. "I dunno. Really, I don't know what it is, but I just want to be with him all the time, and when we are together, it's fucking amazing."

"The sex?"

"Yeah. No! Not just the sex. I mean, the sex is something else, but it's more than that." Dan gestured with the wrong hand, slopping sticky liquid all over his fingers. He put the glass down on the table and attempted to steady himself. It was tricky when the world insisted on slipping sideways all the time. "It's just, spending time together, you know?"

Tris got that funny look he'd had a lot recently. The one where it seemed he was seeing something good, but it wasn't right here, right now. Wistful, that was it. "I think I know what you mean." His lips twisted in a bitter smile. "I was feeling that way about Alex."

"Shit, Tris, I'm fucking sorry, mate." Considering the relationship had lasted only nine weeks, Tris had taken it hard. "I'm a crap friend, and you deserve better. So much fucking better."

"Oh, can the self-pity, darling. It doesn't suit you. Now why don't you finish off that drink, and we can go cheer ourselves up on the dance floor. It's Christmas Eve eve, and we deserve a bit of fun."

It worked for a while, but Dan was too drunk to perform anything other than shambolic gyrations and cheesy, Travolta-esque moves designed to have Tris in stitches. In the end, they stumbled into a cab together, vowing to carry on the party at Dan's flat.

At some point on the ride home, the alcohol reached a critical level in Dan's bloodstream and began working its old tricks. The ones where it made the guy he was with seem like the most alluring man in the universe—except Robin—and sent Dan's libido into overdrive even as his capacity to do anything about it plummeted. He pulled Tris close, mumbling endearments as he pawed at him. Tris didn't seem to mind. He'd played catch-up with the cocktails after Dan had started dancing.

They fell through the front door in a tangle of limbs, giggling hysterically. Tris was still trying to sing something from one of his bloody musicals that was meant to be significant in some way, but Dan was more interested in getting some skin contact. It had been too long. Nearly two weeks since he last saw Robin, and he was desperate to feel arms around him. Right now he didn't much care whose arms. These ones would have to do.

Dan tackled Tris to the sofa and gave him a sloppy, tooth-clashing kiss before standing to strip his T-shirt. He gave Tris his most seductive smile and straddled him. Tris stared with bleary eyes. They widened in alarm. Dan looked down to try and work out what the problem was. Oh yeah. Tris hadn't seen all that yet.

"Shit, Dan! You never told me about this." Tris ran a fingertip over the faded patchwork of bruises and bite marks on Dan's chest.

Dan shivered. Not in a good, I'm-so-fucking-horny-let's-shag kind of a way. No, more of an I-want-my-shirt-back-on-right-now-it's-bloody-freezing kind of shiver. He obeyed the instinct, moving off Tris's lap and curling into a foetal ball at the other end of the sofa.

"He hurts you? You've always said you're not into pain. Are you okay with this?"

Dan squeezed his eyes tight, hoping it might keep the tears at bay. "I love it," he choked out. "I ask for it. When it's Robin, everything's different."

"You want to tell me about it?"

"He just...just makes me feel free. I don't have to try to impress him. Doesn't care what I wear or earn or even if I've had a shower." He snorted. "Dirty boy. Think he prefers it if I haven't. He makes me laugh, Tris. He can be buttoned up so tight sometimes, but when he lets go, he's so..." The right word eluded him. Trying to explain Robin's contradictions made his brain hurt—or maybe that was still the cocktails doing their evil work. "He makes me feel safe." He sniffed and gave a shaky laugh. "Takes control and makes me come so hard I see stars."

Tris gave him a look Dan had never seen on his face before. His drink-addled brain couldn't unscramble it, but there was definitely something uncommonly wise about it. Tris, wise? Ha! How likely was that?

"You love him, don't you, darling?"

Nope, definitely not wise. Dan did not love Robin. He was determined not to. Because if he did, that was the kind of thing you had to fight to protect, and he was terrified of what that might involve. He tried to explain this to Tris but just earned a pitying look for his trouble.

"Go to bed, Dan. It'll seem better in the morning, trust me." Tris yawned and stretched. "Get me a spare blanket, and I'll sleep here. It won't be the first time I've ended up on the sofa, believe me."

But it didn't seem all that much better in the morning, because despite the relief of not having cheated on Robin, Dan had the prospect of the train journey over to Bath, and then on to Cheltenham with him to spend the holiday with his family. Dealing with Rosemary Hamilton while nursing a hangover?

No, Tris really didn't know what he was talking about.

And Dan definitely wasn't in love.

# Chapter Thirty

Robin waited at his customary spot, bouncing up and down on the balls of his feet. He was getting glances from the overzealous platform guard, but he just grinned at him. Nothing could dampen his mood. Not the freezing-cold drizzle that drifted under the platform roof. Not the prospect of spending the next three days at his parents' house. And certainly not a homophobic busybody.

The guard gave him a shy smile as his gaze raked up and down Robin's body.

Okay, maybe not homophobic. Huh, who would have thought? Robin was having to reassess his opinions of so many people. The calm acceptance of his family and most of the other boaters had been such a surprise. For every Nigel with his poisonous barbs and hate-filled eyes, there were at least twenty others who seemed to wish Robin well, and a far greater number who were utterly indifferent. He could do it now. He was ready to take the plunge and ask Dan to move in with him. He'd do it over Christmas, the first chance he had to get Dan alone. Sort everything out before Dan went off for the month. He felt like he was walking on a cloud, and nothing was going to bring him down. Not even the thought of Dan being with Tristan. What did one month matter when soon Dan would be all his, all the time?

It was all so simple. Dan would see it.

Dan would say yes.

Robin's buoyant spirits coloured everything, so he didn't immediately pick up on Dan's mood. They sat in the railway platform café while they waited for the connecting train, Robin chattering about the latest gossip along the canal—he knew it all these days—and his growing enjoyment of the written word.

"I thought maybe I could read some of your articles sometime. I mean, I know it's all stuff about hotels and places I've not been to, but it'd be like listening to you talk. Could keep me company whenever you're away, writing new stuff." Robin smiled at the thought of Dan wielding a notepad on a beach full of sexy men. He mentally dressed Dan in long shorts, hat and shirt, with a good daub of that white sunblock on his nose. And he made sure that Tristan was sitting in the middle of a bunch of tanned men in skimpy swimming trunks to keep him entertained and away from Dan. "Maybe you could send me some to read while you're in Gran Canaria."

"I've got to go and do it, Robin. You won't be able to put a guilt trip on me about this one." Dan wrenched apart of packet of sugar as he spoke, the crystals scattering all over the tabletop. "Shit," he said, brushing them away with his sleeve.

Robin blinked. He took a proper look at Dan, noting for the first time the dark rings under his eyes and the downcast gaze. Dan was fidgeting with his spoon now, stirring the coffee round and round. His misery sent compassion washing through Robin.

"Hey, it's okay. I don't mind. I trust you. It's just your job, isn't it? And I'm okay about Tristan going, really."

"It's not about Tris, all right!"

Dan's voice was loud, and conversations at the surrounding tables stopped as people listened in. He reached out to hold Dan's hand, stopping him from destroying another sugar packet. He ransacked his mind for possible causes of Dan's distress. While thinking, he ran his thumb over Dan's tightly clenched fist.

Dan spoke first. "God, look... I'm sorry. I just, I had a late night and too much to drink. And I'm a bit jumpy about spending Christmas with your folks, no offence."

Robin gave a wry smile. "None taken. I know the feeling."

And because he was in love, and because he could, he lifted Dan's hand and quite deliberately kissed his knuckles. He eased Dan's fist open, licking the grains of sugar from his palm. He didn't give a rat's arse what any of the other customers thought about them.

Dan shivered and squeezed his eyes shut. He must be moved. He looked like he was about to burst into tears. Probably upset about having to go away in a few days. They'd miss each other, but it would be okay. Everything would be better afterwards, when they were living together.

He should try and take Dan's mind off January.

"Did I ever tell you about the year my sister brought back one of her hippy university friends for the Christmas break? She was called Wendy. Bought a microwavable vegan dinner with her and had made us all crocheted hot-water bottle covers as presents. You should have seen Mum's face when she unwrapped hers."

Dan looked up as Robin launched into his tale, and before long, he was starting to smile.

Yeah, it would all be fine.


Dan felt like the world's biggest fraud. He'd been welcomed into Robin's family with open arms—quite literally, in Rosemary's case—and he kept wondering when someone was going to come along and boot him out for being a commoner. It was all alien. The large detached house in its half acre of gardens; the tastefully coordinated furnishings and antiques; even the cats were pedigree—two snooty Siamese who eyed him with suspicion. The cats had it right, at least. He didn't fit in here, and he never would. It made him jumpy.

And then there was Robin's room. His childhood room, still decorated with pictures of boats on the blue walls. Dan sank back onto the bed. That had been changed, at least. A queen-size double with a dark, carved wooden headboard. It was a tacit acknowledgement that they were sleeping together, and he realised he'd been half expecting to find himself given a separate room—let's face it, there were enough spare bedrooms in the house. It seemed wrong for Rosemary and Edward to have so many empty rooms, when he'd grown up squashed into the one tiny bedroom with his older brother. He'd been fifteen before he'd finally got it to himself.

"Mmm, that's a good idea," Robin said, bouncing onto the bed and jolting Dan out of his trance. "Reckon we've got a good half hour before anyone misses us. There's no lock on the door, but I think we could chance it, don't you?"

Dan rolled over to face Robin. What was with him today, being so bloody cheerful? But no matter how weird Dan felt, and how much he wanted to stay annoyed, he couldn't resist that look in Robin's eyes. He'd never really realised just what come-to-bed eyes were before meeting Robin—the man gave a whole new meaning to the phrase with his devastating gazes.

He answered with a kiss, which quickly escalated to a sweaty, half-clothed rubbing off. Lying back afterwards, their mingled come drying on his skin, Dan wondered why it couldn't always be this easy. It was all so simple when it was just them together. None of the outside world coming in to cause conflict.

"I've been thinking," Robin said, running his finger lazily through the mess on Dan's belly, "about when you get back from your trip. It's silly, all this travelling back and forth you're having to do, and you've said yourself you can do most of your work wherever, so long as you have the Internet and a ph—"

"What are you trying to say?" Dan interrupted. Robin stroked his chest, and Dan fought the urge to roll away. He had a hunch about where this conversation was going, and he didn't like it.

"How about moving onto *Serendipity* with me? You could keep the flat in London and just go back there when you need to for work. We could be properly together. It'll be even easier after your trip when you sort out your driving test and get a car."

"You've got it all organised, then, have you? Shit, Robin... There isn't room for me to move onto your boat."

"I can make room. I can build more storage."

"You can't make it twice the size, though, can you? Look, I need my space. I need somewhere that's my own where I can go and work or just be by myself for a bit. Why d'you think I've lived alone all these years?" And even as he said this, Dan knew it was only part of the truth, but the whole truth was more than he wanted to own.

"You were waiting for the right person to come along. You were waiting for me." Robin sounded so self-assured. His self-esteem had skyrocketed since they first met, and Dan hated himself for having to drag it back to the dirt.

Dan groaned and covered his eyes with his arm. Why did Robin have to dump this on him today, when he was already coping with the hangover from hell, the Hamilton family mansion and the lingering guilt about nearly shagging Tris? "I've never wanted to live with anyone, and I don't think that's ever going to change. Sorry, Robin." He felt the mattress shift as Robin got up from the bed, and when he opened his eyes, he could see that familiar figure silhouetted against the window. "It's not you. You just...you don't understand. I grew up in this shoddy little two-bed house with four other kids. My parents had to sleep on a sofa bed in the lounge so that we could have a girls' bedroom and a boys' bedroom. I don't ever want to be that crowded again. I need my own space."

"But I need you." Robin's voice sounded dangerously close to cracking. Dan wished he could see Robin's face, but didn't know if he'd be able to cope with what it revealed.

"I know, I know. Shit, look, I'm doing the best I can here. I'd sell my flat and buy somewhere down in Bath if that made sense, but you'll be moving on soon enough, so I'm best off keeping my place in London. That's where the work is. That's where my friends are."

"You've got friends on the canal."

"Yeah, but I've only known them for a couple of months. I've got friends in London I've known for years. I can't just up and leave them all."

"Friends like this Tristan you're going off with." Robin's voice had an ugly note.

"Yeah, Tris is a really good friend. Look, Robin, if you've got a problem about that, then you should just come out with it."

"You used to shag him."

"Now and again. It's no big deal. You're the one I'm seeing now. I'm not going to start sleeping around again." Dan's face grew hot as he remembered how close he'd come to that the previous night. His guilt burnt fierce and angry. "I thought we'd already been through all this shit. It's not fair to keep dumping it on me."

"Fuck! Look, I'm sorry." Robin came back to the bed and sat heavily, his head in his hands. "I just want you around more. I want you to be there when I wake up in the mornings. I...I love spending time with you and I l-love you."

Robin turned to him with raw need written on his face, and Dan realised he was officially the biggest shit in the universe. He just couldn't respond with the phrase Robin wanted. The one Robin was pleading for with those big blue eyes. He couldn't keep looking into them, so he stared down at the bedcover and flicked away an imaginary piece of lint.

"Fine. Okay, I understand." Robin's voice had gone hard, but Dan could hear the hurt underneath. He wanted to sink down into the bed and have it swallow him whole. It would be a hell of a lot easier than trying to sort out all this. Why couldn't Robin be happy with what they had? It was as much as he could offer.

"It's not that I don't want to be with you. I do. It's just... I don't want to lose my freedom. I don't want to feel trapped and crowded. Don't want to end up like Mum did, giving up everything she could've been to be with my dad. Sorry. I just wish—"

The call for dinner echoed up the stairwell, and they both jumped.

"Shit! Better get cleaned up. We can't go into dinner like this." Dan reached out awkwardly to massage Robin's shoulder. "Come on. We'll never survive your mum's disapproval if we dare to be late." He pressed a kiss to Robin's crown.

Robin heaved a deep sigh, nodded and gave him a tight smile.

It was a reprieve, but Dan knew he'd be kidding himself if he thought of it as anything other than temporary.

# Chapter Thirty-One

Dan watched Rosemary closely as she opened his present to her and Edward.

"Oh, Dan! Thank you so much, darling. Look Edward, doesn't Robin look handsome on his boat?"

Edward Hamilton took the framed photograph and studied it for what felt like hours. Dan's stomach refused to settle. He wasn't sure why he wanted the man's approval so much, but perhaps it was something to do with regaining a bit of Robin's respect after the mess he'd made of things the previous day. Robin had been guarded ever since their discussion, but maybe Dan could charm himself back into his good graces, with the help of his family.

When Edward finally looked up, he had a smile on his face. "It's very striking. The way you've captured my boy's determination and independence." He shot his son an approving look. Robin's eyes widened with amazement, and Edward turned to his wife. "You know, I've always fancied the idea of a boating holiday. We should take one next year. Maybe stop by and visit Robin on his boat. What do you say, dearest?"

Perhaps it was the result of having been on the red wine all day, but Rosemary gave him the most genuine smile Dan had ever seen her use.

"Oh, darling, that sounds wonderful! But please tell me we can hire one with all the mod cons. I hear you can get them with Jacuzzis these days."

Dan almost laughed at Robin's expression. Shock mingled with pride and embarrassment. He reached out to give Robin's hand a quick squeeze before handing him his own present.

Robin tackled the paper carefully, as if he was savouring every moment of the experience. Dan had spent a stupid amount of money on a charcoal woollen coat for him. It was utterly plain, incredibly warm, and the sales assistant in the boutique assured him that wool stayed warm even when wet. Robin looked up from the open package with wide eyes and a soft smile.

"Thank you," he breathed.

Dan tried not to look smug. "Better try it on. Make sure it fits properly."

Robin turned slowly at Rosemary's insistence. The coat fitted perfectly, and while it was smart, it didn't look out of place over his combat trousers.

"Oh, that's perfect," Rosemary said, smiling fondly. "You're such a thoughtful young man. Robin, you make sure you thank Dan properly for that."

His back to Rosemary, Robin rolled his eyes. "Thank you, Dan."

"You can kiss him, you know, darling. No one's going to mind."

Dan saw Robin shoot a doubtful glance at his dad, who seemed utterly absorbed in the photograph all of a sudden. Miranda and Pat were busy cooing over the baby. But Robin did walk over to him and leant down to press a kiss to his lips. It wasn't until the contact ceased that Dan realised he'd been holding his breath. Then the flash blinded him.

"Oh bother! I missed it." Rosemary held the camera in front of her and squinted at it. "Oops, left the lens cap on. Can you do that again please, boys?"

"Mum!" Robin whirled around, and Dan tried his hardest not to snigger. "You can't... Why are you... That's private!"

"Nonsense, darling. I have plenty of photos of Miranda and Pat kissing." She gestured over to the mantelpiece. Now that Dan noticed, there were indeed many photos of couples kissing, including some black-and-white prints of a very young

Rosemary and Edward. "Now come on. Let's have a nice shot of the two of you together. Something I can show the ladies at the bridge club when they ask me about when you'll be settling down and getting married."

"I'm not performing for you so you can laugh about me with your friends."

"Who said anything about laughing? Darling, I'm proud of you. I want to show them all that I'm not ashamed of who you are." Dan and Robin both gaped at her. Dan had to make a quick mental readjustment of his idea of Rosemary.

Robin looked lost, poor thing. Must be hard having to deal with the idea that his mum wasn't the narrow-minded conservative he'd always had her down as. Rosemary put down her wineglass and rose on unsteady feet to give him a hug.

"Now, come on. Dan, you stand next to him. If you won't kiss, then at least let me have a shot of you with your arms around each other's shoulders. That's it."

Dan let himself be arranged into a pleasing pose and turned to smile at Robin. Robin still looked confused, but as their eyes made contact, he seemed to relax, giving a small smile.

"That's lovely," Rosemary cooed. "Hold that pose!"

They did as they were told while she snapped away, and eventually, Robin leaned over and kissed him again. Dan closed his eyes, and Rosemary crowed with happiness. She quietened down when Robin deepened the kiss, holding Dan tight.

When they came up for air, Rosemary was necking her wine and making a point of not looking at them, the camera sitting on the table with the lens cap back on. Robin had a cheeky smile on his face. Dan wondered if he should be keeping score between mother and son. Whatever. It didn't matter. It felt good to be accepted into this family. He trampled down his guilt over yesterday's unresolved argument.

They continued unwrapping the gifts from under the tree. Robin handed out his gifts with flushed cheeks, then sat, staring at his hands.

Dan hefted the gift. It was solid and not too large. He had absolutely no idea what it could be. The shape was somewhat phallic, but he was fairly sure Robin wouldn't have handed him anything embarrassing to unwrap in front of his family. Robin looked nervous but not mischievous. Dan carefully undid the string and unwrapped the paper. He noted the lack of sellotape—that was so Robin. Perfectly neat and precise. Always doing things the authentic, old-fashioned way.

It was a wooden boat. Dan gasped, picking it up and running his fingertips over the smooth grain. It wasn't a perfect replica, but more the idea of a boat—all sleek lines and graceful curves. The pale wood had a soft sheen, and it felt like it had been waxed. He turned it over and found "RH" carved into the bottom.

"You made this? When?" It was hard to believe that Robin's hands could have carved something so beautiful. Dan knew he was a talented carpenter, but this was art, not craft.

"I've had plenty of long winter evenings alone on the boat." Robin cast a worried glance at Dan. "Do you like it?"

Dan squeezed Robin's hand. "I love it. Thank you." He wanted to pull him into a hug, but Robin's family were all waiting to thank him for their own carvings, their faces mirroring Dan's awe.

He'd thank Robin properly when he got him on his own.

Robin awoke on the morning of the twenty-seventh, and a crushing weight settled on his chest. Dan would be leaving, and they wouldn't see each other for a month. The memory of their argument sank heavy inside him. If Dan wasn't willing to move in with him, then what hope did they have in the longer term? Paranoia threaded its way through his thoughts, painting images of Tristan—svelte and oozing confidence—stealing Dan away from him in some tropical paradise. He'd never met the man, but he'd seen the photos. Tristan had the kind of face the cameras adored—all planes and angles, pouting lips and challenging gaze. Apparently Tris had turned down a modelling career to pursue his dream of being a dancer—a piece of information Dan offered that was supposed to illustrate what a great, down-to-earth guy Tris was, but which had only ended up making Robin hate the bloke with a passion.

Robin lay on his side, watching Dan sleep. He wanted to wake him with a caress, to tip them both into that ecstatic state when nothing else mattered outside of their sweat-slicked bodies moving together. Even now, feeling like this, the sight of Dan aroused him more than he would ever have imagined possible.

But he lay there, his erection subsiding, delaying the inevitable moment of waking Dan. Of seeing his eyes open with affection, but not that deeper feeling Robin craved. He thought he'd seen it there, but he must have been mistaken. Dan had made it clear that he wasn't about to give his heart. He wasn't even about to cohabit.

It must have been Robin's sigh that woke Dan.

"Hey," Dan said, snuggling closer and groping him in that lazy way he always did on waking. "Hey, what's the matter?"

Robin had no words. He turned onto his back and stared at the ceiling.

"Come on. You can tell me. It can't be that bad."

He took a deep breath. "You're going away, and you don't want to live with me, and I…I don't know how we can have a future together." He didn't feel any better for voicing his thoughts, and now his eyes prickled dangerously. He blinked and bit hard on his lip.

"Oh. That."

In his peripheral vision, Robin saw Dan prop himself up on his elbow.

"I want to be with you," Dan said, stroking Robin's chest. "I don't think I can make more of a commitment than that right now, but it's a lot for me."

"I need more."

It was Dan's turn to sigh now. "Well then, we're bloody well stuck. What do you want to do about it?"

"I don't know. Can't stand feeling like this, though."

"Like what?"

"Like I love you and you won't give me anything back." Robin's voice shook dangerously. "Like you're going off with Tristan and I'll never see you again."

239

"He's not a threat to us. Really. Nothing's going to happen between us now. Listen..." Dan trailed off, and Robin risked a quick glance at him. Dan's brow was scrunched up, and he looked scared. He continued in a cautious tone. "You remember the day before Christmas Eve? I went out on the lash with him? Well, I got a bit carried away at one point. I kissed him, but that was it. We stopped it there."

Robin sat up straight and glared at Dan. "You fucking what?"

"No, you don't need to be pissed off. I'm telling you that we didn't do anything. Could have, but didn't."

Robin couldn't believe what he was hearing. "And that's supposed to reassure me? That you fucking well snogged him when you were drunk? And now you're going off to some resort full of bars and hot men wearing next to nothing? Well, you'll excuse me if I don't go leaping for joy just because you didn't shag Tristan that time. It's not like you won't get plenty of chances over the next month."

Dan shrank down and bunched the quilt up in his fists. "I'm sorry, I'm... Shit, this was meant to make you feel better. I don't know what to say."

Robin's anger flared hard and bright. "Then don't say anything! There's nothing you can fucking well say to make things any better right now." He ignored Dan's reaching arms, and got out of the bed. "I'm taking a shower. It's nearly nine. You'd better get your stuff together if you want to make your train."

He gathered his clothing and stomped off down the hall to the guest bathroom, leaving the en suite to Dan. He didn't think he could stand it if Dan tried to climb in the shower with him. Didn't want to listen to any more apologies. Didn't want to break down and cry in front of him.

He turned the water up so hot it hurt and held back the tears by sheer force of will. Something precious had been ripped out from inside of him, leaving a raw, agonising emptiness in its place.

Robin made his way down to the breakfast room. Dan was cradling baby Patrick in his arms and had a silly smile on his face. It disappeared when their eyes met.

They were quiet at the table. Well, Robin was quiet. Dan still managed to keep up a steady stream of chatter, but Robin could tell his heart wasn't in it by the way his eyes remained grave and his cheeks undimpled. No one else seemed to notice, though.

After forcing enough turkey sandwiches on Dan to last him the rest of the week, Rosemary drove them both to the station. It was almost empty, and Robin accompanied him onto the platform.

Dan placed a hand on Robin's cheek. "So...I'll ring you. Let you know how I'm doing."

Robin turned away in an attempt to hide his eyes. "Yeah, well, I might want to moor up in the rushes."

"Fine, then, I'll text you."

Robin hunched his shoulders and made a noncommittal nod.

"Fucking hell, Robin. Look, don't go punishing me for one stupid little mistake when I was drunk. I'll behave, I promise. I won't drink any alcohol while I'm away, okay?"

Robin nodded. He couldn't risk opening his mouth in case he started begging Dan to stay and lost every last shred of his self-respect in the process.

"You know you have nothing to worry about, yeah? You're really important to me, and I don't want to fuck things up over something that didn't mean anything."

Didn't mean anything to Dan, maybe, but it meant a whole heap of pain for Robin. He turned away and blinked fiercely, biting down on his lower lip so hard it stung.

The platform speakers crackled and announced that the train was about to arrive.

"Bugger! I wanted to tell you that—" Dan's words were drowned out by the arriving train.

"What was that?" Robin asked.

Dan flushed. "It doesn't matter. Just...just take care of yourself, yeah?" Dan stepped up close and hugged Robin tight.

Robin wanted to avoid those treacherous lips, but his body seemed to think otherwise, and he found himself drawn into a heartbreaking kiss. He was acutely aware of how they'd missed their chance to make love one last time.

But making love wasn't so great when for one of you it was just fucking.

He clutched Dan tight, trying to store up the memory of him in his body. The warm scent of his aftershave, the strong, slender arms wrapped around him. The soft strands of hair, shining like bronze filaments in the weak December sun. And then those eyes—green flecked with gold—that seemed to promise so much, yet kept holding out on him. Betraying him.

Dan wrenched himself away at the last moment, visibly shaken. "I'll call you. I promise. We'll work it out, okay?"

Robin nodded, but he still couldn't believe they would.

His eyes smarted as he returned to the car. For once, his mother didn't say anything but just pressed a hand over his. Somehow, that simple pressure was enough to start the tears rolling. He fell against her, and they sat in the car while he gave in to the sobs that threatened to rip him apart. But they didn't, and eventually he calmed, even if the empty ache inside him was still there.

"He'll be back soon, darling. It will all be just fine. You'll see."

Robin nodded and gave her a smile. It felt tight and false.

He had a terrible premonition that he'd never set eyes on Dan again.

# Chapter Thirty-Two

Dan stared out of the train window, watching the cramped houses and their tiny back gardens spool past in an endless parade of battered fences, peeling paint and dirty windows. His mum's house was the best of the lot; she had standards. He spotted the shiny red back door and the brightly coloured plastic toys that filled the yard. Was that her at the kitchen window? The train went past too fast to tell, but she was generally the one who ended up doing all the chores when Dan wasn't there. It was a shame he'd be around only for the afternoon—she wouldn't be getting much of a Christmas break this year.

The walk from Streatham station took about ten minutes, and as always, Dan felt like he was shrinking in response to the bleak surroundings of the neighbourhood. The South London estate was particularly stark after just coming from the genteel outskirts of Cheltenham. As he turned into his old road, anger boiled up inside him. For fuck's sake, was the family next door deliberately trying to turn their front garden into a haven for every last vicious, disease-riddled rodent in the area? He glared at the piled-up detritus and made a mental note to harangue the local council into clearing it up. Again. They tended to listen to him more than to his mum. Perhaps it was because he'd let them know about his contacts in the media. He'd threatened to use them in the past, he'd been so incensed about the vermin problem.

His mum answered the door in her apron, and he leant down to give her a hug. Jean Taylor was a tiny woman, thin but strong. Her red gold hair had faded now, and her face was etched with lines, but you could tell she'd been a right looker when she was younger.

"You're looking gorgeous, sis. Now where's that mum of ours?"

"Oi, stop it, you! Cheeky boy." His mum giggled and flicked him with a tea towel. Dan thought she looked beautiful, with the lines in her cheeks framing her smile and her green eyes sparkling. "Come on in. It's bleedin' brass monkeys out 'ere. I'll pop the kettle on."

Dan followed her down the narrow hallway. He could hear the television blaring from the living room. It sounded like *Doctor Who*. He glanced in to see an assortment of nieces and nephews sprawled in front of the screen. No doubt his siblings and their partners were all down the pub. Dan said hello, and the older kids grunted, their eyes drawn back to the spectacle of David Tennant outsmarting the Cybermen. Little Chantal rushed over to hug his leg and gave a sticky, raspberry-flavoured kiss to his lips when he crouched down. He rubbed a hand through her frizzy hair and promised her a present when they'd finished watching telly. She giggled and kissed him again, then scampered back to join the others.

His mum had filled a chipped china teapot and covered it with a hand-knitted cosy. Dan sat at the table and looked up at the array of kid's paintings covering the tatty floral wallpaper.

"Where's Chantal's latest masterpiece, then?" He had a real soft spot for that kid. Only four years old and already she was producing beautiful paintings. His mum pointed the picture out. It showed a row of kids with brown skin and crazy hair holding hands with a ginger woman and a dark-skinned man. Dan grinned. "She'll have an exhibition in the Tate before she's twenty, you know."

His mum smiled indulgently, pouring out the brew into mismatched china teacups. Dan really should buy her another set. They never lasted long around here, though. Not with the herds of grandchildren that were always running around the place. Dan's brother and sisters all lived within a half-mile radius and used their mum as an unpaid babysitter so that they could earn enough to feed all those mouths. She didn't seem to mind, though, lavishing her grandkids with affection but still able to lay down the law.

"How's things, then, Mum? You keeping well?"

"Fit as a fiddle, love. You know me." She grinned at him over the teacup. "What about you and this sexy boater of yours, then? Has 'e swept you off your feet, yet? Made an honest man out of you?"

"Mum!" Dan felt an unfamiliar heat in his face. He stared at the steam hissing out of the pressure cooker. No doubt it was one of her famous Christmas puddings. He knew he should be answering her but didn't know how to.

"Well, I never! Never thought I'd live to see the day I could make you blush. Not without getting a photo album out, anyway."

Dan cringed. Yep, there were some seriously embarrassing photos in there. All those youthful fashion experiments. He'd looked like a right twat for most of his teenage years, and it was a wonder he hadn't had the shit kicked out of him on a more regular basis.

"So when are you going to bring this young man around so that I can show them to him? I want to see this tattooed gypsy who's managed to bewitch you."

"Mum! He's not a gypsy. They're called travellers. Or boaters. Or just people."

"I'm not being rude, love, honest. Robin, isn't it?" Dan nodded. "So has he always lived like that? Come from Romany stock?"

Dan gave a wry smile, wondering how Rosemary would react to hearing her son called a gypsy. "Hardly. They're proper upper-middle class, they are. There was a family tree and coat of arms up in the downstairs bog."

"You never! Seriously?" Her eyes were round, sparkling with glee. "You gone and got yourself a sugar daddy?"

"Mum! He's five years younger than me. And he makes his own way doing manual labour. It's just not like that. If anything, I'm the sugar daddy." And that was such a disturbing thought, he blushed again.

"So, when am I going to meet him? Can you bring 'im round for tea once you get back from your hols?"

"Erm, well, I..." Dan trailed off, realising that he had no idea if Robin even wanted to meet his family. Maybe Robin would find them all appallingly common. He doubted it. The guy lived among travellers, also known as the scum of the earth by the right-wing press. Still, he'd hate to think of his mum being looked down on by anyone.

But when he met her understanding gaze, he realised that this wasn't the thing that was making him hesitate. If he brought Robin back here, it would be like making it all official, wouldn't it?

"What is it, love?" Her voice was gentle, and Dan really wanted to unburden himself.

"Oh, it's all gone tits-up, Mum, and I don't know what I'm feeling. He says he loves me, and he wants me to move onto his boat with him."

"And that's a problem, is it?"

"Yes! Yes it is. There's no way I could live in such a tiny space with another guy, no matter how much I...liked them. It'd be a disaster waiting to happen. It'd be like you and Dad." He clamped his mouth shut, seeing the hurt on his mum's face and wishing he could erase the words out of existence. "Shit! I'm sorry, Mum. I'm sorry." He got up and went to hug her.

"Is that what you think, love? You think we was unhappy?"

"You used to row all the time." Okay, they weren't screaming matches like you heard coming through the thin walls from next door. More a constant bickering that sent him running for the sanctuary of his granddad's shed.

"Row? What about?" She looked genuinely puzzled.

"You know. Stuff like you pestering him to repaper the kitchen and calling him a lazy, drunken sod. And him saying you spoilt us kids. And complaining about having to sleep in the lounge." Now that he thought about it, they didn't seem like anything too serious. Not much worse than Robin berating him for feeding the swans out of the hatch.

His mum was giving him an affectionate smile. "You silly boy. That was just life. Nothing to worry yourself about. We used to enjoy our little spats, you know. Especially makin' up afterwards." She had a distinctly roguish gleam in her eye. "We loved each other. If you love someone, you can make it work. D'you love this Robin?"

And that was the thing, wasn't it? The thing he couldn't answer. He stared at her, wondering if he should tell her about the stupid mistake with Tris and whether she'd be able to help him understand his messed-up feelings.

But then the familiar theme tune blared through the wall, closely followed by a mob of children all desperate for their Christmas presents from Uncle Dan. His mum rolled her eyes, saying they'd talk later. It wasn't until he was on the train back that he realised they'd never had a chance to. His sisters had stayed late, chattering about the kids and the latest celebrity gossip—though why they'd thought he'd be interested in the Beckham's love life he had no idea. The only moment alone with his mum had been on the doorstep.

"You look after yourself, hear me? And you make sure you 'old on to this Robin fella. He's good for you. I can see that."

Dan nodded and kissed her before heading back to the station and his empty flat.


Robin cruised away from Bath, looking for somewhere peaceful he could be alone for a while. Trouble was, in the middle of winter, most of the canal was crammed with boats, and he didn't want to deal with all the well-meaning enquiries about Dan from the other boaters. That was the problem with living on the towpath—people were always stopping by to say hello and check up on you. He wasn't sure how well he'd be able to lie when friends asked him if he'd heard from Dan.

Robin hadn't switched his phone on since leaving his parents' place. He didn't want to be reminded of where Dan was and who he was with.

No, he needed somewhere away from gossiping boaters. Somewhere secluded. Somewhere private. He looked with envy at the other side of the canal, where the ends of the carefully manicured gardens of Bathampton met the water's edge.

"Yoohoo! Robin, darling, is that you?"

The call cut through the engine's chugging and snagged his attention. There was a man standing in the next garden waving his arms around. God, it was Charles Wentworth, flapping a handkerchief around like it was some kind of flag. Robin couldn't help but smile at the spectacle and steered *Serendipity* in towards the bank.

Someone who'd owned the house in the past must have had their own boat as there were two wooden jetties extending from the grassy verge. They couldn't have been better positioned for *Serendipity*, one reaching her front deck and one the back, and would be so much safer than tramping over an icy plank in the depths of winter.

He wondered if the offer of a mooring still stood.

"You've come! Oh, that's marvellous. But really, my dear, you should have rung. I haven't got anything in. Well, that's not true, I'm sure I can rustle up a glass of brandy for my favourite young man. Come on in, let me show you what needs your expert attention."

Robin allowed himself to be led inside the large stone house. He didn't shake off Charles's hold on his arm. Right now Charles offered sanctuary, and he'd be a fool not to take him up on it, no matter what the price might be.

# Chapter Thirty-Three

Marek gave Robin an icy glare and muttered something under his breath. Robin forced a smile, stepping around the ladder on his way to the bathroom. It was hard to figure out why the Polish decorator had taken an instant dislike to him, and Marek's English either wasn't good enough to articulate his reasons, or he couldn't be bothered to try. It seemed like an overreaction to the news that he would have to repaint the study once Robin had finished fitting Charles's bookshelves.

He'd been working here for five days now, and apart from the tense situation with Marek, so far things were going well. As well as could be expected, anyway. He worked long hours and kept his mobile switched off so that the outside world couldn't reach him. He had access to Charles's log pile and the use of his bathroom, so he could probably last a month before needing to cruise anywhere to fill or empty *Serendipity's* tanks. It was the kind of seclusion he'd always dreamed of, which made it even more peculiar that he wasn't enjoying it one bit.

Most evenings he'd have a brandy with Charles after finishing up but always made his excuses rather than accepting another. Surprisingly, Charles didn't seem to mind. Either that or he had the good manners not to force the situation. Maybe he had a drink with Marek after Robin left, although God knew what they'd find to talk about. Maybe Marek had other qualities Robin couldn't see. He was certainly very blond and well-built, despite being a couple of inches shorter than Dan.

Robin wondered what he'd do if Charles did make a pass at him. Could he divorce his emotions from his sex drive enough to accept some physical comfort? Dan didn't seem to have a problem doing so. Maybe he should try it. Maybe revenge would give him some satisfaction. It might help to close the raw hole where his heart should be.

He closed the door on the surly decorator and sagged back against it. A big stack of magazines had appeared in Charles's bathroom. He must have been doing more unpacking. Robin leafed through a copy of *Gay Times* until he reached the travel section. A full page advert for a gay resort stared out at him. The photo teemed with scantily clad and well-muscled young men, looking like they'd been oiled. Apparently, clothing was "forever optional".

He threw the magazine back on the stack as if it had bit him. Why the hell did he keep torturing himself with thinking about Dan out there? It wasn't like he could do anything to change the situation. Other than phoning Dan and begging him to come back, of course. But he wasn't going to do that. Not under any circumstances. Far safer just to leave the sodding phone switched off and try to forget all about Dan Taylor.

If only he could convince himself that he wanted to.


Dan took another sip of his virgin piña colada and leaned over the mezzanine railing to give Tris a wave. At the moment, Tris was on the dance floor, sandwiched between two sun-kissed, tattooed gods, and Dan had to swallow the jealousy away with another sip of pineapple juice. Playa Del Inglés hadn't changed much since he'd last visited the island, that time staying in one of the high-rise hotels in the centre of town. At night the central shopping area burst into gaudy mayhem as the plethora of bars and clubs, both gay and straight, competed for trade. Fortunately, this time he'd been set up in a resort at the nearby, yet rather more genteel Maspalomas, just far enough away to no longer hear the pervasive throbbing bass lines and hoots of drunken tourists. However, tempting though it was to mope in the villa every evening, he had a guidebook to update, and that involved visiting as many of the bars and clubs as he could stomach.

"All right, mate? Are you Dan?" an Australian voice asked him, booming over the deafening techno.

Dan stared up at six feet plus of tattooed muscle and attitude, topped with a shock of blond curls. It was one of Tris's dance partners. "Yeah, that's me." His innate friendliness fought with his desire to avoid temptation.

"That's a relief. Name's Shane, and that hunk dancing with your friend is Greg. My boyfriend," Shane said proudly. "I fancied sitting out for a bit, but I'm not in the mood to be cruised. Mind if I join you?"

Dan nodded, and Shane flashed a brilliantly pearly set of teeth. They sat in silence for a while, watching Tris's and Greg's obscene gyrations. The jealousy welled up again, not strong enough to make Dan do anything stupid, just a futile longing. He looked up to find Shane studying him.

"What's up? You look jealous as fuck."

Dan sighed. "That bloody obvious, is it?"

"Sorry, mate, if I'd known it was like that, I wouldn't have danced with him."

Shane looked genuinely contrite, and Dan rushed to explain. "No, it's not that. We're not together. Tris and I are just friends. I just… I wish my boyfriend could trust me like you do with Greg, that's all."

"Your boyfriend?" Shane looked around as if expecting Robin to appear out of the crowd. "Where's he, then?"

"Back in England," Dan admitted.

"You came *here* without him?" Shane's jaw dropped.

"It's not like that! This is work. I'm a travel writer, and I asked him first, but when he wouldn't come, I gave the spare ticket to Tris." Dan stared at his mobile on the tabletop. "Now the fucker won't even answer his bloody phone. He doesn't trust me. Thinks I'm sleeping around behind his back." Dan took a long slurp of his drink as Shane looked on with a puzzled yet sympathetic expression.

"You wanna fill me in on the whole story?"

Shane was a good listener, raising his eyebrows when Dan confessed his fear of water, but making no comment. When he'd finished his saga, Dan sat back and studied Shane, who was again watching Tris and Greg, now snogging and grinding against each other. Shane had an affectionate smile on his face.

"How come Robin can't be like you?" Dan asked, not really expecting an answer.

"God knows, but I'll tell you what, there's no way I'd be happy about Greg doing that"—Shane stabbed a finger in Greg's direction—"if I didn't know he loved me and that he'd be coming back with me later. Not that I mind if Tris comes back too," he added with a leer.

Dan tried to imagine ever suggesting a threesome to Robin. He wouldn't dare.

"Enough of this heavy shit, yeah?" Shane said, standing up. "Reckon it's my shout. What'ya drinking?" Dan filled him in, and Shane grimaced at the notion of alcohol-free cocktails but didn't argue. "All right, I'll get you your lolly water, but when I get back, we're gonna talk about your swimming lessons. Starting tomorrow, I want to see you in your togs out by your hotel poolside at nine. Reckon I can get you swimming like a bloody fish in a month's time."

Dan gaped as Shane strutted off to the bar. Arrogant bastard! Mind you, the idea of being able to swim was appealing, and anything that helped to take his mind off missing Robin had to be good. He mulled it over as he drained the last of his glass. Yeah, it would be great to have a surprise for Robin when he got back. It would do him good to face his fears.

He wished he could contemplate facing the other ones with such courage.


Robin woke to the sound of creaking. He'd been a boater long enough to recognise the sound of a vessel ploughing through ice, but there was still something unearthly about the noise. It reminded him of how there was only a quarter of an inch of steel between his home and the freezing water. He shivered and forced himself out of bed to get the stove going.

He glanced at his phone. Still switched off. But he didn't want to think about why, so he distracted himself with making coffee.

He stood by the hatch with a mug of steaming coffee in his hands and looked out over the frozen canal. It was a proper cold snap; hoar frost rimed every branch of the willows opposite, glittering in the watery sunshine. Looked like every last plant had been dipped in sugar and crystallised. The field was so white, if he squinted it looked like snow. Jagged sheets of ice lined the canal, but the early boat had cut a clear path through the centre, and the ducks were taking advantage of it. They spotted him at the hatch and headed over in a demanding mob.

"I suppose you want some breakfast too."

He fetched the stale end of his last loaf of bread and began throwing them pieces. He could almost hear a ghostly echo of Dan's delighted chuckles when feeding them. Everything reminded Robin of him—especially this hatchway—the one he'd fucked him against until his legs gave way. He bit his lip hard at the thought of Dan letting anyone else do that to him.

But it was inevitable, wasn't it? Eventually, Dan would give in to temptation. He'd get drunk with Tris, and then all thoughts of Robin would be pushed aside. It wasn't like they had a future together. Dan had told him as much when he refused to contemplate moving in.

It wasn't like Dan loved him back.

He punched the hatch frame. It startled the ducks, hurt his knuckles and did nothing to improve his mood.

He trudged up to Charles's house, leaving the phone behind again.

"You sure you don't want to come?" Dan asked.

Tris lifted his head a fraction, then slumped back onto the pillow. "Jesus bloody Christ, how much did I have to drink last night?"

Dan grinned. "No idea. I wasn't there, remember?"

"Can't remember anything."

"Greg dropped you back here and said you'd demolished a whole bottle of Malibu, so if you taste coconut when you chuck, that's why."

Tris just groaned and pulled the pillow over his head. He'd been maudlin the whole time they'd been in Maspalomas. Happy hour at the bar seemed to cheer him up for a while—as did hitting the clubs—and he found someone to keep him occupied most nights, but whenever he and Dan were alone together, all he could talk about was how much he missed Alex. Several times Dan had had to bite back a snappy comment about why the hell didn't he just go back and make up with the guy.

Dan downed a glass of water and started sifting through the pile of clothing on the floor to find his Speedos.

"Ugh, can't breathe!" Tris flung the pillow to one side. "Oh my God, you've grown your pubes. And is that a tan line I can see? Are you having some kind of early midlife crisis I should know about?"

Dan glanced down at his stubbly groin. "Maybe I've decided to go for the natural look."

"Natural? Why on earth would you want to do that? Now be a dear and close that blind before you go. Need sleep."

Dan pulled on his swimming trunks, wrapped a towel around his waist and headed down to the pool. It was early yet, but Shane would be waiting for him. The thought filled his stomach with butterflies. He'd known the bloke only for a week, but already Shane had him doing something he'd never thought possible.

Shane had him enjoying swimming.

This was the pattern of Dan's days. He headed down to the pool early to get his lesson in before any of the other guests woke up. Then, after a shower and checking in on Tris, he'd pick up his camera and head down to the bus station. It never ceased to amaze him how much there was to see on the island. Previous times he'd visited, he'd never ventured far from the bars and clubs of Playa Del Inglés, but there was a whole native community out there. Tiny villages nestled precariously on steep mountainsides. Roadside shrines glittered with votive candles and a bizarre mix of offerings. Hand-painted icons and plaster statues of saints rubbed shoulders with silk flowers and holographic portraits of the Pope. Goats scampered up the hillsides, and giant cactus plants grew through tumbledown stone walls.

He'd take his lunch in some tiny restaurant that usually catered only to locals, then head back down to the resort on the last bus. He'd go out for a couple of drinks with Tris, then spend the rest of the evening holed up in their villa. He'd download the day's photographs and sort through them.

He'd dial Robin's number again and again and again.

He'd sleep alone. Sometimes Tris would fall into bed at a late hour, but they kept to their own sides of the mattress.

He couldn't wait to get back home.

Home wasn't London.

Home was wherever Robin was.

"Robin, my dear, have you seen the *Observer* magazine yet? Oh, you simply must come and have a look."

Robin followed Charles down to his temporary office. He had an idea what he might be asked to look at but was unprepared for just how sharply his stomach lurched when he saw the double-page spread.

Dan's photographs filled the pages like a mosaic. Robin's fellow boaters stared down the lens as if challenging the world to judge them. Charles was still talking, but Robin barely noticed, absorbed in studying the pictures. He lifted the magazine to take a closer look. He'd forgotten about this side of Dan. This side that could see the essence of someone and bring it out. Could help them open up in a way that they never normally would. Could make them feel comfortable in their own skin.

The way he made Robin feel whenever he was around.

The pictures blurred. He blinked to clear his eyes.

"I say, whatever is the matter? There, there, no need to get upset." Charles folded his arms around Robin and handed him a large handkerchief that smelt of cedarwood. "Now come on, you've obviously been working far too hard just lately. You're coming out with me for a drink, and I won't take no for an answer."

Robin nodded, not trusting his voice right now. Strange how easy it was to sink into Charles's embrace. He'd never have expected to welcome it like this. Must be the effect of seeing those photographs.

After what felt like an age, he extracted himself from Charles's arms and risked a quick look at his face. Charles smiled, and Robin couldn't for the life of him work out if it was a leer or simply friendly, or even which one he'd prefer right now, but there was only one way to find out.

"Okay, let's go," he said, wondering what the fuck he thought he was doing.

Robin grabbed his coat on the way out, pulling on a layer of guilt with the woollen fabric—he was going for a drink with another man, wearing his Christmas present from Dan. But he couldn't keep thinking about Dan. It was time to move on. To forget. He drew in deep lungfuls of frigid air and focused instead on the plumes of steam he exhaled.

Charles steered them down through the village, then turned towards the humpback bridge that crossed the canal. Robin balked as they neared the Queen's Head. "Does it have to be here?"

"Do you have a problem with the place? I admit Nigel may not be the most genial landlord, but he does know how to cellar his beers, which is your preferred tipple if memory serves me correctly." Charles held open the door for him, and as ever, Robin found it almost impossible to argue with the man. "Don't worry, darling." Charles lifted Robin's chin with a finger. "You just trust me to know how to deal with Nigel. We were at school together, you see."

"No! I can do it. I'll get the first round in. I owe you a drink."

"Stubborn creature, aren't you?" Charles gave a wolfish grin. "Very well, then, I'll allow you to treat me for a change."

Nigel was his usual, odious self. "Pint of bitter and a double brandy. That'll be six sixty," he said, slamming the drinks down so hard they sloshed into the drip tray.

Robin tried to pay, but Nigel wouldn't put his hand out. In the end, he had to put the tenner down on the bar. The change was shoved back towards him in a similar, begrudging fashion.

"Now, now, Nigel," Charles said, his voice so icy it sent a chill down Robin's spine. "There's no need to treat your customers like that. We expect better service in future."

Nigel muttered something under his breath that Robin didn't catch, but Charles drew in a sharp breath and puffed up with anger.

"Lest you forget, Nigel Truman, I'm still Chairman of the Bath Chamber of Commerce, and I can make things very difficult for you if you carry on spreading vicious rumours about the boating community. I'll have you know this young man has been doing sterling work around my house. I'd trust him with my life."

"Oh yeah?" Nigel's usual ill-tempered sneer seemed to have returned. "I'll bet he's been doing *work* for you. I know your tastes, Charlie. Remember them well."

Robin's rage rose, quick and hot. He'd defend Charles if things turned ugly. There was no way he'd let Nigel pick on the harmless old gent.

But Charles didn't seem to need his help. He pulled out a handkerchief and started polishing up his glasses. Eventually he held them up to the light, nodded and pushed them onto his nose. When he spoke, his voice was quiet and pleasant, but somehow even creepier because of that.

"Nigel, my dear, I can assure you that if you continue to spread your particularly virulent brand of homophobia around here, then I am going to inform all your customers exactly what it was you used to get up to in the boat sheds at school." He paused to look around the pub. It wasn't crowded, but there were at least eight other punters listening in and not bothering to hide the fact. "Now, are you going to apologise to young Robin here, or do you want me to tell everyone your old nickname?"

Nigel stared like he couldn't believe what he was hearing, then turned to Robin and glowered. "Sorry," he forced out through clenched teeth.

"What was that?" Charles demanded. "Speak up, man. Sorry for what?"

Nigel looked mutinous for a moment, staring at Charles. Robin watched Charles mouth something that made Nigel blanch.

"I'm sorry for spreading rumours about you," Nigel muttered, his gaze fixed on the floor.

Robin stared at him. He'd always known the day he saw someone get the best of Nigel Truman he'd be overjoyed, but was surprised to find it tempered by pity for the man, who looked like he'd been kicked in the guts.

"It's okay," Robin said. "Apology accepted."

Nigel looked daggers at him. "How noble of you," he spat out.

Charles took hold of Robin's arm and pulled him away from the bar to a quiet corner table. Robin kept his eyes fixed on Nigel for as long as possible, but then allowed Charles to distract him with his customary genteel flirtation. It didn't creep him out anymore, which was good. In fact, watching Charles stand up to Nigel like that had increased his respect for the man a hundredfold.

There was one thing he had to know, though. "What was Nigel's nickname at school?"

Charles gave a sly grin. "We used to call him Two-Man Truman on account of what he used to get up to after dark, and I hope you don't need me to draw you a picture."

Robin blushed, laughed and drank some beer to try and compose himself. "Are you serious?"

Charles winked, then changed the subject. "Robin darling, have I ever told you how ravishing you are when you're embarrassed?"

"Um, no." And he wasn't sure how he felt about being told, either. It was flattering, and it made his heart beat faster even as he squirmed in his seat.

Charles laid a hand over his. "Oh, believe me, darling, you are breathtaking. You make an old man feel young again."

Robin swallowed hard. What with the way Charles was gazing at his lips, Robin could almost feel the kiss they'd never had.

He was beginning to wonder if he might be ready to find out what Charles really wanted from him.

# Chapter Thirty-Four

Dan stared out at the rolling waves breaking on the sandbank. A lagoon of still, shallow water sheltered behind it, such a startling shade of turquoise it hurt to look at it.

Or perhaps his heart was hurting for some other reason.

He watched the white boats bobbing out in the open ocean.

He'd been here for almost two weeks now, and it was absolutely beautiful. He had a well-appointed villa in a luxurious resort packed with attractive and available men, and by all rights he should be having the time of his life.

But the only place he wanted to be was on a poky little boat with one special man.

The man he now knew he loved.

It was terrifying, this love. It demanded that he change everything. That he give up his independence, his whole way of life and merge it with Robin's. And he was ready to do that. Ready to compromise and move on.

But how on earth could he cope with living together?

He watched the boats, and an idea dropped from the sky, sending his thoughts rippling out from the impact.

Of course! That could work. He'd need to check out some facts and figures, he'd need to run up one hell of a phone bill, but he thought he could probably do it. If Tris would help him, he could definitely do it. He could finish his assignment, and he could get back home and show Robin exactly how much he loved him.

He headed back to his room and booted up his laptop. He spent half an hour checking websites and made a couple of phone calls, then sent a text to Robin. He yanked the covers off Tris.

"Rise and shine, lazybones. I've got a job for you to do. I need you to go back to London for me."

Robin lay back on his sofa, weighed down by Morris on his chest and his constantly circling thoughts. The magazine lay next to him, open on the page of Dan's photos. It was a week since Charles had showed it to him, but he'd been looking at it every day since. A whole week of brooding and indecision and gnawing temptation. He tickled behind Morris's ears, imagining he could hear his mum pestering him to get up and about like she did after Jamie died.

"Robin? Are you there?"

His imagination was more vivid than usual. It sounded like she was right outside.

"Robin? I can see smoke coming out of your chimney. Are you going to stop sulking and help me over this death-trap jetty?"

He sat up. Morris protested, but he pushed him aside and went to the window. She was there, all right, standing next to Charles and decked out in a green waxed jacket and thigh-length wellies like some kind of fancy-dress farmer. Her nose and cheeks were bright red with the cold. Ordinarily he would have laughed at the sight, but right now all he wanted was a hug.

He burst out of the doors and cleared the jetty, almost knocking her over. "Mum," was all he could say. He repeated it again, his voice cracking.

"I'd best leave you to it," Charles said, backing away from them with a fond expression. "If you need anything, you know where to find me."

"Mum, I'm so sorry."

"Oh, you silly boy, how can I stay mad at you when you greet me like this?" She tightened her arms around him. Her face was icy where it touched his. Despite the watery sunshine, it was a chill day. "Now come on, you'd better show me onboard this boat of yours. I'm going to freeze out here, and so are you. You're not even wearing your coat."

Robin gave a small smile. "Come on, then. I'll hold your hand if you want, but you should be fine. It's much safer than the plank was."

He ushered her into his home for the first time. Her eyes were huge, wary, but not disapproving.

"Oh! Isn't it cosy? So warm. I thought it would be cold with the water so close."

Robin watched her taking it all in. She ran her manicured fingernails over the shelving between the galley and saloon. "Did you really build all of this?"

He nodded. Usually he'd want to show visitors around and watch their awed gazes with a quiet pride, but right now he just wanted to look after his mum.

"Sit by the stove. I'll get the kettle on."

He remained silent for a couple of minutes while waiting for the water to boil. His mum was too taken up with removing her excess layers and greeting Morris to grill him, which made a pleasant change. In the end, it was Robin who spoke.

"How did you find me?"

She sniffed, and Robin braced himself for disapproval. However, she just pulled a handkerchief out of a pocket and blew her nose. "It wasn't easy, darling. I had to park in that delightful little village and ask the landlord of that pub. What a pompous, bigoted fool! I gave him a piece of my mind, I can tell you."

"Nigel, you mean? I'd love to have seen that." His mother was not the sort of woman you wanted to cross. Fierce didn't come into it when she was defending herself or her loved ones. "What did he say to you?"

She sniffed again, but this time it really was in disapproval. "Oh, I don't need to repeat it. Some poisonous diatribe against boaters. And you in particular." Her face sagged, the self-righteous indignation giving way to sorrow. "I'm so sorry you have to put up with that kind of thing. Your lifestyle choices are no one else's business."

It would have been rude to remind her of past tirades against Robin's way of life, and besides which, it was too good to see her to risk spoiling the mood. Her presence was lifting the leaden weight inside him. He remembered how he'd kept himself out of contact for almost a month, and shame rushed up inside him, hot and sharp.

"I'm sorry, Mum."

"Don't be ridiculous, darling. You have nothing to be ashamed of."

"I do. I should have called you, let you know I was okay."

"Yes, you should have. Don't ever do that again, darling. I've been worried sick this last month. I kept thinking something awful had happened." She gave him a funny look. "What has happened? Why are you moored up in this Charles fellow's garden? Is Dan treating you properly?"

He laughed, surprised at how bitter it sounded. "Not really. He's gone off with Tristan, hasn't he?"

"What do you mean? Robin, what's going on here?" He watched the realisation dawning on her face. "Is that why you've had the phone switched off all this time? Have you been avoiding Dan's calls?"

"No! Yes. I don't know. I just—I don't want to know what he's doing out there with all those other blokes. With Tris."

"But what makes you think he's doing anything? I don't understand."

"It's a gay resort, Mum. You know the sort of things that go on somewhere like that."

"I certainly don't!" She pulled her cardigan around her primly.

"No, okay, maybe not. But trust me, there'll be sex on offer everywhere. It'll be a meat market."

"What makes you think that, darling? Have you ever been to one of these places?"

"No fucking way!" She flinched, and he made a conscious effort to calm down. "Sorry. No, no I haven't. But I know what gay blokes are like. They're sluts."

She frowned at him, and Robin busied himself making the tea.

"Are you like that, Robin?"

"Like what?"

"Like you said," she enunciated carefully, "a slut."

He gaped at her and was about to say it was none of her fucking business, but something about her expression warned him not to. He thought about it. Thought about how he'd been out on the prowl when he first met Charles. Thought about how readily he'd leapt into bed with Dan and how he'd recently started flirting with Charles. But then there were all those years of staying faithful to Jamie. And then he hadn't gone near a bloke for years, and he'd been faithful to Dan so far, even though they weren't really together anymore. If indeed they ever had been.

"No," he whispered. He cleared his throat and spoke louder, clearer. "No, I'm not like that."

"But you think Dan is?"

He didn't want to answer that one, so he turned back to the mugs of tea and slopped milk into them. "Jamie was."

"Jamie was a manipulative little S-H-one-T and I don't think you should be judging Dan by *his* standards." She looked shocked at her outburst, but then her shoulders sagged as she sighed. "Look, sweetheart, I don't know Dan's history, and I've no idea what it's like in these gay resorts, but I don't think you do either. Besides, it's plain to see that no matter what, that young man is besotted with you."

Robin grimaced. "I don't think so. He doesn't love me."

"Nonsense! Of course he does. You can see it every time he looks at you. If that's not love, then I'm the Queen of Sheba."

Robin wanted it to be true. He saw the conviction blazing in her eyes. But just because his mum said it was love, didn't mean Dan would agree.

"Here's your tea, Your Majesty," he said, handing her the mug.

They drank in silence for a while.

"I'm sorry I made you gay," she said out of nowhere.

He spluttered on a mouthful of tea. "You what?"

"I'm sorry. I know I wasn't the best mother in the world. I did everything wrong when you were young." She looked sheepish, her eyes lowered.

Was this really his mum? Robin had never heard her admit to being in the wrong before. "You were a good mother. I've always known you love me."

"You do? That's good." She seemed genuinely relieved, and Robin wondered how she could ever have doubted that.

"I did everything wrong, though. I know that now. Reading all these attachment parenting books Miranda lends me and seeing how happy little Patrick is being carried around in a sling and breastfed on demand... Well, it makes me wish I'd been able to do that with you. You were such a difficult baby, always crying. You must have needed me to hold you, you must have been trying to tell me that—"

She broke off, and Robin saw the tears start to fall. In an instant, he was by her side, holding her tight and rocking gently. "Hey, it's okay. I turned out all right, didn't I?"

"You don't understand! I was told the *proper* way to do everything. The midwives said if I picked you up when you cried, you'd end up being a real mummy's boy. They told me that breastfeeding could turn you queer. Well, just shows you what they knew! Brought up on the bottle and still gay."

The bitterness wounded him, but sympathy for her soothed the sting. "I don't think it's connected. And even if it is, I don't care. I'm happy with who I am."

"Are you?" She pulled back to look at him. Her mascara had made smudgy marks under her eyes, and she looked about ten years younger without her usual mask of confidence. "You don't sound happy about it. You talk about gay men like you don't have any respect for them. That makes me think you can't possibly respect yourself."

Robin didn't reply. He watched the flames dancing in his stove. He thought about Jamie, and about Dan, and how totally different they both were. He barely noticed when his mum got up and went through to the back of the boat. When she returned, she had her usual war paint back in place and a resolute expression.

"I want you to check your phone."

He stalled. "I can't. There's no reception here."

"Fine, then we'll go for a walk. There was definitely reception in that pub. You can check your messages, and then we can have something to eat and show that petty-minded little fool that we're not ashamed of anything."

Robin was about to point out that a boycott would hurt Nigel more, but then he thought about how reluctant he'd be to cause a scene in front of the Sunday lunch crowd. He'd have to put up with Robin sitting in his pub. A homo boater sitting at his own bar and polluting it with his foul depravities. One who knew his secret nickname.

He grinned. "Yeah, all right, then."

There was a side passage around to the front of the house, and Robin headed that way to avoid disturbing Charles, but then Charles called out after them.

"Robin! I say, do you have a moment to spare? I really need your help with something. In private, if that's not too much to ask."

"I'm just on my way out..." he began, but the plea in Charles's eyes made him pause.

"Mum, would you mind going on ahead and getting us a table? I'll catch you up."

"Of course, darling." His mum furrowed her brow. "I do hope that dear man is all right. He's quite a character, isn't he?"

Robin smiled. "Yeah, he is. Don't worry, I'll help him sort it out."

He followed Charles in through the back door.

# Chapter Thirty-Five

Dan steered the *Jolly Roger* through the swing bridge, waving to the dogwalker who'd stopped to open it for him. He looked out over the shiny blue roof of his new boat and gave her a pat. Yep, he could understand now why Robin caressed *Serendipity* in that way. Already he'd fallen in love with her, and he just had to hope Robin understood her significance—the proof that Dan trusted in their future together so much he was willing to sell his flat and buy a boat instead.

Best decision he'd ever made.

Now he just had to find Robin.

A familiar figure with blond dreadlocks appeared on the roof of a boat moored up ahead. Dan waited until he was nearly parallel, then went into reverse, bringing the *Jolly Roger* to a stop alongside Aranya's boat.

"All right, mate? I don't suppose you know where Robin's moored up, do you?"

Aranya gave him a cool stare. "Haven't seen you around in a while."

Shit, had Robin been telling the other boaters about their problems? It didn't seem likely, but it was hard to read Aranya's expression. Dan went for a half-truth. "Yeah, I've been busy with work, but now I'm back, and I'm one of you lot." He patted his boat for emphasis. "I can't get hold of Robin on his mobile. Do you know where he is?"

The stare turned pitying. "You mean you don't know?"

"I wouldn't be asking if I knew, would I?" Jesus, had Aranya always been this irritating?

It was a moment before Aranya replied, and when he did, he sounded reluctant. "Same place he's been all month. Some rich bloke's garden down in Bathampton. Look, Dan, I don't like having to be the one to tell you this, but I think Robin's got a new man. I've seen him heading back to his boat really late at night, and they've been seen drinking together down the Queen's Head."

Dan's head spun. "They? Who are you talking about?"

"The old bloke who owns the house. Absolutely loaded, fruity dress sense, wears a cravat—you know who I mean? I think his name's Charlie or something."

The penny dropped. The old guy from the pub, all those months ago. Dan dug up an old memory of Robin's tale of how Charles had tried to seduce him into mooring up at the end of his garden. He laughed. "Oh yeah, I know who you mean. Nah, Robin's not interested in him. Besides, I'm back now, and I'm here to stay this time."

Aranya didn't look convinced. "I'm just letting you know what people have been saying. Robin's given up working at Smiler's, and he's been avoiding everyone. Looks pretty suspicious if you ask me, but I suppose you know him better than I do."

"That's right." Dan smiled and waved good-bye, but his guts gave an uneasy twist, and he put the *Jolly Roger* into second gear despite being in an area where boats were lining the canal. He didn't care if they caught his wash—he needed to get to Robin and find out what was going on.

In another five minutes, Dan rounded a bend and caught sight of *Serendipity*. His heart stuttered. There was a telltale rippling in the air over her stovepipe. Robin was home.

Dan brought his boat to a stop alongside her and fastened the two boats together. He was blocking the whole canal, but he just had to see Robin right away. In fact, he was surprised Robin wasn't out on deck, wondering what was going on.

He walked down the roof of his boat and jumped onto *Serendipity*'s front deck. The doors weren't locked, but it took only a moment to search the boat and come up empty-handed. There were two mugs sitting on the side. Dan paused for a moment, wondering who Robin had been entertaining. Surely there was only one option, if he hadn't been socialising with the other boaters? Peering out through the kitchen porthole, Dan could see that the back door to Charles's house was standing open, Morris loitering just outside it.

Dan made his way up through the garden, his stomach twisting itself in knots. Could Robin really have decided he'd be better off without him? Better off throwing his lot in with Charles? Surely not.

But then again, Robin had been acting strangely, taking himself right out of contact with everyone else.

Dan told his mind to shut the fuck up and walked the last few paces to the back door. He could hear voices from inside. Charles's voice. Moaning. Slurping noises.

"Yes, that's it. Good boy. Suck it down. Mmmm, feels so good in your hot little mouth."

Dan leant his forehead against the doorjamb and tried to ignore Charles's dirty talk. It served him right, didn't it? Leaving Robin on his own for this long. The man had needs, and it was only natural to find someone to fill them.

But no, that wasn't right. Dan had coped for a month without straying. Robin always acted like Mr. High-and-mighty-and-bloody-well-purer-than-thou, but here he was, caught in the act. Dan gave a grim smile that hurt his face. The betrayal was sickening. His insides burned like he'd swallowed acid. He had a feeling there were worlds of pain lurking behind this sharp edge, just waiting to catch up with him.

To pay him back.

But he'd bought a bloody boat!

Charles was still talking. "That's it, get your cock out. I want to see you beat yourself off."

Dan had heard enough. Sod this. He wasn't going to stand around like a pillock while Robin got his rocks off with his new sugar daddy.

He stepped into the room. It took a moment to adjust to the shade inside the kitchen, but then he caught sight of the figures up against the fridge. Charles was standing, his back resting against the appliance, his hands on the head at his crotch.

The blond head.

"Marek, darling, that's the way. Christ, yes!"

Dan backed out silently, unseen. He leant back against the stone wall, waiting for his breathing to calm. Why'd he have to doubt Robin like that? Going behind his back to give some other bloke a blowjob was far more Dan's style than Robin's—the old Dan, anyway. He could do better than that now. Robin had shown him how.

Through the open door came the familiar sound of skin on skin, slurps and grunts, insinuating its way into Dan's thoughts with an unwelcome flicker of arousal. Feeling like a voyeur, he headed back down the garden and took out his mobile with shaking hands. There probably wasn't any point, but he tried Robin's number anyway.

It rang.

"Dan." Robin's voice was cautious, but it was so good to hear it again.

"Hello, stranger, I'm back. Thought you must have dropped your phone in the canal." Dan aimed for a light tone but felt the emotion thicken his voice. Bugger it, he was still pissed off with Robin for putting him through so much worry. "I've missed you so much, you stubborn git."

Robin was silent for a long moment. There were voices in the background—the muted polite conversation of a restaurant, perhaps. Dan started to worry that he'd bollocksed things up again.

"You missed me? Really?"

"God yes! The whole time I was there. Every night when I sat there drinking fruit juice and turning away hot men, every night when I went to bed on my own. Why the hell didn't you answer your phone? And more to the point, what's all this I hear about you shagging Charles?"

"What? I'm not shagging Charles." Robin was emphatic. Almost too emphatic, but Dan wasn't about to argue with him.

"Well no, I can see that. He's got some blond lad sucking his cock right now, and it sounds like you're in a pub. Are you going to fill me in on why you haven't been answering your phone, then?"

Robin gave a long sigh. "It's going to sound stupid."

"Yeah? Well, maybe it was stupid, then. It's a good thing I'm not a worrier or I'd have been up every night wondering if you'd gone and drowned or burnt your boat down or something."

"I know, I—"

"Do you have any idea what you've put me through?" Now that he'd started, the words kept on bubbling out. Must be the relief of knowing Robin was okay, letting all the worry and suppressed anger vent. "And all because of what? Because you didn't trust me? I fucking love you, you idiot!"

Shit! He hadn't meant to say it like that. Dan sat down on a bench at the bottom of Charles's garden.

When Robin finally spoke, his voice shook. "Do you really mean that?"

"Of course I bloody well mean it! There's no way I'd have said it if I didn't. Looks like you're stuck with me." Dan waited a long time for a response. "Well?" he asked, his indignation giving way to nerves. "Do you have anything you want to say, seeing as how I've gone and laid it all out for you?"

"I—I've been a stupid prick, and you don't deserve me."

Dan grinned, most of the tension leaving him in a dizzying rush. "Yeah, you have, but I reckon I've been one too. How about we call it quits? I'm rather hoping I do deserve you, especially after what I've gone and done. Where are you right now?"

"Uh, Bathampton. Sitting in the Queen's Head with Mum."

"Blimey, that's definitely not something I ever imagined I'd hear from you. Okay, that's good. Can you stay there for a bit? I reckon I can be there in about five minutes. Just wait in the pub, and I'll be there. I've got a surprise for you."

"Surprise? What surprise? Why aren't you still in Spain?"

"Got back on Wednesday, and I've been busy sorting things out, but I'm all done now. I'll tell you more when I get there. Just wait in the pub, okay?"

"Okay." Now Robin sounded tense too.

Dan gave a nervous chuckle. "See you in a minute."

Robin couldn't tolerate another moment inside the pub, and now he was pacing up and down the towpath outside. He remembered teaching Dan to steer properly down this stretch of canal. He recalled the way he'd still been able to smell him over the stench of the diesel, the way Dan had felt when Robin pressed up against him. The memory made his skin tingle, and for a moment he forgot where he was. Then he stubbed his toe on one of the mooring rings and swore as he nearly fell into the canal. He hopped, washed by waves of embarrassment, irritation and horniness. But most of all, churning anticipation.

A dark blue wide beam emerged from under the bridge, and Robin straightened, admiring the sleek paint job and shiny brass of the window frames. She had the look of a hire boat about her, luxurious but not lived in. There wasn't anything on the roof, for Christ's sake. Not even a sack of coal, at this time of year! She even had one of those nautical names that the hire companies seemed to find amusing. The *Jolly Roger*. He'd have to tell Dan about that later. No doubt he'd come up with some filthy joke involving the skipper.

Robin turned away from the boat, looking down the towpath towards Bath. Where the hell was Dan? He didn't even know what direction Dan would be coming from.

The *Jolly Roger*'s engine slowed as she steered in towards the bank, and Robin figured he might as well help them out by grabbing a line when they came alongside. He raised his gaze to check out the skipper and see if he'd be the sort of guy who might enjoy a jolly rogering.

Robin's eyes widened and his mouth fell open. "Dan?"

Why on earth had Dan arrived on a hire boat? But Robin grinned, because he didn't really give a toss so long as Dan was here, and he helped grab the boat and pull her in. He heard Dan cut the engine as he looped the rope around the mooring ring twice, but that was all he could manage before Dan was on him and everything else faded away.

They kissed, hungry lips and tongues tangling as they tried to climb into each other's skin.

"Hey." Dan pulled back. Robin tried to chase his lips. "Good to see you too, but aren't you going to ask me about the boat?"

He looked unbearably smug, and Robin wanted to eat him alive. He tried to concentrate his thoughts above the rushing of the blood in his veins and the pounding of his heart. "Boat...why'd you hire a boat?"

Dan threw his head back and laughed. Robin wanted to lick the skin of his neck, still pale under his chin despite the tan elsewhere. He didn't have that sunbed look anymore. The freckles on his nose were even more plentiful, his hair bleached almost blond by the Spanish sun.

"I didn't hire her. She's mine. All mine."

Robin looked from Dan to the *Jolly Roger*. "Yours? I don't get it... How can she be yours?"

"I bought her, fair and square. She's mine."

"But you can't afford a boat like this."

"Oh, can't I?" Dan raised his eyebrows and grinned. "What about that nice little pile of equity I was sitting on top of back in London?"

Robin scrunched up his brow. What was Dan trying to tell him? It was bloody hard to concentrate with him right here looking and smelling and feeling so excruciatingly sexy.

"My flat. Bought it back when prices were low, didn't I? Even with a rushed sale, I had enough to pay off the mortgage, buy this beauty and about twenty thousand left in the bank to tide me over." His eyes crinkled at the corners. "You know what that means? I can pick and choose my work, try to get together a book of my own. I'm thinking some sort of guide to the Waterways of Britain, written and photographed by Dan Taylor, live-aboard boater."

Robin was having problems wrapping his head around it. "You sold your flat?"

"Yep... Well, nearly, but I got a bridging loan to cover the cost of the boat until the sale's completed. It was the answer to all our problems, wasn't it? We can be together, but we don't have to share that tiny little boat of yours."

"*Serendipity* is not tiny!"

"Yeah, but my boat's bigger than yours."

Dan looked so bloody smug again that despite the delight flooding through him, Robin wanted to protest. He looked over

Dan's shoulder and smirked. "She may be bigger, but you don't seem to able to keep her under control."

"What? There's nothing the matter with my steer— Oh shit!"

The *Jolly Roger* was drifting slowly away from the bank, and the end of Robin's rope dropped off the edge as they watched.

"You could have tied it," Dan shouted as he threw himself towards the bank and plunged his arm into the water.

"Someone was distracting me." Robin watched Dan pull out the dripping rope and attempt to secure it with fumbling fingers. "I'll do this one for you." He sauntered over to the line at the bows and knelt down to make it fast, while Dan still struggled with his.

Robin watched in amusement. What on earth possessed someone so inept with boats to go and sink all his money into one? But that was Dan all over: reckless when going after what he wanted. And right now, what Dan wanted was Robin. The thought made his heart pound. Then he noticed the boner Dan was attempting to hide. Oh yes, it had been way too long for both of them. Robin gave a salacious smile. "Need a hand with that, do you?"

Dan's eyes followed Robin's gaze, and he smirked.

Robin crouched down next to him and took over, deftly tying off the line and taking Dan's hands. He tutted. "Your sleeve's soaking. Mum's going to have to wait. I think we'd better get you inside and take these wet clothes off you."

"Yeah." Dan's voice squeaked as he started to reply. He cleared his throat. "Yeah, sounds like a great idea."

# Chapter Thirty-Six

Dan climbed up onto the deck and turned the key in the door while Robin tied the stern line. It opened into a narrow corridor the width of the boat with a porthole at each end. There were hatches down to the engine, and an assortment of dials and switches on the wall. A door led through to the main boat, and if Dan remembered the plans correctly, it opened directly into the master bedroom with its king-size bed. He picked up his bag and opened the doors.

He forgot to breathe. Light poured in through the large windows on each side and bounced up off the ceiling. It was lined with pale wooden panels, giving the illusion of size even though it was only about a quarter of the size of his old bedroom. But it was beautiful. And it was his—he didn't owe anyone a penny.

"Wow!" Dan breathed, sinking back when he felt Robin step up behind him.

Robin nuzzled at his neck. "You're acting like you've never seen it before."

"I haven't. Not properly anyway. I wanted us to do this together."

"You didn't even look inside? You're just a daft romantic really, aren't you?" Robin said, pulling Dan close so that he could feel a stiff cock pressing against the crease of his arse. "I bet you didn't look over the engine, either." Dan shivered as Robin nipped his earlobe. "Hmmm, chilly. We should get you undressed and into bed."

Dan looked at the bare slab of foam rubber and laughed. "No arguments here. No, wait, windows."

Fortunately curtains were included in the sale, even if bed linen wasn't. They stripped in moments, too ravenous to take the time to undress each other. Dan stumbled as he tried to take his jeans and boots off at the same time. He landed on the mattress, and Robin fell on top of him, kissing and licking and grinding and devouring. Hard muscles and rough stubble and metal piercings and hot cock pressed into Dan's skin and turned him into one giant puddle of need. That incomparable scent of woodsmoke and musk that was pure Robin filled him up and drove him wild.

"Hmm, scratchy," Robin murmured, rubbing his hand in the crease of Dan's groin. "You've been letting yourself go."

Dan gave him a gentle slap. "Oi! I just couldn't see the point in going through all that pain if you weren't around to appreciate it. And then I thought you're such a big hippie freak, you might prefer the natural look."

"Cheeky." Robin nipped at his earlobe, making Dan gasp. "Thought you liked a bit of pain."

"Only if it's you dishing it out."

Robin chuckled into his neck. "I hope you're not saying you want me to start waxing your pubes for you."

"I'm just saying I want you. No one else. Nothing more."

Robin growled and ground into him, hot and needy and oh-so-good.

"Stop! Wait!" Dan was going to come from this alone if Robin didn't let up. "I want you in me, please." He tried to find the words. "I've been wanting you, dreaming about you." Robin was propped up on one elbow, looking down at him with something like lust, something like indulgence and something an awful lot like love. Dan felt awkward. He still hadn't said it face-to-face. He traced a finger over the lines of Robin's tattoo, wondering if he had it in him to say those words again.

There was something else he wanted to say too, and by comparison, that was far easier, even though he was nervous about Robin refusing.

"Please, I had a test before I left. I'm negative, and I've not been near another man since. Could we go without the rubbers? I want to feel you properly. Feel you come inside me."

Robin made a strangled sound in his throat. "Fuck yes! I want that so much. Oh God, I want to feel you around me."

"Well then, what are you waiting for?" Dan gave him a shove, giddy with relief and desire. And more than that, with the knowledge that Robin trusted him enough to take his word for it. "Lube's in my bag—down there somewhere. Got strawberry flavour, for old time's sake."

"You're an evil, evil man."

Robin was back within seconds, brandishing the lube. Dan sat up to kiss him some more while Robin slicked up, then fell back and spread his legs. But Robin moved with him, bruising Dan's lips with a demanding kiss even as he breached him with those strong fingers. The sudden burn made Dan hiss and arch his back, but Robin just grinned and shoved in farther, past the knuckles.

Between the pain in his lip and the pain in his arse, Dan was in heaven. He'd forgotten just how intense this always was with Robin. "Bite me, please!" His bites and bruises had all faded while he'd been away, and he'd mourned their passing.

Robin obliged, moving down to suck up marks on his neck as Dan thrust against the invading fingers. Dan grabbed hold of Robin's head, crushing him closer while lifting his hips to try and take him deeper.

"I can't hold on! Please!"

Robin instantly stopped sucking and pulled out his fingers, leaving Dan a writhing, whimpering wreck.

"You'll wait until I say you can come. You hear me?" Robin's voice was stern enough to command Dan's attention, but his eyes still shone with affection.

Dan grinned, then winced as Robin pinched his cock hard. "Ow! Aye-aye, Captain."

Robin's stern expression crumpled as he laughed. His body shook, the vibrations taking Dan even closer to his climax. Then the pinch came again.

"Guess that makes you my insolent cabin boy, then." Robin's voice rasped, his breath scorching Dan's ear. "Think you need to be disciplined. Shown who's boss. Even if you do have a bigger…boat." Robin rubbed their cocks together.

Dan thrust up against Robin's hand, spreading his legs wider still. "Oh yeah. That's just what I need. Come on, then. You're all promises. I want some delivery."

"Cheeky boy." Robin nipped at Dan's neck, then pushed himself up on his knees and lined them up. "Christ, you look so fucking gorgeous."

Dan heard the need roughen his voice. Saw the love shine through the lust in Robin's eyes. Took in the sight of the man about to fuck him bareback. He never thought he'd trust anyone enough to do this. Never thought he'd love anyone enough.

"I love you, Robin." The words spilled out as Robin entered him, slowly, inexorably filling him inside and making everything feel just right. He kept staring into Robin's dark eyes, and when he felt Robin's hips hard against him, he said it again. "I love you."

Robin fell on him, kissing him so thoroughly Dan's jaw ached and his lips stung.

"Love you too."

"Quite right. Now screw me so hard I won't ever forget it."

"My pleasure."

Robin kept his word, starting with long, slow pulls out, followed by slamming in so hard and fast his balls slapped against Dan's arse. They both gasped, the breath forced out of them.

"So good," Robin panted. "I've missed this so much."

Dan had to agree, but he couldn't form the words. Every pull and thrust sent Robin's piercing sliding over his prostate, so much more intense without the latex in the way. Pre-come dribbled onto his belly and rolled down his sides. He reached out to grip the sheets so he didn't touch himself and come too fast. But there were no sheets. He balled his fists instead, then clutched at his hair. The burn on his scalp felt good, helped ground him. The heat pooled inside him, sizzling out until every thrust sent charges right through his body. Dan felt it from his toes to his crown. He wanted to tell Robin, but all he could manage was a garbled noise.

"Dan!" Robin's rhythm stuttered, and Dan felt his own balls drawing up.

"Please, kiss," he asked, curving his back to meet Robin halfway, reaching out with his arms.

And that was all it took. Robin inside his mouth, simultaneously claiming him with tongue and cock. Dan groaned and shuddered as his balls pumped hard, covering their chests with come. The wave rolled through him again and again, gaining power from Robin's jerking hips and the delicious sensation of Robin coming inside him, filling him with hot seed.

The kiss didn't end. Robin's sweat-drenched body was sticking to his, Robin's softening cock still inside him, Robin's tongue mapping out the inside of his mouth, then moving on to his neck. He could stay like this forever, drifting on the current, letting it take him where it may.

Robin, on the other hand, seemed to have more purpose. Dan felt him withdraw; then that exquisite mouth resumed its attentions, stirring him from his torpor. He wriggled, then squirmed as he felt teeth teasing his nipple.

"No, don't stop! That's good." He saw Robin smile, his teeth still gently nibbling. Now Robin's hands were moving on him, rousing other parts of his anatomy, those lips moving ever lower until it felt like Dan would fly apart when they finally made contact.

"Arrgh, you tease!" Dan flung his head back, and the tremors ran right through him as Robin licked down the crease of his groin and circled his balls. "Come on, suck mmm—" His words dissolved as he felt Robin's tongue rasping over his tender hole. It stung and it soothed and it felt like he was in paradise. He spread his legs wide and thrust up his hips, thrust against Robin's tongue, urging him deeper.

The loss of sensation and the sound of Robin spitting snagged his attention.

"You wouldn't have a drink in that bag of yours, would you?" Robin's face was twisted in disgust. "I love you 'n' all, but not enough to rim you when you're leaking strawberry lube and jizz."

The laughter bubbled up in Dan's throat. In the end, he could only gesture weakly towards the bag, but Robin was already there, pulling out the bottle of water and then chugging it back. The long column of his throat was exposed, and Dan watched his Adam's apple bobbing before taking a slow visual ramble over Robin's body. Hard to believe that after all this time—and three months with one guy was unprecedented for him—he still found Robin every bit as attractive as he had to begin with.

No, more attractive. Now he was seeing so much more than the surface.

Now he was seeing everything.

When his gaze meandered back to Robin's eyes, he found them sparkling with amusement.

"You've got tan lines."

Dan looked down at the telltale lines from his shorts and T-shirt. "And what of it?"

"I thought clothing was optional at those sorts of places."

"Might be for some, but I was saving myself for you."

The smile Robin gave him was so sweet it might have been tooth-rotting if it hadn't been for the hint of lascivious promise.

"You know what I want right now?" Robin asked.

"Ask anything and it's yours." Dan really meant that, as well. It wasn't a line—he'd do anything for Robin just to see him smile like that again.

Robin leaned down, licked Dan's cheek and murmured into his ear, "I want you inside me."

Dan's cock seemed to think that was a great idea too, twitching with interest as it started to fill. His breath escaped him in a long, shuddering moan. "Yeah, I want that too."

The only other time he'd topped, Robin had still been the one in control, but this time he seemed to be waiting for Dan to take the initiative. And that was good too. It was all good when it was him and Robin together, no matter who was in charge. Dan pushed down on Robin's head.

"Think I might need a little help before I'm ready."

Robin gave him a grin which seemed to promise all manner of good things, before swiping that pierced tongue up his cock. It was exquisite torture, Robin teasing the head and finding the particular spot to rub his tongue stud against that always made him crazy with lust. He was going to have to put a stop to this if he was going to be able to give Robin what he wanted.

"Okay, enough!"

Robin nuzzled into his thigh. The light in those deep blue eyes was almost enough to make Dan lose it there and then.

"Where do you want me?" Robin asked.

And there were so many possibilities it could have been hard to decide, but Dan had a particular fantasy that had been plaguing him the whole time he was away. It had seemed so impossible, but maybe Robin would go along with it this once. He was unusually pliant today.

"On your knees, facedown."

Robin raised his eyebrows but did as he was told. "You realise this is going to make a mess of your mattress?" he said, the words distorted by him having one cheek pressed into the foam.

"It'll wipe clean." And even if it didn't, who cared? All Dan could focus on was the vision of Robin offering himself in such a wanton pose. He ran a hand from Robin's neck down his arched spine and over his buttocks. They were raised in a deliciously obscene spectacle, and Dan couldn't hold back any longer. Heart hammering, he positioned himself behind Robin and pushed his legs farther apart.

Robin trembled and made a muffled sound.

Concern flooded through the haze of lust, "Are you okay with this?" Dan asked.

"Yeah, why'd you ask?" Robin's voice was uneven, quivering, making Dan even more worried. Much as he wanted this, he didn't want to have it at Robin's expense.

"You're shaking."

"I'm excited," Robin said, the emphatic tone of voice wiping all doubts away.

"Excited is good. Okay, yeah. Oh Christ." Because if Robin was excited, then Dan was in some kind of delirious frenzy. But he stopped his own hands from shaking enough to slather his fingers in lube and push one into that waiting hole.

He wasn't sure what he'd expected from Robin. Maybe a hiss, maybe some kind of movement away from him. He certainly didn't expect the heartfelt groan and surge back against him as Robin attempted to impale himself on Dan's finger. And although he was tight, it didn't take long to get him ready. Get them both ready. The sight of Robin pressed down on the mattress with his arse in the air combined with those needy sounds had Dan sweating and panting along with him.

He waited, poised to push in, awestruck at the sight of his naked dick about to breach Robin. He'd never done this unprotected. Everything had been stripped away, all the barriers between them demolished—physical, mental, spiritual.

This was how it was meant to be. He didn't want to fuck Robin. He wanted to make love to him.

"Come on, I'm ready," Robin pleaded.

Dan pushed in, inched through the tight muscle into that perfect heat. Every thrust was like a revelation, the knowledge that there was nowhere he'd rather be and no one he'd rather be with filling him with incandescent joy.

The knowledge that he was home.

He gathered Robin up—pulled him until he was sitting back against his thighs and he could kiss his neck. He reached around to clasp Robin's cock, thrilling at the sensation of Robin's body pulsing around him.

It was a perfect give and take. Perfect balance. Balance that disintegrated as he tried to tell Robin just how much he loved him. Felt him stiffen, felt his cock swell and his body clench hard. Heard him cry out.

He wasn't Dan anymore. He exploded into Robin, and they were one, rocking together in that radiant moment that lasted forever.


Robin surfaced through layers of bliss to find Dan's lips on his. They were lying side by side, Dan pressed up against him in what felt like an attempt to have as much of their skin in contact as possible. They kissed lazily, drowsy on love and each other. He could feel the aftermath of their coupling as a sweet ache. It had been incredible to let go like that. To trust Dan so completely that he could.

At the sound of voices outside, Robin stirred.

"We should probably get dressed or something. Go see Mum before she drinks the pub dry. She'll be wondering where we've got to."

Dan ran a hand down his flank. "I'm sure she has a good idea. Hey, did I ever tell you how amazing you are?"

"Not in a while." Robin blushed. Compliments always made him embarrassed, but he loved hearing them from Dan.

"I'll have to remedy that. I'll be telling you every day, just so's you know and start believing it yourself."

Robin could probably believe anything Dan told him with his beautiful eyes so full of truth, but he changed the subject. "So you're really staying? Travelling with me, wherever I go?"

"Yep, we can work out a system. One night in my boat, one night in yours. You'll have to get up pretty bloody early in the morning to shake me off."

"Or just cruise to a bit of the network your boat's too wide for."

Dan pouted, but his eyes still sparkled. "You wouldn't."

"Only if you buy strawberry lube again."

Dan chuckled, the sound sweeter than any birdsong.

"The *Jolly Roger*? Tell me you didn't pick her just because of the name."

"It was a sweetener, but it was the Jacuzzi that did it."

Robin gaped. "You have a Jacuzzi?"

Dan gave a maddening grin. "Oh yeah. Care to try her out? I've been assured she's just about big enough for two, provided you don't mind being *intimate*."

"Is there any way to share a bath without being intimate? No, don't answer that. So long as you have towels, you're on."

Dan sat up and went to the window. He peered through the crack in the curtains. "Oh look, there's your mum. Hi, Rosemary!" he called. "And Charles, and that must be the lad who was sucking him off. Hmmm, cute, isn't he?"

Robin groaned. So much for the Jacuzzi.

"Are they a couple, then?" Dan asked.

"Charles and Marek? Yeah, I guess they must be now. I only found out today. Apparently Marek got it into his head that Charles and I had something going on and was insanely jealous. Charles had to get me to talk to him, tell him I was seeing you and didn't have anything going on with the boss. They were in the middle of making up when I left for the pub."

"No, they were in the middle of that when I walked in on them," Dan murmured.

Robin started pulling on clothes after cleaning up with Dan's wet wipes. He had to hand it to Dan—he'd thought of everything. Except bed linen.

"Where's all your stuff? How did you manage all this? You were in Gran Canaria."

Dan grinned. "Amazing what you can do over the Internet and phone, isn't it? Plus I had Tris as my man in London. Oh yeah, I sent him back early to help me out. He was driving me nuts moping over Alex anyway. They've patched things up now, so it's all come up roses."

Suddenly, Tris didn't seem so threatening. "So he sorted out your flat?"

"He took my keys to the estate agents and sold all the furniture. Not much else to do until I got back. Finished the assignment a few days early, came back and packed what I needed into a couple of suitcases. They're on the front deck. A few things with sentimental value are in a box in Mum's attic, and the rest went to charity. I never had all that much stuff. I've always travelled light."

Robin stepped up behind Dan, wrapping his arms around him and letting him fall back. He murmured into Dan's ear. "To think I once thought you were a vain, materialistic wanker who couldn't be trusted."

Dan chuckled. "I used to reckon those were my best qualities. Took someone special to make me realise there was more to me than that."

"There's always been more to you."

"Maybe. Mum always said there was. Hey"—Dan's tone brightened—"she's dying to meet you. We're going to have to go and visit soon. I want to show you off to everyone. Be warned, they'll all think you're a posh git despite the hippie camouflage."

Robin smiled against Dan's neck. "Can't wait. Sounds like a riot. Now let's go see my mum before she explodes with curiosity."

Robin stepped down from the deck of Dan's boat. His boyfriend's boat. He held out his hand to help Dan down. It wasn't necessary, but it was worth it to see Dan's nose crinkle up and his cheeks dimple.

People were walking up and down the towpath. People were watching from the pub windows. He couldn't care less. He was with the man he loved, the one who had barged into his life and turned it all upside down and now put it all back together in a way that made perfect sense.

He pulled Dan to him and kissed the tip of his nose.

"What was that for?"

"Don't ever change. You're just perfect."

Dan grinned. "Can I have that in writing, please?"

"You can have anything you want," Robin assured him.

"Oh, I'm definitely holding you to *that* promise."

They walked into the pub hand in hand, grinning like love-struck fools.

# About the Author

Eccentric Englishwoman, absent-minded mother, proud bisexual, shameless tea addict, serial textile craft hobbyist, iconoclastic logophile and writer of homoerotic romance—Josephine Myles is all these things at once. She has held down more different jobs than any sane person ever should and is fundamentally rebellious, preferring the overgrown yet enticing path rather than the wide and obvious one.

Jo once spent two years living on a slowly decaying narrowboat, and was determined that she would one day use the experience as fodder for a novel. It may have taken a few years, but she got there in the end. She usually does.

Jo would love to know more about her readers and you can contact her via email: josephine_myles@yahoo.co.uk. For regular blog posts and saucy free reads, visit her website at www.josephinemyles.com

*The bigger they are, the harder they fall...in love.*

# Muscling Through
## © 2011 JL Merrow

Cambridge art professor Larry Morton takes one, alcohol-glazed look at the huge, tattooed man looming in a dark alley and assumes he's done for. Moments later he finds himself disarmed—literally and figuratively. And, the next morning, he can't rest until he offers an apology to the man who turned out to be more gentle than giant.

Larry's intrigued to find there's more to Al Fletcher than meets the eye; he possesses a natural artistic talent that shines through untutored technique. Unfortunately, no one else seems to see the sensitive soul beneath Al's imposing, scarred, undeniably sexy exterior. Least of all Larry's class-conscious family, who would like nothing better than to split up this mismatched pair.

Is it physical? Oh, yes, it's deliciously physical, and so much more—which makes Larry's next task so daunting. Not just convincing his colleagues, friends and family that their relationship is more than skin deep. It's convincing Al.

*Warning: Contains comic misunderstandings, misuse of art materials, and unexpected poignancy.*

*Available now in ebook from Samhain Publishing.*

*It's all about the story...*

# Romance

# HORROR

www.samhainpublishing.com